The Bar Harbor
Retirement Home
for Famous Writers
(And Their Muses)

The Bar Harbor Retirement Home for Famous Writers (And Their Muses)

A Novel

Terri-Lynne DeFino

WILLIAM MORROW
An Imprint of HarperCollins*Publishers*

HarperCollins books may be purchased for educational, business, or sales promotional use. For information, please e-mail the Special Markets Department at SPsales@harpercollins.com.

FIRST EDITION

Designed by Leydiana Rodriguez

Library of Congress Cataloging-in-Publication Data has been applied for.

ISBN 978-0-06-274267-4

20 21 22   LSC   10 9 8 7 6 5 4

For William and Gioia

❦

Today you're a boy catching frogs in the marsh.
Tomorrow you're an old man listening to stories
told by other old men. Life. It happens just like that.

—CORNELIUS TRAEGAR

"I'm driving into oncoming traffic. My thinking is clear. I imagine every detail before it happens. Headlights kissing. Crash. Shatter. Metal twisting. Done. It's quite vivid."

Cecibel folded the bedsheets fresh from the line, just like Mrs. Peppernell liked them. The old woman's vivid dreaming unsettled her, unsettled them both. So, too, did the new doctor drawing the recurring dream into the light. For Mrs. Peppernell, Cecibel would futz about the room, pretend to be diligently working. For her, Cecibel would do most anything.

"Done, you say? Do you die in your dream, Olivia?" Dr. Kintz's pen paused. "Olivia?"

"I have asked you to call me Mrs. Peppernell."

"We try to be a little less formal here."

"Informality is for intimates. You are not my friend. You're my shrink—"

"We don't use that word, Olivia."

"Mrs. Peppernell!" She slammed her knotty hand on the arm of her easy chair. "And don't interrupt me, you impertinent boy."

Setting the sheets into the hope chest, Cecibel tried to make eye contact and, failing that, let the lid slip just enough to make an audible click. Olivia's gaze flicked her way. Their eyes met. Her wrinkled cheek twitched. "If you insist upon calling me Olivia," Mrs. Peppernell said evenly, "I shall call you Richard. Or Dick, if that is your preference."

"Would it make you happy to call me Richard?"

"It would make me happy if you would use the title I earned with sixty-two years of marriage. And it would make me even happier if you would stop speaking in the royal 'we.' Now go away, Dick. I am finished being monitored for today."

Dr. Kintz heaved a sigh. Not the first psychiatrist to do so over Mrs. Peppernell. He would learn, or he would earn every lash of her wicked tongue. Tucking his pen into his pocket, his notebook under his arm, he leaned a little closer than experience would soon warn him against. "Forgive me, Mrs. Peppernell. Feel free to call me Richard, but please don't call me Dick. We—you and I, not the royal 'we'—can pick up on this conversation tomorrow, if you're up to it."

The old woman brushed imaginary lint from her impeccable trousers. "That would be agreeable, Dr. Kintz. Good day."

"Good day." He bowed his head. If he glanced Cecibel's way, she didn't know. She turned her face to the wall before he could. Then he was gone with a soft click of the door. Poor Dr. Kintz. Only a week in the Pen and he still had no idea what he was in for. Those who left made sure not to tell. Those who stayed knew better.

"Fetch my medicine, will you, dear?"

Cecibel lifted the lid of the cedar chest again. Once a place to store hopes for the future, it held only the past now. And sheets. And marijuana. The scent of it permeated everything. Moving aside the cotton—always cotton, never polyester—quilt awaiting winter, Cecibel pulled the baggie from its folds. "You're running a bit low."

"I'll have more ready soon enough." Olivia took the baggie from Cecibel's outstretched hand. "The last crop is all but ready. Join me?"

"No, thank you, Mrs. Peppernell."

"Don't be silly, child."

"Olivia," Cecibel amended, smiling openly. The old woman

never grimaced, never winced. *Ghoulish is as ghoulish does.* She'd said it without a trace of condescension or pity. Without apologizing afterward.

"Do you have a moment to walk me outside, dear?"

"Of course." Cecibel gave her arm. "You could do that here if you want to. No one would care."

"What am I? A barbarian? Gentle people don't smoke indoors. It's rude." Olivia leaned on her, light as breeze. The power of her wit, her words, those ice-chip blue eyes, did not extend to her physical form. Once, long ago, she'd been a driving force in literary New York, a crusader for women. Longer ago, she was what all debutantes skating the last sharp edge of Victorianism were—a wife, a mother, a homemaker. Before that, for so short a time, a gifted nurse who married a doctor and gave up her career. Longer still in the years beyond years, Olivia Peppernell née Stuart was a little girl from rural Connecticut, one with dreams of being an equestrian, a concert pianist, anything but what she became.

"How about the arbor?" Cecibel asked once they were outside. Mornings were chilly in Bar Harbor, whether June or September. "The sun hits it just right this time of day."

"Lovely."

An orderly and an old woman toddled across the green lawn, down the dirt track to the arbor overlooking the sea. Cecibel lifted the ruined side of her face to the sunshine, petitioning the gods of sunlight and warmth to undo what those of darkness had done. Deaf ears. Blind eyes. No compassion. Not for her.

"Have you heard anything more of our new resident?"

Cecibel gave her companion's arm a little squeeze. "He's supposed to arrive today. Did you know that?"

"I did, yes. But, why now? Is he ill or simply old? I thought I read something about a memoir in the making."

Cecibel laughed softly. "Bar Harbor Home for the Elderly is a lovely place—"

"The Pen is east of nowhere," Olivia corrected. "He belongs in New York. Or Paris. Or Rome. He must be losing his marbles and his handlers want it done out of sight."

"His medical records are private." Cecibel settled Olivia into an Adirondack chair, blocked the wind while the old woman lit her joint and inhaled. The scent conjured friends forgotten, better days, coaxed a rare smile. Sitting on the footstool at Olivia's feet, Cecibel pulled her sweater tighter. "I read about the memoir, too."

"It'll be ghosted." Another long drag. "I'm certain. None of us writes once we come here."

"That's not true. You do. All the time."

"I scribble. That's all any of us do. Our best writing has been done."

"How do you know?"

Olivia patted Cecibel's knee. Kindly and condescending. "Did you read Switch's book yet?"

The Sleeper and the Slumber. Raymond Switcher's last novel, published in 1976. Switch mostly painted now, images that reached nostalgically back to a childhood in New Hampshire that never actually existed, considering he'd lived his whole life in Philadelphia. Occasionally, he penned short stories for obscure literary journals no one read.

"I did," Cecibel said. "Well, I haven't finished yet. It's wonderful."

"The *Times* got it right for a change." Olivia nodded. "It's truly his best. Possibly because he was wise enough to end on a high note."

"And what about you? What is your best work?"

The old woman's medicine, the only one she would use, had relaxed her shoulders, the set of her jaw. She slumped a little in her chair, able to now that the ever-present pain in her back was eased. "If you go by what the critics and sales figures say, my greatest work was *And the Ladies Sang.* A good book. One I'm proud of, naturally. Nineteen eighty-four was a powerful time for women, and the book spoke to several generations fighting the good fight. But if you're asking which book rests most kindly in my heart, it's *Green Apples for Stewart.* Barely made the best-seller list, but"—she patted her thin chest—"it still pitter-patters my shriveled old heart."

"That was your last novel, right?"

"Second to last." Olivia inhaled, held it, exhaled slowly. "No one's heard of my last one. I, unwisely, didn't know enough to quit."

"What's the title?"

"Look it up in the library if you're so curious. I'm tired now, dear. I think I shall nap in the sun for a while." Olivia closed her eyes. The ocean breeze whiffled her spun-sugar hair. The perfect white, Cecibel thought, just as it had once been the perfect copper red. Book jacket photos had never done her beauty justice. Stiff. Posed. Untouchable. Unapproachable. Unlike the ones displayed in her rooms, those including old friends and lovers. Olivia in wilder times.

"I'll sit with you," Cecibel offered.

Olivia's eyes, tiny slits made by slumber and cannabidiol, found hers. An old hand reached out, into the breeze-tossed tendrils of Cecibel's hair, and fell again. "'Lean out the window, Goldenhair,'" she whispered. "'I hear you singing, singing . . .'"

Her head lolled. Cecibel shrugged out of her sweater and gently covered her with it. Olivia Peppernell softly slept. Her face to the sun. Her dreams gently kept. What did she dream? Outside of twisted metal and headlights?

Such a life she'd lived. Famous. Infamous. So much glory. So much pain.

Hugging herself, Cecibel hurried back to the main building. "Mrs. Peppernell is napping in the arbor, Sal," she told her fellow orderly behind the maintenance desk. "Could you please send someone to keep an eye on her, and help her back to her room when she wakes? I have to go finish getting Mr. Carducci's room ready for him."

"Sure thing, buttercup." Sal chuffed, waving her away with his big sausage fingers. Pink nails, today. Subtle. For Sal. "Doubt she'll be waking up anytime soon. You reek, girl."

Cecibel sniffed at her hair, wrinkled her nose. "Oh. Okay, thanks. I have some perfume in my room."

"It ain't gonna help," Sal called after her as she hurried away, head down and face burning. Dodging residents, doctors, nurses, and other orderlies all the way to her room. No one would accuse her of smoking up on the job—everyone knew about Olivia's medicine—but it wasn't acceptable for her to reek of marijuana either. She changed her clothes, sprayed her brush with rose perfume, and gave her hair a good brushing.

Long and golden and lovely. The only remnant of a beauty shredded and burned away nearly a dozen years before. Even that was flawed by a hairline slipped too far off her ruined face. While the rest of the staff at the Pen was required to bind their hair off their faces, she was not. A kindness to her. To everyone.

She rolled an elastic band onto her wrist and dashed out of the small space belonging to her and her alone within the grand beachside mansion now a home for the elderly. Once in Mr. Carducci's room, she'd bind it back and work unencumbered. She could cut it, of course, to a length that would hide the worst of her scars and still be manageable. The last vestiges of vanity kept it long and always longer. Vanity she no longer had a right to.

Mr. Carducci's suite of rooms smelled of pine cleaner and lemon wax, leather, and wood. Cecibel had worked hard to make it perfect for him. Just the right light in just the right crooks and corners for reading, sleeping, writing. Soft blankets, softer pillows, a desk in the window facing the sea, and a healthy stash of paper and pens and notebooks. Of course, he worked on a computer; all writers did these days. But there wasn't one of them who didn't get sentimental and dreamy at the sight of a blank page and a waiting pen.

When she was a young woman, whole and hale in her twenties, Carducci's novels opened her dreams to places and people beyond her ken. After the accident, his words kept her company through the darkest of the dark, through the pain, through the chaos of thoughts. Cecibel hadn't read anything of his in years—she was done dreaming and he was done writing—but for what he'd once obliviously given her, she owed him her best effort. For what he gave the world, he deserved to finish his own story in peace.

Alfonse Carducci was overdue. She'd been told to have all in ready by ten. Perhaps she'd gotten the day wrong. Or perhaps Dr. Kintz's enthusiasm for so auspicious a resident kept the famous man in the office once belonging to Cornelius Traegar himself, and vacated by too many in the dozen years since his death. Old writers didn't fade into that good night. Not those populating the Pen. Their wits got sharper while their bodies betrayed them, their tongues sharper still. Cecibel rarely kept up with their banter; her mind was not quick or mean enough. It was more often that later, alone in her room and trying to sleep but for dreams, she'd laugh aloud at a joke or gibe given and taken hours before.

One last swipe along the polished wood of the bookshelf, and Cecibel called her job done. Tucking the rag in her back pocket, she scanned the titles there. Mr. Carducci's books, of course. Every one. And Olivia Peppernell's. Raymond Switcher's, even those that didn't make it to the best-seller list. Many of the residents, past and present, were represented upon those shelves. Authors. Editors. Illustrators. Cover designers. It was the only necessary requirement to apply for residency in the Bar Harbor Home for the Elderly— they had to have been in publishing. Cornelius Traegar's will stipulated this one condition be kept, and it had been for more than fifty years.

Cecibel pulled a book—*Wicked Tongues*—and took it to the window. She flipped to the back cover. Alfonse Carducci, there a man in his fifties, smiled the half smile of an attractive, talented, successful man fully aware of his charms. The perfect smattering of white flecked his temples. And though the photo was in black and white, she knew his eyes were amber, like a lion's. Cecibel remembered clearly, from an interview he did with Johnny Carson, the silky-deep tone of his voice, the Italian accent never lost though he'd lived his adult life in the United States. How enamored she had been of him during his heyday, of this man in his prime in every sense of the word. Now she stood in this window of his new residence, holding her favorite of his books in her hand, and the twittering, teenage lust chased her across the years.

"Ah, good afternoon, Cecibel," Dr. Kintz called from the entrance. "I see we caught you—"

Spinning to the shelf, pulling the elastic band from her hair, she nearly tripped over her own feet. She pushed the book back into its space, smoothed the hair over her face, and hurried toward the door. A hand caught hers before she could make her getaway.

"No need to hurry off." The voice, still silky-deep, was only slightly less robust.

Cecibel turned her face to the doorjamb. "I was just finishing up and . . . and . . . I'm sorry. Good afternoon, gentlemen."

She didn't rip her hand from his. Alfonse Carducci simply let her go. Their voices carried after her, Dr. Kintz's the louder. "The residents love her, but she's shy. She was in an accident, you see, and . . ."

Cecibel ran full pelt, oblivious to where she was going or how fast. Away. Where she didn't have to hear the pity in Dr. Kintz's voice. Or worse, in Alfonse Carducci's.

"Whoa! Hey, hold on now."

Hands gripped her arms, steadied her. Cecibel instinctively turned her face from the voice familiar enough to know doing so wasn't entirely necessary. Finlay Pottinger had been working the Pen longer than she herself, and had as much to hide.

"You all right? Seen a ghost?"

"No. I'm fine. Thank you, Finlay."

He let her go, bent to pick up a bouquet of flowers tied up in a bit of twine, and held them out to her. "Happy birthday."

So close, a flicked glance was all she'd hazard. She liked Finlay too well to offer a full-on view. Taking the flowers from his hand, she brought them to her nose and inhaled. "Thank you, Finlay. How did you know?"

"Your birthday?" He chuffed. "It's not a secret, is it?"

"No, but I've never celebrated it here."

"Ain't it time you did? Thirty-five is kind of a big year."

"No bigger than any other." She started away.

"Cecibel?"

And stopped.

"I thought maybe you'd like to do something, seein's it's your birthday and all. Maybe go into town for a burger and fries? What do you think?"

"No, thank you, Finlay. See you." Her heart pounded so loud in her ears she could scarcely hear her own words. Or the mingled garbling that might have been his response. Or the wind. Or anything at all.

Bar Harbor, Maine

MAY 15, 1999

✦

If at first you don't succeed, get a ghostwriter to do it for you.

—CORNELIUS TRAEGAR

"You have to open your door sooner or later, Alfie. You know better than to hope I'll just go away."

Money, fame, and respect bought many things. None of it, gleaned over a lifetime of achievement, would spare him Olivia Peppernell indefinitely. Two days of him hiding away in his very comfortable, well-appointed suite in the Bar Harbor Home for the Elderly seemed to be her limit.

It was nice, while it lasted. Alfonse would never have imagined himself content in his own company after a lifetime surrounded by fans, colleagues, friends, lovers. Age did strange things to a man. As did a failing body. When the mind was the only part left functioning, it had more than enough time to remember, reflect, regret. Two days, it appeared, was his limit, too.

Laboring to the door, he took deep, even breaths. He rested his hand on the knob. Shoulders as straight as he could get them, he opened the door. "Livy." Her name gushed out of him in a breath he hoped she heard as the joy it was, and not his failing lungs. "You gorgeous creature. Come in, come in."

Old. So old. Weren't they all? But Alfonse saw her still, that menace with her red hair and whipcrack blue eyes, transposed over the frail frame. He recalled curves and softness and a willingness to let him explore every lovely inch. Were he not so withered himself, he might even have entertained the notion of seeing how much of it remained.

"Sit, sit." He gestured to a leather chair set in the sunshine streaming through his massive window. "Shall I call for tea? Coffee? Anything at all?"

"I'd ask for a bourbon but I guess that's not in the cards for either one of us."

"Sadly, no."

"I'm fine. Sit, Alfie, before you topple over."

He did as he was told. Alfonse had used up all his energy to deny her in his two days of solitude.

"So you're finished avoiding me now, are you?" she asked.

"I have not been avoiding you, Livy. I simply needed time to acclimate to my new surroundings."

Her gaze traveled the length and breadth of the room, came to rest on him. "This was Cornelius's suite, you know. It's been vacant nearly a decade. Waiting. Shall I wonder why?"

"You can wonder, but I will tell you it was in his will. This was not just his dream. It was our dream, this home where old writers go to die."

"For fuck's sake, Alfie. I was there, too. Or is it true you're losing your marbles and don't remember?"

"My marbles are all accounted for," he said. "Cornelius was content to be here to usher in those old greats who came before us. I wasn't."

"He was one of those old greats."

"And I was the protégé he took under his wing."

"Protégé?" Olivia chuffed. "Still in denial, I see."

"I deny nothing. Cornelius was . . . I loved him. Just not only him. As you know." He wagged a finger at her. "Intimately."

"And yet you didn't come to his funeral, and have not visited me even once since I became an inmate here. That is what I wonder why, Alfie. Why it is you waited so long."

"Inmate?" Alfonse laughed softly, the only way he could. "You are free to leave, my dear. No one demands you stay."

"And where would I go? My children despise me. And don't think you can sidetrack me. Why didn't you come?"

Alfonse let his shoulders slump. It was too much effort to keep them square and talk at the same time. Memories and regret took their toll, too. "We had not seen one another in a long time, Livy. It was better for him that way. I couldn't give him what he wanted. What he deserved. He understood that. He loved me, not what he wished I would be."

She chuckled softly. "You still haven't said why you didn't come for his funeral."

Love. Respect. Regret. Relief. "He was already gone," he said. "What was the point? Let this go now, Livy. Please. I am here now."

Olivia's chin raised. He knew that combative look. So well. So dear. The spun sugar of her hair still held the gentle waves he used to lose his fingers in for hours, for days. Her face was that of an old woman, but within the lines he found her youth.

"It's good to see you, Livy."

"It's good to see you, too." Her smile melted a little of the ice in her eyes. "So what's wrong? Why are you here?"

"I'm dying, of course," he said. "My heart and lungs are failing slowly every day. My liver and kidneys are shot to hell. One day, something will simply stop. I've had DNR orders written up. It won't be long I'm a resident here."

"How long?"

"A month? A year? No more."

"You never know," Olivia said. "They didn't give me long when I got to the Pen. It's been almost six years now."

"You did not abuse yourself the way I did." Alfonse inhaled carefully. Slowly. Already he was light-headed with the exertion of speech. "A lifetime of cigarettes, bourbon, and bad choices takes its toll."

"You lived well, Alfie. Would you change anything? Really?"

Would he? Alfonse shook his head. "No. I wouldn't. We were the music makers, for a time, the dreamers of dreams, were we not?"

Olivia nodded. "The world is so different now."

"As those we once took it from thought as well, I imagine." Pain, soft and stealthy, rippled across his chest. Alfonse quelled the urge to clutch it. "Forgive me. I tire easily. I need to rest."

"Then rest." She patted his knee. "I'll sit here and read."

"You don't have to keep an old man company."

"No, I don't. Which is why you should be grateful I offered. Don't be a martyr. It's unbecoming."

"Vanity prohibits any argument from me."

"As if you'd win." She chuffed. "Shall I read aloud?"

"I'd like that."

"What shall we read?"

"You pick. Something new. Something I've never read. Or written."

Olivia moved, slowly, to the extensive bookshelves he himself had not had the energy or will to inspect. Pulling a book from the stacks, she made cooing sounds, like a mother to her child. "This one." She handed him the book. "I'm surprised they included it in your collection."

"This is a children's book."

"Only an old man would say such a thing." Olivia's eyes twinkled. Ah, he remembered that, too. "You mark my words, this is going to be bigger than even the greediest publicists have ever dreamed about. You'll want to be ready when the next one releases. If you've not expired, we shall read that one together, too."

To the rustle of turning pages, the whisper of her practiced voice, Alfonse Carducci closed his eyes. A boy who lived, under the staircase, in the home of his terrible relatives. A book he'd never have read but for coming here to this place he'd always known he'd die in, alongside all those others who once ruled the world.

Sunlight, warm on his face. Sweet humming. Disoriented musings involving an owl perched upon his armrest and a giant riding a motorcycle. Alfonse slipped from slumber, certain he'd died in his sleep. The proof was in the humming, and the angel reaching into the sunlight. He'd seen her before. A fleeting glimpse sometime in his past.

She was, now, warm and lovely on his arm. An unfamiliar gift. A grief to come. Always and always, his . . .

The words filled his head the way they once had; in those days words came so swiftly his pen could not keep up. Notebooks filled with scrawl and scratch he could scarcely decipher days later, but could only coax out of memory in fractured bits and jagged pieces.

"Please," he said. "My laptop. There, on the desk."

He shouldered higher in his chair. Olivia was gone, but the young woman who'd first been in his rooms upon his arrival in the Pen was already grabbing the laptop computer from his desk. He reached. She handed. Words already sifted out of dreaming, out of the world.

"Damn this thing!" He pounded on keys as if that would boot it up faster. "Please, write this down. Hurry. Hurry!"

The young woman yanked the band from her hair as she darted back to the desk, but not before he saw what she tried so valiantly to hide. Beauty and Beast. Jekyll and Hyde. Proof of the duality in every human soul—hers was simply worn in the open. Or not so open. She hid her face behind her hair, angled the worst of it away from him.

"Go ahead. I'm ready."

Alfonse gave her his words, a mad jumble that didn't sound as lovely coming from his mouth as it would have flying out of the tips of his fingers. There was enough to pull the beauty back from oblivion, later when his computer finished booting up.

"Thank you," he said, holding out his hand for the notebook. "And forgive me. I was dreaming. I didn't want to forget."

"It's an honor, sir," she said. "Is there anything else I can do for you?"

Head bowed, gaze on the chair leg or her shoes or the pattern in the carpet, she was a golden cascade standing before him. Model tall, but not model thin. Voluptuous, like the bombshells of his lusty youth, when he fell as hard for the feminine curve of a hip as he did for the masculine cut of a shoulder. She'd been in his rooms quite often; he'd caught her several times lingering. Young Alfonse would have opened his eyes, caught her hand, and seduced her into his bed. Old Alfonse had to be content imagining it.

"Tell me your name?" he asked.

"Cecibel," she answered. "Cecibel Bringer. I'm an orderly here."

"A pleasure to meet you, Cecibel. A lovely name, for a lovely young woman."

A sound, something like laughter. A slight shift of her shoulders. A small exhalation of breath. "Charming. So the stories are all true."

"I imagine most of what you may have heard about me is true," he said. "The good and the bad."

"A lifetime of hearing things. Some must be lies."

"Some." Curiosity burned. Not the desire to see her face; that, he'd already seen. Dr. Kintz's assessment of her was all wrong. The man was sincere if not very astute. Alfonse's ability to read body language well enough to transpose it onto a page deduced she was not quiet and shy, not potentially addled by the accident that took half her face. Not mousy and ugly and all those things a first glance would have seen. Alfonse Carducci did not put much stock in first impressions. Human beings were far more complicated. "Would you sit with me?"

"I only came in to collect your breakfast tray. I should go."

"Of course, you have duties." He waved his hands over his head, an old gesture once full of sarcasm and humor, now one that took his breath away. "Forgive me."

"It's not that." She nearly looked up. Only nearly. "I don't want to go all fangirl on you, and I will if I get half the chance. You probably get that a lot."

"Fangirl." A soft chuckle. Another moment of breath gone. "I have not heard that one before. Yes, I used to get it a lot, and I loved every moment of it. These days, I do not warrant so much attention. I'm a relic of a bygone day."

"There are whole college courses dedicated to your work."

"Alfonse Carducci as a subject to be studied, not a writer to be admired."

"Do you need admiration to be proud of all you've accomplished?"

"That, my dear," he said, "is what we call a loaded question. I don't need the admiration to feel pride in my work, but do I need it in general? Yes, I do. I'm a vain man, Cecibel. A vain man who happened to have the talent to continuously feed that vanity."

"I think you sell yourself short, sir."

"Alfonse, please. And I can assure you there is not a being on the planet who thinks more highly of me than I do."

A glance through lashes. Progress made. "An enormous ego is a handy shield, Mr. Carducci."

"Slain by my own words." Alfonse clutched his heart, part drama, part need. "Touché, my dear. Touché."

"I've read everything you wrote. *Wicked Tongues* has always been my favorite."

"Everything?" He sifted through dates and releases. "Even after *Night Wings on the Moon*?"

She nodded, her gaze again on a chair leg or shoes or carpet.

"A dark story, full of unlikable characters," he said. "Do you believe it is true, what the critics said of it? That I betrayed my loyal readers writing so dark a tale?"

"I've read it more times than I can count," she said. "I keep it on my bedside table."

"Didn't you say *Wicked Tongues* is your favorite?"

"Yes." Cecibel picked up his breakfast tray. "I should get back to work."

"If you must." He let go a deep breath. Alfonse was tired. Always tired, but Cecibel was right; he lived for admiration. He absorbed it like sunshine, like the drugs keeping his ill-used body going. Waking to words conjured by her presence revived his body, pulled his soul back from the brink of oblivion like nothing had in far too long.

"Cecibel?"

She turned her head, fair side, hand still on the lever of his door. The round blush of her cheek, the slope of her nose, lashes so thick and long they cast shadows, waves of blond hair cascading down the curves of her waist, her back, Cecibel was a fairy princess stepped out of an old German folktale.

"Would you visit me again?" he asked. "When duties don't conflict?"

Her hand fell from the lever. "Me?"

"Yes, you."

"Switch . . . um . . . Raymond Switcher has been asking after you," she stammered. "Many of the residents have. Perhaps you'd like to have one or two of them come visit. Or your nurse can bring you down to the gathering room for a little while."

"I'm not quite up to that just yet," he said, and it was true. "I don't wish to dwell in the past. Not yet, at any rate. And that is what will happen. Reminiscing about the old days when we were young and immortal. But I am lonely here. Indulge a dying old man, my dear. The company of a lovely young woman, a fangirl at that, is exactly what I require to make it through another day."

A soft chuckle. Musical, from her. "I see the drama hasn't been embellished either."

"Not even slightly."

Her pause lasted far too long. The blush of her cheek burned brighter. "All right, Mr. Carducci. After my shift. As long as you're still up for it."

"I will nap the rest of the day to ensure it."

Cecibel opened the door. "Your nurse will be up soon with your lunch, but can I get you anything before I leave?"

A new heart? A fresh liver would do in a pinch. "No, thank you. I'm content as a cat in the sun right now."

⌒

How silly it was, to be so aflutter. The man was seventy-nine, and dying. She was enamored of a reputation, of years of hero worship, of a past so grand and wild. But it felt so good. She was new, to him, even if Cecibel felt as if she'd known him all her life. As, in fact, she had. The familiarity, bred in a past long before the one that took everything from her, freed her somehow, from something she'd stopped noticing.

Infatuation offered to gather his breakfast tray when Sal groused about schlepping all the way out to that far wing of the residence to do so. For the third day in a row. Sal thought he was playing her. Or maybe he knew. Infatuation had lingered longer today, tidying up while he slept. It stood beside his chair watching the rise and fall of his chest, even if that felt like crossing the line between fan-girl and stalker. He didn't know. And if he did, Cecibel was pretty certain Alfonse Carducci would get a kick out of it.

Gripping her copy of *Dark Wings on the Moon* tighter, she smoothed the front of her dress, the hair against the side of her face. She lifted her hand to knock, and froze. In all her years working at the Pen, she'd rarely gone into Dr. Traegar's private suite; it had already been closed up and waiting when first she was hired. Rumors varied as to why that was so, but all included Alfonse Carducci. Mentor and protégé. Lifelong friends. Lovers. In the weeks since reading of the famous author's failing health, Cecibel had been in there quite often, tidying. Preparing. Snooping. Dr. Traegar hadn't only left the suite, but all its contents, to his old friend. Inscriptions in many of the books left little to wonder concerning the nature of their relationship.

"Don't just stand there, Cecibel," she muttered. A quick knock before her nerve gave out, and she opened the door.

"You are here, at last." A diminished but still regal Alfonse Carducci sat in the same easy chair, now moved closer to the fireplace kindled to the perfect flicker. In the lines of his face, she saw the man from book jackets, on *Johnny Carson*. He was there. Oh, he was there. And Cecibel's heart fluttered all over again.

"Come, sit beside me." He gestured to the chair opposite. "I took the liberty of making tea. It's not quite the proper time for tea, but not so far off."

The second easy chair loomed. Cecibel sat on the edge of the cushion, ankles crossed. She didn't have to angle her face away; the chair had been set to do that for her. "Can I pour for you?"

"No tea for me, thank you. I'm afraid my doctors don't allow me caffeine, and I despise that herbal nonsense. I have my glass of water with lemon. And your company. I have all I require."

Cecibel set her book on the tea table, pleased that her hands didn't tremble the way her insides did. Pouring herself a cup, she coaxed herself calm. He was just a man. An old, dying man. A resident, and she, one of his caregivers. The fangirl shit had to stop.

"Your copy has seen better days." He picked up the book from the table, turned it over in his hands. "It is like me. Battered. Dog-eared. Still intact but falling apart."

She laughed softly. "I suppose it is. Does that bother you? Your book being in less than stellar condition, I mean."

His smile spread. "A book is like a woman. She should leave your bed with her hair tangled and her clothes on backward. A book without creases is a book that has never known passion."

She stirred cream and sugar into her tea. There was fire in the old man's eyes. He'd been waiting all day for this, just as she had. "What about people who love a book so much they want to keep it pristine?"

Alfonse leaned a little closer. "Love is not passion, my dear. Love is sweet and good and righteous. Passion is wild and messy and dangerous."

"Dangerous?"

"Yes, very dangerous. Passion is all impulse, and impulse is rarely rational."

Cecibel sipped. "I don't know that I buy that."

"No?"

"What about passionate love?"

"Ah!" He thrust a finger in the air. "A wonderful thing, but not what we're discussing."

"We're not?"

"No, we're discussing the difference between love and passion, not a combination of the two. Let us take this copy of *Dark Wings* for example." He hefted the book, fluttered the pages. Again. And again.

The scent of old paper made soft with wear wafted into her face. Glue long-past cracked along the spine threatened to give way completely. An oft-read book, yes, but not a well-loved one. Cecibel's heart thumped, measure for measure. Her skin prickled.

Arms. Neck. Scalp. She steadied her breathing, succeeding only in making it stunted and obviously labored.

"The critics were wrong about this book, Cecibel." Alfonse spoke so softly. "It did not betray my fans. It fed them what they needed. Love it or hate it, people were passionate about it. You were passionate about it." He handed her back the book, tapped the cover. "What does your copy of *Wicked Tongues* look like?"

"Not like this, I swear."

"Because you love it. Cherish it. This one?" He shrugged. "The passion is in the creases. Why is this the book you brought for me to inscribe?"

She tried for casual. "It was on my nightstand, and only the first of many I hope to have you sign." And held her breath.

Alfonse thumbed his lip. "It would be my honor to sign them all."

Cecibel exhaled, slow and softly.

"Leave this with me," he said, "Bring me the rest tomorrow. It will occupy my time until you visit me again, thinking up the perfect inscription for so lovely and indulgent a young woman."

Leave it? Her own hands placed the book upon the tea table, her own voice said, "Of course. Thank you," from far, far away, where another voice was screaming. Always screaming. Years and years and years.

"Let us talk of other things." Alfonse Carducci's hand upon her knee silenced the distant screaming. She focused on the long, straight fingers. Trimmed, pink nails. Wrinkled, yes, but the hand of a much younger man. He pulled it gently away. "Forgive me. I meant no offense."

"Pardon?"

"My hand. Your knee. You were staring."

"Oh, no." Cecibel managed to laugh without smiling. "I was . . . was just thinking that you have nice hands."

Alfonse held them out. "One of my few still-functioning body parts. A writer depends upon his hands. I have never been able to dictate more than notes. There is a magical, even sacred bond between my mind and my fingers."

"Mrs. Peppernell has said much the same."

"Olivia is of the old school." He sipped his water. "I suspect most of the residents are."

"That will probably be so for some time. Do you know everyone here?"

"Not everyone." Another sip. "Olivia, of course. And Raymond. If one is older than sixty, which I imagine everyone here is, we've probably met or worked together."

"Our youngest resident is sixty-seven. Judith Arsenault. I believe she's Canadian."

"Judi?" Far, far more romantic and lyrical when he said the name. "Yes, she is Canadian. A point of contention, back in our day. I didn't know she is here. She was my editor many times. Brilliant. And so young to be locked away with the rest of us."

"Everyone is here for a reason," she said, and no more. Judith could tell him what she wished, or nothing at all. "And no one is locked in anywhere."

"A figure of speech you will understand when you are as old and decrepit as I."

"Are you fishing for compliments?"

"That depends." His eyes twinkled when he smiled. They really did. "Are you offering any?"

Cecibel watched him carefully while they chatted, for batting eyes or labored breathing. As one of his many caregivers, she knew his medical history, his medical facts. As one of his many fans, she knew a whole lot more. Alfonse was more interested in listening to her talk than he was in talking, possibly because breathing took enough effort without adding more.

How he managed to steer the conversation away from himself and to her, Cecibel couldn't figure out. Standing outside his suite an hour and some after she'd gone in, she pressed palms to burning cheeks. Had she chattered too inanely? Of course. She could scarcely remember anything she said, but what she did remember was about her. Coming to Bar Harbor, practically falling into the job she'd held for eight years. The patients met, loved, and lost. Her duties. What she loved. What she hated. Everything about her life on a superficial level, and nothing whatever of life before coming to the Pen.

"Will you come back tomorrow?" he'd asked before she left. Cecibel agreed in a rush of breath, a dash for the door, and as graceless an exit as ever there had been.

Bar Harbor, Maine

May 22, 1999

There are many yesterdays. With any luck, many
tomorrows.
But there's only one today. Don't fuck it up.
—Cornelius Traegar

Cecibel's copy of *Night Wings on the Moon* sat where she'd left it upon the tea table, and still he hadn't inscribed it. She'd brought him others that he easily found the right words for, but for this one? Words failed.

It opened to one specific page every time he set it on its spine and let it do as it would. Someone had written in the margin—pencil, too faded to read—beside a bit of text.

We fell free from on high, like dragons mating. We snapped and roared and bit. And we loved. The ground came at us. I saw it and didn't care. She never saw it coming at all. I covered her eyes; if she saw, too, she'd have banked her great and powerful wings. I didn't want to be saved, and so she couldn't be either. Both, or none. I was content to fall.

Alfonse tried and tried to remember writing those words, but couldn't. It was like that. Writing. First rounds of revisions never failed to surprise and delight him. A book was always new, no matter how many years he'd worked on that first draft. *Night Wings* had taken six. Not his longest affair with a book, not his shortest. That he remembered. And the pain of all that honesty.

~ 23 ~

Cecibel would arrive any moment, just as she had every day since that first. He picked up the tattered copy, flipped to the title page, set it down again. Instead, he opened the drawer of the table where there should have been teaspoons and cloth napkins, and retrieved from it the nearly blank notebook Cecibel had jotted his rambling into almost a week ago.

She was, now, warm and lovely on his arm. An unfamiliar gift. A grief to come. Always and always, his . . .

He picked up his pen.

That was the deal. The pact. The promise written in kisses and on long walks. In screeched battles and hours of makeup sex. Cecilia and Aldo. Aldo and Cecilia. The stars had proclaimed it; either they or the storm clouds always so thick over Buffalo, New York . . .

Buffalo? Alfonse shrugged. He'd been there, he was certain. At some point. Maybe. Underlining the city, he placed a question mark above it just as Cecibel knocked on his door.

"Come in." He placed the pen and notebook back into the drawer, closed it softly. In she came, as always, wearing a dress, the glory of her hair strategically covering half her face.

"Good afternoon, Mr. Carducci."

Still Mr. Carducci. "Good afternoon, Miss Bringer."

She frowned. Strange, how she would do that but remain stingy with her smiles.

"What happened to Cecibel?" she asked.

"I should not have been so forward," he said. "That you call me Mr. Carducci leads me to believe you prefer formality. Thus, Miss Bringer, I shall not use your given name unless you do me the honor of using mine."

"I was taught to address my elders with respect."

He waved a hand over his head. Caught his breath. "An elder? I'm not certain my poor heart can take such reverence."

She dropped onto the chair set beside his. "Don't say that. It's not funny."

"Add humorless to the list of my shortcomings." He patted her hand. "I think it is time you were forced to see the real me, my dear, not this image you have of me. I have never been respectable."

"That's not true."

"Then take me to the gathering room, and you will see."

Cecibel sat straighter. "You want to go to the gathering room? Now?"

"I do. Now."

"Let me get a nurse."

"No, no." He grabbed her hand as she started to rise. "You. Or I do not wish to go. I need you to protect me. I trust no one else here."

"Not Olivia?"

"Who do you suppose I need protection from?"

That made her laugh. Excellent. Even if she kept her lips together.

"Unfortunately, I'm just an orderly. It's against the rules."

"Rules?" When did his laughter start sounding like paper rustling? "Here? Ah, my dear, whatever has been since Cornelius's death will be no more. He and I dreamed up this place when we were young men conquering the literary world. We took it from the greats. Faulkner, Joyce, Cather, Parker. We robbed them blind and flew their tattered flags in their faces. Cornelius is gone and now I am king. Look around you if you need proof. Will you refuse the king?"

She leaned back in her chair, studied him with that one, marble-blue eye. What a beauty she had been, still was. Shame was the only ugliness he could see; but he was a writer, a weaver of words, and his reality was not hers.

"I suppose not," she said at last. "But if I get in trouble, I'm throwing you under the bus."

"Excellent. Thank you." He started to rise, caught his breath, and made it the rest of the way to his feet. The wheelchair, state-of-the-art, sat unused in the corner. "I suppose being wheeled in by a goddess powering my chariot is not a terrible way to greet my subjects."

"It's the chair or I'm getting a nurse. That's the deal."

"I will not argue." He gestured to it. "Would you?"

Cecibel fetched the wheelchair that he could have powered on his own with nothing more than a little effort from his fingers. Still, he let her take control, folding his hands obediently in his lap while she maneuvered him out the door.

"Tell me about my kingdom," he said. "Dr. Kintz is a good man, sincerely invested in his patients, but he doesn't have an artist's soul."

"I don't have an artist's soul either," she said. "I'm an orderly. A caregiver."

"That doesn't mean there is no art in you, Cecibel. If that were true, you could not exist here. You would never have stayed."

"Then how will Dr. Kintz?"

Alfonse glanced up at her over his shoulder. The buckled and pitted skin along her jawline nearly undid him. "See how long he endures," he said, proud there wasn't even a hitch in his voice. "As I understand it, there have been several head doctors since Cornelius's death."

"Yes," she said. "I didn't get here until just after he died. I always wished I'd known him."

"He was an extraordinary man."

"Olivia tells me stories." Cecibel leaned lower to whisper. "I've always believed it was Olivia scaring off all the doctors."

Alfonse chuckled. "I will not disagree, but if you tell her I said so, I'll deny it."

"Good call."

She wheeled him silently, slowing closer to the gathering room. Alfonse attempted to control his breathing, trying vainly to keep his beleaguered heart from hammering. In the days he'd been in the Pen, there had been no need to step out of his suite. Olivia, Cecibel, his medication and food came to him. Too late to turn back. Alfonse Carducci never backed down. Schoolyards still bled his exploits, decades after he left Italy for the States. For a boy like him, it had been fight or fall.

The halls and public rooms on the first floor looked much the same as they had when Cornelius first opened the place. Rich wood, gleaming granite, polished brass. The Pen had been built during the early 1920s by one of those haphazardly rich families who lost everything in the Crash. By the time he and Cornelius found the mansion, it had been left to rot.

Nineteen forty-five was not kind to men of their ilk. Bar Harbor had been the perfect sort of obscure. Warm days swimming in the freezing sea. Cold nights burrowed warm in down quilts. Cornelius bought the mansion for a song, a dance, and a few pretty seashells. They spent four years restoring it, planning its future. Their future. And then Alfonse sold his first book, and everything changed.

"You ready?" Cecibel's voice startled his poor heart into beating uncomfortably fast. Her hand on his shoulder steadied him. Cornelius was gone. So were most of those the Pen was built for. Only he was left, barely. Olivia. Raymond. Judi—thank goodness, Judi. How fast the years flew by, and yet, their youth was eons ago.

He covered her hand with his. "Do I look . . . old?"

She bent low. "Yes, you do. And so do all the other residents here." The spicy scent of her perfume excited him. "That's why they call this an old people's home."

⌐

No cheer went up. Some tears were shed. Judi Arsenault. Switch. A few of the others who remembered Alfonse, though he did not remember them. Not Olivia, who'd been keeping Alfonse company whether he wished it or not. She'd scowled at Judi's tears, taken the handles of the wheelchair, and rolled her old friend among his subjects. Alfonse didn't object, though he did look back at Cecibel with a plea in his eyes.

She made herself comfortable within hearing distance, and watched the king at his court. If anything happened to him, she was in trouble. While he was technically free to roam as he wished, unwritten law insisted that none of the residents were permitted to do so without authorization. This foray would never be authorized.

Cecibel checked her watch. Fifteen minutes gone. Alfonse looked all right. Maybe a little pale, but he smiled that heart-pattering smile he'd been famous for. Olivia sat closest to him, her back to Cecibel and her hand resting lightly on Alfonse's arm. Raymond Switcher, lined face lifted ten years in the past, sat on his left. Judi, still comparatively young and elfishly lovely, finished the circle at his knees. The gossip all over the tabloids years and years ago bloomed there in the intimacy of hands on his knees, in the ownership Olivia took, in the fact of the crown invisibly worn. Alfonse Carducci and Judith Arsenault. Alfonse Carducci and Olivia Peppernell. Alfonse Carducci and Cornelius Traegar. It wouldn't surprise Cecibel to discover he'd also had a torrid affair with Switch despite the thousand stories Switch had for every picture of his Bethany gracing his room. But Switch was another storyteller in this place where such a thing was a given. For all Cecibel knew, there was never a Bethany to begin with.

"You're a brave one. Yes, you are." Sal had a way of sneaking up on people, a true gift, considering his ample size.

Cecibel pretended he hadn't startled her, smoothed her hair over her face even though he'd seen it more times than she caught him. "I won't let him stay long," she said. "And I'm watching."

"If Dr. Dick catches you—"

"Hush." She shook her head. "You're so bad."

"You know it, honey. The nurses will tattle, but I won't. You can bet your skinny, white-girl ass Dr. Dick already knows. Probably on his way over right now."

"My ass isn't skinny."

"Honey, please." He turned around, brandishing the pride of the drag queen circuit. "This is an ass."

"You got me there." She patted the chair beside her. "Dr. Kintz is having his dinner. He always eats early so he can make rounds before the residents settle in for the night. If the nurses tattle and he disapproves enough, he'll come down and chastise me. If he's okay with Alfonse being among his subjects, he'll pretend he didn't hear anything."

Sal raised a perfectly plucked eyebrow, pursed plump lips. "Your funeral, honey."

"You performing this weekend?"

"Does a drag queen shit in the woods?"

Cecibel nudged him. "Gross."

"You coming this time?"

"Where?"

"If I tell you, you won't come."

Portland. Had to be. Cecibel crossed her arms over her chest. Uncrossed them. "You know we can't both leave," she said. "Who'd watch over the residents?"

"Their nurses, maybe? Come on, honey. Road trip, just us girls."

"Maybe," she said.

Sal shrugged. "We both know that maybe means no. It always does."

Cecibel didn't argue. He was right, of course. But he would ask again, another day, for another show, until she said yes.

⟨~

"You're looking a little blue around the gills, there, Alfie." Switch circled a finger around his mouth. "You okay?"

I'm dying, you fool. "I'm fine," he said.

"Maybe you should rest." Judi fussed. Like a bird, she was. Always had been. He'd been almost afraid to make love to her that first time. So delicate. So crushable. How wrong he had been. Birdlike, indeed. A raptor who'd more than once shredded the skin of his back and buttocks, and his manuscripts. Memory stirred what little libido Alfonse still retained. A valiant twitch rather than the sharp salute of his youth, but something.

"He can rest when he's dead, Judith," Olivia grumbled. "Carpe diem! What he has left, at any rate."

Judi glared. "Will you have dinner in the dining room this evening, then? Are you permitted?"

"They can't keep him locked up against his will. Of course he'll have dinner with us. Won't you, Alfie?"

"Are they always like this?" Alfonse asked Switch.

Switch grinned. He rubbed the back of his neck. Nodded. Winked. Darling Switch. Brilliant writer. Exquisite and inventive.

Not even in their wild youth had his tongue obeyed those eloquent words inside his head.

"Tell us more about your memoir." Judi wriggled closer. "I understand you're working with someone?"

"I'm not working at all," Alfonse said. "It's a memoir in name only."

"A ghostwriter." Olivia shook her head. "I knew it. I would rather never see it written."

"It was contracted ages ago, before my health deteriorated." A long, shallow breath did little to alleviate the woozy feeling. "I anticipated spending my golden years writing it. A swan song, no? But I don't have it in me, Livy. Be kind."

"You don't write anymore either, Olivia." There was his raptor. Judi's narrow, exotic eyes gleamed. "Don't fault Alfonse for—"

"Ladies." Switch nodded toward the door, and the stern and unhappy-looking nurse stalking their way. Judi shifted in her chair, hid her dangerous bite behind a smile. Olivia did nothing of the kind.

"Is there something wrong, Yana?" Cecibel intercepted the nurse.

"You know very well that Mr. Carducci needs to have a nurse with him outside of his room. It's very dangerous to—"

"Hush your nonsense, child." Olivia darted to Cecibel's side faster than she should have been able to. "Alfonse is not a prisoner. I can take him anywhere he asks me to take him. Any of us can."

Cecibel bowed her head, cheeks blushing red. Did her shoulders shake with laughter? Or rage?

"You are responsible for this?" Yana pointed to Olivia, who smacked her hand away.

"It's rude to point. And yes, I am. Cecibel was good enough to accompany us, and keep her trusted eye on Alfonse even though her shift ended long ago."

Yana's prim lips set. She'd already lost, and would pretend she hadn't. Alfonse kept a straight face. Oh, Olivia. Had she obliged and divorced the husband she abandoned, she could have made an honest man of Alfonse Carducci, writer, rake, miscreant. Perhaps.

"You should have contacted me, Cecibel," Yana murmured. "I'd have come."

"I know how busy things get just before dinner," Cecibel answered. "It was no bother at all."

"Well, then." Yana stood taller, checked her white wristwatch. "Dinner begins in twenty minutes. If Mr. Carducci wishes to eat in the dining room tonight, I'll take him. Understood?"

"Sure, Yana."

"Nurse Yana."

"You got it."

Yana made a show of checking his pulse, her eyes on her watch and a thin smile on her lips. Alfonse obliged obediently. Without his chart there to consult, she had no idea what was normal for him, and what was not. She let go his wrist and patted his hand, as if he were a small child, not a man diminished to the size of one.

"Insolent cow," Olivia grumbled at the nurse's back, resuming her perch at Alfonse's side. "What do you think, Alfie? Dinner with your old cohorts?"

"That would be lovely. And Cecibel, too?"

She glanced up, eyes wide. "I'm not allowed to eat in the residents' dining room. But thank you, Mr. Cardu . . . thank you, Alfonse."

"Oh, I have a much better idea, then." Judi Arsenault bolted to her feet and flittered from the room.

"What is she up to now?" Switch stared after her, a look of longing softening the lines of his face. How old was Raymond Switcher? Younger than he; healthier, that much was certain. *There is still time. Don't waste it, my friend.* But Alfonse said no such thing.

Bar Harbor, Maine

꧁꧂

Holidays are nothing more than excuses
for gluttony, drunkery, and debauchery.
Here's to Left Sock Day!

—CORNELIUS TRAEGAR

Even sitting in the sunshine was too much for him. The breeze, warm and steady, coming off the ocean, snatched his breath. He would persevere through the lobster-bake luncheon—of which he could not partake of a single claw, mollusk, or cob—and ask to be returned to his room. Quietly. He didn't want to ruin the festivities for Raymond or Olivia or Judi. He didn't want them to know how truly feeble he was.

The faint scent of marijuana rolled over him like the surf, tickled out the past. Damp sheets. Silken copper splayed across his shoulder, his chest. An ivory leg tossed across his dark and hairy one, trapping him in a room, in a bed. They'd been fifty-two—she—and forty-nine—he. Indomitable. Not by time. Not by critics. Not by one another. They hadn't known, then, what the years would bring. His continued rise. Her fall from grace. Distance even immortals such as they could not surmount.

Alfonse spotted her in the arbor overlooking the sea, the telltale smoke wafting over her head, sparking those olfactory memories that let him forget, for a moment, how difficult every breath had become. Olivia's fondness for weed wasn't a new one, of course.

Simply, now it was also necessary. The fall (or push) down the stairs all those years ago made it so.

"I really ought to do something about that." Dr. Kintz pulled a folding chair up to Alfonse's wheeled one, turned it around, and sat with his arms draped over the back. "We could find ourselves in trouble."

"She is an old woman," Alfonse told him. "This is Maine. No one cares what she does."

"It's not good for her."

Alfonse chuffed. "And the butter with lobster you provided for her is? And the ice cream? Rolls? And the—"

"Point taken." He laughed. "Did you know it'll probably be legal in a few months? Medicinally, anyway."

"I did not. Is that truly possible?"

"It's on the ballot. You can't vote on it, because you're not a resident yet, but Olivia, I mean, Mrs. Peppernell can."

"The question is, will she?" Alfonse sacrificed a few more breaths to laughter. "She likes being a rebel."

"Gee, I hadn't noticed."

No more laughter. He couldn't spare it. Richard Kintz could and did, the sound fading from his lips but remaining in the corners of his eyes. Nice eyes. Brown and warm and inquisitive. Alfonse enjoyed his company. He appreciated Richard's genuine wish to make the lives of his patients better, more comfortable, or at least tolerable. Kindness went further than acumen when dealing with those so close to the inexorable. In any other place, such kindness would be appreciated. Here, where dwelt resentful artists still and never to be understood, Richard's kindness would trip him up. Unless that glint now and then spied behind the smile, in the corner of his eye, was something meaner than amused patience.

"I understand Cecibel has been watching over you." Ah, there it was. The glint.

Alfonse nodded sagely as he could. "She is my guardian angel."

"An orderly, not a nurse. You are aware."

"Of course. Richard, my boy, a nurse's care is appreciated, but it will not buy me another moment longer than my allotment here on this earth. Cecibel, on the other hand, allows me to pretend there is a way to cheat."

Richard rested his chin to his forearms on the chair back. "Why?"

"Why?"

"Yes, sir. Why?" He straightened. "She puzzles me. Your interest in her puzzles me more."

"I don't understand."

"Let's be frank. There's the obvious that shouldn't matter, but whether we like it or not, it does. She's a good worker, a hard worker. A worker, period. And that's kind of my point. Don't get me wrong, I appreciate her. But why would a man of your fame and reputation, surrounded by his peers, break every unofficial rule here concerning the necessary line drawn between residents and staff to spend so much time with her?"

Ah, so he did know of the dinners taken in his room, the four of them and Cecibel (who never ate a thing). Of course. Nothing happened in the Pen that the nurses didn't report to their head doctor—a single man, pleasant to look at, with a respectable job, and still young enough to entice. Even Salvatore seemed smitten, the dear boy. Girl? Despite his own appetites, Alfonse was ever unsure as to how Sal viewed himself. Herself. Salself.

Dr. Kintz obviously did not know Cecibel. The nurses didn't either. Alfonse would take that out and dissect why it was so, later when Richard was not sitting beside him waiting for curiosity to be appeased. Waiting for a reason to let him continue ignoring the breach in etiquette.

"Her scars tell a story," Alfonse said. "Every action, every reaction speaks to me as an artist. In short, she inspires me to create. And creation is the only purpose of life, after all. I have very little left of this one, my boy. Leave me that, and don't put too much stock in rules that don't really matter."

Richard scrubbed a hand across the back of his sunburned neck. "I don't mean to give you a hard time. And I don't mean to belittle

Cecibel in any way. She intrigues me in the same way she inspires you, I suppose. She makes me want to *know*."

"Then you understand more than you think you do."

"This position . . ." Richard blew a breath through his lips. "It's very different from what I was expecting."

He wanted to say more. It was there in the tension of his body, on the edge of his voice. All the good doctor needed was the opening he craved, the opening Alfonse did not have the energy to provide. "May I beg further indulgence, Dr. Kintz?"

"Of course. What can I do for you?"

"The sea air is a bit too much for my poor lungs. I need to rest, if someone could escort me back to my—"

Dr. Richard Kintz scrambled out of his chair, summoning a nurse with an urgent flick of his fingers. How amusing, this, after all these years. Alfonse had no kin to sue should someone mistreat him, accidentally or not. Fame still lingered, overshadowed its failing subject. Alfonse would use that, as he always had, to mold things to his liking. In this tiny corner of so grand a life, the world still rested gently on his palm.

Sunlight beams reached in, casting long shadows like bars across his room. Once, slumber had been ponderous and soothing. No longer. Slumber was a cat twitching ears at the smallest noise. The soft tread of rubber-soled shoes in the corridor, the click of a gently opened door, breath held and shallowly released.

"Don't go, Aldo. Please."

"I have to."

"I can't do it. I'll kill myself. I swear."

"Say that again and we're through."

"You're a liar. You'll never be through with me."

"I didn't mean to wake you."

Cecibel's voice superimposed over those skirting between awake and asleep. The ones so clear they spoke directly into his brain. Joy prickled in bursts along his skin. He remembered the feeling, and yet it was new. Bigger. Brighter. More magnificent than it had ever been in his ungrateful youth.

"I was only dozing." Alfonse checked the clock. "Are the festivities over?"

"Until dark." Cecibel sat on the arm of his chair. "Most everyone is resting so they can enjoy the fireworks."

"Ah, the fireworks."

"It's kind of amazing," she said. "I understand Dr. Traegar always did it up big for Memorial Day, the Fourth, Labor Day, and New Year's."

"And Valentine's Day," Alfonse added. "It was his favorite holiday. Always red and white fireworks."

"I have a feeling he was pretty fond of any reason to celebrate." Cecibel picked at a thread on the hem of her shirt. "We only do the three summer ones now, but it's still nice. When I was a kid, I loved watching the fireworks over the falls. Nothing like over the ocean, though."

Alfonse's breath hitched. This tiny insight. This show of faith. "Falls? Niagara?"

Cecibel chuckled. "Nothing that grand. The Paterson Falls. In New Jersey. That's where I was born. St. Joe's Hospital. We moved to Portland when I was a baby, but we always went back to my grandparents in Paterson for their big Fourth of July picnic."

"Silk City."

"You know of it?"

"Of course, of course. It is where I lived when I first came to this country. It's where many Italians had family already established. I was a bricklayer, back then."

"Really? I never read anything about that. Is this a story?"

Alfonse put up his hands in surrender. "Yes, and no. I did live in Paterson for three months working as a bricklayer before I left it for New York City. It is not glamorous, and hardly worth mentioning. I don't know that I ever have."

The clock ticked. A chime sounded. Cecibel looked at the clock and started to rise.

"Something wrong, my dear?"

She shrugged.

"Tell me."

"It's nearly time for dinner."

"And?"

Cecibel bowed her head. "I'm an ungrateful idiot, but I'm not going to have dinner with you and the others anymore."

"Why not?" *If Dr. Kintz said anything to you . . .*

Her shroud of hair blocked both the freakish and the fair. "It's horribly uncomfortable." Her voice, barely a whisper. "I eat alone in my room for a reason, Alfonse. Please let it go at that."

And she was gone, flying from his room like wind through his window. Like air from his lungs. Alfonse drew in slowly, exhaled long. Dr. Kintz had been right, in the completely wrong way. There was a necessary line between residents and staff, but not for the residents' sake alone. Not for propriety or even to keep authority where it belonged. Cecibel sat with the king and his court, but never a morsel ate. She sipped water with a lemon squeeze. Safe enough. Alfonse had been certain she'd become more comfortable, trusted them not to be repulsed by her. Such a fool he was. A self-centered, insensitive fool. She'd known Olivia for years and still hid her face. Switch. Judi, even Salvatore. Known them. Loved them. And still hid from them. Not for them, for herself.

A cold fury sent dangerous prickles of electricity to his extremities. Her proximity, even when he was sleeping, lit words inside him. Candles along a darkened path once so bright and eager. Cecibel was not her accident, and not what resulted from it. Dr. Kintz's grazing assessment of her was right only on the surface. Beneath it, she was all things beautiful and bright. Bringer of words. Muse of creation. Alfonse didn't know why or how, only that she was. So late in life, at the end of all things, Cecibel gave him back the thing that mattered most.

Rising, creakily and carefully, Alfonse held enthusiasm on a short leash. When he could move without bones and flesh shaking apart, he got the nearly blank notebook from the drawer where teaspoons and napkins should have been. He took it to his desk set against the huge windows looking out onto the sea, and picked up a pen.

Paterson, New Jersey

WINTER 1953

She was, now, warm and lovely in his arms. An unfamiliar gift. A grief to come. Always and always, his. That was the deal. The pact. The promise written in kisses and on long walks. In screeched battles and makeup sex. Cecilia and Aldo. Aldo and Cecilia. The stars had proclaimed it; either they or the summer storm obscuring the Paterson Falls when first they met.

Pressing her up against the cinderblock wall, Aldo fumbled with panties he'd yet to see. There was never any time for lingering, peeking, caressing. Stolen moments at the falls, behind the hot dog joint where he worked, in parked cars that didn't belong to either of them. Quick and desperate and explosive. And done. She, pulling down her skirt. He, zipping up. Hands smoothed over hair. A smile, a laugh, a kiss. Until the next time they collided.

Silk against his fingers. The elastic snap. Lace trim. He was in. Gloriously inside the heat of her, moving and groaning. The greasy-good stench of hot dogs and french fries spiked Aldo's libido. Cecilia had no more modesty than a cat in an alley. It's what he liked about her. Loved. Wild. Uninhibited. His, every scorching bit of her.

Cecilia's leg hitched over his hip. The other. Aldo clung to her flesh and pushed deeper. She groaned against his shoulder. "My God, Aldo. My God." He was her God with all the power she imbued. In her, he could change the course of the Passaic River, turn the falls upside down. With her, he wasn't a closet case still flipping burgers and dogs two years after outgrowing his high school job. Without her, he was nothing. Less than nothing. Aldo didn't exist at all.

His brain emptied, washed out of him in orgasmic spasms shuddering every muscle in his body. Cecilia crushed herself to him. "Not yet. Don't stop." And it was enough to let him finish her. Then she was sliding off of him, her legs unhitched, her skirt pulled down.

"I'm going to end up pregnant at this rate."

"Then you'll have no choice but to make an honest man of me."

"I'm not marrying you, Aldo, one way or another. My dad'll see you dead first."

"Even if I put a bun in your oven?"

"Especially then. He'll marry me off quick. When the baby comes a month or two early, we'll all say what a miracle it was he came out so big and healthy." She touched his cheek, tucked a strand of hair behind his ear. Those fingers, what they did to him. "You know I love you."

"Then let's go. Right now. We can get married in Maryland, head down to Florida. No one has to ever see us again."

She glared. Five foot nothing, all dark hair and darker eyes. Aldo cringed inside. Yearned.

"Easy for you," she said. "You have no one but me. It'd kill my mother if I disappeared. She's counting on me to care for her when she's old. And what about my brothers? Who's going to teach them how to treat a lady without me?"

Not her father. He treated his wife like shit. Not her mother, who pretended otherwise and drank away the lies. Aldo reached for her. She molded her body to his.

"What's going to happen to us?" He kissed her hair like magic against his lips.

"In a few years, I'll marry a nice Italian boy from a good Italian family. He'll adore me. Worship the ground I walk on. Or he'll be just like my dad and forget I exist. Either way"—she grinned up at him—"you and I'll have a torrid, lifelong affair. The children I have will be yours, but we'll keep it a secret until my father and husband are dead. Then you and I will marry and make everything right."

"And what if I find a nice Italian girl to marry, one who'll give me kids without secrets?"

Cecilia leaned away. Her grin turned cold. A hand whipped out, cracked like doom across his face. "You'll never," she said. "You'll stay true to me. I have no choices. Not what I wear or who my friends are or what man I fuck. You have every choice. If you make that one, I'll never, ever forgive you. Do you hear me? Never."

Aldo clutched his stinging cheek. Moments ago, he'd been a Roman candle lighting up inside her on Independence Day. Now he watched her walk away, picking over garbage in her saddle shoes, cold and dead inside. Because he would do exactly what she demanded, no matter how it tore him apart.

Bar Harbor, Maine

❧

Love is a beast with sharp teeth, bad breath, and no conscience.

—CORNELIUS TRAEGAR

Olivia looked everywhere for Cecibel. She'd sat among them at the fireworks, but no one had seen her since. No one but Salvatore, who said she wasn't feeling well. And yet when Olivia knocked on her door, no one answered.

There would be no more dinners in Alfonse's elegant suite. If Cecibel wouldn't come, he said, there was no point in supping in private. Judith and Switch had sadly agreed; Olivia would not argue, though it had been wonderful, keeping separate. The last of the new-old greats, glitterati no longer forced elbow to elbow with the peasants. For a little while, time turned backward, set her on the stage she once claimed to despise. No true artist produced art for fame's sake, but when fame arrived, ideals snuck out the back door. Olivia accepted this truth, embraced it in her decrepitude.

She didn't knock on Alfonse's door but opened it softly, slipped inside. He was sleeping, of course. Always sleeping. Saving every burst of energy for entertaining, being entertained. There he was in his armchair set beside great windows whose glass waved in the sunlight. Cornelius had spared no expense in this space he created for himself. For himself and Alfonse, who never came. No reproduction glass for these windows, but salvaged from other dilapidated places built in a more elegant time.

A notebook, turned spine up, fanned on Alfonse's lap. Olivia's heart pittered. A blank page. A pen in hand. Was there anything as exciting? The endless possibilities, the potential for beauty, even genius, waiting for that breath of life.

Carefully, so carefully, Olivia lifted the notebook from his lap. Alfonse didn't stir. She checked to make sure—thank goodness— still breathing. Moving closer to the window, she flipped through the pages. Mostly empty. His handwriting on those first few. Black pen. Some words in the margins; others hovered over those crossed out. Alfonse Carducci revised as he wrote rather than letting it flow out of him in a creative burst. Funny, Olivia never imagined he'd be disciplined or cautious in his art. Wild. Chaotic. Art imitating life, but not so. Not so at all.

Computers had changed everything. No more crossing out. No notes in margins. Clean, even in revisions. A simple delete, words replaced, scenes rearranged, and wobbling characters solidified. It made the process efficient. Fingers could fly without fearing the indecipherable scrawl, without cramping. No more writer's bumps (though hers was mighty, ancient, and earned). No need for an assistant to decipher and type out a clean manuscript when all was said and done. A slower process, one given to care and distance no longer necessary. Something lost. Something found.

Respect let her eyes take in his scrawl as a whole. Decorum demanded she set it back onto his lap unread, fanned and waiting. Old love begged her to read. Rekindled jealousy taunted. Oh, how weak virtue when baser instincts flexed.

~Buffalo, NY~ Paterson, New Jersey
Winter ~1939~ 1953

She was, now, warm and lovely ~on~ in his arms. An unfamiliar gift. A grief to come. Always and always, his. That was the deal. The pact. The promise written in kisses and on long walks. In screeched battles and ~hours of~ makeup sex. Cecilia and Aldo. Aldo and Cecilia. The stars had proclaimed it; either they or the summer storm ~storm clouds always so thick over Buffalo, New York thick over encasing~ obscuring the Paterson Falls ~on the day they met~ when first they met . . .

She read to the end. And again. Already Cecilia and Aldo bloomed *in substantia grisea*. Sparked images of a skinny young man sporting a greasy ducktail-doo. A pack of cigarettes rolled into the sleeve of his white T-shirt. No. Too cliché. Aldo was tall and skinny but muscular from lifting and carting crates of bottled soda. His hair was long only because he couldn't afford regular haircuts. And he didn't smoke. Cecilia would never stand for it. He wore an oil-spattered apron over a blue button-down, and jeans. His grin? Lopsided. His teeth? Endearingly crooked. His face was a collection of chiseled edges and angles, and blue eyes that could cut or coddle, a Roman nose he'd have to grow into, and a cleft in his chin that would become popular—Kirk Douglas, *Spartacus*—within the next seven or so years.

Cecilia—oh, glory. Alfonse gave her five feet of hellion, dark hair and eyes. Olivia's conjuring turned those eyes slightly almond-shaped. Catlike, not Oriental—Asian, so sorry. The vernacular of youth slipped in now and again. Her cheekbones were high, her lips pouted even when she smiled, and her nose punctuated the drama of her face like a button. Sixteen to Aldo's twenty—trouble no matter what state or era from a parent's perspective—Cecilia was soft and curvy and rich. She wore all the right clothes, had all the right friends, and hated her father with the burning passion of a teenager given everything but love. For her mother, she had only pity edged sharp with scorn. And loyalty. Misplaced. Unappreciated. Lonely. She was only a girl. Girls didn't matter until they bore sons who would be turned into men who felt the same. She would marry such a man, though he would love her in his way. To make him completely unlikable would give applause to the future misfortune Olivia would give him, if this were hers to give him anything at all . . .

Olivia dropped the pen in her hand, horrified. Blue pen beneath Alfonse's black. Her neat, calligraphic script like the sea beneath his stormed scrawl. Fingers cramped. Writer's bump ached. Shame! How could she? Another writer's work, purloined. Closing Alfonse's notebook with a soft snap of pages, she scurried for the door.

"Bring it back when you've finished." His voice came from the slumbering corpse in the easy chair set against sunshine-waving windows. The corpse smiled. Cheeks pinked. Olivia Peppernell darted out the door before he opened his eyes.

∽

Cecibel ached. A short span of elegant dinners she never tasted, taken with the kings and queens revered by even those who'd never read a single one of their books, or any books at all, had been a dream. A dazzling one of wit. A nightmare of worry. Had Judith seen the water dribble down her chin? Had Switch sat beside her to spy the monster hiding behind her hair? Could she hope that none had noticed she never ate a morsel? No, she couldn't, and that was worst of all.

The first dinner had been glorious. The second, less so. By the third, Cecibel could not even eat once she got back to her room, her stomach being far too traumatized. Alfonse had seemed genuinely sad when she said she'd not dine with them again. It was all too grand. All too nauseating. Far too frightening to do again.

And yet, the ache of depriving herself of their company itched like healing wounds. How had she never realized how starved she was? Work, eat, sleep, work again. The occasional conversation with Sal. Olivia. They'd been enough for so long. And now? Alfonse Carducci had ruined everything. He'd drawn her out. He'd made her think thoughts she'd forgotten. He acted as if she weren't flawed beyond repair and made her believe it was so. But it wasn't. Not when she couldn't even share a meal with him. With them.

Cecibel worked in corners, in avoided glances and ignored calls. Given a few days, she'd be able to face them again, whether singly or as a collective. Time would lift her shame, dull the fear. Just a little time.

In her room, alone once again, Cecibel tossed her scrubs into the hamper. She walked naked to her tiny bathroom. The mirror taunted. Her bugbear. And as she did once—no more—every day, she looked. And looked away. No change, of course. Magic didn't exist, and only magic could mend what had been torn away. Several plastic surgeries she couldn't afford and still paid for with every paycheck had done what could be done. At least she had a face to frighten away children, small dogs, and the squeamish. Most of what she'd been born with got left on windshield and asphalt.

I saw it and didn't care . . . I didn't want to be saved . . .

The words, Alfonse's words, tumbled from the showerhead.

Both, or none. I was content to fall.

Cecibel closed her eyes against the water falling, her mind from the shattered thoughts. A book salvaged from the wreckage, left at her bedside. For when she felt strong enough to open it, to hold it, to read. To find the note in the margin, and wonder why she'd made it there. Years and years left wondering. Answers too monstrous to seek.

Drying, dressing, disremembering, Cecibel hummed a song she maybe remembered from the past, maybe made up on the spot. She'd go down to the commissary, snag a tray from the kitchen, and eat in her room. Routine. Comforting. If she spied any of the kings and queens, she'd wave and hurry on if she couldn't duck fast enough. Just another few days. That's all she needed.

It was still an hour before the official dinner bell. Kitchen staff scurried. The *garde manger* and the *potager;* the *entremetier* and *saucier; poissonier* and *rotisseur.* Even the *pattissier,* creating decadent but harmless tapiocas and puddings, light cakes and sorbets. *Le personnel gastronomiques* hired and maintained to the exacting standards of Cornelius Traegar ran like a well-olive-oiled machine. Cecibel ducked and dodged, apart from but a part of the routine. Filling her plate and loading her tray as she had been doing since her first days in the Pen, she thanked and pardoned her way down the line.

In the vestibule between kitchen and formal dining room, Cecibel placed a cloche atop her tray. Early-bird diners were already making their way to tables, unassigned but daily claimed. Olivia and Alfonse would arrive five minutes after six. Judith and Switch would be with them, modestly pretending it was not a staged thing. Their table of four, never five or six, would be empty even if it was the one closest to the hearth, near to the bathrooms. Such a short time ago, before Alfonse Carducci arrived, those arriving after six o'clock took what seats remained, in usual places left by the infirm, or the dead. How long before their newly celebrated table of four dissolved back into unassigned but daily claimed? Cecibel didn't want to think about that, so she put it out of her mind.

Hurrying across the commons separating the dining area from her room, Cecibel wished a tiny wish she could set her tray upon a picnic table there and eat her bland-gourmet dinner in the cooling warmth of June's sunshine. Wished and discarded quickly.

"Cecibel! Girl, wait up!"

Another few steps and she was safe behind the hedgerow that shielded the entrance from the wind. Sal panted, one hand up in surrender, the other on his cushioned heart.

"Never make me run, honey. My heart's about to burst."

"Don't you dance as part of your act?"

"I sway, sugar dove. Something you'd know if you ever came to see me. I sway and I sing." He sang the words, a rich contralto that always took her a little by surprise. And his grace for so big a man. He'd learned to dance sometime, way back. When? Cecibel didn't know, and never asked. One didn't ask questions of others when answers would be expected in return.

"I see you perform every New Year's Eve," Cecibel said. "And last year, you danced a cha-cha."

"Me? Cha-cha? Honey, I couldn't even cha. That was a rumba. Much sexier. And slower."

"I stand corrected." She lifted her tray a little higher. "I was about to have dinner. Did you need me for something?"

"I need you for everything." He smiled, a six-foot, three-hundred-pound coquette. "But not this moment. It's Finlay."

"What about him?"

"He's a big baby, is what he is. A splinter, well, it's a pretty big one, in his hand and he won't let any of the nurses look at it. I tried, but my hands aren't quite . . . delicate enough." He waved those sausage fingers, nails painted red, white, and blue. "Would you see to him? After you eat?"

Cecibel's shoulders sagged. She hadn't spoken a word to the man since he tried to get her out on her birthday. "Sure." At least she'd be where no one—Olivia—would think to look for her. "I'll go see him after I eat."

"You're a lovely, lovely thing." Sal bent and kissed her fair cheek. "Tomorrow, your shift ends at three. Don't worry. I'll keep you on the clock until four."

Dinner eaten, tray returned, Cecibel walked across the dusk-dewed lawn. Finlay lived over the maintenance barn, in a rustic apartment that had once been an artist's studio when the haphazardly wealthy family had the place built. She'd read about them in a book she found in the Pen's library. A coal miner from Pennsylvania and his seamstress wife. The diamonds mined and absconded with, the small fortune turned into a bigger one. New-money feuds with old-money snobs who'd been new money only decades earlier. The abundance, and the fall. The suicide of a man first made old in the mines, then older by the Crash. The children left behind. The wife left to fend. It was all very sad. Better to have nothing than to have it all and lose it.

She shuffled up the steps, knocked on the door. Footsteps on the other side. A whoosh, and Finlay stood there gaping. "Hey, Cecibel. Something I can do for you?"

"Sal said you had a splinter but wouldn't show the nurses."

Finlay laughed. He showed her his bandaged hand. "He said he wouldn't tattle if I let him have a go at it."

"Well, he lied." Cecibel peeked around him. "I'll take a look at it, seeing as I'm already here. If you want."

"You don't mind?"

She shrugged. He moved aside. Cecibel stepped into the apartment that smelled of old cedar and the ghost of oil paint past. Nothing was new. Nothing was tattered. Homey. Lived in. Clean. She'd never have guessed. Finlay always seemed so disheveled. "Come here in the light." She beckoned from afternoon's slanting rays streaming through the window. He didn't move, only stared, mouth slightly open. If she turned her face, let that sunlight blaze the monster into being instead of the fairy tale she showed, would he cringe?

Cecibel held out her hand. Waited. Unwrapping the bandage, Finlay obliged. A thick sliver of wood lined the palm of his hand, red and angry-looking already.

"When was your last tetanus shot?"

"Not sure. I'm probably up-to-date." He wiggled his fingers. "Sal got out part of it."

"I can see that." Cecibel prodded gently. "You should really have one of the nurses do this."

"Nah. It'll be fine."

Cecibel felt his gaze on the crown of her head. *Look up,* it said. *Just once.* "You have tweezers?"

"Nah. I got a razor, though."

"No razor. Jeez, Finlay. You want to lose your hand?"

"I healed after worse." His hand fell. "Don't worry about it. But thanks for trying."

"I didn't do anything yet." Chancing a glance up, through lashes and a fringe of hair, she caught the slight grimace of fear ripple across his features. "Wait here."

"Where are you going?"

"Just wait here," she called over her shoulder. "And ice it while I'm gone."

A pilfered splinter kit, bottle of peroxide, roll of gauze, and tube of antibiotic ointment later, Cecibel tromped up the steps to Finlay's apartment. The door stood open. She went inside. Finlay stood at the sink, shoulders hunched. An open bottle of whiskey, half consumed, sat on the counter beside him. He wasn't a big man, or a small one. Neither slim nor stout, clever nor slow, beautiful nor unappealing. Brown hair, slightly thinning. Brown eyes, if she remembered right. Average in every way there was to be so.

"It's only a splinter." She tapped the bottle. "Do you really need to get drunk to have it removed?"

Finlay glanced once over his shoulder. "I'm not drinking it. I'm killing germs. Like in those movies when we were kids."

Disco, *Star Wars,* Pet Rocks. Childhood was so long ago. "Soap and water'd do just fine. Here, let me see. Did you ice it like I told you?"

"It was a while ago. It's not numb anymore."

Cecibel fished slim ice cubes from the sink. She wrapped them in a paper towel and pressed it gently to his palm. Finlay's breath wafted warm, and smelled of the whiskey he said he hadn't drunk. *Look up. Just once.* Focusing hard on the black line beneath skin, she picked and pricked until the skin gave up its claim. No pus, thank goodness. But it looked sore enough to warrant some.

"Hold it over the sink." She poured peroxide on the wound that bubbled white, patted it dry, and did it again. A smear of ointment, a little gauze, and he was good as new. "See the internist tomorrow. I'm not sure who's on call. You should have a tetanus shot, just to be safe."

"Will do," he said, but he wouldn't. His choice. His problem if he got lockjaw.

Cecibel gathered what was left of her pilfering. Finlay stopped her at his door. "We've worked at this place a lot of years. How come we ain't friends?"

Aren't friends. "What makes you say we aren't?"

"Maybe because this is the longest we've ever spent together."

"That's not true at all. We've worked together many times."

"That's work, not conversating."

Conversing, for goodness' sake. Cecilia bit her lip to keep yet another correction in her mouth. College got her a minor in English, and a bad habit of silently correcting people's grammar. How long ago that was. Time wasted. Effort fruitless. She'd never written the novels planned from childhood. Many wanted to be writers. Few actually ever wrote. How sad, she'd become one of the latter. She'd blame the accident, but that would be a lie. She'd switched her degree to nursing long before, and never finished.

"Is it because of what I done?"

Cecibel struggled back from old regrets. "Pardon? What?" She processed his words. Old gossip. Decades-old newspaper articles read on microfiche. Her face warmed. "Oh. That. No, of course not. You were a boy. That wasn't your fault."

"Wasn't my fault I bashed a man's brains in?" He chuckled, rubbed a hand across the back of his neck. "I guess you're right. It wasn't my fault. Too bad the jury didn't agree. But I'd do it again and pay twice the price, and that's the absolute truth."

"Well, I don't hold it against you. That man was a monster."
Takes one to know one.

"I agree." Finlay leaned against the counter. "So if that's not it, why shouldn't we be friends?"

"We are."

"Then let's go grab a beer."

"I don't drink beer."

Another chuckle. "You don't leave the property neither, much as I can tell."

"I do so."

"How about a walk on the beach? Tomorrow, after your shift. Sal tells me you get off at three."

Sal's going to have a hard time telling anyone anything after I cut his tongue out. "I have to get this stuff back to the infirmary, Finlay—"

"Fin," he corrected. "If you don't mind."

"Whatever. Fin. If you'll excuse me." Cecibel shouldered past him and hurried for the door.

"Is it because of your face?"

She stumbled on the stair, caught herself. Caught her breath.

"I seen it," Fin said more softly now. "It makes no nevermind to me. I'm not looking for anything, Bel. Just a friend. I swear. I'll be on the beach at three thirty tomorrow. Come walk with me. Or don't. I'll understand."

Breath caught, face flaming, Cecibel flew the rest of the way down the steps—*Bel, Bel! Stop! You're killin' me!*—through the maintenance barn, across the lawn now evening-dewed, straight to her room without putting back the gauze, the ointment, the peroxide, or the splinter kit. Back pressed to the door, holding too many demons at bay, Cecibel wept hot and silent tears out the one eye that still worked properly, down the one cheek that still could feel them.

Paterson, New Jersey

SPRING 1954

❦

Cecilia

In March, when coy Winter lifted her skirt for Spring, Aldo informed her he'd joined the navy. Just like that. No warning. No discussion. Cecilia had told him he had all the choices in the world to make but one. She never expected this. If she had, she'd have forbidden it, too.

"I have no family," he said. "And I can't flip burgers the rest of my life."

His couch smelled like his clothes—hot dog and burger grease. The scent would arouse her all her life. Cecilia used to keep perfume in her purse, to hide the condemning odor of him. Unnecessarily. As a kid always in trouble with the law, her father'd hung out at Falls View, too. He remembered it fondly enough to indulge her, as long as she didn't get fat.

"What about college?" she asked. "I could visit your dorm on weekends and holiday breaks. It would be so much fun."

"You need money to go to college. I can barely afford this room. It's too late anyway. I can't back out. I signed the papers. I leave in—"

She covered his mouth, her Florida-tanned hand dark against his winter-pale skin. "You did this while I was away. You waited for me to leave, and you did this terrible thing."

Aldo pulled her hand away, gently. "It wasn't like that, exactly."

"Then tell me what it was exactly like."

She waited while he fidgeted, while he fumbled with her hand. She waited for words that would make sense, and somehow lift the pain.

"When you were away," he said, "it was kind of exciting. At first, anyway. I marked the days on my calendar. Every red *X* meant one day down, one day closer to seeing you again."

A smile shivered to her lips. Cecilia snuggled into him.

"After that first week, it stopped being exciting. The closer it got to you coming home, the more I understood the truth."

"What truth?"

"That this is going to be my life," he said. "Always waiting for you to come to me. I can't ever go to you. Not for any reason. Ever. After you graduate, your family might send you to college, or they might marry you off, and the waiting is just going to get worse. Harder. This way, we'll be waiting for each other, and when I come home again, I'll be an officer if I work really hard. Maybe then, I'll be good enough."

They've already chosen him, she didn't say. *Long before I ever knew he existed. Probably even set the date.*

Cecilia burrowed deeper into him, her arm snaking about his waist. Aldo kissed the top of her head, the corner of her eye when she lifted her face. Sorrow pricked resignation into heat. They made love on his couch as they had dozens of times before, and only weeks left to add another dozen or so times more. Cecilia straddled him; he held her hips, eyes only slits, ecstasy burgeoning. She preferred being on top, it was true, giving him access to her breasts, being able to control him, herself. Everything. This time, it was different. She even hoped—stupid, foolish, insane—she'd get pregnant. But it hadn't happened yet; it probably never would. Maybe she'd be lucky and turn out to be barren. No man would want her then. No man but Aldo.

Three sharp bangs on the floor. Agnes, the aging waitress doomed forever to Aldo's escaped fate, signaled for them to come down. She was the only one who knew, and Cecilia paid her to keep it that way, just like she paid for these rapped warnings. Aldo didn't know. He thought she was an old romantic with a soft spot for him. Whatever softness Agnes once had leached out of her when, a decade ago, a Purple Heart and a U.S. flag were delivered to her door. That was all Cecilia knew. Husband? Son? She couldn't tell, by the look of her. Agnes might be thirty, or sixty. Grief taxed a body far more than time.

"I'll go in through the back door," Aldo said, tucking in his shirt. "You go over a few lots and come in from down the street, through the front."

"I know the drill." She kissed him, lingered. "I love you." And out she flew before she said anything about the navy or how little time they had left whether or not he had made that choice. Whether or not he knew.

Her father sat hunched at the counter. Of course. Dominic Rafaele Tommaso Giancami. Cami to friends, family, and enemies in both camps. He allowed her afterschool visits to the hot dog joint of his youth, but checked on her from time to time, just in case. Trust, he always said, was something earned only after a lifetime of obedience and good choices. She was only sixteen, and had a long way to go.

All shoulders, her father. Once upon a time, they were all muscle. Cecilia remembered riding on those shoulders, feeling like the princess she was born to be. He loved her then, she thought, when she was small and innocent and pure. Her hero. Her daddy. The love of her life. Until the advent of breasts and hips confirmed she was, after all, female and not to be trusted. A temptress. A slut. By virtue of body parts she had no idea what to do with, she'd been cast out. Planned for instead of played with. Punished whenever a man or boy whistled at her on the street.

For a split moment, seeing her father through the window, the tiniest surge of that old love, that wish to please rose up. And then he turned and—maybe? Oh, maybe! But no. If anything surged in her father's heart, it was squashed before he waved her inside.

"Hey, Daddy." She kissed his cheek. "What are you doing here?"

"Just chattin' with my old pal Agnes." He jutted a thumb over his shoulder. "She says you're usually here by now, already stuffing hot dogs down your throat with your friends. Where you been?"

"I had to take a makeup test in history," she lied, "from when we were away in Florida. I'm starving now. You going to stay and buy me a dog?"

"No can do, kiddo." He slid from the stool, his massive frame still muscular under all the cushion gained since youth. Tossing a couple dollars on the counter, he towered over her. "Half hour," he said. "Then you're home. Got me?"

"I gotcha, Daddy."

"Good girl." He kissed the top of her head, his attention already on something outside. All eyes followed him out the door. A collective exhale whispered mouth to mouth.

Cecilia climbed onto the stool her father vacated. She added a fiver to the two bucks he left and slid it all to Agnes. "Thank you."

"You're going to get yourself in trouble, Cecilia. Cami'd have me killed if he knew."

"Then he can't know, right?"

Agnes's rounded shoulders drooped lower. She slid the money into her pocket and pushed through the swinging doors to the kitchen. Aldo emerged two heartbeats later with a hot dog all the way in its little paper sleeve. "On the house," he whispered.

"No, thanks. I'm going home."

His hand twitched, a thwarted reach for hers. "You mad?"

"Yeah, I am," she said, and left.

Bar Harbor, Maine

JUNE 6, 1999

◦◦◦◦◦

Give Dinesen her sweat, tears, and sea; I'll take bourbon, neat.

—CORNELIUS TRAEGAR

It was late—nine o'clock. Gone were the days of deep-pocket slumber after champagne nights. Hours bent into one another now, some being dark and others light. All moments ticking by. Slowly. Relentless. Until the Cecibel-shaped story brought Alfonse Carducci back to life, and with him Olivia Peppernell, who sat beside him trembling, though she would deny it.

He couldn't speak for the labored beating of his heart no longer accustomed to the swell of joy. His words, and hers, embraced like the lovers they'd once been to create . . . what? Surely not the genius of their younger selves, but something else. The joy nearly tore his heart in two.

"You've made a mistake." Alfonse tapped a finger on the notebook. "You put them on a couch in an apartment above the hot dog place. Read my first paragraph. Go, go. Read it."

Olivia paged back in the notebook. She cursed under her breath. "Ah, I see. A simple fix. I'll put them in Agnes's car behind Falls View. She can slam the back door instead of rapping on the floor. Writing is rewriting, Alfie. You know that. Tell me honestly. What do you think?"

"I like where you took it," he said.

"Give me more, Alfonse. These are the first real words I've written in years."

"You maintained the core voice while giving Cecilia her own."

"More."

"You made Aldo too articulate. He's twenty and flipping burgers in 1950s New Jersey."

"Not going to college doesn't mean he must be poorly spoken."

"He has no family, Livy. He's a poor boy with little schooling. He will speak like other boys of his time and station, to survive if nothing else."

"Like you did?"

Surprise warmed him through. Alfonse wagged a finger. "Touché, my dear. Touché."

"We'll work out the kinks as we continue on." Olivia placed the notebook on his desk. "No planning ahead. We work from whatever came before. Sudden inspiration, Alfie, like when we were young and had no idea all the ways we were doing it wrong. What do you think?"

Bring it back when you've finished, he'd said, when he woke to her scribbling in the notebook no one was meant to see. The words had fallen from his mouth like Icarus from the heavens. Foolish. Reckless. Aflame. "I think you have shanghaied my manuscript." He chuckled. "But there is magic here, no?"

"Yes."

"And it is marvelous to be writing again."

"It is."

"But is it truly magic? Or are we old fools who don't know the difference anymore?"

Olivia patted his hand, leaned forward, and kissed his cheek. "Does it matter, Alfonse? We grasped for great literature and climbed those great heights. We weren't just part of the literati, we *were* the Literati. But this? This is writing for the joy of it, nothing more. I'd forgotten how extraordinary that is."

"Acclaim exacts a price we never anticipated, eh? Way back in the beginning."

"It does, but it's what we wanted. Then. Now, we have this." Olivia rose slowly to her feet, her hand moving to though not reaching her back. There was a time he'd have leaped to his feet, assisted her to the door she headed for.

"It's your turn," Olivia said from the threshold. "Shall we put a time limit on our contributions?"

"One week," Alfonse answered. "And if I expire before then—"

"I'll dig you up and prop you at your desk if you dare."

"Sorry to thwart your efforts, my dear, but I'm to be cremated."

"Nevertheless." She grimaced at him, and closed the door.

Under his palm, the smooth cover of the notebook warmed. Brown leather. Gilded edges. How many gifts he'd received of such quality. He'd always preferred a simple composition notebook—black and white—for that first stream-of-consciousness draft, before the typewriter snap and hum of the second. Third. Tenth.

Alfonse thumbed through the pages already a mess of cross-outs and insertions. It would have to be keyed into the computer once the first draft was done. He no longer had the leisure to indulge in the comfort of old ways. For this part, though, this first draft, he'd make the sacrifice.

⌒

Finlay sat alone on the beach, leaning back on his arms, face to the sun. Four days he'd done so. Possibly three. It'd rained the day prior and Cecibel hadn't gone out to the arbor to spy on him. What he was waiting for, she wasn't exactly sure, considering she hadn't shown up that first requested day. He'd seen her in the arbor; that she knew because he waved. Cecibel hadn't waved back—*I'm not looking for anything, Bel. Just a friend*—but kept her arms crossed, as they were now.

Warm sunshine on her skin, the cold breeze lifting the weight of her hair from her neck, the wish for freedom pricked tears that dried instantly. She remembered this feeling already bunching her muscles, shrinking her around the tiny ball living in the pit of her. To live unafraid would be astonishing, peculiar, and impossible. To live unafraid meant to die.

"'When last the winds of heaven were unbound—'"

Cecibel spun to Olivia's voice, automatically plastering what hair she could gather to her face.

"'Oh, ye! who have your eyeballs vexed and tired'"—Olivia gently pried Cecibel's hair from her fist—"'feast them upon the wideness of the sea.'" The old woman smiled. "Keats."

Cecibel fought the urge to cover herself. Tears burned. She looked away. "I was just going inside."

"Sit with me." Olivia held up a joint. "You're off duty, if you want to . . ."

"No, thanks. But I'll sit with you." Cecibel took the spot beside Olivia, in a double Adirondack chair, positioning herself strategically.

Cupping, lighting, expertise years in the making, Olivia took a pull. "I've noticed you out here the last few days."

"The weather's been pretty nice. Not yesterday, though."

"Not yesterday," she said on the exhale. "I also noticed Finlay down on the beach."

"It's a free country."

"Just making observations." Olivia smoked in silence. Swift inhale. Long exhale. Over. And again. Hypnotic, like the tumble and crash of the sea. Cecibel slumped lower in the chair. Legs outstretched, leaning, leaning. Her head came to rest on Olivia's shoulder and she let it stay. Small comfort, sincerely given. Hard to accept. Fear wormed, even now, even with this old woman Cecibel loved so very much. "He asked me to walk with him."

"Oh? And you said no?"

"I just didn't show up."

"And now he waits every day."

Cecibel nodded.

"Why don't you walk with him?"

"What's the point?"

"Friendship."

"I have friends. I have you."

"I won't live forever, my dear."

"There's Alfonse, too."

"Who won't live out the year."

"What about Sal? He's my friend."

"A good one, yes. A gay man. And old people. Safely dissimilar, these friends of yours." Olivia slid her arm around Cecibel's shoulders, stroked her upper arm with fingers like lioness claws. Gentle. Fierce. "I have a secret," Olivia said. "Want to hear it?"

"Is it something you should tell?"

"Of course not. Then it wouldn't be a secret." Olivia chuckled. "Do you want to know or not?"

Cecibel wriggled against her. "Spill it."

Olivia took another long drag, a couple little sips, and stubbed the joint out. "Alfonse and I are writing. Together."

Cecibel jerked upright. "Really? What are you writing? What's it about? Will you publish it?"

"Hush, child. It's only just begun and there's no telling how far it will go, but it's . . . it's astonishing is what it is."

Cecibel's heart thumped. "Can I read it?"

"Oh, I don't know. Alfonse would never allow it, even if it's you. But . . ."

"But?"

Olivia squeezed her arm. "If you happened to find a brown, leather notebook with gilded edges on my desk or his, I can't be responsible for what you do with it. He has it now. It's his turn to create. Just make sure you put it back the way you got it. Exactly."

"Olivia! You're wicked."

"I'm nothing of the kind." She winked, looked beyond Cecibel and back again. "Finlay's coming. Stay." Olivia grabbed Cecibel before she could bolt. "I'll be with you. All right?"

Frantic eyes darted from beach path to old woman, back and again. To run now was worse than staying, than walking, than pretending the screaming didn't deafen all. Cecibel yanked her gathered hair into place.

Finlay called and waved.

Olivia responded in kind.

Cecibel bolted awkwardly to her feet, forcing fight before flight.

"Hey, Cecibel."

"Hey, Finlay."

"Beautiful afternoon, isn't it? Lots of shells on the beach after yesterday's storm." He reached into his pocket, jiggled the contents, opened his palm to her. "Pretty, right?"

Snail and clamshells. Muted and pink. Pale, blue sea glass. An orangey pebble washed smooth by the sea. Finlay plucked the sea glass from the cluster and held it out to her. "Matches your eyes."

She took it from his fingertips. He smiled and let it go. "Keep it," he said. "I have a whole jarful back at my place."

"Thanks . . . Fin."

"You're welcome . . . Bel." He grinned. "There's plenty more where that came from."

"I imagine so."

"Low tide's around five tomorrow, if you're interested."

The sea glass on her palm was nothing like her eyes. Hers were not pale blue, but cornflower, bright like marbles, not matte. Still, it was lovely, and it made her look away and smile. She curled her hand around the offering, and tucked it into her pocket.

"Well, see ya." Fin's back was to her when she looked up, already walking away, but there'd been a lightness in his tone that let her hope she hadn't insulted him with silence, or frightened him with a smile.

Cecibel breathed slowly in. And out. Heading back to the main building, she hummed a song she maybe remembered from the past, maybe made up on the spot. She'd put the sea glass in the jar of treasures in her room, then she'd go see Alfonse for the first time since Memorial Day, maybe get a glimpse of a brown leather notebook with gilded edges all around.

⌒

Gravel crunched beneath Olivia's sensible shoes, her footsteps slow. The pain in her back—righteous penance—was bearable now. Thank all the heavens for her herbal medicine. Cecibel hadn't even noticed her leaving, though Finlay had. The man had patience, for right and certain. Nine years in prison might've had something to do with that.

She'd read all about it in the local paper, after his release. A boy abused. A pedophile acquitted. Justice taken into seventeen-year-old hands. There was only so much the law could do when confession was made without remorse, when the murder weapon was delivered to the police station still dripping fresh blood and brains.

"Justice has been served" was the quote, Finlay's own, in the papers. Across headlines. Coast to coast. Both before the trial and after the inevitable conviction. Olivia had been, at first, appalled by his cool, then sympathetic, and finally curious about the polite young man Cornelius hired shortly before his death. Cruel gossip called it a crime of passion, an affair gone wrong, a lover spurned. But Finlay had been a boy of fifteen when the local teacher had his way with him, and only after more abuses came to light and got brushed aside had he acted. He'd paid the price for his actions—almost a decade of his youth, gone—and for all she could tell, he was a happy-enough man.

She found Alfonse in the house library, without his wheelchair, chatting with devotees. A couple of editors, a proofreader. Olivia barely knew them outside of titles they once held. Gesturing to Alfonse, she finally got his attention by dropping a book on the marble floor. He startled, hand to his heart, and Olivia feared for that instant before he smiled and started her way. The man loved his drama; she had to remember that.

"I don't think I've seen you walk more than a few steps," she said as he approached.

Alfonse waved a hand over his head. "I must walk a little every day or lose the ability completely. As long as I take it slow, I'm fine. Have you come to walk me back to my suite?"

"Actually, no, but I will. I've come to tell you, the bait is laid and the mouse is sniffing."

"My darling, Livy, what in the hell does that mean?"

She giggled, almost girl-like, as if she'd ever been such a one. "It means I'm stoned. I'm happy. Cecibel now knows about our endeavor. She thinks it's a secret you're not to know."

"Why would you do that? How can I discuss it with her now?"

"You can't. Now you have to go without her praise of it. Can you bear it?"

"I'll try."

"It's all for her," Olivia said. "Such a little thing to give the child, this bit of intrigue. You should have seen her glow."

"Just how stoned are you, my dear?"

"Quite, but that's beside the point. She loves me like a dear grandmother, but you? She is as enamored as any of your groupies, past and present. She is your muse, and you are mine. See? It all works out."

"I will pretend there is logic in there, somewhere." Alfonse sipped at the air, his shoulders going slowly back. "She returned to me my words, but Cecibel is a child in comparison."

"When has that ever mattered? To you, or anyone infatuated with you. She is a woman. A woman locked away far too long, and ready to live again. You did that for her, Alfonse. All these years, I've tried to accomplish what you have by simply appearing in her world outside of the pages in a book. Like she gave you back your words, you gave her back the longing for life. Let her have that. It feeds your ego more than you'll ever admit to anyway."

Alfonse chuckled, a wheezy, breezy sound. He offered his arm, and Olivia took it, resting her head to his stooped shoulder and remembering days gone by. A similar setting. A sanctuary, they called it. His shoulder broad and sinewy. Her hair like fire. Fans waiting. Gossips, too. But in there, safe from them. From *him*. Her injuries healing. Her memory daily and diligently erased by drugs and electrical shocks. Dreams of tumbling turned to headlights and twisted metal. No one visited. Not the man who refused her a divorce. Not the children he kept from her. Only Alfonse, and sometimes Cornelius, though never at the same time. Now, decades hence, decades older, decades lost, they bookended the fame, the fury, the sweetness and safety and solitude. They'd give to each other, to Cecibel. And maybe it would be enough this time.

Bar Harbor, Maine

JUNE 9, 1999

❧❦❧

*It's not always about what you need; sometimes, it's just
about what you want.*

—CORNELIUS TRAEGAR

Alfonse had been as happy to see her as Cecibel was to see him. Her silly heart, and how it fluttered when he smiled at her. How foolish she'd been, staying away. She promised to resume her daily visits, after work, and though she spotted the brown leather notebook with gilded edges fanned on his armrest, not even the desperate fangirl within her had the nerve to swipe it.

From Alfonse, Cecibel went to the beach, where Finlay waited as he had promised without ever speaking the words. Hair in a side ponytail, hoodie up, she kept to his right, offering him her left, and was able to enjoy hunting for sea glass with him. It was June. Days were long. They walked until even the late sitting for dinner had passed. When he asked her to raid the kitchen with him, Cecibel became an armadillo. A hedgehog. A pill bug. She ate granola bars alone in her room, washed them down with water from the tap. Lying in her bed that night, staring at the ceiling lined by moonlight and windowpanes, she wondered what cruelty Finlay had in store for her. What mockery. What malice. By morning, shame opened her eyes. Finlay was good and kind. So he had killed a man; that didn't make him evil. Not like her—*I didn't want to be saved, and so she couldn't be either*—who had such wicked thoughts, whose outside matched her inside, though no one seemed to know.

"Meet me here tomorrow?" Finlay had asked after that first walk, before hedgehog-Cecibel exposed her prickly back.

"I can't tomorrow," she'd answered, "but how about Wednesday? We both have off. We can ramble a good long way. No telling what we'll find."

He'd smiled, nodded. Cecibel hadn't seen him since. And now it was Wednesday. Banishing armadillo and hedgehog, pill bug and wicked thoughts, she tied her hair in place, grabbed her bucket from the shelf, and headed out to meet Finlay.

He wore a red baseball cap, working the brim of a matching one in his hands. Cecibel held her hair against the force of the wind, trying so hard to appear casual her teeth ground together.

"For you." He offered her the worked-in cap. "It'll keep the sun out of your eyes."

"It is bright out here. Thanks." She took the cap, turned her back, and placed it on her head. Not only did it keep the sun from her eyes, it helped to hold her hair in place.

"Ready?" Finlay lifted his bucket, a metal thing half rusted through.

Cecibel held up her plastic yellow pail by the bright orange handle. "I'm hoping for some sand dollars today."

"Haven't come across one in a while. I'm hoping for shark teeth."

"Shark teeth? Really?"

"Ancient ones," he said. "Prehistoric. I got lots of them. Been collecting since I was a kid. I'll show you sometime."

And so they walked along the beach, searching for sand dollars and shark teeth, sea glass and shells. Cecibel stayed to his right, always to his right. If Finlay noticed, he didn't say. Low tide had passed hours before, not the best time for such hunting. By noon, they'd each found treasures enough to add to their collections, and Cecibel had worked up an appetite she hadn't anticipated.

Her stomach rumbled, loud enough to hear above the hissing surf and breeze. They'd been walking in one direction for more than two hours. She sipped water from the bottle she'd thankfully thought to fill earlier. Not much left now. She snapped closed the cap and shook it. "I guess I didn't prepare very well. Maybe we ought to head back."

Finlay grinned. He tossed his backpack in the sand, set down his bucket and then himself. "An Eagle Scout is always prepared," he said. "Sit."

Cecibel obliged. "An Eagle Scout?"

"Yup . . . well, unofficially. Jailbirds ain't allowed to be Scouts. I was almost done before I went to juvie, finished before they sent me to Buldoc." From his backpack, he pulled two deli-wrapped sandwiches, two bottles of iced tea, and two bags of chips. "I didn't know what you like. I figured turkey was safe."

Her empty belly clenched. "I . . . uh . . . I'm not hungry. But thanks all the same."

Finlay placed one of everything on the sand beside her, smiled, nodded, and rose to his feet. He resettled himself closer to the tide and, his back to her, unwrapped his lunch. Cecibel stared at the plaid pattern of his shirt stretching shoulder to shoulder. His hair curled around the edge of his cap. Nice hair. Nice shoulders. Nice. In her periphery, the white deli paper waved surrender. Tears threatened. *Why* was he so nice? What did he want? Just a friend, Bel. Just a friend. Hideous, suspicious, she was a coward, too. Picking up the sandwich, iced tea, chips, and herself, Cecibel forced down the fear ripping her into tiny pieces and replaced it with anger. For what happened. For the result. For being afraid of eating a sandwich with so kind a man. She dropped down onto the sand beside him and unwrapped the sandwich. She'd eat it with him, or not at all.

"Don't look at me."

"I ain't."

"The scarring is tight and the muscles in my face don't work right and I'm missing a bunch of teeth. It's disgusting."

He kept his gaze on the sea. "Nothing you do could be disgusting."

"You don't know me."

"I'm trying to change that."

"Why?"

"Because I like you."

"Why?"

"Do you ask Mrs. Peppernell that question?" He glanced her way out of the corner of his eye, took another bite of his sandwich. To be so free! Cecibel could weep with wanting it. No one knew. No one understood. To worry over a zit, a wrinkle, wide-set eyes, or a big nose or a chin that owned its own chin—oh, the joy that would be. To be able to go out among people without the monster in tow, without fearing she'd be seen. The anxiety. The derision. The pitying, averted glances. The silent wondering about what she'd done to earn a face like hers, or how the monster inside got out of its cage to ravage her face. Once so beautiful. Everyone said so.

Thoughts tumbled over themselves, over her. Cecibel bit into the sandwich. She chewed and she spewed and she wept until it was gone. Not once did Finlay look her way. Not a single word did he utter. He simply uncapped the iced tea and handed her the bottle. She drank, liquid running out the corner of her mouth. He handed her a napkin. "You ever hear the story about Tatterhood?"

Sniffing, Cecibel wiped her eyes, her chin, her neck. "Huh? Um . . . no."

Fin settled back onto his elbows, eyes on the sea. "It was my favorite story when I was a little kid. Kind of obscure, I guess. You remind me of that story."

"Not sure if that's a compliment or not," she tried to joke.

Eyes closed, Fin tipped his face to the sun. "That's pretty much the gist of the whole story, when you get down to it. Tatterhood and her sister were twins. One ugly and smart and brave, the other pretty and sweet and kind. Couldn't separate them for nothing. Tatterhood knew what she was. Calling her ugly only made her hoot and holler and bang her wooden spoon on a pot like a drum.

"One day, hobgoblins came knocking at the door and the pretty sister ended up with a calf's head in place of her own. Tatterhood rode off on her goat, her sister went, too, and they got the pretty sister's head back. On their way home, they met two princes. One fell instantly in love with the pretty twin and asked her to be his wife, but she wouldn't marry anyone unless Tatterhood got married, too. Prince One talked Prince Two, who was actually a pretty nice guy, into marrying Tatterhood. He liked her goat and her wooden spoon. He liked her hair all wild with birds and shit living in it. He liked that she was smart and brave and didn't mind that she was ugly when there was so much more to her than that.

"On their wedding day, Tatterhood wouldn't fancy herself up. She trotted her goat down the aisle. Prince Two just kind of smiled, thinking he was in for some strange life with this woman, but happy. Then she got a little closer, and he saw she wasn't riding a goat, but a really fine horse. Her wooden spoon was a ruby-crusted scepter, and she wasn't ugly and tatty anymore, but way prettier than her pretty twin was on her best days."

"And they lived happily ever after." Cecibel chuffed. "Is there a moral to this story other than the obvious commentary you're making about my face?"

Fin sat upright, brushing his arms free of sand. "That's not it at all. I thought you was smart."

Were smart. "Enlighten me."

"Enlighten yourself," he said, but he smiled when he did. "You just remind me of both sisters all rolled into one. And I can picture you riding a goat and waving around a wooden spoon."

"I'm honored," she drawled. "Thanks."

He shifted in the sand, facing her now. How kind his smile. Sincere and warm. It made Cecibel feel even meaner, even lower, for putting her own unkindness on him.

"Nothing about you is as bad as you seem to think it is," he said. "You don't see yourself clear, is all."

"Did you get your psychology degree along with your Eagle Scout badge when you were in prison?" Even lower. Even meaner. Cecibel thought she would vomit.

"Doesn't take a degree to know any of that. You ain't got to be afraid with me, Bel. I seen things, done things. Nothing about you scares me, or grosses me out. Okay?"

Another sniff, this time accompanied by a shrug. Finlay handed her a bag of chips. Cecibel took it and, this time, ate without weeping. She drank the rest of her iced tea and hardly spilled any. Like when she ate alone in her room, away from stares and gasps and pity. And even that was easier to take than Fin's gentle kindness, than Olivia's love, than Alfonse's pretense that her appearance didn't matter. Those things hurt far worse than anything, because they looked beyond her scars, and still didn't see her at all.

Fin had moved closer to the tide line, throwing scraps of bread and turkey to the gulls that shrieked and dove. He dodged and laughed. After all he'd suffered, all he'd done, how was he so carefree? What battle had he waged and won against all those demons born in abuse and murder? If he had, could she?

Something in Cecibel's chest dislodged. It fluttered like a moth inside her. She opened her mouth and out it flew. Whispering, feathery wings beat about her face. She didn't grasp it back but let it flutter, let it fly, let it vanish on the wind.

Alfonse wasn't in his room when Cecibel got there, right on time, despite her day with Fin. She'd only had enough time to freshen up, change into a dress, and brush some of the windblown tangle from her hair. The treasures she'd collected remained in her bucket, on the vanity in her bathroom. She'd see to them later. Compromising the precious little time she spent with Alfonse was not an option.

Instead of checking with the nurses, who usually looked down their noses at the lowly orderlies the way the doctors looked down on them, Cecibel went straight to Sal, who knew everything that went on in the Pen.

"He's in the hospital," he told her. "Don't look like that, honey doll. He's just having some kind of treatment they can't give him here."

"I wonder why he didn't tell me."

Sal's penciled eyebrow arched. "Why would you need to know that, hmm?" He waved a finger up and down. "And why you so dressed up? Huh? Ceci-bel-bellissima, you got an old-man crush going on?"

"He's someone I like spending time with. Someone I respect."

"Fine, fine. But you know you ain't getting any from Mr. Casanova, right?"

Cecibel shook her head. "Just tell me when he'll be back, will you?"

"By supper's all I know," Sal said. "Now, since you don't got no place to go, how about you tell me where you been all day, and why I saw Fin swinging a bucket and whistling his way to the maintenance shed a little bit ago."

"Bye, Sal." She waved over her shoulder. Try as she did to fuel the indignation, she couldn't. Cecibel felt lighter and, if she let herself, maybe even happy.

Heading back to her room, she halted at the corridor leading to Alfonse Carducci's suite. He'd gone and hadn't told her. Strange. And yet, the opportunity presenting itself like the Yellow Brick Road straight to his door turned strange into fortuitous.

Her scalp prickled. Could she do it? Had she ever intended to? Well, yes, of course she had, but not this way. Not sneaking into Alfonse Carducci's private suite and swiping the notebook from his desk. But how much more exciting than waiting for Olivia to accidentally-on-purpose leave it for her to find?

Another day, Cecibel might have ignored fortune's call. Another day, she'd barely consider it. But today was today, no other. Without even a glance over her shoulder, she answered.

Paterson, New Jersey

SPRING 1954

❈

Aldo

"Don't go, Aldo. Please."

Hot tears scorched his chest where she'd whispered her passion and then her plea. Gathering his arms tighter around her, he kissed her hair, still damp from their bath. A risk, a splurge, taken on this last night together. Motel on the Mountain. Hillburn, New York. Her parents thought she was at Denise Pagano's pajama party, and she had been. Until ten. Aldo had waited in a borrowed car for all the lights to go out.

"I have to," he said. "If I don't show up, I'll be arrested."

"They can't do that."

"Yes, they can. I signed up. I passed all the tests, had my physical. I have to go, Cecilia. I'm going. But I'll write you letters every day and send them to Agnes. She'll give them to you."

"I can't do it," she told him. "I'll kill myself. I swear."

He kissed her hair again, her eyes, her mouth. "Say that again and we're through."

"You're a liar, Aldo Wronksi. You'll never be through with me."

"Just don't say it again. Please."

"Then st—"

Aldo devoured her words and swallowed them. He returned her words to her in soft moans that she breathed back into his mouth. They kissed and caressed, plunged and sucked. Her body, slick and scented, writhed beneath him, on top of him, on hands and knees before him. Drained and desperate, he took her, gave to her, satisfied her as many times as she would have him. As many times as he could. At twenty, his stamina was mighty, and even Cecilia lay spent in the end. An arm across her eyes. Hair, sex-curled, splayed on the white and tangled sheets. Breasts rising and falling, slower, lower with each breath caught. Aldo sat cross-legged on the rented bed, unable to look away. Unwilling.

"It's getting too close to morning." She moved her arm. "You better get me back to Denise's."

Aldo crawled to her. Pinned her hands above her head and covered her body with his. He kissed her once. Twice. So tenderly. And rested his brow to hers. "I swear to you, I'll be true. No matter how long I'm away, there's never going to be anyone for me but you."

"And I'll never love anyone but you."

His heart ached. Aldo kissed her until it eased. "I swore I'd come back someone your dad can't object to. Someone he will respect, but—"

"No. Don't say it. No vows, Aldo. No conditions or demands. I'm yours and you're mine. Forever. When you come home, no matter what happens to either one of us in between, that's still going to be true." She wriggled beneath him. "We have to go. If I'm not in my sleeping bag by the time Mrs. Pagano calls us for pancakes, Denise'll tattle."

Cecilia rolled out from underneath him. Aldo flopped onto his back. Empty. Cold. And only moments out of her arms. Four years was so long.

She'd dressed in the lace-and-flannel pajamas her mother bought her for Denise's party and put her hair in pigtails before Aldo got his pants on. Out of the motel room he'd paid for with his last week's paycheck, into the car he'd borrowed from Agnes, along dark and rural roads to the new Garden State Parkway he'd only driven on twice.

He parked on the street parallel to Denise's. Dawn pinked the edges of day. Through the backyard, he saw a light in the Pagano kitchen go on.

"Shit." Cecilia hunkered low in the seat, as if someone were watching. As if someone would see. "Who the hell gets up this early?"

"Is there another way in?"

"The front door." Cecilia yanked open the glove box. "I know she's got some stashed in here."

"What?"

"Cigarettes. Agnes smokes. There has to be— Aha!" She fished out a cigarette from the metal case, flicked the lighter. Her face illuminated. She inhaled, sputtered.

"What are you doing?"

"Picking up an unladylike habit." Cecilia shouldered open the car door. "I'll pretend I sneaked out for a smoke and got caught before I could sneak back in. Better that than the truth." She came around to his side of the car. "I love you, Aldo. Never forget that. Write me soon."

"I love you, too," he told the air outside his window. Cecilia was already climbing over the low wall separating the Paganos' yard from the one behind it. He didn't watch her go in. Better to not be seen, even momentarily through the yards. Mrs. Pagano would buy her story. She'd tell Cecilia's mother, who might or might not tell her father. Aldo guessed no, she wouldn't. Dealing with her daughter's dip into hooliganism was better done privately.

He drove back to Falls View in silence. No radio. Only the engine's hum and the cold wind coming through the window. After parking the car in the lot behind the establishment, he left the keys under the dustbin, just as Agnes asked him to. Though she'd teared up when he told her he was leaving, she had to be glad she'd no longer be forced to lie to her old and dangerous friend Cami. Delivering letters between the two of them was simple and safe enough. She couldn't be blamed for what the U.S. mail delivered, from whom.

Morning was near, and Aldo hadn't slept. He had to catch his bus to Illinois at seven o'clock. Illinois. So far away. He'd rarely been out of New Jersey, barely ever left Paterson. A few trips down the shore when he was a kid and still had a family. Mother. Father. Brother. Two sisters. Only one sister now, and she lived in Florida with a distant cousin who had wanted a little girl to raise but not a teenage boy. Did she remember him at all? She'd been six, he thought, but wasn't sure. Blond hair. Blue eyes. Tessa. Or maybe it was Theresa. Or was that the one who died in the car with his parents and brother?

Aldo would get no sleep. It had to be after six already. Time enough to head to the rented room over the garage where he'd been living since the orphanage set him loose at eighteen, get his belongings, bus ticket and go. Walking past the falls, he paused. One last look. One more time with his feet on the iron railing, looking down into the roaring swirl. By the time he came home from service, he'd be twenty-four. Maybe older. The falls would look the same.

A shaft of sunlight hit the mist, sparking dozens of rainbows into being. Aldo smiled. "Goodbye," he said, and turned away.

"Pretty, ain't it?" Dominic Giancami stood so close behind Aldo he could have reached out and grabbed him. But he didn't. Hands clasped in front of him, the man rolled his shoulders, tilted his head side to side.

Aldo's insides itched and squirmed. "Excuse me."

"Excuse you what?"

"Excuse me, sir."

"Nah." Mr. Giancami waved a cinderblock hand. Aldo flinched and Cami smiled. "I meant what're you asking me to excuse? That you're blocking my view? Or that you fucking my *putan'* daughter?"

Cold shivered through Aldo. He couldn't move. "Sir?"

"You think I'm an idiot? You think I didn't know you been sniffin' around her since last summer? I got eyes, *stugots*. I got a dick, too, and I know what it wants. You get what you wanted? Feels good in there, ah? I hope it was worth it 'cause I'm gonna kill you now."

Massive, slow, Giancami lunged. Aldo danced to the side, tried to get around him, but the man's reach was long. He swung again, this time nearly clipped him.

"Where's Cecilia?" Aldo shouted. "What did you do to her?"

"Nothing. Yet." They danced the ancient dance of combatants

poorly matched. Cami's face was beet red. Anger. Exertion. Both. "She'll get hers after I finish with you. I'm gonna beat you out of her. Every drop of you."

"Don't you touch her!" Aldo dove into the wall that was Dominic Giancami. The man grabbed him around the waist, flipped him over his shoulder. Kicking, punching, Aldo was already dizzy trying to catch his breath while Cami squeezed and squeezed. A lucky strike found Cami's balls. Hitting the gravel hard knocked out what little wind was left in Aldo. He rolled to his feet.

Doubled over, his face purple, spittle flecking his lips and chin, Giancami croaked, "I'm gonna fucking kill you."

"I love her!"

"Fuck you!" A roar, gravel scattering underfoot, and Dominic Giancami came at him like a wrecking ball.

Aldo scrambled backward, slipped, fell. He covered his face with both arms—"Hail Mary, full of grace"—and missed the sight he would forever imagine of Dominic Giancami flying precisely through the iron railings surrounding the falls. The man's screams opened Aldo's eyes, lowered his arms. He crawled to the railing and stuck his head through. Only the mist, the rainbows sparkling, and the crushing rush of water on rock where Cecilia's father was, this very moment, drowning.

Aldo put his back to the railing, his head between his knees, and sobbed. What had just happened? What would he do now? And Cecilia? He'd just killed her father. It didn't matter that he'd otherwise be a bloody heap of bones and flesh, that he saved her from the same, or that he hadn't meant for it to happen. Dominic Giancami was dead. He killed him.

And nobody knew it but Aldo.

Cool morning stole over him, washed through his veins, washed them clean. He pushed to his feet. Aside from the disturbance in the gravel, there was no sign of the altercation. No car he could see in the lot. He brushed off his pants. Straightened his hair. Cecilia was safe. Or, at least, safe from her father, but he could never face her again. How could he? She'd never know why he didn't write, only that he didn't. She'd go to college, get married, have children. Without her father's influence, she might even marry for love.

Love. He'd promised her forever; he would give her that. A vow made in passion and now, written in blood. Aldo Wronski left the falls. Paterson, New Jersey. His home. Every mile on the bus took him farther from home, from Cecilia, but not even an ocean would ever take him far enough from what he'd done to forget.

*Some say there are only two certainties in life—death and
    taxes;
but there are three—death, taxes, and heartbreak.*
—CORNELIUS TRAEGAR

"He's Polish?"

Alfonse chuckled carefully, took the leather notebook from her hands. "I just killed a man and that's what you ask?"

"Don't evade the question."

"It just happened. Surprised the hell out of me, too."

"But his name is Aldo."

"His mother was Italian."

Olivia tsked. "You can't invent a character's background after the fact, Alfie."

"Of course you can. I did it all the time. Writing is rewriting, remember? And what happened to no planning? Writing as organically as we did when we had no idea what we were doing?"

"Don't you throw my words back at me, Alfonse Carducci." Olivia thumbed her lip. "Polish. Hmm. I do like it, actually. And the addition of his family, the sister still alive. You're going to have to add that in, further back. You made it a point, in your earlier chapter, that he had no family. Remember? This sister will have to come into play, of course."

"There is no point to keeping her alive, otherwise."

"What do you have in mind?"

"Nothing whatsoever." Alfonse tapped the notebook. "But it

will come to me when the time is right. Or to you. We must trust."

"My mind is already percolating."

"Good. Because it's your turn." He handed her back the book. "I think it needs more period detail. What do you think?"

"A few small ones wouldn't hurt. The setting could use some fleshing out."

"Maybe a little more detail on the naval training center. I guessed at Illinois. I know it's on Lake Michigan, and I vaguely recall it being near Chicago."

Olivia took a pencil from his desk, scratched a note in the margin. "We can add it later, if we find it necessary. How about Agnes's car?"

"What about it?"

"Give it a make, a model." Olivia sparkled. "A 1946 Pontiac Streamliner."

Alfonse wrinkled his nose. "Why?"

"Don't you remember?" She waited. "Your first car. You were still driving it when we met, that old heap."

"Ah, yes. A glorious old heap it was." Alfonse's heart quivered. "Cornelius bought it for me, brand-new, to celebrate the sale of my first novel. I was twenty-six."

"So young. I wish I'd known you then"—she grinned—"before fame made you insufferable."

"I was born insufferable." He held out his hand for hers. Olivia gave it, and Alfonse brought it to his lips. Cornelius. How many ways he'd betrayed him. How many times he'd hurt him. With women. With other men. But then there'd been Olivia Peppernell, whom they both loved in their separate ways. "He forgave you, didn't he?"

"I did nothing that needed forgiving."

"I suppose not." Alfonse kept her fingers against his lips. "He never forgave me."

"Of course he did."

"He might have, at one point," he said. "But in the end, I didn't come. I abandoned him completely."

"Cornelius understood. He loved you."

"He shouldn't have. I didn't earn what he gave me. I couldn't give back what he gave."

"Alfonse." Olivia tugged her hand from his lips, but not from his grasp. She clasped his in both of hers. "Cornelius couldn't help loving you any more than you could help not loving him in kind. We don't control such things, no matter what anyone says."

"He was a good man."

"A very good man. And if you need proof of his love and forgiveness, look around you. He wouldn't have willed this suite to someone he despised."

Alfonse did look around at all the sunshine on all the polished wood. Perhaps Olivia was right. Or perhaps it was he who couldn't forgive.

"So?" Olivia let him go. "Did she read it?"

Alfonse shifted in his chair. "She took great pains to hide the evidence, but yes, she did. Or someone did. The match I slipped into the binding was on the floor when I got back from the hospital."

"She'll tell me. I can hardly wait to hear what she thinks."

"Something I'd dearly love as well." Alfonse chuffed. "You wily witch. You did it on purpose, keeping Cecibel's adoration all for yourself."

"I thought only of her," Olivia countered. "Besides the lark, think about it logically, Alfie. Imagine how she would feel, reading the first work you've done in over a decade, knowing you were awaiting her response? Especially considering she fancies herself in love with you. She'd never read a single word."

"You're just thinking that up now, on the spot."

"Is it any less true?"

He grunted.

"Don't be so cross." Olivia got to her feet. "I'm going back to my room. My brain is buzzing, and not from the excellent weed I smoked a little while ago. Cecibel will be around for her daily visit later on."

"You're leaving already? You only just got here."

"For goodness' sake, Alfonse. Surely you can entertain yourself. Watch television."

"I loathe daytime programming. It's for old people and the unemployed."

"You are an old person. And you're also unemployed."

"I still get royalty checks every quarter."

"That doesn't make you employed. Go down to the gathering room," Olivia suggested. "There's always someone lingering in there."

"Will you take me? The nurses talk to me as if I were deaf, or a simpleton."

"Oh, fine, you big baby." Olivia moved his wheelchair closer. "You know you're perfectly capable of doing this on your own."

"I like to be waited on." He caught her hand and kissed it. "Especially by a beautiful woman who captured my heart decades ago and kept it all to herself."

"Liar." Olivia bent to kiss his cheek. "But charm will get you everywhere. When I'm stoned. I'd leave you where you sit, otherwise. Consider yourself warned."

Alfonse kept his hand on hers as she wheeled him down the corridor. Their passion had been legendary, but now? Love and passion, as he'd told Cecibel, were such disparate things. What he felt for Olivia now intricately entwined with what they had been, with all they'd shared. Love, still. Passion, faded. Remembered. Cherished. And gone.

"Look, there's Judith," Olivia said close to his ear. "Sit with her a bit. She can feed your ego for a while."

"Are you jealous, my dear?"

"Oh, I was, Alfonse. I was indeed, all those years ago when I had become too old to be enticing, and she was still young and fresh. But that's all in the past now."

"Livy?" He put the brake on his chair.

She nearly tumbled over his shoulder. "For goodness' sake!"

"You can't believe that," he said. "Please tell me you were joking."

Olivia came around to face him, arms crossed over her bony chest. "Isn't it true?"

"Not even slightly. You were never too old, only too loved. You must know that."

"You loved me too much to desire me?"

"I loved you too much to cause you more pain." Alfonse grasped her hand and tugged until she sat in the chair just behind her. "We both know you didn't fall down any stairs, Olivia."

"That is also in the past. No need to—"

"It was because of me he did that to you."

"You were the dalliance, not the cause. And it wasn't the first time he laid hands on me. What cause would I have had to seek solace in another—in many others, I'll have you know—if my life had been happy or even adequate?"

Alfonse let go her hand. "And I'll have you know, those weeks we were together, you were the only one."

"You've had many 'only ones.'" She rose to her feet. "I know the intensity of your attention. When we were together, I was your sun and stars. Few will ever feel that important, that cherished. It's why everyone loves you, and none of us ever despised you after your attention focused elsewhere." Olivia patted his shoulder, kissed his cheek. "You can make it the rest of the way to Judith. Have a lovely afternoon, my friend. I'll see you at dinner."

The motorized hum grated on Alfonse's sense of himself. That he would end up so reduced had never dared venture into his reality. An active life and fortunate genes had always kept him fit, but his vices were many. Alfonse Carducci had never expected to see fifty, let alone eighty. Moderation hadn't seemed worth the sacrifice.

"Alfonse!" Judith stood, waved him over. She bent to say something that made her companions laugh. Still lovely, so elfin. Hair white as a dove's breast, her face unlined and her eyes bright, she was a softer version of the woman he'd known before his body's comeuppance. He'd been close to sixty when she was assigned to him, an editor far more brutal than any he'd ever worked with before. Alfonse loved her for that, for putting his story above his monumental ego. Olivia believed it was Judith's comparative youth, her beauty that attracted him; it was every blue-penciled stroke that made her desirable. Every cut to his prose aroused. It was there on the desk in her New York City office they first made love, amid arguing over whether or not the serial comma was passé. Their affair waned when the novel went to galleys, cooled before it hit the stands. Now she was coming toward him, an affectionate smile on her lips, and Alfonse could not help wishing for wings that worked.

"You're looking well." Judith kissed both cheeks. "You've a rosy glow about you."

"Seeing you brings out the best in me."

"Always the charmer."

They settled in the sunlight by an open window. A walk outside would be so nice; going back to retrieve his oxygen apparatus wasn't worth the effort. June's pollen would not be the death of him. September's, maybe, but not June's. He had a novel to write.

"What brings you to the gathering room this time of day?" Judith asked. "I haven't seen you outside of dinner in a week."

"I've been . . . otherwise occupied this past week. Today, I am at odds. Have you had your tea?"

"Several cups, but I could do with another. You?"

Alfonse grimaced. "Chamomile, please."

She returned moments later, balancing two cups. Handing him one, she settled into a chair. A breeze lifted her hair. "Lovely, isn't it?"

"Entirely." He sipped. Grass and flowers. Disgusting. "Thank you."

"So what had you occupied last week that deserted you this one? Olivia?"

"In a sideways sort of way, yes. But no, not the woman herself. Though she has deserted me today."

"I saw her come in. She didn't say hello."

"Don't take it personally. She's distracted."

"I know Olivia Peppernell well enough by now not to take insult, even if she means to give it. Is what's distracting you the same thing that's distracting her?"

Alfonse sipped his tea again. Maybe it wasn't so bad. At least it was warm and sweet. He looked at her over the rim of his teacup. "Why would you ask that?"

Judith laughed softly. "Were it a decade earlier, I'd accuse you two of picking up your lusty affair. Things being as they are, I'd say that's not it. Knowing you and knowing her, being the keen observer that I am, I'd say you two have a secret, and that secret involves the only thing you two have left in common. You're writing."

Alfonse's cup clattered on his saucer. "How in the hell could you possibly deduce that?"

She leaned forward. "I spotted her in here a couple of weeks ago, madly scribbling in a notebook. And she just left clutching a notebook like the devil himself was after it. Tell me, Alfonse. Are you two geniuses collaborating on something?"

Lying required energy Alfonse didn't have to give. He handed her his teacup. Judi set it down, her face no longer teasing but concerned. "I shouldn't have pried. I'm sorry, Alfonse. Forget I—"

"It is nothing genius," he said. "Just a story sprung to life one day as I woke from dreaming."

"Alfonse, that's wonderful!"

But it was less wonderful now. A secret told sent the magic already leaching into the ether. "It has given us both reason to open our eyes in the morning."

"And you're writing long hand?"

"For the first time since the eighties," he said. "It seemed . . . required."

Judith slumped back in her chair, the look of wonder he once saw in her younger self surfacing. "Of course it is. You've gone back to the beginning."

He smiled. "Yes. You're exactly right."

"This is truly wonderful, Alfonse. What will you do with it when you're done?"

"We haven't thought that far," he said. "I may not make it to the end, after all."

"Of course you will. Don't say such a thing."

"Why not?" He shrugged. "Denying the truth doesn't make it

any less so. I'm dying, Judith. But here, in my last days, I've found the kind of joy I haven't known in a very long time."

She lunged forward, grasping both his hands. "Let me transcribe it for you."

"Pardon?"

"Let me key it into the computer. I can clean it up as I do. I swear I won't change a thing of plot, pace, or character. And I won't push for publication even after you're gone. I'll even put that in writing. Please."

Alfonse licked suddenly dry lips. "The work of a copy editor? A . . . an intern? You're one of the most respected editors in the country."

"I was," she said. "Just like you were one of the literary giants. Like Olivia was. Now we are here in the Pen, living out our last days in the shadows of our former glory."

"You are hardly in your last days, my dear."

"You don't know that." She slumped back again, a fist under her chin.

Alfonse's poor heart stuttered. "Are you ill?"

"Ill?" She shook her head. "No. I'm tired. My nerves are fried. I burned brightly, and burned out. Isn't that what we all did? We spent our lives chasing words and stories and rising stars and then one day woke up and realized our best years were done. We're tired and getting older and there's no one in our lives outside of colleagues we've spent more time with than family who gave up on us years ago." She gestured, encompassing the whole of the Pen. "Where else would I go but here? Where else do I belong?"

"You miss the world outside."

"Don't you?"

"I miss the past. I miss my youth. I don't miss the world at all."

"But you no longer miss writing, because it has found you again." Judi picked up his teacup, handed it back to him. "Let me be part of it. This small, small part. For all I once was to you, professionally and personally. Please."

Something of the leaching magic stoppered. Sparkled. Olivia would fume—what delight! She kept her secret with Cecibel. He might keep a secret of his own. It would mean giving Judith some of his allotted writing time, but he'd crushed deadlines before. Electric joy prickled his skin. He raised his disgusting, grassy tea, which really wasn't so bad with enough sugar. "How could I possibly refuse such a plea?" he said. "We'll work out a schedule. Just don't tell Olivia. No matter how old or sick I may be, she'll have my most tender bits in a vise if she finds out."

Paterson, New Jersey

SUMMER 1954

✦

Cecilia

The short walk from Falls View took forever. A whole month, and still no letter from Aldo. No phone call. A month and still no period.

Where could he be? What could have happened? Whatever it was, it had to be huge. A secret assignment (because her Aldo was just that brilliant and brave). Maybe a drill sergeant who had it out for him (wasn't there always one in war movies?) never gave him her letters. He wasn't dead, that much she'd been able to find out through phone calls to the base. But her letters went unanswered. Her phone calls were never returned. If she could leave her mother, Cecilia would take a bus all the way to Illinois and wait in whatever holding room they put her in until Aldo showed up. But she couldn't leave Mama. Not with Daddy missing.

Opening the kitchen door, Cecilia let the cool air inside hit her like a little bit of heaven. Air-conditioning. What a glorious thing, and one of the many well-to-do perks of being a Giancami she was grateful for. Were it not for those perks, life with Daddy would have been unbearable. Sadly, happily, life had been sort of good with him gone. Easier. Mom wasn't always cowering, or angry. The boys were another matter. Without their father's adoring guidance, they stuck closer to their mother, who babied them mercilessly. They'd been bratty enough before. At least they were no longer torturing mice and crickets. How much better it would have been had Dominic Giancami vanished before Aldo left for the navy. Maybe she'd have broken free. Maybe she'd have gone with him.

Maybe Aldo doesn't want you anymore.

No. No! Cecilia wouldn't betray their love with such thoughts. She never imagined she was bluffing when she said she couldn't marry him, even if this happened. She'd marry him in a heartbeat, live in some tiny apartment in Chicago while he trained, follow him all over the world if necessary. How foolish to make him think otherwise. How sad she ever thought she should.

And now, no letters, no contact, after all the promises he made. Had she been so convincing? Cold sweat beaded her upper lip, her brow. What was she going to do if another month passed and still no period? There was no way she was going to some coat-hanger surgeon. She already loved the baby she feared. It came first now. Not her. Not Aldo.

"Cecilia? Is that you?"

Maria Antonette Giancami, born Maria Gallo to immigrants who'd never learned to speak English before dying too young to meet their grandchildren, breezed into the kitchen. Dressed, coiffed, perfectly powdered, wearing heels, Maria hadn't touched a mop or dustrag in more years than Cecilia could remember. They'd already been on their way to *respectable* by the time she was old enough to notice. Angelina did the housework and the cooking. Her husband, Giuseppe, took care of the grounds and upkeep on the house. Cecilia and her brothers didn't even have to tidy their rooms to earn the ridiculous allowance that she wished, more than anything, she'd thought to save instead of squander.

"Why didn't you answer me?" Maria scolded.

"Because you walked in and saw it was me."

"You still owe me the courtesy of an answer, ah?"

Such pretty speech, so touched by the past, by an accent she'd never cultured away.

"Were you looking for me?" Cecilia asked. "Mama?"

Maria's shoulders rose and fell. She lifted her head. Cecilia's skin beaded up all over again.

"Sit, Cecilia."

"Can I get a glass of water first? I just got home from school."

Maria waved her to the sink, pulled out a kitchen chair. She sat with her back to Cecilia, who took her time filling a glass, gulping it down, and filling it again.

"What's up?" she asked, sitting across from her mother. "Is it something about Daddy?"

Maria's face scrunched. Holding back tears? Or disdain? Cecilia couldn't be sure.

"Your *father* won't turn up until he wants to be found," she said. "I imagine he made a bad investment"—code for a gambling debt—"or ran off with an old friend"—Trudy, his mistress, whom he didn't even attempt to keep secret—"and is having himself a grand time in Cuba, ah? No, it's not about him. He's disappeared before. It's about you."

She imagined the sudden guilty pallor pulling all the blood from her face. "Me? What'd I do?"

"It's not what you've done," Maria said. "But what you must do. With your father . . . gone, certain covenants are being called into action. I am honor bound to see them through."

Cecilia sipped her water. "Covenants?"

"You know you've been promised in marriage to the Parisi boy, ah?"

Cold again. Enzo and Virginia Parisi's drippy son, Enzo Jr. She'd known him since they were babies. He was nice enough. He might even be handsome one day. Now he was a math nerd on the chess team and she was one of the most popular girls in school. They moved in different circles. Always had. Always would, if she had anything to say about it, which she did not. Cecilia knew what was coming, saw that train barreling down on her, and had no idea how to get out of the way.

"I wanted you to have more time," Maria went on. "I got your father to agree to college first, but things have changed."

"I still have a year left of high school," Cecilia blurted. "I can't get married now."

"Not married. Engaged. Enzo Jr. is off to college in the fall. The courting is being moved up, as a show of faith that with or without Cami's influence, you'll uphold the promises made." Maria leaned across the table, took her daughter's hand. "Without your father, this family won't survive. Not you, me, or your brothers. We need protection. Do you understand? They'll take everything from us."

"You'll sell me off to save this?" Cecilia waved her hand over her head. "Is that all I'm worth?"

Maria looked at her long and hard. "You were promised when you were just a little girl, Ceci. Don't pretend you didn't know. We're in America, but among our kind, the old ways still hold." She squeezed Cecilia's hand and let it go. "Enzo's a good boy. You'll have time to grow into one another, maybe even fall in love. Though love isn't all it's cracked up to be. I married for love, and look what came of that."

"But what if I fall in love with someone else?" Cecilia asked. "While I'm at college, I mean."

"You won't. You can't." Maria pushed away from the table. "Ginny and I have set up a date for you two. Tonight. Go upstairs and rest. Make yourself pretty. Enzo will be here at six to pick you up."

Cecilia sat where she was after her mother left, sipping water she didn't feel go down her throat. She would refuse to do it. No one could make her.

Yes, they could. They would.

She would run away.

To where? With what money? And if she managed to find Aldo and marry him, he'd be dead before the ink dried on their marriage license. She'd been so cavalier, lying naked in Aldo's arms, telling him she could never marry him. Telling him she'd be married off. It hadn't felt real, even then. And now?

The truth settled in the pit of her stomach. She was a girl in a world that favored boys. That catered to them. Obeyed them. Hadn't she known that all her life? But knowing and *knowing* were such different things. And she wasn't a girl anymore. She was a woman. Aldo had proven that to her, as the baby growing inside her proved now. Knowledge was power and, girl or not, Cecilia was Dominic Giancami's daughter.

Dumping the rest of her water into the sink, she watched it trickle down the drain. Daddy was missing. Aldo was missing. She was on her own to make her future, and her baby's. Enzo Parisi Jr. would arrive in a couple of hours. She'd be ready for him, but there was nothing on the planet capable of making him ready for her.

Night came through Cecilia's open window. Mama insisted on switching off the air-conditioning on cool summer nights, just like she used to insist the heat get lowered on all but the coldest winter nights. It was one of the few arguments she made and won. The fact that Daddy spent many nights elsewhere probably had something to do with that.

Naked, supine on top of her pink, dotted swiss bedspread, Cecilia smoothed her hand over and over her soft, flat belly, telling herself over and over that she'd done what she did to protect her baby. She'd had no choice.

The kissing was the worst part. It felt so wrong. Enzo's mouth tasted like garlic and cigarettes. She focused on that to get through the pain worming out of her heart. After that, it wasn't so bad. Nothing like the frenzy Aldo made of her insides, but Enzo was sweet and awkward and grateful. She pretended to be a virgin, like he was, even crying out in pain when he first pushed inside her. It did hurt, truly, deeply, far worse than the first time with Aldo. Then she'd barely felt a thing.

They talked afterward, her head on his soft shoulder—so unlike Aldo's muscular one—his fingers caressing circles on the small of her back. He'd be leaving for college in a few months. Princeton. Some mathematics degree she didn't understand the use of. But Enzo was passionate, and that was a good thing. If she couldn't love him, at least she could like him for that.

"I'm glad you like me," Enzo said, after they were dressed. "I didn't think you did."

"We've known one another since we were babies. Of course I like you."

Enzo blushed then. "I mean." He gestured to the bed. His bed in his room in his house where his mother slept just down the hall. "I never expected anything like this to happen to me."

"Like this?"

"A beautiful girl doing . . . you know . . . with me. I'm not exactly Rock Hudson."

You're not Aldo Wronksi either, but you'll do. "We're going to be married, Enzo. This was bound to happen." She sidled up to him, her best impression of a movie vamp, and on tiptoes kissed his lips. "Is it wrong for a girl to find her fiancé irresistible?"

He put his arms around her. Did he tremble? "Do you? Really?"

Yes, he was trembling. His lip quivered. Cecilia's heart gave a little jolt. *Keep going. You can do this.* Winding her arms around his neck, she kissed him long and luxuriously. If he wondered where her experience came from, he didn't say. *Sweet Enzo. I'm sorry.*

"I love you, Cecilia," he whispered. "Not because of tonight. I have for a long time. Even before my dad told me you'd be my wife someday. You're so pretty and popular. I never thought you could actually—"

"Shh." She placed a finger to his lips. "Let's get out of here before your mother catches us. Before your father gets home. We have all the time in the world to talk."

"All our lives," he had said.

Naked, supine on top of her pink, dotted swiss bedspread, smoothing her hand over and over her soft, flat belly, telling herself over and over that her baby was safe now whether Daddy ever came home again, whether Aldo ever wrote her back, Cecilia smiled.

Bar Harbor, Maine

❧❦❧

You can rarely tell the real thoughts behind a smile.
—CORNELIUS TRAEGAR

"If you go to him looking like that, he's going to know." Olivia took the notebook back from Cecibel, a crooked smile on her lips. Wicked woman. So dear. Cecibel's giddy heart overflowed.

"I'll be the epitome of sedate decorum." She kissed the old woman's cheek. "I promise. But Olivia, how amazing it is."

"Hardly amazing. It's just a story."

"A wonderful story."

"Of little literary merit, I'm afraid. Genre at best."

"You say that like it's a bad thing."

"After a career like mine, child, it is." Olivia tucked the notebook away. "Thank you for getting it back to me so quickly. There are a few little tweaks I'd like to make before giving it back to Alfonse."

"Like?"

Olivia shrugged. "I want to put a little more flesh on Enzo's bones before my cowriter gets ahold of him. He must be solidly likable, sweet, and naive if his character is to go where I want it to. Alfonse has a habit of making all his boys dark."

"Will he do that to Aldo?"

"He's already begun." Olivia stretched carefully. "One cannot kill a man without it changing him. Goodness, my back is stiff today. I should go for a walk."

Cecibel grinned. "Out to the arbor?"

"Now that you mention it . . ." She moved carefully to the cedar trunk. Cecibel readied herself to assist, but Olivia opened the lid, shuffled about in her linens, and found her own stash tucked within. Would wonders never cease?

"I'll walk with you," she said.

Olivia waved her off. "You'll be late getting to Alfonse. He so looks forward to your time together. You know he fancies you his muse, don't you?"

A blush crept up from Cecibel's neck. "Is that why he named her Cecilia, do you think?"

"Oh, sweetheart." Olivia laughed. "That you believe you even have to ask is dear. You're as smitten as he is."

Cecibel chewed at her lip. Aldo and Cecilia. Cecilia and Aldo. It was written in the stars. "I'm not smitten, I'm starstruck. He's Alfonse Carducci."

"And I'm Olivia Peppernell." She sniffed. "I think I've been insulted."

"Don't be silly. I've known you for ages, but I was starstruck by you at first."

"Were you?"

"Of course."

"Well, that's better." Olivia patted her hair, struck a pose that made Cecibel laugh. But the old woman's hand fell along with her pretended pout. "He won't be with us long enough for that awe to fade, I'm afraid. It breaks my heart."

"Don't say that."

"As Alfonse says, denying the truth doesn't make it any less real. Go to him now. Be his muse. I'm off to the arbor to visit with my dear friend Mr. Weed."

Cecibel waited for Olivia to turn the corner. How amazing, the change, since Alfonse arrived. Since their story began. Not just in Olivia, but in herself. Perhaps Cecibel *was* his muse; what did that make him to her?

Hurrying along the corridors, she didn't see Dr. Kintz until it was too late to avoid his quiet summons. She stumbled slightly, but didn't have the nerve to pretend she hadn't heard. "Can I help you, Dr. Kintz?"

"A private word," he said. "It won't take long. I know you're off duty and by your lovely dress I can guess you're on your way out."

"Just visiting with a friend."

Dr. Kintz gestured to the wingback chairs set face-to-face before a massive window fronting the courtyard. He waited for Cecibel to sit before doing the same. "I've been going over all the employee records and I came across something in yours that gave me pause."

Cold dread knotted her belly. "Oh? What's that?"

He pulled a little notebook from his pocket. "I want to get this right." He read, "Cecibel Bringer . . . la-dah-dah . . . Oh, here it is. 'Patient released against recommendation of primary physician.'"

"I'm sorry," she said. "What's the question?"

"I'm trying to put this delicately."

"No need."

"Considering this is a private care facility, I'm within my rights to ask, but you don't have to answer."

That cold and dreadful knot spread to her chest. "All right."

"What year was your accident, Cecibel?"

"Nineteen eighty-seven. Why?"

"Because Dr. Marks, the physician who wrote that note, did so in 1990."

Shoulders, thighs. Her fingers tingled. "My injuries were extensive, as you can imagine."

"Dr. Marks is not a surgeon, Cecibel, she is a psychiatrist. The hospital was a mental health facility, and you were there against your will. Must we play this game?"

She was a block of ice, barely able to move her lips enough to speak. "If you have a question, Dr. Kintz, ask it."

He waited. Quietly. Patiently. Cecibel was all too aware of the technique. Dr. Marks never asked her a thing outside of how she was feeling, and if the medication she prescribed was plaguing her with side effects. She always waited, that same quiet patience now applied by Dr. Kintz. It hadn't worked back then. It wouldn't now.

"All right, then," he said. "Thank you for your time, Cecibel. My door is always open."

She rose, and he did, too. Dr. Kintz smiled kindly, a little sadly. "Have a nice afternoon."

"Thank you." What had frozen now flamed. Slow, deliberate steps quickened. She was running full pelt. Where, she didn't know or care. Away was all she wanted.

What records did he have, and where did he get them? She'd been very careful not to provide more than the absolute minimum on her employment questionnaire. So minimal she'd been surprised to have been hired at all. No experience. A nursing degree never finished. She'd been no one, from nowhere, hired as an orderly in one of the poshest nursing homes in the country, and only now did she wonder how that had happened at all.

Unhirable. Like Salvatore. Like Finlay. Both hired when Dr. Traegar was still alive to collect misfits no one else would have. But who had collected her?

Stuttering to a halt, Cecibel nearly lost her footing. She leaned against the wall, hand to chest, and gained her bearings. The service corridor. Between living spaces and kitchen. Safe enough. Familiar. She tilted her head back, not caring, momentarily, if her hair fell off her face. Outrunning the past was as impossible as hiding her disfigurement, but she kept at both anyway.

"Cecibel, what are you doing here?" Salvatore stood in the doorway, his hand propping back the swinging door. He looked at his watch. "Aren't you supposed to be with your boyfriend?"

She looked at hers. Four thirty. Alfonse would be wondering where she was. Letting her arm drop, she stepped closer to Sal. "Dr. Kintz stopped me on my way. He asked me some unsettling questions."

"You too?" Sal pished. "He's been going through everyone's rap sheets—"

"I've never been arrested."

"I'm being dramatic, darling." He pulled her nearer. "No sooner did he uncover my alter ego than I got put on probation."

"What?"

Sal let her go, waving a hand as if shooing a bug. "Oh, he said it was because I left the supply closet unlocked and demented old Mr. Gardern got caught stealing toilet paper again, but I know the real deal. He fires me, I'm going to sue him for discrimination."

"Sal." Cecibel shook her head. "You know that's not true." Dr. Kintz was a snoop, not a bigot. "You're a fixture here"—*like me and Fin*—"not in any real danger. So he really is going through everyone's files?"

"Yes, he is."

"But I didn't have a file. At least, I didn't know I had one. He seemed to have . . . information about me from before I was ever hired."

"Who knows how they gather what they do or why?" He raised a fine, thin brow. "You got a skeleton or two I don't know about?"

Or three or four. "I guess he knows all about Finlay by now, too."

"I'm sure he knew before he ever got here. It's not like it wasn't scandalous and tragic and in all the papers for years and years."

"I get why Dr. Traegar would hire him," she said. "From all accounts, Dr. Traegar was a good man, kind. He probably knew Fin as a kid or something and felt bad about what happened. But . . ."

"But Finlay bludgeoned a man to death," Sal supplied. "So why didn't anyone since Traegar let him go? Your guess is as good as mine."

"I have no guesses," she said.

"Speaking of Finlay." Sal batted his eyelashes. "I noticed you two are getting chummy."

"Stop."

"Oh, come on, honey. It's nice."

"We're two of the only three on-site staffers," Cecibel said. "It's time we got to be friends."

"You're getting no fight from me. I been saying it for years. Now that it's happening, I think I'm feeling a little jealous."

Cecibel blew a breath through her lips. "Don't be an idiot. I'm really late now. See you later, Sal."

Sedately, as she'd promised Olivia, Cecibel walked to Alfonse's suite on the other side of the mansion. Her conversation with

Dr. Kintz had drained the exuberance from her anyway. Whatever information he had didn't matter anyway. Old news. Way in the past. Done. *But not forgotten. Never ever. Apparently.*

Hand resting on the lever of Alfonse's door, Cecibel took deep breaths. She was good at her job. Most of the residents loved her, and those who didn't had no cause to dislike her. The nurses snubbed her, but they left her alone for the most part. It'd been a while since one tried to get her fired, anyway. She was safe. Nearly a decade safe. If Dr. Kintz kept Fin on without qualm, he'd keep her for sure. He couldn't know anything about her outside of, somehow, getting files from Dr. Marks, and Dr. Marks hadn't known anything. Because Cecibel never told her, never admitted she didn't know if the accident had been on purpose, never confessed that whether or not it was, she'd been more than willing to die. More than willing to take Jennifer with her.

ᵔ

Cecibel was never late. Nearly twenty minutes to five and Alfonse feared he'd begin hyperventilating if she didn't appear—think the thought, crook the finger, smile the smile—now! She didn't. If ever he believed he had magical powers concerning his desires and the fairer sex, his current attempts disabused him utterly. Or perhaps his memory faded with his heart, lungs, liver.

The door swung open and in she rushed, her hair hanging in a thick braid over her shoulder. Alfonse's stuttering heart changed tack but not rhythm. Magic, indeed. Before he could gather himself to rise as a gentleman did for a lady, Cecibel threw herself to the floor at his feet, her golden head upon his lap.

"Cecibel?"

"Please. Don't talk. Don't ask. Just . . . please."

No shaking shoulders. No sobbing. Cecibel took slow, deep breaths he felt in his knees, against his shins. Even in distress, she'd been careful to turn the fair of her face to him. His heart stirred, maybe even locations south. He couldn't be sure. It had been so long. Strange spasms racked him all the time. Petting her tenderly—hair, shoulder, back; hair, shoulder, back—he crooned soothing sounds out of the past. *It's all right, my darling. Hush. I'm here. I'm here.*

"I don't know what's going on with me." Her whispered words scattered his thoughts, like a hand through smoke.

"What do you mean?"

"I'm thinking things."

"Things?"

She nodded against his knee. "Things I haven't thought in a long time. Things I haven't been able to. Things I shouldn't. And it's because of you."

Another change in tack. Could Olivia have been right? Alfonse quelled the need to clutch his chest. "Because of me, how, my dear?"

"I'm not sure." Cecibel picked up her head, and for a split moment, he saw her whole. A trick of the light, of failing eyesight. Whatever the reason, it was fleeting. The scars were there, behind the stranded curtain obscuring but not quite hiding them from the world. Never hiding them from herself. That Alfonse knew with a certainty settling painfully in his beleaguered heart.

"I don't know what to do," she whispered. "I don't know how to turn it off, or if I should. I'm . . . scared."

"Fear can be a good thing, Cecibel," he said. "It means you're facing down a demon."

"But what if I don't want to? What if I want to let it win?" Cecibel lowered her gaze, waited for absolution. Benediction. Condemnation.

Alfonse lifted her chin. "If that were so, you wouldn't be asking."

Cecibel flinched but she didn't pull away. The fingers of a man much younger than his body felt trembled. He lifted her braid, tested its weight. A fortune in gold, in silk, this beauty. He pulled the elastic from the end and, tenderly, undid its glorious length. Cecibel closed her eyes. Alfonse traced the contours of her fair half, a lover coming to know his beloved. In a novel, perhaps. Real life was never like a novel written to pull at heartstrings, to frighten or to thrill. Real life was so much more complicated. The emotions skimmed or embellished for a reader's pleasure could never be truly expressed. In a novel, Alfonse would be a younger man. Cecibel's scars would be somehow and strangely beautiful. In a novel, he would touch her and she would lean into his hand and an understanding would be reached without either of them uttering a word. In a novel, all obstacles could be overcome.

He pushed the hair from her face, all of her face. Now Cecibel flinched. A tear slipped out from between closed lids and rolled down her soft, lovely cheek. The other eye could not weep. The lid was a slit of borrowed skin. No lashes. She was a melted candle of cobbled flesh from eye socket to jawline. Her plump, kissable mouth did not end in a delicate corner, but in a thick, shiny scar that drew a line up to her ear. An ear that had no lobe, no flap. The insides of a seashell broken on the rocks.

Leaning low compressed lungs too weak to compensate, but Alfonse held his breath and did so. He kissed her brow. He kissed the fair princess's cheek, and the monster's. He dropped back in his chair, gasping. Cecibel opened her eyes, blue marbles, even, impossibly, the ruined one. The moment froze. One heartbeat. Two. Three. Four. She was rising, towering over him. A wounded Valkyrie fresh from battle. Alfonse felt so small in that gaze. A withered old man who'd trespassed into places he didn't belong, and couldn't survive.

Cecibel's hand came to rest on his shoulder. A swoop of hair dropped into his lap as she kissed his brow, his cheeks, his lips. She lingered there though he didn't respond, couldn't respond without breaking the spell. A thousand sweaty nights, languid afternoons, fresh mornings careened through his body, his brain. To pluck even one of them from the parade would undo him. Instead, his fingers curled into that hair pooled in his lap. He fingered it, concentrated on the thick softness Cecibel took with her when she pulled away.

He didn't call her back. She didn't glance over her shoulder. The metallic click of his door was the only indication that she was gone; he hoped, not for good.

Head back, eyes on the ceiling so high above his head, Alfonse counted breaths until he could do so calmly. He couldn't have written the magic of these moments, not if given another century to try. Life could never be contained by words. It could only be expressed to the best of one's ability, in the hopes of capturing a tiny spark and giving it away.

Off the Aleutian Islands, Alaska

※

Aldo

No matter how cold it was on deck, the kitchens broiled. Aldo didn't complain. Low man on the totem pole in the kitchen was far better than holding that position above. He worked hard, but he was warm, fed, and he was learning.

The monotony of prep work in the galley gave him good knife skills and too much time for his mind to wander. To Cecilia. What she was doing. Where she was. Who she was with. Life had to have changed drastically after her father's death; for the better, he hoped. Criminal that he was, Dominic Giancami was small stuff and not newsworthy. At least, Aldo hadn't read anything about it in Chicago newspapers. The only news they got onboard was radio broadcasts concerning movie stars, and the ship newsletter.

A year, already, since seeing her last. Touching her. Tasting her. Even so he could still close his eyes and conjure her entirety. Nearly six months since completing all his training and being assigned to the galley crew on the USS *Greenwater*. A whole continent away from Cecilia, in a world where even summers were cold. It was an important ship playing a vital role in keeping the citizenry of the United States safe. The communist threat across the Bering Strait was as real as the Japanese threat of a little more than a decade ago. Diligence, his commanding officers claimed, was the key to freedom.

"Never saw a man chop an onion so fast without nicking himself." Dooley's big, dopey grin rarely faltered. Aldo liked that about him, even if some of the other fellas picked on that trait. The man wasn't stupid, just perpetually cheerful.

"It's nothing," Aldo said. "Mindless."

"It's more than the chopping. You got a way with food. That's what I heard."

"From?"

"People." Dooley leaned closer. "I heard Zigs say something about you getting bumped up to the officers' mess."

"When'd you hear that?"

"Today. Just a little while ago."

Pride warmed him through. Meals during boot camp were nothing to write home about, if he had a home to write to, but far better than Aldo had ever been able to provide for himself. It sparked something in him he'd never tapped before. His experience grilling dogs and frying potatoes at Falls View got him a foot into the culinary world the military might not be known for but ran on. He learned the basics, discovered a palate he'd never noticed before. A whole new world appeared on his horizon, not simply one of food, but of cuisine, because aboard the USS *Greenwater,* even the crew ate well.

All these months hanging around the kitchens, lending a hand even when he wasn't on shift, Aldo had taken pride in helping to prepare meals the men could look forward to. Imagining the culinary delights he'd be able to provide the officers tweaked the glands in his jaw. He wasn't sure what the rungs on the ladder were just yet, but he did know the highest he could go was the White House, if he stayed with the military. Aldo hadn't thought that far ahead. Join the navy, do his stint. From there, it had been a blurry thing that swirled around Cecilia. No more. She was part of the blur of his past now, leaving his future completely without focus.

Until being in the kitchen.

Aldo finished his shift amid daydreams of cooking for the president of the United States, opening a restaurant on the Mag Mile, in Manhattan, maybe even in Paris. He headed for the berthing compartment. Being tall got him stuck with the top rack, but he didn't mind too much. At least no one had to climb past him to get to the floor. It did put him farthest from his gear stowed in the locker below, and Aldo didn't trust Cavanaugh one little bit. Sneaky little runt was always somewhere he wasn't supposed to be, usually with someone else's stuff in his pockets.

Checking his locker, he found everything where he'd left it. Not that he had much. Navy-issue socks, underwear, T-shirts, pants. A uniform, in case they ever got the promised shore leave that hadn't happened yet. A copy of *From Here to Eternity* sent as a high school graduation gift by the cousin who was raising his sister but hadn't wanted him. He'd tossed it in a drawer of his banged-up dresser in the tiny, lonely room he rented. Two years later, the movie came out. He took Cecilia to see it. One of their first dates. The scene with the kiss on the beach sparked their first kiss. It was for that and that alone he packed the book when he left Paterson. Aldo had no intention of ever reading it; he'd already seen the movie.

He took the book from his locker, sat on Cavanaugh's bunk, and thumbed through the pages. Stuck into the middle, a letter. Unopened, postmarked December 16, 1954. The letter caught up to him just before he left Illinois for the West Coast. It had seemed like kismet, the letter arriving when it did, and it was the only one he kept; the rest went in the garbage, unopened. Unread. Pulling the letter from the pages, he let the book fall back into his locker.

The letter sat flat on his hand, pristine. A holy relic. A talisman as magical as King Arthur's sword. The contents a mystery. Words of love or of anger. Maybe both. Until he opened it, the possibilities were endless, and far safer than knowing.

"Off my bunk, you dumb Polack." A small, quick hand snatched the letter. "What's this? Letter from your mommy?"

"Fuck you." Aldo tried to snatch it back. "Give it now, or—"

"Or what?"

"I'll smear your mick ass from here to the brig."

"That'll get you bumped up to the officers' mess." Cavanaugh snickered. "Oh, sure it will. Pickin' on a runt half your size. Might even be worth the ass-kicking."

Aldo halted midgrab. "What'd you hear?"

"Same as everyone, you fuckin' kiss-ass."

Aldo grabbed for the letter. Cavanaugh yanked it away. "Now let's see what Dearest Mommy has to say."

His bunkmate ripped the envelope. Aldo lunged. Cavanaugh was quick but small, and comparatively weak.

"Get off!"

"Give me the letter." Straddling him, Aldo wrestled the no-longer-pristine letter from Cavanaugh's fist. He pushed off and away, kneeing him in the chest for good measure.

Cavanaugh scrambled for safety. "I'm reporting you!"

"Make sure you suck Ensign Trotters's dick after you're done kissing his ass."

"Dumb Polack," he grumbled, rubbing his chest. "Can't take a fucking joke."

Aldo grabbed his parka and took Cecilia's letter, and himself, above board. Cavanaugh wasn't going to report him. The idiot was always in trouble; the less contact he had with his commanding officers, the better. Aldo didn't put it past him to steal the letter in retaliation, read Cecilia's words, and taunt him with them. That wasn't going to happen either. He'd throw the thing overboard first.

On deck, cold wind so stiff he had to shoulder through it, Aldo zipped his parka up as high as it would go. How could it be summer? He'd rarely experienced a winter so cold in New Jersey. He pulled gloves from his pocket and nearly lost the letter tucked in with them, nearly let it go. *Watch it flutter. Consign it to the sea.* That life was over—had it ever been real?—even though he would love her the rest of his life. He'd made his vow in kisses and sweat, sealed it in churning water and blood. Aldo wouldn't break it even if he could. There had to be special places in hell for a man who could do that.

Holding the letter up to the wind, Aldo watched it flutter and flap. His grip tightened. He couldn't let it go. Cavanaugh had already ripped it open. The spell was broken. No longer a talisman of possibility, it was an old letter from a girl he'd loved, broken, and left. After killing her father. It was a sign. He had to read it now. Aldo would believe that the rest of his life.

Tucking the gloves back into his pockets, he held the letter in his teeth. He moved to the lee side of the ship nevertheless buffeted by the constant arctic wind. Aldo fit his finger into the tear Cavanaugh had made. The breach. The desecration. He pulled it out again and opened Cecilia's letter from the other side.

My Aldo,

I've given up hope that you'll answer. There are a million dumb reasons I can make up to console or torture myself with, but the end-all-be-all is that you won't. I don't care. I love you anyway.

How did everything get so fucked up? Dumb question. Things have been fucked up for me since I was born a girl. I'm sorry you fell for me and got fucked up, too. Maybe you figured that out. Maybe that's why you don't write me. Or maybe you're really upset about me having to drop out of school to get married. There I go torturing myself.

I hope you believe me when I say I don't love Enzo. I'm fond of him. He's a good man. At least my father didn't promise me to an asshole like himself. We live in a little apartment off campus. Being away from my family is the only good thing right now. That, and the baby. Enzo will be good to me. He adores me. He'll be a good father. I will still never love him. Not like me and you. If he and I are married fifty years, and have a dozen kids, I won't.

I love you, Aldo Wronski. I will love you every day for the rest of my life, but this is the last letter I can write to you. It's too dangerous for you. For me. If anyone ever found out, Enzo's heart would break, and I'm not so cold a bitch that I want that either.

Someday, we're going to see one another again. The last time can't have been the last time. Me with my hair in pigtails, wearing flannel pj's, the smell of your cologne on my skin. I'll see you, you'll see me, and it'll be like only a few minutes has passed. I believe that with all my heart.

Yours eternally—Cecilia

P.S.
You were wearing a blue shirt. You'd done the buttons up wrong. I thought it was so cute, I didn't correct you. And your hair was sticking up a little. Love-tossed is how I like to remember it. Forever, my Aldo.

P.P.S.
I bought Enzo that cologne for Christmas and make him wear it all
the time even though he doesn't really like it much. It's wrong of me,
but he doesn't know. At night, in bed, I pretend he's you. Forever and
a day.

Aldo crumbled the letter in a fist. Enzo? Married? Baby? A hole
opened up under his feet. He hovered above it while the chasm
deepened, swirled, threatened. She must have told him in prior letters. He imagined her on her wedding day, waiting for the priest to
ask if anyone objected, waiting for Aldo to cry out "I do!" from the
back of the church. She was pregnant, and that meant she'd been
with another man. A man who was now her husband. A husband
she would never love. Aldo was glad she married a good man who
adored her even if his own heart was suddenly full of more holes
than it had been before reading her words, before learning her truth.
Whatever his hopes when he joined the navy, he'd blown it all to
smithereens when he fought with Dominic Giancami and won.

Cecilia was married.

Cecilia was going to have a baby.

Maybe it had already been born.

Cecilia was lost to him forever, and had been since the day they
met. Only now he knew it with a certainty those vague notions
caught in that blur of his past never made clear.

"I love you, Cecilia," he said. "I will love you every day for the
rest of my life."

And Aldo opened his fist. The arctic wind snatched Cecilia's
letter, lifted it up, tossed it about, took it away. Jamming his hands
into his pockets, he made his way down to the galley. Zigs would
know how to go about making it happen, and if he didn't, he'd find
out how. Tonight, Aldo was taking a step into a future suddenly
as clear as the cloudless sky above his head, one in which Cecilia
was the blur that might or might not ever come into focus again.
Tonight, he was cooking for the captain.

Bar Harbor, Maine

❧❦❧

Is a kiss ever just a kiss?

—CORNELIUS TRAEGAR

Alfonse paced outside Judi's room, in his head, at any rate. In fact, he leaned against the door, head back and eyes closed, waiting. He'd shushed her when she'd tried to talk about the manuscript in the gathering room, reminded her it was a secret she couldn't spill. It had been her idea to stroll from there to her room, farther than he'd walked since his episode—code word for dying and being brought back before he knew what a DNR order was—last winter.

Judi hadn't invited him in, but asked him to wait outside while she got the notebook for him. Alfonse found that strange, considering they were to discuss the manuscript she'd pleaded to be part of. There were no wingback chairs in this hallway. Perhaps the younger residents, those with fewer health problems, lived here. What remained of his machismo forbade him to ask if he could sit in her room a little while.

"Alfonse?"

He lifted his head. Switch's broad grin appeared like Cheshire Cat's, heralding the man forming around that single point of focus. Alfonse cleared his throat. "Hello, Raymond. How are you this afternoon?"

"Right as rain. You're not looking so good, though."

"An unfortunate and perpetual state of being, I'm afraid."

"You waiting for Judith?"

Alfonse nodded. "She's getting something for me. I didn't know you lived in this wing."

"It isn't as fancy as your place, but it's quiet and close to the gardens."

"The Pen isn't exactly a circus of noise and attractions. And, to be clear, no one's place is as fancy as mine." Alfonse chuckled, or attempted to. He wheezed instead. Lungs failed him. Lips tingled. His knees buckled.

Grabbing Alfonse's arm, Switch shoved open Judith's door. "Judith, quick. He needs to sit."

She was already leaping up from her desk chair. "Oh, Alfonse. I'm so sorry. I'd forgotten you were waiting. Switch, put him in my chair. I'll call a nurse to come with a wheelchair."

So much fuss. So humiliating. Emasculating. Dehumanizing. And yet he had no breath to protest, and more sense than to try. Judith got him water he couldn't drink. Switch murmured into the phone. Alfonse closed his eyes. Sparkles crackled behind his lids. He smiled. It wasn't a lack of oxygen; it was the sunshine on a summer day. It was magic. It was memory dancing in better times.

"I've got him, Mr. Switcher, Ms. Arsenault." Angelic voice. One that conjured sunlight on gold. Words whispered between his ears—*In all his travels, across the world, he'd never seen a woman nearly as lovely as Cecilia in a lacy bathrobe, rollers in her hair and a dab of overlooked cold cream on her chin*—and were already fading away.

Plastic jammed up his nose, behind his ears. Oxygen hissed. Alfonse sipped at it, first, then took bigger drafts. He was in a wheelchair, though how he got there, he didn't know. Someone had lifted him into it. Cecibel? Masculine pride could not accept that. It had to be Switch. He was older, but not old. Still mostly hale. Yes, Raymond eased him into the wheelchair. Alfonse could almost remember him doing so.

"I'm fine," he managed to whisper. "Please. I'm fine."

"You will be in a moment." Cecibel squatted down in front of his chair. Back was the side ponytail veiling her monster half, but she smiled. Truly smiled. "I'm . . . we're not ready to let you go just yet. Take easy breaths. Let me know when you're feeling better and I'll take you back to your rooms."

"I feel awful." Judi spoke in soft tones behind him. "I completely forgot he was waiting."

"It's okay, Judith," Switch answered in tones just as soft. "We all forget sometimes."

"You're kind." She sniffed, and sniffed again.

If he opened his eyes, Alfonse was certain he'd see Raymond Switcher taking Judith Arsenault into his ropy arms, soothing her. No jealousy. Not the kind he might have once felt seeing another man embrace his once-lover. More like envy. Alfonse could no more take a woman into his arms to soothe than he could to love. "Cecibel?"

"Yes, Alfonse?"

Alfonse. Not Mr. Carducci. *Heart, no! Don't pound so.* "I'd like to go back now."

"I'm so sorry, Alfonse." Judi hugged him from behind. "I'm so sorry."

"Don't fret, darling." Alfonse patted her hand, brought it to his lips, and kissed it. "I'll see you at dinner."

"Of course. Oh, just a moment, Cecibel." Judi darted to her desk and grabbed the brown notebook. She whispered into his ear, "Outstanding, my friend. We need better detail on navy life. The military is something you simply cannot get wrong. I'll make some notes."

He only nodded. The story wasn't about being in the navy. It was about love, the kind reserved for Gatsby and Daisy, for Tristan and Isolde. Forever and tragic and flawed from the start. He'd tell her, but Judith wouldn't listen. She didn't create, she perfected. In all his years writing, Alfonse never got used to his vision being altered, even when it was for the better.

"I'll walk with you." Switch's gentle voice replaced Judi's in his ear. "Okay?"

"I'd like that." Though he wouldn't. He knew what they were up to. Cecibel was on duty, and no one wanted him to be alone or, worse, left with the nurses who'd fuss so. What he needed was to sleep, and yet it was the last thing in the world he wanted to spend any of his precious time doing.

"Where would you like to be?" Cecibel asked as she wheeled him into his suite.

"Jamaica?" he answered. "Saint Martin?"

"Very funny." She squeezed his shoulder. "How about there, in the sunshine? Close enough?"

Alfonse nodded. Cecibel wheeled him closer to the windows. She took the leather notebook from his hands and set it onto his desk. "Can I get you gentlemen something?"

"I see an electric kettle there." Switch pointed to the contraption on Alfonse's sideboard. "And all the fixings for something warm to drink. Looks like we're all set."

"All right, then. Alfonse, I'll see you later."

He closed his eyes rather than watch her go. It pained him, somehow, since he kissed her days ago, since she kissed him in kind. There'd been a shift he couldn't explain. Or, perhaps, it was the lack of a shift that perplexed him. His muse, his fair monster, altered his world, and her unchanged manner toward him seemed to suggest he had not altered hers. Vanity had ever been a close companion, as had foolishness and recklessness. And yet, having her rescue him from Judi's room left him bereft of even the semblance of what he'd once been, what he still was, sometimes, inside his head.

"She's a good one, isn't she?" Switch was already at the electric kettle, filling it from the bar faucet. "Good girl."

"She's a woman, Switch."

He picked up his head, smiling. "Ah, so now I'm Switch. Why do you call me Raymond most of the time?"

Alfonse shrugged. "In public, out of respect."

"Well, thank you for that." He plugged in the kettle. "You want tea?"

"Tea, tea, and more tea. I'm fucking tired of tea. Why is it we're made to drink it so much?"

Switch chuckled. "Because we can't drink booze. We're old men, Alfie."

Alfie and Switch. Once young writers, then giants, now not so much at all. "Remember the days of Long Island iced teas over hors d'oeuvres and Manhattans with steak, followed by port and cigars?"

"They were good days," Switch agreed. "We're lucky we had them. There's many who never do."

"I'm not feeling quite as generous as you are today." Alfonse tilted his face to the sun. "I'll have tea, thank you. Peppermint, if there's any left."

Switch stood over the kettle, arms crossed, waiting for it to boil. Didn't he know it wouldn't if he watched it? Why would a man even do such a thing when the whistle would shriek loud enough? But that was Raymond Switcher, always content to stand still. To observe. He'd never been the one with a witty comeback, only with a humble smile. Witty comebacks were Alfonse's territory. Scathing ones belonged to Olivia. To those outside their royal court, Switch might have even seemed a simple soul thrown in over his head, but he'd never gone under. Never once. Alfonse came to understand he was the wisest, had the keenest intellect. The old saying was true—it was the quiet ones you had to worry about.

"Here you go, Alfie." Switch handed him the steaming cup. Square hands. Callused and cracked. The hands of a farmer, not a writer. "Peppermint. You're almost out, though."

"Thank you."

"I have a whole bunch that I grew and dried myself, if you're interested."

Ah, the farmer's hands. "I'd love some. Thank you again."

"You feeling better now?"

"Do I look better?"

"Much. Want me to get rid of the oxygen thing for you?"

"Oh, I'd forgotten it's there," he lied. "I suppose I should let it stay."

Switch sat back in his chair and sipped. "So what were you doing over on my side of the tracks, anyway?"

Alfonse pointed to the notebook Judith had just returned to

him. "She was looking at something for me. I was too vain a fool to tell her I needed to rest." He sipped his tea. At least peppermint had a bite to it. "Honestly, I hadn't realized going out meant I had to get back, too. I'm still not accustomed to thinking in terms of my limitations. And then she forgot I was there."

A grim nod, and Switch set his cup onto the coffee table. "It's why she's here, you know."

"No, I don't know. She didn't say. Is it . . . Alzheimer's?"

"Sadly, yes."

"But she's so young."

"Early onset. One day, she went out to meet one of her writers for lunch, and never showed up. She was missing for two days before she finally turned up at St. Luke's."

"What happened?"

Switch shrugged. "No one knows, really. Thankfully, some nice kids saw her wandering and confused and got her to the hospital. She didn't know who she was, who anyone was. A couple days later, she woke up and was herself again. Well, mostly. Her sister convinced her she shouldn't live alone anymore."

Judi had a sister and still she was here in the Pen? Alfonse quelled the disdainful chuff. All families had their issues. "I imagine it's best for her. She's safe here, and among friends. She's always been the distracted sort. I'd never call her ditzy but . . . ?"

"Disorganized."

"Exactly."

"It's a shame she never married, had kids," Switch said. "Judith would have made a good mother, I think."

Judith would have made a terrible mother, just as Alfonse would have made a terrible father. They were selfish people, centered on their work. Much as he enjoyed children, he never saw the point of producing them. Olivia had four, after all, and that had earned her nothing but heartbreak. "Speaking of children," he said, "how is my goddaughter?"

Switch's whole face crinkled. "As of February, Lizzie's a grandma times two. I got a great-grandson and a great-granddaughter. Twins."

"That can't be. She's just a teenager."

"She was when you saw her last."

"Not true. I attended the wedding."

"She married when she was nineteen."

"Oh, right." Tears welled. A little pixie, all dimples and flyaway curls and frilly dresses. Now a grandmother. "How quickly time flies by. It's not possible I haven't seen her in, what is it, thirty years? That child was the apple of my eye."

"She's missed you. Asks about you whenever we talk. In fact, she's coming up for the Labor Day picnic. It's open to families now, though few ever come. She wants me to meet the twins. I think knowing you're here now pushed her from a maybe to a definite yes."

"I highly doubt that."

Switch grinned. "Bryce is coming, too."

"Her husband?"

"Bryce is Lizzie's son. James died back in, oh gosh, just after Bethany was diagnosed. That'd be 1980? Yeah, January of 1980. Traffic accident."

"I'm sorry. I didn't know."

"You were too busy being famous your whole life." Switch laughed softly. "Bethany used to call you the comet. You came around once every twenty years or so."

"Always the comedian, your wife." Alfonse sipped his tea. Bethany had been a bank teller until she became Mrs. Switcher. Wife, mother, then real estate agent. She rarely read—a point she loved vexing Alfonse with—and when she did, it was nonfiction. She was the love of Raymond Switcher's life, and the one woman Alfonse could not have seduced even if he'd tried—which he never did. "I was devastated to hear of her death all those months after the fact. I'd have come, Switch. I hope you know that."

"There's that famous thing again." Switch shrugged. "It was a long time ago. But thanks."

Silence crept out of the shadows to bask in the sunshine with them. Alfonse sipped his tea already growing cold in the air-conditioned room. Switch was as prone to silence as he was to observing. It settled around him comfortably in a way Alfonse had always envied, but not enough to strive for.

"So," Alfonse said, "do I detect another reason your room is way out by Judith's in the newer wing?"

Switch's lips twitched. "Maybe."

"You surprise me, my friend."

"How's that?"

"You've been a widower for nearly twenty years now."

"Eighteen, but who's counting. I'd say that's long enough, wouldn't you?" Twitching lips became a huge smile. "Besides, couples get better rooms with kitchenettes and everything."

"So she can make you pies?"

"So I can make her fried chicken. It's my specialty."

Ah, to eat something with too much fat and salt and spice. Alfonse looked into his teacup and set it aside; the click of porcelain on wood echoed a tight rap on his door.

"I got it," Switch said.

Olivia pushed into the room as he got to the door. "What's this I hear about you collapsing?"

"Greatly exaggerated." Alfonse waved her off. "I got a little winded."

"You're wearing an oxygen tube, Alfonse Carducci. Don't you dare tell me it was exaggerated."

"Ask Raymond. He was there."

But Raymond Switcher had already, wisely, left. Olivia pulled a chair closer to his. She took his hands. "What were you doing all the way out there?"

"I'd been chatting with Judi and walked her to her room. Blame my chivalrous nature. I didn't think of the consequences."

"But you have to, Alfonse. For once in your life."

His heart pinched. "It *is* my life now, Livy."

Olivia squeezed his hands. She got up and made herself a cup of infernal tea without asking if he wanted a refresher, thank goodness. Alfonse would have, beyond all doubt, put his head in his hands and bawled. Dunking the tea bag, blowing steam across the lip, she sat on the edge of his desk.

"Have you finished your part?" She tapped the notebook there. "Or do you need until the end of the day?"

"I've finished," he said. "On the short side, but complete. Take it."

She set her teacup down, picked up the book. "Where did you start them?"

"You ask as if you don't know how to read what's there in front of you."

"Just making small talk." Olivia scanned the pages. "Good. I was afraid you'd dwell too long in Paterson. It's a love story, not a murder mystery."

"I know what it is. We agreed to keep focus where it belongs."

"Well, you do tend to linger on things, Alfonse. You make your point a thousand different, lovely ways, but they are, after all, the same point."

"It's part of my voice."

"Indulgent is what it is, but I do love your style. For the most part."

"Then why that crack about lingering on the same point?"

"Just making an observation. Come now, Alfie. Don't get your ego in a twist. This is a creative endeavor, the last we will ever do. Don't get bogged down in ego now."

"If you haven't noticed in the centuries of our friendship, my dear, I spend most of my time bogged in my own ego."

"Don't be silly. You wouldn't be worth your salt as a writer if that were true." She tucked the notebook under her arm, emptied their teacups in the tiny bar sink, and poured him a glass of water. "Now you need to rest." She set the glass close enough for him to reach. "Will you be down to dinner?"

"Of course."

"Would you like me to come for you?"

"I'll manage on my own." Or Cecibel would help. Again. "Draw the shade before you go, Livy. The sun feels good but it's a little too strong."

Olivia did as he asked, kissed his cheek, and left him. Alfonse didn't want to rest. It was barely two in the afternoon, for goodness' sake. He wanted to call Judith and have that discussion they hadn't gotten the chance to have. He wanted to explain to Olivia that he made the same point a thousand different ways because there were a thousand different ways to see the very same thing and either you got that or you didn't, but either way the words were lovely. He wanted to do those things over a glass of wine, some cheese, and a nice chunk of crusty bread. Falling asleep in the wheelchair, oxygen tubes still hissing up his nose, Alfonse wanted and wanted and wanted.

❧

Secrets are all fun and games until someone loses an eye.
—CORNELIUS TRAEGAR

~~The baby never slept. It was as if she knew all about the lies she was~~
~~being force-fed and was having none of it.~~

Olivia's pen tip nearly went through the heavy stock paper. She'd written the line a dozen times, each in almost the exact same way. The story wanted to begin with the baby and Cecilia's guilty conscience and the longing—part postpartum, part a lifetime in the making. But she couldn't get past the dead father.

Alfonse had to go and kill the man, derailing Cecilia's motivation to do as she was told instead of getting on a bus to Illinois the moment she discovered she was pregnant. Olivia had created Maria Antonette capable of taking over the family business until she could quickly remarry. She should have written that part, dammit! She'd simply wanted to draw out Cecilia's evolution into the kind of woman who chose her own fate despite the conventions of her time. Instead, Alfonse made her obedient to her dead father's promise. A young woman protecting her child, and the man she truly loved, by sacrificing everything she wanted for herself. Typical man. Instead of trapped, she appeared obedient, and no Cecilia of hers was going to be so without some really compelling reasons.

Of course, Cami's death forced Aldo to stay away. Olivia had to admit, she'd been thrilled about that twist. How could a man face the woman he loved when he'd killed her father? The tension promised down the road, when Aldo and Cecilia finally met again, was delicious. But what the hell was she supposed to do now with half the heroine's motivation missing?

"Good morning, Olivia."

Olivia gasped and bolted upright, a hand to her chest. "Raymond Switcher, has no one ever warned you not to sneak up on an old person like that?"

"I didn't sneak. I've been sitting right here watching you take vengeance on that poor notebook for the last ten minutes."

The library was, of course, a much frequented place within the Pen. No computers. No electronics whatsoever. Just books, the kind of leather chairs one could get lost in, and sunshine coming in the giant windows all along the back of the mansion. Comers and goers arrived and left unnoticed. Book clubs met and spoke quietly but animatedly. In the early years of her writing career, Olivia had gotten used to writing in coffee shops and public libraries, at her son's basketball games, or her daughters' tennis matches. Anywhere her husband wouldn't catch her and demand she put an end to her nonsense and focus on the children. On him. And thus had learned how to tune the noise into the white kind conducive to creation. She couldn't write in solitude if she tried.

Closing the book, pen trapped inside, she glared at Switch. "You might have made your presence known."

"Watching you write was entertaining."

"I'm glad I amused you, now if you don't mind . . ."

"What are you writing?"

"None of your business, dear."

"Come on, Olivia." He nudged her. Winked. "I'd hate to see the new crop of indicas get mites or something."

"Don't even joke."

"Okay, okay." He slumped back in his chair, grinning, pointing. "Alfonse has a notebook just like that."

Olivia pursed her lips. She bit the inside of her lip until the sour-lemon sensation eased. "Does he, now? I imagine we all have one of these. Somewhere."

"I don't."

"Do you want one? I'm sure I could find—"

"You looked like you were having trouble." He leaned forward, hand outstretched but not demanding. "Maybe I can help."

Holding the book tighter was all that kept Olivia from pushing it into his hands. "I'm sorry, Switch. You're right. I am having trouble, but this isn't something I can share."

"Why? Because Alfonse wouldn't like me nosing in on your project?"

"Alfonse has nothing to do with it."

"You're a terrible liar, Livy." He chuckled. "Curse of the redhead, no matter if your hair is white now. You two writing together?"

She looked away. "It's just a little project."

"Nothing Olivia Peppernell and Alfonse Carducci write will ever be little."

"It's nothing like our past work."

"That's good, no?"

"Well, yes. Yes, it is. In a way. But really, it's nothing I can share with you."

"Why not?"

"Because we agreed to keep it between the two of us." *And Cecibel. He's not supposed to know, but he does, only she doesn't know he knows . . .* Olivia sighed. "It's rather complicated."

"How about you just tell me? It's really not a secret anymore."

"Why do you want to know so badly?"

Switch grimaced, and that grimace turned into a grin—the humble, gentle kind that graced every book jacket, every author interview, every review ever printed about his work. "I'll tell you; it's because I watched you scribble and scratch out and scribble again, and it filled me up in a way I haven't been in way too long. It reminded me of that feeling I used to get when a story bubbled under my skin."

"Then write."

"Maybe all my stories have been told," he said.

"Nonsense." But hadn't she thought the same?

Another signature Switch shrug. "I stopped writing when Bethany got sick. Back then, I figured it was temporary, until she got better. But she went and died on me when she promised not to. I lost that spark. I lost the stories. Until just a minute ago when I saw it burning in you. I just thought, maybe, since we're such good old friends, you'd let me in on whatever lit you back up again, is all."

No sour-lemon sensation, but her lips pursed all the same. Damn him for being sincere, for speaking her own sentiments back to her. "Raymond Switcher. I never thought you were the manipulative kind."

"If it helps your moral dilemma," he said, "Alfie showed it to Judith."

"He did what?"

Switch nodded. "That's why he was out her way, I think. She put it in his lap and whispered something about the navy as we were leaving."

"I might kill him."

"Please don't."

Retaliation for keeping Cecibel's enthusiasm all to herself? Curse the man. Of course he'd go to Judith Arsenault to assuage his bruised ego. History repeating itself. Olivia gripped the notebook tighter. Damn it all, why not? If it was acceptable for Alfonse to seek advice, he couldn't object to her needing the same. Well, he could. He would. The great Alfonse Carducci was the do-as-I-say-not-as-I-do kind. Still, in his state, it might not be wise to shove her righteousness in his face. She did love the old bastard, after all. "You have to swear you won't tell him I showed it to you. That you had any input at all."

Switch raised his hand, put the other atop the notebook. "'I solemnly swear I am up to no good.'"

She pressed a hand to her chest, batted her eyes. "You're a fan?"

"Rabid. I got an advance copy from the UK. Hardcover, of course. You?"

"We must have the same sources." Olivia laughed. "It's good to be the queen. Or king, as the case may be."

"There's word of them being made into movies," Switch said. "Not sure how I feel about that."

"They won't be nearly as good. Movies never do the books justice. Well, rarely." Olivia laughed softly, leaned in. "Have you ever been bestowed the honor of hearing Alfonse go on and on about *From Here to Eternity*?"

"A few times, why?"

She flipped through the notebook scrawl. "Because he slipped it in." She showed him the passage. "At least he didn't go into his tirade about taking out the brothel, venereal disease, and homosexuality to appease the Production Code office."

Switch scanned the page, his grin faltering. "The navy. So Judi has read it."

"Apparently."

"I wonder why."

Olivia spread her fingers wide. "Editorial feedback. Alfonse has ever been needy that way."

"He hates editorial feedback."

"When it's critical. I'm certain Judith had nothing but praise."

"Didn't sound like it." Switch turned another page, flipped backward, then forward again. "So you write in parts. He has one point of view, you have the other."

"Yes. No planning ahead, just going from what has already been written. It's rather exciting."

"But now you're stuck."

She nodded. "Because Alfonse went and killed off my heroine's father and robbed her of the motivation that . . . It's hard to explain. I'm a little lost. To make this work, my character has to become someone I never intended her to be."

"Hmm . . . maybe not."

"What do you mean?"

Switch closed the book but kept it in his lap. "Let me read it. There's not all that much so far. Maybe I'll see an angle you're missing."

"Oh, I don't know about that."

"You know the process, Olivia. Sometimes you need new eyes on something to really see it."

He was right, of course. Ego resisted. This was her story. And Alfonse's. And apparently Judith's, damn it all. Had he, like her, gotten stuck? Whatever else she was, Judith had always been an excellent editor. It was all about the story, after all. Isn't that what she always preached?

"All right, Switch," she said. "But I need it back right away. We only give one another a week to write our respective parts. I've already wasted almost four days."

"I'll have it back to you tomorrow. Maybe I'll be able to come up with an answer for you. In the meantime . . ." Switch reached into his pocket and pulled out a baggie. "First of the newest crop. You're going to love this one. It's a new hybrid. Won't make you as sleepy. At least, that's what the seed catalog said."

Olivia took the baggie from him, fingered the contents through the plastic. Opening the bag, she inhaled deeply. Sweet, slightly skunky heaven. "My word."

Switch nodded. "Let me know how it helps with your pain. I have more of the old stuff if you need it."

"I still have some." She pocketed the baggie. "Thank you. I'd have probably killed myself by now without our little herbal miracle."

"That's what Bethany used to say." His smile turned sad. "I wish I knew then what I do now. I wouldn't have had to risk jail to buy her relief."

"Times change," Olivia told him. "People learn. If November's vote goes well, you won't even have to hide our plants in the peppermint anymore."

"Don't have to hide now, really. No one cares what old people do. Unless it's driving. Everyone has an opinion about that." He got to his feet, patting the notebook's cover. "I'm excited about this."

"Just keep it to yourself. And to me. No telling Judith either. Not that she's likely to remember. Is Alfonse aware of her . . . memory issues?"

"He is now." Switch saluted. "See you later, Livy."

But Switch didn't appear in the dining room that evening. Judith hadn't seen him all afternoon. Alfonse told her not to be such a hen. Olivia held her tongue. Despite the oxygen tubes in his nose, Alfonse still looked rather blue around the gills. He barely ate the soup she harangued him about so forcefully Judith had to kick her under the table.

"I'm sorry," she said, rubbing her shin. "I just worry about you, Alfie."

"You're going to worry me into the grave," he grumbled. "Leave the doctoring to the professionals."

"Yes, dear." She batted her eyes. Alfonse's gaze narrowed, but whether he was appeased or too tired to care, he didn't challenge her.

Once dinner was done, she and Judith walked him to his suite, where the night nurse took him from them with a smile and the assurance he'd be taken care of. Not all the nurses were snooty. In fact, one-on-one, they were quite nice. It was only when thrown together in an us-against-them power struggle that they turned ugly. Or when Cecibel dared overstep her bounds. There was nothing quite so waspish as a nurse usurped of her duties. Or when Dr. Kintz was around. The preening among the unmarried women would be laughable if it weren't so pathetically cliché. Or maybe Olivia was just remembering herself, once upon a time.

"I'll walk back to your rooms with you, Judith." She hooked her arm through the younger woman's. "It's a lovely evening for a stroll through the gardens, don't you think?"

"That would be nice." Judith patted her hand as if they'd never been anything but dear friends. Maybe a failing memory wasn't such a bad thing. Judith had arrived in the Pen slightly confused and quite grateful to have so many familiar faces around her. Olivia had to admit she'd never despised the woman, only her place in Alfonse's past. Maybe Judith never knew they'd both loved the same man. Maybe she did once, and no longer remembered. Or maybe she just pretended, to keep the peace. Whatever it was worked for them both. Olivia didn't hold a grudge. Not one she'd admit to, anyway.

"Would you like to come in for a nightcap?" Judith paused with her hand on her door. "Cognac?"

"No, thank you, dear. I don't drink. It gives me headaches."

"Oh, that's a shame. All right, then. Good night."

"Good night, Judith."

Olivia started slowly away, listened for Judith's door to close, then turned on her heel and made a beeline for Switch's room down the hall. She knocked softly. At first. Then harder. Was that the shuffle of slippers on carpet? Olivia listened harder. "Raymond? Are you in there?"

The lock tumbled. The door opened. Switch looked as if he'd been hit by a bus, or thoroughly kissed. He pulled her inside. "I didn't mean to."

"Didn't mean to what?" She recovered her step. "What have you done, Raymond?"

He lunged for the notebook fanned on the arm of his chair, pressed it into her hands. Olivia opened the book, paged through Alfonse's scrawl, her own neat hand. His, hers. And another.

Not cursive. Print. All caps. Some bigger, some smaller. In pencil, no less. Pages and pages of it.

"You wrote my part?"

"I wrote mine." Breathless. Raymond Switcher was actually breathless. "It just happened. I swear I didn't realize what I was doing until I'd nearly finished. I was . . . appalled. I really was. But look." He pressed the notebook closer to her. "I figured it out, Livy. It works. He's not—"

"Hush." Olivia pushed past him, eyes on the notebook. She sat in his armchair. "I'm reading."

Enzo

Enzo Parisi was the luckiest guy in the world. He didn't always think so. When he was a pimply kid discovering all the ways he could make Little Enzo happy with his hand or a ripe cantaloupe, his pop had sat him down and said, "Enzo, between now and when you graduate college, get all the pussy you can 'cause after that, your dick belongs to one girl and one girl alone. Cecilia Giancami. Got that?" Enzo said he did and smiled when Pop nudged him in the ribs with that "Eh? Eh?" thing he did. Mama stood in the doorway, wringing her hands.

Enzo didn't think he was the luckiest guy in the world then, mostly because he wasn't sure what cats had to do with his recently gratified dick and why it would one day belong to Cecilia Giancami. She was just a little kid. He didn't think Uncle Cami would want her to even know he had a dick, let alone that it was hers one day.

When he was a sophomore in high school, he was the luckiest guy in the world again. Cecilia wasn't a little kid anymore. She was a freshman, and she was pretty, too. Prettier than Susan Carruthers, who knew from the minute Cecilia Giancami set foot in Eastside High she'd been deposed as reigning beauty queen. Cecilia wasn't just prettier. She had better clothes, bigger boobs, and she was rich. Susan didn't have any choice but to take the demotion gracefully. Cecilia's father was Dominic Giancami, and not even cute little high school girls could cross him without consequences.

By then, Enzo was firmly entrenched in Math Nerd Kingdom.

Cecilia wouldn't even say hello in the halls, let alone date him. He tried to follow Pop's advice, once he figured out what "pussy" meant, but upon seeing Cecilia descend into the halls of Eastside in all her exceptional magnificence that September day, Enzo didn't want any other pussy but hers. Ever.

He was the luckiest guy in the world from then on, if only in his head. No one ever had to tell him not to talk about the arrangement Pop and Uncle Cami came to when he was twelve and Cecilia nine and a half. It was a given. Enzo knew. So did Cecilia. This secret even they didn't speak of made it all the more exciting, made the wait more exquisite, less excruciating. He always had the cantaloupes, after all. Or a nice, ripe pumpkin.

Senior year came to an end. Enzo was off to Princeton come the fall. Only four more years, and Cecilia would be his. Maybe she'd come visit him in college. Didn't high school girls love boasting about their college men? In the midst of that daydream, Uncle Cami disappeared.

"Cami's gonna turn up, Ginny. You'll see," Enzo overheard Pop say, days later.

"That's not good enough," Mama growled at him. "Our boy is going to marry that girl, just like Cami promised. You know how fast things shift when power changes hands."

That night, he had his first date with the girl who would be his wife. He also got his first kiss. Not to mention the little added bonus of losing his virginity. Best of all, Enzo lost his heart, the one he thought lost long ago, but holy cow if he didn't manage to lose it more completely than he ever dreamed possible.

Cecilia had been sweet, sexy, and, much to his virginal delight, a bit naughty. After the first go, she'd coaxed him into another, a third. And his mother down the hall, asleep in her bed. Enzo didn't know which way the floor was by the time Cecilia finished with him. Way better than a melon. In fact, he'd never cheat on her with one again. Yup. Luckiest guy in the world.

July 4, 1954. Best day of his life, and would remain among the top ten until the day he died. Picnic at the D'Argenios' cinder block pool—Italians could work miracles with concrete—and Cecilia in a polka-dot bathing suit with a cute little skirt that accentuated every curve. Hot dogs, burgers, potato salad until it was coming out his ears. The whole day topped off by fireworks up at Lambert Castle. Sparkle, flash, rumble, and pop in every direction, and Cecilia's perfect face illuminated red, green, gold.

They were sitting apart from everyone else, up on the hill. Best spot in town. Her friends had been alternately horrified and impressed by her college-man boyfriend who'd been too drippy to even acknowledge at Eastside. But Princeton was a big deal, and anything Cecilia Giancami did was the new cool. Some of his math-club friends even got dates with her friends. If Jeremy Stubbins could be believed, he'd scored a smooth second with Vonnie Beretti.

"Today was fun, right?"

"Very." A tight smile. Flat tone. Cecilia's gaze drifted back to the sky.

"Something wrong?"

Now a sigh. "I suppose that depends."

Enzo would never, ever forget the sorrow in her eyes, the tears welling, the way she bit her lip so adorably he had to kiss it or die. He didn't want to die. Not when he was going to marry the most amazing, perfect, beautiful girl in the world, so he kissed her. "What is it?"

"I'm pregnant."

His blood crackled. The fireworks boomed. Words failed. Utterly. Enzo pulled Cecilia into his arms. She squealed and she laughed and she cried at the same time. He kissed her long and he kissed her tenderly. No four-year wait. They'd be married before summer ended.

Standing before their parents and Monsignor Gallo, because good Catholics didn't do anything important without a priest present, Enzo held Cecilia's hand so tightly. "We want to get married now. We have to." And Cecilia put a hand to her beautiful belly. Pops looked a little scared, a little proud. Mama and Aunt Maria gasped, fell into one another's arms, and wept. The last reaction was the one Enzo feared most. Eternal damnation. A stay in the hospital. Maybe he'd be lucky and suffer only a few broken bones. It'd all be worth it for Cecilia, for their baby.

The shadow rose up, loomed closer. Cecilia's grasp on Enzo's hand tightened. He put a protective arm around her, as if that would save either of them. Instead of the anticipated pain, gentle arms went around them both.

"You kids," Uncle Cami said, then turned to Pops. "I told you, didn't I, Enz? Match made in heaven. Couldn't even keep their clothes on a coupl'a years, eh? Monsignor, how soon can we tie this knot?"

Enzo nearly wept, but he held it together. Wherever Dominic Giancami had been all those weeks before turning up at St. Joseph's Hospital had changed him, at least somewhat. As far as Enzo knew, he still maintained his kingdom with a healthy dose of fear and respect. But he and Aunt Maria held hands in church. Her face wasn't pinched all the time anymore. He overheard Mama tell Pops that Cami's longtime mistress had finally been given the boot. And with Cecilia? Holy cow. Uncle Cami doted on her the way Enzo promised to when they had their future father-in-law/son-in-law chat.

"I feel like a little girl again," she'd confessed one night after supper with her parents and little brothers. "I didn't think he loved me anymore."

"You're his little girl," Enzo said. "Of course he does."

She'd only nodded then, tears in her eyes. Enzo had pulled her close, kissed her cheeks, her nose, her lips. He would never tire of worshiping her. Never.

And then they were married.

And then they were off-campus apartment hunting.

And then they were moved in, just days before Enzo started classes. Cecilia got a job at a local dress shop, though she needn't have. Between the allowance Pops gave them and the heaps of money Uncle Cami tossed their way, they lived well. Better than well. Enzo was happier than he ever imagined during those erotic daydreams he used to have as a pimply teenager gratifying himself with cantaloupes and a yearbook picture of his intended. Those daydreams were ghosts. Ghost dreams. Flimsy wisps blown away by the joy of his reality.

And then it was Christmas. O! Holy Night. Their little apartment decorated with lights and tinsel and a too-big tree. Cecilia attempted to make the holiday meal for his family and hers, despite her already cumbersome belly. The turkey was dry and the gravy too salty. The stuffing could have broken a tooth had anyone had the courage to eat any. To Enzo, it was the best Christmas in his life. Next year would be even better, with a baby in the house. Toys under the tree. In time, a bicycle he'd struggle to put together on Christmas Eve. All the Christmases to come spread out before him like a Rockwell promise.

And then came January. Cecilia cried a lot.

And February. She cried almost nonstop. Mama said it was baby blues. Enzo wasn't so sure.

And March 3, 1955.

Patricia Edith Parisi roared into the world, a whopping twelve pounds. Cecilia and the baby were healthy and resting. The nurses said he could see his wife and daughter soon. Enzo handed out cigars. Uncle Cami beamed, handing out little bottles of Scotch. No one said anything about the extra-large baby born only seven months after the wedding. It wasn't really a secret, though everyone pretended otherwise. No one but Enzo knew his first time with Cecilia had been closer to July than May. Eight months was long enough to cook a twelve-pounder, he was sure.

Hours later, Enzo quietly entered the private room Cecilia and his daughter had to themselves. St. Joe's, same hospital both he and she had been born in. The princesses of Paterson would have nothing less. Dominic Giancami wasn't letting any grandchild of his be born in central Jersey, anyway. Tomorrow, her parents, his, the whole damn town would be there with flowers and chocolates and little pink baby clothes. Tonight, they were all his.

The baby at her breast, her face tipped down, gaze so loving Enzo thought his heart would break, Cecilia hummed softly. No formula for his child. Nothing but the best, and whatever Cecilia could provide her was just that. Enzo moved in, suddenly shy. Cecilia looked up. There were circles around her eyes. Tiny, broken blood vessels spidered her face. Hair in a ponytail grown so long. She'd never been more beautiful.

Enzo sat on the edge of the bed. He looked down upon his daughter suckling at his wife's breast, and this time when tears threatened, they fell. She was so small, yet gigantic compared to the other infants in the nursery—a room his daughter had not and would not see, courtesy of King Cami.

Her face wasn't puckered like an infant's. Patricia was a chubby little cherub, complete with dimples that deepened as she suckled. Curls framed her busy face. Thick. And blond. Blond, not brown like his, like Cecilia's. There were no blondes in either of their families, were there? Maybe it was a baby thing. Weren't they all born blond and blue-eyed? That had to be it.

Patricia stopped suckling. She let go her mother's nipple and stared up at Enzo, that wise infant gaze telling him all he should have known from the start.

"Tell me now, Enzo," Cecilia said softly, so tenderly. "Is she my daughter? Or is she ours?"

He couldn't look away from the tiny being his whole world had revolved around all those months. Patricia. He'd loved the name. If she'd been a boy, he wanted Patrick, but Uncle Cami said no grandson of his would have a mick name, so they'd decided on Thomas instead. Enzo had secretly wished for a girl. He'd call her Patsy, and she'd be his angel. His princess. His pride and joy. Just like Cecilia was to her father. But the beautiful baby staring up at him wasn't his.

"I'm sorry, Enzo," she whispered. "I never meant to hurt you."

"Cecilia, please. Just . . . just please don't say anything."

Is she my daughter? Or is she ours? Could he do it? Enzo's heart was a drummer in his belly. Patricia Edith Parisi. That's what the birth certificate said. He'd spent months loving her, dreaming about her, planning for her. His gaze moved inch by excruciating inch from baby to mother. "Do you love him?"

She nodded. His drumming heart ripped in two.

"Do you love me?"

She nodded. Traitor heart. It started up again.

Enzo closed his eyes. "Does he know?"

"No. He's gone. For good. I'm your wife. I chose you. Do you understand?"

Yes, he did. Too horribly well. He held out his arms for the baby now asleep. Cecilia handed Patricia gently, confidently over. Enzo cradled the child close. He leaned low, breathed in her milky scent. She'd been his, all these months. He couldn't not love her any more than he could not love Cecilia.

Enzo reached for his wife, the mother of his child. He cupped her still-exposed breast before tucking it into her dressing gown. She didn't flinch, didn't pull away in revulsion. Cecilia smiled that same smile she'd been conquering him with since asking if she could see his room, way back last June-almost-July. She might not be entirely his, but he was entirely hers.

And he was the luckiest guy in the world.

Bar Harbor, Maine

❦

Few of the wrong turns you make in life are actually wrong. Sometimes, you just don't know you're going the right way until you get there.

—CORNELIUS TRAEGAR

"He's alive?" Alfonse gasped. "Giancami survived?"

"Genius, isn't it?"

"But, Olivia, how could you? This is *our* story."

"You gave it to Judith before I ever let Raymond see it."

"She only *looked*. Besides, we need her. I don't have the leisure of time, for transcription or editing. What you did wasn't fair. It wasn't fair at all."

"You're such a child, Alfonse." Olivia laughed softly. Cecibel could barely hear her through the door. Thank goodness Olivia, in her hurry, hadn't noticed her chasing after her with her forgotten sweater, or that she'd left the door to Alfonse's room open a crack. Cecibel touched it, barely a feather's weight of pressure, and it opened just enough to hear Alfonse's chuckled response.

"Well, I suppose it could be worse. You might've given it to Georgette."

"Bite your tongue! The woman's a hack, at best."

"She's had more best sellers than you and I combined."

"She is . . . was prolific, I'll give you that. But her kind of best seller isn't the same as ours. Romance!"

"Is this not romance?"

"Heavens no. Romance must end happily ever after. This will not."

"Won't it?"

"Not if I get the last chapter."

Alfonse sighed. Or maybe he wheezed. Cecibel quelled the urge to rush in and make sure it was the former.

"Then I suppose this must mean we are in it together," he said. "The four of us."

"The four of us," Olivia echoed. "And thank goodness for that. Raymond pulled us from the brink of disaster."

"He pulled you from disaster." Alfonse sniffed. "My part was right on track."

"Too bad you derailed mine."

"You'd have figured out something just as brilliant."

Silence, then, "Thank you."

"I never doubted it for a moment, Livy."

"Well, the point is moot. Raymond added his brilliance, and this story will be the better for it." She tsked. "Could you imagine if the media got wind of this? Alfonse Carducci, Raymond Switcher, and Olivia Peppernell writing a novel, edited by none other than Judith Arsenault? There would be a frenzy."

"Wait until I die to share the news," Alfonse said. "Whether our efforts turn out well or poorly, there will be publishers across the globe bidding on the rights."

"That's not what we're doing this for."

"Of course not. But that's what will happen nonetheless."

Cecibel rolled to the side, silencing her laughter inside Olivia's sweater still in her hands. They bickered like Statler and Waldorf. Like Edina and Patsy. Neither could outdo the other, and neither actually wanted to. It fed them, this bickering. It proved their deep and abiding love. She wished for a little of that for herself, even if her wit would never be so sharp, or her tongue so biting.

"Cecibel? What are you doing outside Mr. Carducci's room?"

She bolted upright, her hand, as always, smoothing her hair against her face. "Good afternoon, Dr. Kintz. I followed Olivia down here. She forgot her sweater. I overheard the two of them . . . chatting in there and didn't want to interrupt."

"Looked to me like you were listening in."

Snagged. "Maybe a little. But not in a bad way. I was waiting for a break in the bickering to knock on the door."

Dr. Kintz chuckled softly. "They are pretty funny when they get going." And he cleared his throat. "But eavesdropping isn't ethical. You're a care provider, not a journalist."

"Understood. Sorry, Dr. Kintz."

"See that it doesn't happen again."

"Yes, Dr. Kintz."

"You may call me Richard." He wagged a finger. "But not Dick."

Cecibel smiled her half smile. "After hours, Doctor. During working hours, it would be better to stick to formalities. The nurses would have a cow if they heard me use your given name."

"The nurses around here are prone to cow-birthing, I've noticed. Ah!" Another finger wag. "I got a laugh out of you."

"It was more of a snort," she conceded.

"I'll take it." He looked at Alfonse's door. "I came to see Mr. Carducci, but I suppose he and Mrs. Peppernell will be at it awhile."

"They tend to. I'll leave Olivia's sweater on the doorknob. She'll find it when she comes out." Cecibel hung the sweater, being careful to close the door all the way without the audible evidence ratting her out. "Entertaining as they are, I have another few hours before my shift is over. Guess I better get back to work."

"You heading that way?" He pointed.

It was the only way to go, but Cecibel answered, "I am."

"Good, I'll walk with you. I wanted to apologize for my questioning the other day. It was out of bounds, and I am sorry."

"You have a right to ask questions of your staff, especially if they seem a risk to our patients."

"You are in no way a risk to my patients. I know that. Curiosity should never dictate a psychiatrist's actions, and I allowed it to.

I know you're the most reliable employee on staff, the residents love you, and the nurses resent your competence. Anything else I needed to know is all there in your charts. Can you forgive me?"

"Nothing to forgive."

"Thank you."

"This is me." Cecibel stopped in front of the supply closet she didn't really need to get into as much as she wanted to part with his company. The newly rigged lock was, once again, swaying on its hinge. She groaned. "Not again."

"Mr. Gardern?"

She pulled open the door. Toilet-paper rolls, what was left of them, littered the ground. "Apparently. What is it with him and toilet paper?"

"I'll see to him," Dr. Kintz said. "You stay and clean up here. I'll have someone bring back whatever I'm able to retrieve."

Cecibel bent to the task. What hadn't unrolled, she put back on the shelf. What had, she put in a garbage bag. She wouldn't throw it away; it was perfectly usable. Just not by the residents. Though she was tempted to use it to refill supplies in the nurses' lounge, she'd give some to Sal, to Finlay, and save some for herself. Before she finished straightening up, Sal arrived carrying a garbage bag full of what she assumed were more toilet-paper rolls. He flung the sack to the floor like Santa coming out of the chimney. "We need more orderlies around here."

"We have six."

"Six part-timers, honey." Sal huffed. "I'm a manager. I shouldn't be toting stolen toilet paper around."

"Susan and Jill are here today."

"They're on break."

"Together?"

Sal pursed his glossed lips.

Cecibel shook her head. "You let them get away with it, Salvatore."

"It wouldn't have mattered. Dr. Dick found me, not them. We orderlies all look the same to him, even if I wear my little name tag that says I'm managing staff."

"He's still learning his way around. And don't call him that if you want to keep your title."

Sal waved her off. "He can't fire me. I'd sue his ass."

"Not your job, your title. Insubordination is a big offense. He'd be within his rights."

"You taking his side?"

"I'm taking yours. If you lose your title, who's left to fill it, huh? Me, that's who. No thanks."

Salvatore pulled her into an off-the-ground bear hug. "You're a lamb, you know that? A sugar lamb."

"Put me down."

He obliged, but not before pinching her. "Mmm-mm! Sweet ass."

"Salvatore!" She slapped at him and missed. "You can't do that!"

"Oh, sugar, please. It's just between us girls. You know I like me some fine male-tail." He put his hands on his hips, studying her behind. "Skinny as it is, yours is fine. You should be getting some male-tail yourself."

"Not currently in the market for any, thank you."

"Not even for Finlay's?"

"Of course not. We're friends."

"Mm-hmm. Wouldn't be some old-ass tail you got a hankering for, would it?"

Cecibel's face flamed. "Don't talk about him that way. Have some respect."

"But you knew exactly who I was talking about."

"Knock it off."

"Oh, lord in heaven, looks like I struck a nerve."

"You're pissing me off is what you're doing." Cecibel snatched up the garbage bag full of toilet paper and started stacking. She'd kissed Alfonse's brow, his cheek, lingered on his lips. She let him see her when she let no one else, because there was admiration and there was love, and there was something else that transcended both. Slamming the garbage bag down, she turned away from Sal before he saw her tears. "Alfonse Carducci is a distinguished artist, and a very sick man. Don't denigrate all his accomplishments and my respect for him by making him some old-ass tail."

"Hey." Salvatore touched her gently now, a fleshy hand turning her around. "I was just playing with you. I'm sorry."

"Fine. Whatever." Sniffing, she averted her gaze. "Fin and I are going to light a fire down on the beach tonight, maybe roast marshmallows. Want to come?"

"I have a gig," he answered. "But you two have fun."

"We always do."

"He's a nice man, that Finlay."

"A very nice man. See you later."

"And I'm dismissed." He spun off, striking that injured pose he'd perfected. Cecibel couldn't help laughing, internally at least. Salvatore was a beast but she loved him. He was one of the few constants in her life.

Cecibel finished stacking the salvageable toilet paper and filled stray grocery bags with what was not. One she left at Sal's door, one she tossed into her room, and the third she brought out to Finlay's place over the maintenance barn.

The metallic tap of equipment repair sent her to the barn rather than his loft. Finlay was headdown under the hood of an enormous tractor-mower. Cecibel tried not to stare at the end sticking out, but it was, as Salvatore would say, a fine bit of male-tail. She checked herself. Quickly. Firmly. She wasn't allowed to have those kinds of thoughts.

"Don't want to scare you," she called.

He bolted upright, slammed his head on the open flap. "Oh! Ouch! Too late." He rubbed his head, looked at his greasy fingers, and grabbed a rag. Cleaning his hands, he came her way. His hair stuck up straight and mucky where he'd rubbed it. "What's up?"

Cecibel held up the grocery bag. "Mr. Gardern got into the supply closet again. I brought you the salvageable toilet paper."

"That's a strange sort of love token." He laughed, took the bag. "Thanks. We still on for tonight?"

"I already bought the marshmallows."

"Good, because I grabbed some chocolate bars and graham

crackers while I was out earlier." He peeked out the crusty window. "Looks like we're going to have a clear night. Should I bring my telescope?"

"You have a telescope?"

"A real nice one. Dr. Traegar left it to me when he died."

Curiosity, once sparked, kindled anew. "Really? You were that tight?"

"Pretty much."

"Did you know him when you were a kid?"

Finlay tossed the rag onto his toolbox. "Yeah. He took me in when my parents gave me the boot."

After all he'd been through. Cecibel crossed her arms over her chest. "Your parents? Why?"

"Before I got arrested and all that," he answered. "After Mr. Bennet . . . after he did those things to me, I . . . I wasn't myself. Then he went on trial for doing stuff to that other kid, and I guess I was kind of out of control. I tried to tell them, my parents, what he did to me, but they were on the side of most other adults in town, saying the kid was lying because of a bad grade." He grunted. "As if a kid would admit to being butt-fucked for a better grade. Sorry. Language."

"It's okay. I had no idea."

"It was a long time ago." He shrugged, and like that it was dismissed back into the past. "So, yeah, Dr. Traegar took me in. He set me up with one of the therapists here. She testified for me, at my trial, but, well"—he rubbed the back of his neck—"we all know how that went. I was glad I got out before Dr. Traegar died. He hired me and said I'd never have to worry about finding work ever again. I always had a place here. Good man."

"I wish I'd known him." Cecibel leaned on the tractor wheel. "You and Sal are lucky. Other than you, Sal, and some of the residents, I don't think anyone here now knew him."

"You're probably right about that."

"Sal says Dr. Kintz is just looking for a reason to fire him." Cecibel laughed. "I love him, but Sal does plenty to get himself fired all on his own."

"He won't be fired," Fin said. "You, me, Sal. We belong here. Everyone who comes through here knows it."

"Seems that way, huh? Well . . ." Slapping hands to thighs, she pushed herself off the tire. "I guess I should get back to work. See you at eight?"

"You bet."

The metallic tink followed Cecibel out of the barn. Her mind churned, brought back earlier conversations, earlier thoughts. About Dr. Traegar. About Sal and Fin. About Dr. Kintz's questioning and apology. Something wanted to connect, but wasn't sitting right in her head. It coaxed that old itch out from under her skin, the one she got when anxiety was building to a point of no return. An itch she thought lost long ago in a past she tried to forget. Until recently, when Dr. Kintz questioned her about Dr. Marks and leaving the hospital without her consent. It had sent her running without knowing where she was going, straight into Sal, who'd been likewise questioned with information found in a file neither he nor she knew existed. It had been the first time in years she'd even thought Jennifer's name.

Stay put. Don't come out. Please, just stay dead.

Cecibel stopped in her tracks. She inhaled deeply, exhaled long, forced thoughts onto a different, safer, but connected path.

File? Or chart? Sifting through their recent conversation, Cecibel was almost certain Dr. Kintz had said chart. Employers kept files on their employees. Doctors kept charts. Dr. Kintz was, after all, a doctor. A slip of the tongue? Had to be. Her heart's hammering kept double-time rhythm to the metallic tink still audible in the distance. Whether file or chart, Cecibel hadn't known of its existence, and that wasn't acceptable. No one in the Pen knew anything about her outside of who she was since coming to work there, after the ruin. Anything else wasn't simply unacceptable, it could prove fatal. For someone. Cecibel had killed before; there were no guarantees she wouldn't snap again.

～

We fell free from on high, like dragons mating. We snapped and roared and bit. And we loved.

Alfonse read his own words from the pages of Cecibel's mangled copy of *Night Wings* over and over again. Unrequited love was too easy, too ordinary, and not at all his golden Valkyrie. Whatever horror of her past had been visited upon her face had nothing to do with a broken heart. Not that sort, at any rate.

The ground came at us. I saw it and didn't care. She never saw it coming at all. I covered her eyes; if she saw, too, she'd have banked her great and powerful wings.

Whether Cecibel was the one covering or covered, he couldn't say, but she was definitely, intimately one of them.

I didn't want to be saved, and so she couldn't be either.

Had she been the one who needed salvation, or the one who didn't want it at all? Perhaps she was both.

Searching the passion in the creases, within the rips and tears and worn-away pages, Alfonse conjured an image of his Cecibel before half her face had been left on the road. A girl, in a car, a book on the seat beside her. His book. And after the accident, bandaged to hide the worst of her pain, that book on her bedside table, waiting. He imagined her picking it up one day, finding the passage that spoke so loudly, reading it over and over, rolling the cover onto itself, her grip as fearsome as her hidden face.

A soft knock. Four twenty. Right on time. Alfonse smoothed the haggard copy as best he could and tucked it into the cushion of his chair. "Come in, Cecibel."

The door opened, and there she stood. His golden Valkyrie. His Cecibel. Alfonse reached out his hand, and she came.

Bar Harbor, Maine

JULY 4, 1999

There is no I *in t-e-a-m, but there is an* m *and there is an* e, *so go to hell.*

—CORNELIUS TRAEGAR

They could come to no agreement. Big surprise.

It was Cecilia and Aldo's story. Though Enzo was a vital point-of-view character, his part was minor in comparison, and thus, passing it from Olivia to Alfonse to Switch would only topple the balance necessary to tell their tale. Alfonse argued that Switch's voice didn't quite match up, being more folksy and lighthearted. But no—Olivia defended—that wasn't true at all. Switch's seemingly lighthearted style only served as contrast to deepen the impact of Enzo's understanding and love. Switch let them go at one another, feeding their frenzy with a grumbled comment now and again. They each argued for their characters, their styles and voices. No one was right. No one was wrong. Great minds thinking alike was a beautiful thing. Great minds at odds was not.

"Staying true to the whole doesn't mean abandoning your unique visions," Judith told them, late one night. Late for them. All of nine o'clock. "The story will dictate which point of view will come next, and the correct author will be given the notebook to write in. You three know better. It's about the story, not which of you gets more face time."

Duly chastised, they agreed. Switch's part had deftly changed the story's tack, perfectly solidifying Cecilia's motive while keep-

~ 140 ~

ing the dead-father-distance Aldo needed for his arc. Next point of view had to be Aldo's, and while Olivia grumbled over missing her turn, she handed the notebook to Alfonse. He accepted it graciously and, he thought, not at all smugly. But Olivia's glare insisted otherwise.

"I know exactly where it needs to go right now," he tried to console her. "And it will lead right back to Cecilia. You'll see."

"No planning!" Olivia scolded. "And no discussing it on the side or the whole thing is shot to hell. It must be organic and different and new or it's just another boy-meets-girl-loses-girl story that has been written and read a million times."

"I told you she's a literary snob," Alfonse whispered loudly behind his hand.

Switch did the same. "You didn't need to tell me."

Olivia glared at them both. "Well, pardon me for attempting to maintain a little author integrity."

"What happened to doing it for the joy?" Alfonse asked. "Wasn't that what thrilled you first?"

"I am, and it still does." Olivia sniffed. "I can't help being good at it."

"She's insufferable." Alfonse tucked the notebook down the side of his chair cushion lest she attempt to steal it. Again. Switch remained wisely noncommittal.

Darling Raymond. Keeping Cami alive truly had been a stroke of genius. The scenes played behind his eyes. Dominic Giancami going into the water, washing up somewhere downriver, barely alive. Recognized. Hidden away while schemes played out and coups were attempted. He wouldn't remember the events leading to all that; if he did, Aldo was as good as dead no matter where he was. Amnesia. Brain damage. Blackouts that would plague him the rest of his life, along with the dark moods that whispered someone had pulled something over on him and gotten away with it. But a kinder Cami, as Switch had made him. A more loving man, maybe the one he'd once been before crime hardened him. It wouldn't all make it out of his head and onto the page, but he had to know the details to make the story come alive, to make it authentic.

Eight o'clock. Fourth of July. Alfonse was almost asleep in his chair set up to give him the perfect view over the ocean, where the fireworks would erupt once the moon had fully risen. It had been a long and lovely day at the Bar Harbor Home for the Elderly. No writing today, even if his time with the notebook was almost up. As promised, the story would lead directly to Cecilia. He hoped Olivia picked up on enough of his cues to take it in the right direction. Right being *his*. No, today was about sunshine that exhausted him and food he couldn't eat without suffering the consequences. At least there had been friends all around him, pretending he was still the one-and-only Alfonse Carducci. There had even been a few moments he fooled himself.

He was so tired of being tired. The dearth of oxygen. Every hard-won heartbeat. It cost him dearly simply to eat, because eating required the bodily energy to digest one's food and Alfonse had such precious little to spare. If it weren't for the book, he'd have no reason to live. If it weren't for Cecibel, there would be no book. Thus he lived on love, for Cecibel and Cecilia, Aldo, and Enzo. He would live on love until the day he died, in the room that love provided him, in the house that love built, and gladly. Gratefully. Alfonse Carducci did not want to die.

A knock on his door woke him from his doze. He straightened in the chair. "Yes?"

"Alfonse?" Cecibel opened the door. "I didn't wake you, did I?"

"No, my dear, no. Please, come in. I'm trying to stay awake for the fireworks."

Cecibel closed the door softly. She came to him barefoot, wearing cutoff shorts and a tank top under her flannel shirt. How Alfonse enjoyed the grunge look. Laid-back and edgy all at once. Feminine despite the high-top hiking boots she'd earlier worn and now held in two fingers by the laces. Her hair, as always in an obscuring braid, was wind-tossed into curls whispering along the princess cheek, temple, throat. She sat on the arm of his chair, rested a hand to his shoulder. "I thought I'd watch the fireworks with you, if that's okay."

"Why would it not be okay?"

She laughed softly. "Olivia said you wanted to be alone."

"She should have been honest. I simply wanted to be away from her."

"You adore her."

"I do. Absolutely. But she exhausts me far more than the sea air that chased me back here to my room."

Cecibel pulled the other wingback chair up to his. She sat facing the same window, looking out at the same sky. "What was she like, when you first knew her?"

"Much the same as she is now." No, he could not laugh. Best to save his energy for talking. "Beautiful. Volatile. Brave."

"Just younger."

"Just younger, yes. I'd have done anything for her."

She turned her head, offering him only the fair. The monster left in shadow. Cecibel smiled. "Then all the old gossip is true?"

"Scandalously so," he said. "Olivia Peppernell was one of the two great loves of my life."

"And the other was Cornelius Traegar."

"The love of my youth," Alfonse agreed. "A fragile thing, yet an enduring one."

"Why did you end it?"

"With?"

"Either," Cecibel answered. "Both. Can I ask that?"

"I might not answer, but you can ask." He grinned. "It was no small thing to be a man who loved a man, back then. I was a rising star, too new to withstand the scrutiny and condemnation our relationship would cause. It was Cornelius who told me to go, to win the world and come back to him when I was big enough to eclipse the rest." *Oh, Cornelius, you glorious fool. Did you know, even then, that I never would, never could be true to only you?* "Great loves are not meant to be forever, only great."

Cecibel nodded, her expression so somber. "And Olivia?"

"That, my dear, forgive me, is one question I cannot answer. Cornelius is dead and gone. Olivia is not."

She looked away. "Sorry."

"Don't be." Alfonse took her hand, curling his fingers between hers. Cecibel's eyes followed the movement. Fingers curled. They fit together like shoelaces, crisscrossing, containing. Alfonse could not help himself. He brought her hand to his lips and kissed her fingers, one at a time. Some instincts could not be squelched by age and decay. She moved him and, by the birdlike trembling of her muscles beneath her skin, he moved her right back.

"I . . . I've never been in love. Before."

Blood surged to parts of his body it had not visited in far too long. Alfonse wouldn't read too much into her choice of words, in that moment, though he wanted to. So badly. Cecibel was young and starstruck and somehow broken inside. Whatever balm he could be to her, he gave gladly. She'd never been in love before, didn't know the difference, but Alfonse had. He knew the feeling, knew the power, and knew that, wise or foolish, he was in it again.

"But you've had a great love," he said. "No?"

"Why do you say that?"

Alfonse pulled the tattered copy of *Night Wings* from the cushions of his chair, curled the passion-creased pages open to that one that told the truth of her tale. Cecibel's lip trembled, her gaze moving from the book to their joined hands, up his arm, shoulder, chin, cheek, nose, and finally, to his eyes. The shadows and the wingback took away half her face, the half she shared with everyone, leaving him the half she shared only with him. Alfonse reached out, hesitated. Cecibel didn't even blink. He tucked her golden shroud behind what remained of her ear, bared the monster to the moonlight.

"She was my sister," Cecibel whispered. "I couldn't save her."

"From?"

"Herself."

"I imagine that wasn't your job."

"Maybe not, but I was the only one."

"Younger sister?"

"Older. By three years."

"And your parents?"

Cecibel's good eye blinked. "They weren't strong enough."

"Only you were?"

She shook her head.

"But you tried."

"I failed."

Beyond the window, a rocket whistled to the stars, sparkling flowers bloomed. And boom.

Cecibel untucked her hair and let the shroud fall. She turned back to the window, said nothing more. But she let him keep her hand curled into his while Independence Day blared and rocketed through the night sky over the ocean.

Alfonse fell asleep before the last crackle, woke up hours later in his bed. He didn't have to wonder how he'd gotten there, tucked into pajamas and under the sheets. Dreams and reality mingled. Wants and wishes. Sorrow and love. He'd undressed her as she undressed him, slipped into bed, tugging him along. He made love to the monster. She smoothed the covers over his shriveled frame. He kissed her and caressed her body. She checked his pulse, put the oxygen tube in his nostrils.

"Good night, Alfonse," she'd whispered, and kissed his cheek, tiptoed away, and flicked off the lights.

In the darkness beyond dreaming, Cecilia whispered Aldo's name. Their bodies joined. Their heartbeats synced. *Good night, Aldo,* Cecilia said in Cecibel's voice. *Good night, good night, good night.*

Paterson, New Jersey

✬

Aldo

It was impossible, and yet there he was, whole and hearty if slightly older than the night he went over the falls and drowned. Aldo had taken a huge risk, returning to Paterson. Not because he was afraid of ghosts, or old enemies made without meaning to. He risked seeing Cecilia. Married Cecilia. Never-again-his Cecilia. Running headlong into the dead father instead—who was not, in fact, dead—toppled him completely. Quite literally.

"Sorry, there." Giancami had hauled him to his feet, looked him in the eye, shook his hand—"Ah, a man in uniform. Thanks for your service. Better you than me, eh?"—and hadn't recognized him. Yes, Aldo was a man now, not a boy of twenty. He was taller, broader, made of sterner stuff. But—gracious God in heaven!—no recognition whatsoever. And he'd have never known it without a chance return to Paterson, brought about by another impossibility smacking him out of the past.

Her letter arrived along with the orders for his second tour of duty. From Chipley, Florida. Aldo looked it up on a map. The tiny town sat between Alabama and the Gulf, tucked into the tiniest part of the Florida panhandle. He'd thought her name was Theresa, but his sister's name was Tressa—two syllables, not three. He thought she lived in Florida-Florida, not almost-Alabama. But the last name—DiViello—was his mother's maiden name. The name of the cousin who'd wanted a little girl to raise, but not him. That, Aldo remembered clearly.

Dear Aldo [the letter began]. *Do you even remember me? I remember you. Not a day has gone by in the last fifteen that I haven't thought about you. I try to picture you in my mind when I add you to my prayers at night. Sorry, I keep remembering you as you were. But I never forgot. A girl doesn't forget her big brother, especially when he was her favorite person in the whole world.*

Mama and Daddy (our cousins, who raised me) wouldn't let me contact you. They said it would be too hard on me. Too confusing. It was harder and more confusing to go without you all these years. I always knew I'd find you the moment I came of age and they couldn't tell me what to do anymore. I don't mean to be ungrateful, but I'm all grown up now and I still don't see why they wouldn't let me stay in contact with you. I know you finished high school, joined the navy, and worked your way up in the kitchen ranks. (Dooley Higgins says you make the best mashed potatoes this side of Idaho!) I know you're a fine man, a good man. I'm proud you're my brother. I think Mama and Daddy were just afraid they'd lose me sooner rather than later if you were in my life.

I'm twenty-one now, a woman in my own right, and all I want for Christmas is to see my big brother. I want to hold you in my arms and hug you fifteen years' worth of hugs. I know you re-signed with the navy, and I know you have two months of leave before you ship out again. (The Mediterranean, how utterly divine!) Please, please, oh please, meet me at the falls in Paterson. It's the only place I remember from when I was little. Didn't we picnic there all the time? December 20, 2:00 P.M. If you're not there, I'll be back every day at 2:00 P.M. until you show up or ship out. You'll come. I know you will. I'll be the one wearing a red carnation and a white winter coat.

Your loving sister—Tressa

P.S.
Maybe you're wondering how I found out all that information about you? Can you guess? I'm studying journalism in college. I want to be an investigative journalist, even if I'm the only girl in my class and no

*one takes me seriously. I don't want to write about fashion or family
or the Society Page. We'll talk all about it when we see one another.
Toodles!*

And that's where Aldo was when he bumped into Dominic
Giancami at 1:54 on December 20, 1959, in the same parking lot
of the same falls where he'd left the man to drown. Only Cami
hadn't, somehow, but was there instead with two teenagers who
had to be Cecilia's little brothers.

"It . . . it's all right, sir. I'm fine."

"Let me make it up to you. Buy you a beer?"

"Thank you, no. I'm meeting my sister. She should be here any
minute."

Giancami pointed to Aldo's trousers. "You're all muddy, and
there's a rip in the knee. Come on. At least let me have those
cleaned and mended."

"Thank you, sir, but it's really fine. No harm done."

"Aldo! Aldo, is that you?"

Both men turned to the girl in the white, wearing a red carnation and waving. Tressa bounced on the balls of her feet tucked into
perfect red pumps. Blond curls tumbled out her red beret, down
the lapels of her coat.

"That's your sister? Holy jeez." Giancami whistled softly before
smacking both his sons in the back of the head. "Quit gawping and
have some respect, eh? *Mamalukes!* That's the man's sister."

"Sorry, Dad."

"I'm not. She's some dolly."

"Nicky, you're not so big I can't put a strap to you."

"If you'll excuse me, sir." Aldo nodded to him, to the boys.
"My sister's waiting."

"Wait a minute, there." Cami pulled him back by the sleeve
of his jacket. Aldo forced his heart back down his throat. Cami
leaned closer, his gaze still fixed on Tressa. "What say you come to
the shindig I'm throwing at my place tonight? Christmas party. It's
gonna be big doin's. All Paterson high society, eh? My wife does the

cooking. Days, she's been at it. Can't get food like hers nowhere, not even in the city. Come on. Let me do something to make up for knocking you down."

A dead man. A lost love. Old sacrifices made irrelevant far too late to do anything about them. What would he do if he saw her again? What would Cecilia do?

"My . . . my sis—"

"Yeah, yeah. She's starting to frown, eh? Can't make a pretty girl unhappy. Well, the offer stands." Cami pressed a business card into Aldo's hand. "Come. And bring your sister. Nicky. Joseph. Shake the man's hand."

Nicky's handshake was firm. He looked Aldo in the eye. Joseph's grip wasn't quite as confident, but he, too, met Aldo's gaze, his narrowing. "Don't I know you?"

Aldo flinched, recovered quickly with a grin and a shrug. "I lived here when I was a kid," he said. "Maybe."

"What's your name?"

"Al . . . DiViello."

"Ah, *paesan',*" Cami said. "Let the man go, boys. Looks like his sister is gonna pop a gut in another minute." He started away, walking backward. "Six o'clock. See you there."

"Aldo?"

He spun back to Tressa, still standing in the same spot, no longer bouncing. Her hands were tucked into a white fur muff. She was a vision of all things golden and beautiful, this once-frizzy, freckled, snotty creature who asked him to meet her in the one place he'd planned on never returning to again. There hadn't been time to attempt contacting her, requesting an alternate meeting place. One glance over his shoulder at the dead man who wasn't dead, then Aldo hurried to her.

"Tressa." Her name fell from his lips as easily as if it had been doing so all their lives. He caught his little sister in his arms. She squealed and he spun her around. He could almost forget Dominic Giancami and the party he couldn't possibly go to, even if Cecilia sang like a siren inside his head.

"Aldo! Oh, my Aldo." Tressa took his face in her hands and smooshed his cheeks. "Look at you! Such a handsome man, my brother. You look just like our mother."

"Do I?"

"Don't you remember?"

He smiled sadly. "Not really. I don't have any pictures or anything."

"I do. Scads of them. Oh, Aldo, we have so much to talk about." Tressa looked down at the little suitcase at her feet.

He dutifully picked it up, offered her his arm. "When did you get in?"

"Last night. I stayed at a little hotel over that way." She pointed. "The one with the fountains out front. Do you know it?"

"I've been gone awhile." But he knew it. Les Fontaines. Posh, even if it was owned by the same family that opened it as Downtown Gardens when he was a kid. "Let's go someplace warm and catch up. We can figure out what we want to do."

Tressa squeezed his arm, rested her glorious head to his shoulder. "This is the happiest day of my life." *Ma laff,* not *my life*. Tressa had been raised so far in the south it erased every shred of New Jersey she might have taken with her.

They walked to Woolworth's and took a seat at the counter. The years fell away—the wrong years. His sister, his only surviving family, sat beside him, a woman grown, and all he could think about was meeting Cecilia for malteds and egg creams at that same counter. He expected Margaret Mary Donahue to come out from behind the counter, her chewed-up pencil between her teeth. She always eyed them like they'd just robbed the place. She didn't trust guineas or Polacks as far as she could throw them and, considering her size, that wouldn't have been far. But Margaret Mary didn't take their order for a root beer float and coffee. No one walked in that Aldo knew. When he left Paterson, he'd known only Agnes from Falls View. And Cecilia.

She'd be there for the Christmas party. He knew it like he knew his sister sat beside him, chattering about her life down south with the people who'd rejected him. He should have been listening, but his mind wouldn't stick to her while it was chasing love through the years. All the adrenaline that should have had him hightailing it out of Paterson swished around in his body, through his brain. Maybe Dominic Giancami wasn't dead, but he had to know someone had tried to kill him. The younger son—Joseph—recognized him. Aldo tried to remember if he'd ever met the kid back in the day. Maybe he'd seen him with Cecilia. Somewhere. Somehow. They hadn't been discreet until the first time they made love. God, making love to Cecilia was the closest to heaven he'd ever gotten. There had been other women through the years. Every size, shape, color. None of them had been memorable. None of them had been her.

What would he have done if he'd known, back then, he hadn't killed Dominic Giancami? Would he have read any of her letters? Returned them? Could he have stopped the marriage she'd been forced into?

"Do you want to go to a Christmas party tonight?"

Tressa's chatter stopped, her mouth still open. "A party? Where?"

"Remember that guy in the parking lot at the falls?"

"The one who bumped into you?"

"That's the one. Dominic Giancami."

"Why would he invite us to a Christmas party?"

Aldo grinned. "Maybe because he and his boys think you're the prettiest thing that ever set foot in Paterson, New Jersey."

"Oh, you." She waved him off. "I don't know about—"

"He's a gangster," Aldo added. "Richest guy in town."

Tressa grasped his arm, squealing softly. "A gangster? Really?"

"Think of the story you could write, Miss Journalist. High society *and* crime. An age-old combination that never gets boring."

"You had me at gangster." She pouted. "But I haven't a thing to wear."

"You look gorgeous just the way you are."

Tressa plucked at the baby-blue dress, all pleats and pearl buttons. "Goodness, no. This is a traveling dress and will never do for a soiree. If I'm to go to a party at a wealthy gangster's home, I need appropriate attire. Where does one go to buy something pretty around here?"

"That depends on what you have to spend."

"Money is not a concern," she said primly.

"Then Meyer Brothers," he answered. "Come on. We can walk."

Aldo paid for her float and his coffee, even if money was not a concern for her and was for him. Anticipation robbed him of all caution. He hadn't seen his sister in fifteen years, in truth, hardly even thought about her, and now, together at last, he couldn't keep his attention on her either.

He tried. They walked and they talked. He told her about the orphanage and Falls View and joining the navy. She already knew a whole lot about his military career, how he'd impressed his commanding officers with his culinary skills. Her daddy, the cousin who didn't want him, had done his time in the navy, too. And what a coincidence that was, after all. But she'd cooed proudly when he let it drop that he'd been assigned to a diplomatic ship more like a yacht in the Mediterranean, cooking for officers, dignitaries, and politicians of all kinds.

"Will you cook for me?"

"If I can find a kitchen to do it in. When do you have to go back to school?"

"Around the same time your leave is up. Maybe we could sublet an apartment somewhere. Oh, New York City!"

"Don't your parents—"

"Cousins."

"Guardians. Don't they want you to come home?"

Tressa burrowed her hands deeper into the white fur muff. "They can't always get what they want, now, can they? I wanted to see you, and they wouldn't let me. I'm a grown woman, and if I want to stay up north with my brother until he ships out, that's what I'm going to do."

He didn't remind her about the money she spent being of no concern, or that her guardians were footing the bill for her college degree, not to mention this trip north to see him. Did she think of such things? No, of course not. And he was glad she'd never had to. Better a spoiled, southern princess than the girl she'd have been had he been old enough to raise her.

Aldo left Tressa squealing madly over the New York, Paris, and Milan fashions coloring the racks in Meyer Brothers Department Store and headed back toward the bus depot where he'd stashed his duffel bag. Somewhere far, far in the reaches of his memory, he remembered a jewelry box his mother kept, MEYER BROTHERS embossed in gold. The box her engagement ring came in, maybe. Something small and precious. But that it was from Meyer Brothers was even more important. It meant she'd warranted the expense. At least, that was what his adult mind told him. When he was a kid, he simply liked tracing the gold letters with his finger.

Aldo unlocked the rented locker at the bus depot and put Tressa's tiny suitcase in with his duffel. Staying at the YMCA wasn't going to be an option, he decided. Not with his sister in tow. Somehow, he'd thought she'd have relations to stay with. Wasn't that what young women did when traveling? Did they stay in hotels on their own? It seemed rather scandalous to him. And dangerous. But she had done so the night prior. Worse came to worst, she would do so again. Apparently, she could afford it. At least her guardians could.

Letting that old dog lie, he set out for the only place he might still find a familiar, safe face. Head down and collar up, he hurried along the once-familiar streets to Falls View. He could smell the grease and the meat long before he got there. The scent tugged a smile from his lips. Life might have been a little grim, back then, but it wasn't all bad.

He pushed through the door with a whoosh of cold air and heads lifted to see who'd just come in. Aldo took off his hat, as an officer and a gentleman did when entering a building where ladies were present. High school girls were ladies, nonetheless, and several of them were still looking at him, a man in uniform, like he was the daily special on the menu. A woman came out of the kitchen, pad and pencil in hand. A woman not Agnes.

"Excuse me," he said. "But do you know if Agnes will be on duty today?"

The woman chuffed, her chins wagging with the shake of her head. "Agnes died two years ago," she said. "You want food or something? Otherwise I got things to do."

Aldo looked up at the menu board. Prices were largely the same, as was the menu itself. Even he could afford to splurge on this old memory. "I'll take a dog all the way, fries, and a chocolate malted."

"You got it, kid."

She called the order through the window. Aldo rested his chin to the heel of his hand, eyes fixed on the menu board so the girls still ogling him wouldn't get any ideas. Agnes was dead. Strange how little that actually mattered to him when once she was his only friend.

He'd been the only one of his navy buddies to earn a spot on that diplomatic ship. Aldo said good-bye to Dooley and Zigs and even Cavanaugh without much more than a handshake and a half-hearted promise to keep in touch. He'd left the orphanage, high school, even Paterson in the same manner. Seventeen years parted from the little sister he thought he'd never see again, and he could leave that moment and not look back. There'd been only one anchor in his life. Maybe that was all his heart had room for.

He paid for his food, nodded to the ladies staring, and headed back out into the cold. Tressa had to be done, didn't she? How long could a girl shop? He checked his watch, an Omega waterproof Admiral Salfrank had taken off his own wrist and put on Aldo's despite such gifts being taboo. Rules were rules for some, not all.

Five o'clock. He headed back to Meyer Brothers. Tressa, face flushed and beaming, was waiting for him. "Oh, you're here. I got the most glorious dress. Just wait until you see it." She motioned to a young man dressed like a bellhop, who handed Aldo garment bags, shoe boxes, and what appeared to be a velvet treasure chest. "Have you gotten us lodging?"

"No," he said. "I wasn't sure what was proper. I was going to stay at the Y. I didn't know you were . . ."

"I was what?"

Aldo smiled. He kissed her cheek. "A lady," he said. "Until today, you were still a toddler to me."

"Oh, Aldo." She squeezed his arm. "We can always get a room at the hotel I stayed in last night."

"I can't afford—"

"Nonsense." She waved him away. "You're my brother. You'll stay with me."

"That's not such a good idea."

"It's not?"

Aldo leaned in close. "No one is going to believe we're brother and sister. This is a city, Tressa. There's no such thing as innocence here. I'll walk you to your hotel and go get a bed at the Y. How long do you need to get changed?"

"Oh, an hour or two."

"The party starts at six."

She laughed again, the sound so merry Aldo couldn't help laughing himself. "What's so funny?"

"Darling, no one arrives on time. That's so gauche. You want to make an entrance, not stand around like a wallflower waiting for all the who's who to get there. Trust me. I know these things."

Tressa led the way back to Les Fontaines. Crystal chandeliers, crushed velvet upholstery on the chairs and couches, gilded crown moldings, at least eight stories high. He'd love to know what she'd think about some of the rattraps he stayed in. A bellhop took her garment bags and boxes.

"You need to change." She pointed to his torn and dirty trousers. "Do you have dress blues or something?"

"This is my dress uniform."

"Hmm."

"What does that mean?"

She plucked at his jacket sleeve. "Are you required to wear it?"

"No, but I don't have anything else."

Tressa looked up at him through her lashes. Her grin began in one corner of her lovely mouth, spread slowly to the other. Dimples deepened. Blue eyes twinkled. She motioned the bellhop over and pulled free one of the garment bags. "Yes, you do." Now she handed him a shoe box from the pile in the young man's arms, giggling madly. "The tuxedo should fit perfectly. I've a good eye for such things. And if the shoes pinch, we can send out for another size if you're quick enough."

"But—"

"No buts, mister. No brother of mine is staying at the YMCA."
She handed him a key. "Don't argue. Go shower and change."

The bit of brass on his palm glinted in crystalline light. The
muscles in Aldo's throat constricted. He'd never been too proud to
accept a handout. He'd relied on it far too much since the accident
that took his family from him. His life had been a series of making-
dos and thank-you-kindlys. He cleared his throat. "Our stuff is in
a locker down at the bus depot."

"Key?" Tressa held out her hand. Aldo fumbled about in his
pocket and handed it to her. Holding up a five-dollar bill in one
hand, she handed the locker key to a second bellhop with the other.
"Fetch our bags and have them brought to our rooms."

"Yes, miss."

"Do it quickly." She handed him the five. Imperial, and beautiful. He'd never have guessed she'd be so, until today, if given a
million years of trying.

Aldo took her hand, turned her to him. "Thank you."

"Don't thank me. I'm your sister." Tressa's brilliance faded, her
lip trembled. She took both his hands in hers. "I never forgot, Aldo.
Not them. Not you. I always knew no matter how happy my childhood, no matter how cherished I was, that you were in the world
maybe not so happy, or cherished. I can't make any of that up to
you, but I can spoil you while I have you in my clutches."

He kissed her hands. "I'm glad your guardians did good by you,
but I'm pretty sure they'll be angry if they find out you're spending
their money on me."

"Whatever do you . . . Oh, dear." She touched perfectly manicured fingers to her lips. "Is that what you think? That I'm a spoiled
debutante off spending Mommy and Daddy's money?"

"I . . . No?"

"Oh, Aldo. Well, of course you wouldn't know any better."
She kissed his cheek. "I see we still have oodles and oodles to talk
about, but for now, don't worry about the money. It's mine, all
mine, thanks to my granny and pawpaw and being twenty-one. I
can spend it any way I wish without ever worrying it'll run out.
Honest Injun. All right?"

"I sup—"

"Lovely!" Tressa squeezed his hand and let it go, brushed a tear from her eye. "Now that that's settled, I'll go make myself presentable for the gangster Christmas party. I'll meet you down here at a quarter to seven."

"Yes, ma'am."

She laughed, calling behind her as she hurried to the elevator, "And don't forget, if those shoes don't fit, call down to the store and have them bring you new ones. You'll never enjoy the party if your shoes are too tight."

Aldo watched the doors slide closed on Tressa and the stupefied bellhop. He looked down at the key in his hand, the garment bag, the shoe box. How could it be? Tressa, his baby sister, a young woman of twenty-one and already far more sophisticated than he would ever be.

He closed his hand around the key. What the hell. He was already risking his life to attend a party; might as well sell his dignity in the process.

Bar Harbor, Maine

JULY 6, 1999

❧

Be the light in someone's darkness.

—CORNELIUS TRAEGAR

Clouds billowing and white by day swirled into sunset's palette—yellow ocher, vermilion, alizarin crimson, a line of ultramarine blue where night slipped fingers over the edge of the world. Olivia had learned to see a sky the way an artist did, to better understand the words necessary to a sunset, a sunrise. The Prussian blue of storm clouds. The gray of a moonglade on the ocean. She'd never been a great artist, but she was the best among the others in the watercolor class she took. Olivia Peppernell née Stuart was never anything but the best.

She took a long drag, willed the cannabinoids to soothe the demons along with the pain. It had done the trick, not so long ago. Now, whether chemical resistance or stronger demons, it wasn't working quite as well. It didn't soothe as much as distance her from them, let her see, so clearly, that a life doing what she wished as long as she did what she was told was not independence; it was a bigger cage with sturdier locks not even love could pick.

A final drag, a long exhale, and Olivia put the roach out on the rubber heel of her sensible shoe. She'd never been one for stilettos, but orthopedic was definitely not her style either. Thank Charles for that, too. Sixty-two years waiting it out for him to die first. At least she'd outlasted him. The bastard.

She started to rise, flopped back into the Adirondack chair. An electric shock of pain shot through her mighty buzz and pulled a gasp from between tight lips. Switch had been right about the newest crop; it didn't make her sleepy, but it did fuddle her a bit. That was fine by her. She deserved the cushion between her and the world at this point in her life. Anyone who had a problem with that could suck her dick.

"Olivia?" Cecibel's disembodied voice cascaded from the darkling sky. "Are you okay?"

"I'm fine, dear. Just fine."

"Why are you on the ground?"

Olivia patted the scrubby grass. "Oh. I . . . I suppose I am."

And then there she was, Olivia's fallen angel, lifting her gently to her feet, holding her until she steadied.

"Hey, Sal?"

The static crackle of Cecibel's walkie-talkie vibrated Olivia's nose. She sneezed.

"What's up, chicken butt?"

"I need you to come out to the arbor with a wheelchair. And what's with your obsession with my butt lately?"

"It's an old expression. I think it's from a cartoon. Who's the wheelie for?"

"Just come out, will you? Alone. Unless you want me to do it and miss my date with Fin."

More crackling. Or maybe it was Salvatore cackling.

"So you admit it!"

"I'm manipulating you."

"Fine, fine. I'll be there in a minute or three."

Olivia allowed Cecibel to help her into the Adirondack chair, suppressing the desire to giggle. Olivia Peppernell did *not* giggle. Not even as a child. It was entirely gauche and utterly unacceptable. Clearing her throat, she attempted to smooth the ridiculous mess the wind made of her hair. "I'm fine. You can run along."

"I don't really have a date. Just meeting Fin on the beach for our nightly walk."

"Daily tea with the infamous Alfonse Carducci, and nightly walks with a handsome murderer." A giggle disobeyed. She gulped it down. "When did your life become so thrilling?"

"Olivia . . ."

"Oh, come now, dear. Alfonse is infamous and Finlay is a murderer. What did I say wrong?"

"You're way too smart to pull that off." Cecibel pointed. "Is that the notebook?"

Olivia had forgotten she'd brought it out with her. She clutched it to her bony breast once as plump and white as a dove's. "Yes. I was going to read it back again before handing it off."

"Who's next?"

"Enzo, it has to be."

"I still haven't read the part Switch added," Cecibel said. "Can I read it before you give it to him?"

"I don't know. Can you?"

Cecibel rolled her eyes. "May I?"

"Of course you may." Another disobedient giggle. She held the notebook out to Cecibel. "Be sure to get it to Raymond tomorrow. And don't let Alfonse see you."

Cecibel took the notebook. "Are you feeling all right?"

"A little loopy, but otherwise, grand. This new weed makes me almost forget the pain. Almost. It hurt when I fell off the chair, but not a fraction as much as when Charles tossed me down a flight of stairs like a little raggedy doll." More giggles. "He thought he was such a man, doing the things he did to me." Threatening giggles. "Couldn't come if there wasn't pain involved, you know. His pain. Mine." The giggling churned in her belly now. Gurgled. "Is it any wonder I could not love my children, conceived the way they were? I tried. I tried so hard."

"It's all right," Cecibel crooned. "Hush."

"And then he turned them against me. He bought them, the ingrates. I should have stayed with that monster? I should have let him continue misusing me, humiliating me?"

"Take a deep breath, sweetheart. Deep, deep breath."

Her head resting against Cecibel's breast, Olivia was nearly overwhelmed by the desire to bury herself in so maternal a haven. Mama. Sweet Mama. "She told me I'd regret it," Olivia whispered. "She said I'd rue the day I let jealousy dictate my heart. I only wanted him because Lucille had him. He was so handsome and charming and wealthy. I didn't listen, and then I could never, ever admit it. Not until she was gone and couldn't say she told me so. Not until Alfonse . . ."

"Shh, Olivia. It's all right. He's long gone. You're safe."

Giggles tamed, the tears she'd so seldom shed in life replaced their blatant disobedience. "They pay my bills with money I earned," she blubbered. "My money, from my books. But do they know that? No. They think their sainted father provided for his errant, evil wife. They have no idea his family money was gone long before I ever left, that it was my success that kept them in boarding school and university and homes in the Hamptons. They don't know his cruelty, though ask any woman who'd ever fucked him. Ask them. There were plenty. And I got a broken back for loving a man who loved me in return."

Doubling over, Olivia ignored the shock of electric pain. Momentary, absorbed by the cannabidiol, and gone. She'd smoked too much. Too, too much. Stupid, stupid woman. She knew better than to overindulge in a new product.

"Just get her back to her room," she heard Cecibel say. "Don't tell the nurses or Dr. Kintz. Let her sleep it off."

"You got it, sugar."

"Sal's going to take you home, Olivia." Cecibel was at eye level now, Olivia in a wheelchair. She nodded obediently, banished tears with a mercurial swipe of her once-elegant hand. Now it was old, liver-spotted, like crepe paper. Fingers were twigs sticking out, at odd angles, of knuckles like golf balls. She'd been so beautiful. Once. Beautiful. Talented. A force of nature only one brick wall had ever stopped. She learned her lesson well, paid the price for the only freedom open to her. But she'd taken it. By God, she had! Charles Peppernell, her ungrateful children, would all be lost to time. Olivia Peppernell née Stuart would be remembered, dammit.

Dusk had already tipped nearer to night, the line of ultramarine blue edging over the world now a fat band splashed with alizarin, aubergine, cadmium yellow, and indigo. Words, ever hers to conjure and recall, filled her head, her heart. Dear companions. Greatest loves. They'd never failed her. They never would.

∼

"'Do you see in yon sunset sky, that cloud of crimson bright?'" Olivia's singsong drifted on the sea breeze. "'Soon will its gorgeous colors die, in coming dim twilight.'"

Sal wheeled Olivia away. Cecibel clutched the notebook to her breast. Interesting lives exacted a price, one that nobody actually elected to pay but that all were forced to. All that pain, the heartache. At least Olivia set her story to the music of her prose. What did Cecibel do with hers?

Weaving down the path to the beach, sand still warm between her toes, Cecibel tried to let it go. Tea with Alfonse was always thrilling in ways she didn't quite understand, but her walks with Finlay were just the opposite. Comforting. Relaxing. A long sigh after a hard day. All the pent-up and confusing emotions released into the simplicity of their friendship.

"Sorry I'm late." She trot-slid her way down the dune to him. "I had to get Olivia taken care of."

"I seen her in the arbor." Finlay chuckled. "Woman smokes a lot of weed."

"She's in a lot of pain otherwise. You know she broke her back about thirty years ago."

He nodded. Cecibel didn't elaborate. Whatever Fin knew or didn't, he could keep to himself.

"Can you—" She amended, "Will you put this in your backpack for me?"

"Sure." He took the notebook from her without asking what it was. "Ready?"

"Ready."

They walked in companionable silence, flashlights at the ready. They picked up shells and sea glass, pebbles smooth and white. The wind blew and the surf hissed warm over their toes, sucked the sand from under their soles. The rhythm, the pulse of the sea soothed and electrified. Maybe it was this that made Finlay Cecibel's comfort after a long day, and not the man himself.

"Want a beer?" Finlay shouldered the backpack off, dropped down into dry sand just beyond the tide line. "Before they get too warm."

"Sure." Cecibel flopped down beside him, a little too close. Her hip brushed his. Shifting away would be too obvious. She stayed where she was, trying to pretend she didn't notice the intimacy.

Fin twisted off the cap and handed her the bottle. She sipped, fizz tickling her mouth, her nose. Drinking out of a bottle was easier than from a can or cup. Had he noticed and planned accordingly? The thought made Cecibel smile secretly.

"How's about we go out, Bel? I don't mean a date or nothing. Just out. I know dinner won't work for you, but what about a movie?"

"Don't you enjoy our walks?"

"Sure I do. It's just, I'd like to get off this property once in a while, wouldn't you?"

When was the last time she'd set foot off the Pen's grounds? Cecibel was certain it hadn't been all that long ago, but for the life of her, she couldn't remember when. "Maybe. What's playing?"

"Funny you should ask." He grinned so big. "You like *Star Wars*?"

"Why not simply ask if I enjoy breathing?" She laughed. "Oh, you mean the new one?"

"Well, no. I meant the originals, but yeah, the new one is still playing in town. One final week. I just thought, maybe, you'd want to go see it."

"I hear it's terrible."

He shrugged. "So what if it is? We're the *Star Wars* generation. It's part of our American culture. We kinda have to go. It's our patriotic duty."

"Well, when you put it that way . . ."

"Yeah?"

It would be dark. She'd be extra careful with her hair, maybe even use hair spray to make sure it didn't slip out of place. Fin was right; they both needed to get off the property now and then. "Yes. Let's do it."

The blush was instant and furious. Thank goodness for the dark and her hoodie.

"How about Friday night?" he asked. "Movie starts at eight-something."

"Uh—yeah, sure. Friday night. I don't drive, by the way."

"Then it's a good thing I do." He pulled a paper bag from his backpack, took both their empty bottles, and put them inside. Rising, he offered her his hand and didn't let go once she was on her feet. Instead, he led her to the rocks, where, come high tide, the sea would crash.

"What are you doing?"

Fin handed her his backpack and climbed farther out onto the rocks. He held up the paper bag, then dashed it once. Twice. The bag split. The shards scattered. Crumbling the bag up carefully, he joined her where she stood.

"Sea-glass seeds." He took his backpack from her and put the bag inside. "Ready to head back?"

Climbing the dunes to the arbor, they walked side by side. His backpack bumped her shoulder each time he stepped with his right foot, until she synced her pace to his. Rhythm again. A pulse set to the music of the sea. A man and a woman, both broken and somewhat repaired. Stepping left foot, right, left, right. Swaying like sea grass buffeted gently by the wind.

"Oh, your book." Setting the backpack on the chair Olivia had been sitting on, Fin pulled it from within. "Sorry. Looks like it got a little wet."

Cecibel brushed the droplets of water from the cover. Condensation from the beer, or maybe the sea. The pattern of drops long sitting and swirls just made with the side of her hand looked a little like pussy-willow branches swaying in the wind. With any luck, no one would notice. If anyone did, Olivia would take the blame.

"G'night, Bel." Fin squeezed her shoulder. "If I don't see you before, I'll see you Friday night. Meet me in the lower lot?"

Of course he didn't offer to pick her up. He knew better, and how she loved him for it. A good friend, Finlay. Why in the world had it taken her so long to discover such a thing? The answer nudged her from behind but she ignored it. Not now. Just, not now.

"Sounds perfect. Seven thirty?"

"Make it seven. We want good seats. Line might be long, considering it's the last week."

"Seven, then. See you, Fin."

He went one way, she the other. Another balmy July night stuck to her body, her clothes. Sand coated her feet and toes even after rubbing them in the scrubby grass. Salt tightened the skin of her face and bound the individual strands of her hair into clumps like thin dreadlocks easily brushed smooth. If she closed her eyes, it could be another July night, Cecibel walking sticky by the sea. She was seventeen. Portland, Maine, not Bar Harbor. Her face was whole and beautiful. Her hair even longer, even thicker. Her body was new and ripe, untouched but ready. She was meeting Dennis on the beach. A bonfire, just the two of them. First love. First time. It was supposed to have been the best night of her life.

"Jen." She choked on her sister's name. Of course she'd been at the same beach. Wasn't it where everyone hung out? There, where police and parents gave a little leeway to the amorous and intoxicated? No bonfire. No lovemaking. Sirens and an ambulance. Police and questions she couldn't answer.

What did she take?

How much?

How long ago?

When did she lose consciousness?

All the friends who could have answered such questions had long since fled by then. No one wanted to be associated with such a thing, not even for a girl universally loved. Pitied. They all knew what she'd been through, knew her pain. They'd been standing over her, panicking when Cecibel happened upon them. Stand her up. Get her breathing. Call 911. They did, and they'd fled, leaving only the little sister who didn't meet Dennis after all, who never saw him again once he heard what happened.

Who are you to her?

What's your home address?

Do your parents know where you are?

Did you take anything?

Will you submit to a drug test?

Those were questions she could answer and did. She rode in the ambulance with Jen, who didn't die completely, but did a little bit. Every time.

Wiping the tears from her cheek, Cecibel opened the door to her room, blinked away the pink-and-yellow frill of her youth and found the homey comfort of the present. She leaned against it in the dark. Breathing slowly in and out. Her grip on the notebook clutched to her chest eased. She tossed it onto her bed, went to the bathroom, and rinsed herself free of the salt and sand.

After so many years spent forgetting, blocking, pretending, Jennifer was so clear Cecibel could almost see her reflected in the mirror, right behind her. Not the Jennifer she'd become, but the Jennifer she'd been before.

"I miss you," she told the phantom. "You don't think so but I do. You never got that it didn't matter, that as long as you were alive, there was a chance you'd get better. I'd have lived every day of that horror over again for that chance."

Cecibel dried her face. When she looked up again, only she looked back. More than a decade since the monster's birth. More than a decade since finding Jennifer that last time. More than a decade spent forgetting, after all, for nothing, because there was no forgetting. Any of it.

A crisp, cotton nightgown from her drawer felt good against her skin. Fresh. Clean. Scented with sunshine, dried on the line. Cecibel scooped up the brown notebook, sat on the edge of her bed. The watermarks had dried, but left behind their shadows. Settling between the July-damp sheets, she switched on the bedside lamp.

꙰

Cecilia

Sucking in, Cecilia Parisi pulled the all-in-one girdle into place, leaned over to arrange her breasts in the strapless cups. She groaned upright. Excruciating, but it did the trick. The lumps earned with two babies in less than four years smoothed.

Enzo loved her softness, earned giving him the children he adored. He'd run his hands over her plush belly and it would arouse him faster than any slinky lingerie. Cecilia used to be self-conscious about it. He was a strange duck, the man she married. A better man than she deserved. But what was fine and dandy behind closed doors would never do where her Christmas dress was concerned—a little black dress like the one Marilyn Monroe wore in the publicity shots for *The Asphalt Jungle*. Cecilia had the exact picture, torn out of a Hollywood magazine, taped to her mirror. She even had the white fox stole to go with it, though wearing it in the house was a little ridiculous. She'd find a reason to go outside, maybe for a seldom-smoked cigarette. How glamorous she would look in that outfit, hair swept off her neck, smoking a cigarette from a holder. Enzo couldn't possibly object, looking the way she would.

In her old bedroom of her parents' house on Derrom Avenue, Cecilia slipped her dress over her reshaped frame, her feet into black satin pumps, and grabbed the stole from the back of her chair. A quick swipe of lipstick and her makeup was done. Babies might have stolen her body, but they'd robbed nothing of her beauty. She was only twenty-two, after all.

She tiptoed across the hallway to the nursery that was once her brothers' playroom. Joe and Nicky had taken up residence in the old servants' quarters over the kitchen. The rooms were small and not so fancy, but they were private—a definite perk for teenage boys and their paternally encouraged libidos. But heaven help any girls caught in their beds. Mama was happy enough to turn a blind eye, as long as it could remain blind.

Baby Frankie slept in his crib, the image of his father. Dark hair, thick lashes, the little cleft in his perfect chin. Enzo Francis Parisi III. It had been Enzo's idea to call the child by his middle name while holding on to the tradition of the first. Cecilia wasn't overly fond of either name, but at least calling her son Frankie avoided the confusion in a family full of uncles and cousins named for the common grandfather dead longer than any of them had been in the United States.

"My God, you look gorgeous." Enzo's arms slid around Cecilia's cinched waist before she could turn around. "I may have to follow you around with a bat or something."

Cecilia placed a finger to her lips and gestured to the door. She closed the nursery, her sleeping son inside, and twined her arms around her husband's neck. "Your chivalry astounds me, darling."

"Caveman chivalry." He laughed softly, kissed her nose. "How'd I get the most astonishing woman in the world to love me?"

"Our dads arranged it."

He squeezed her closer. "They got the ball rolling is all."

"True enough. I guess it must have been the last several years of you brainwashing me."

"That must be it. Hell, whatever works, right?"

It was ever thus. A game they played. He had no idea, so it was fine. Her conscience could survive her lies, but not his pain. "Where's Patsy?"

"Downstairs with your mother." Enzo let her go. "We really should get her to bed. She's too little to stay up late."

"It's barely seven, and it's Christmas. Let her be."

"As long as you're the one putting up with her whining all day tomorrow."

"Deal." They both knew she was lying. When they were back on Derrom Avenue, Patsy belonged to her grandmother. She'd take the child shopping and come home with a new holiday dress and a doll and buggy slightly different from the ones back at their home in Princeton. Too many sweets, too much indulgence, it would be days before the child recovered from the visit. As always. Cecilia didn't much care. Her blond-haired, blue-eyed cherub of a child was universally loved; that was all that mattered.

"Where's the sitter?" she asked. "I don't like leaving Frankie alone too long."

Enzo sighed almost imperceptibly. "He's ten months old. The doctor said—"

"I know what the doctor said, but he wasn't there. I was. If I hadn't checked on him . . ." She couldn't say the words. Cecilia had never once checked to make sure Patsy kept breathing in her sleep. The child had been born the size of a three-month-old and slept through the night almost from day one. Frankie had been half her size, bluer coming out than Cecilia remembered her daughter being. A son for Enzo to make up for the secret he kept, for the love he showered on Patsy as if she weren't his secret shame. But for a frightening article she read in a waiting room magazine after her second child's birth, she'd never have started monitoring Frankie's slumber.

Enzo ran a finger along her bare shoulder. "I'll fetch her myself and escort her up here, okay?"

She nodded.

"Are you ready to make your grand entrance, then? Everyone must be here by now."

Cecilia checked her watch. Seven o'clock on the dot. If she stretched it any further, Mama would lay an egg. *"Vini, vidi, vici,"* she said. "Help me with this, will you?"

Enzo dropped the stole across her bare shoulders, kissing the curve of her neck. Warmth tickled, raced along her skin. She did love this man. She really did. They'd been happy, and he adored her beyond reason. What more could a girl ask for?

The quiet upstairs gave way to the riot going on below. People.

Everywhere, people. In the grand foyer and the ballroom, in the music room where a jazz singer crooned carols and the adjoining dining room where hired staff would be setting up the buffet. There were more people than there were tables and chairs, a circumstance that never deterred Dominic Giancami from inviting more people than the year prior. Since his brush with death, there was always room for more.

Descending, on her husband's arm, Cecilia kept their pace slow. Deliberate. Eyes turned to them. Fingers pointed. Enzo's hand covered hers. A good hand. Square and strong but soft. No man of the trades, he was a college graduate, in the process of earning his doctorate. Any woman would be proud, and she was. So proud. Where had the skinny, gawky boy gone in the few years they'd been married? Cecilia once suspected he'd be a looker one day, but she'd never dared to hope for what she got. They made a striking pair, and she knew it even if he didn't. Sophia Loren and Carlo Ponti, if Carlo had thick, black hair when he was twenty-four.

Enzo nodded to those calling and waving Christmas cheer. The front door opened. Cecilia's attention moved, along with everyone else's, to the woman stepping over the threshold and shedding a stole. White ermine, no doubt about it. She handed it to the doorman.

"Who's that?" Enzo asked.

"I have no idea," Cecilia answered. Her brothers were falling over themselves to reach her, this vision in red satin. Fair skin, elegant in the way of Audrey Hepburn in *Roman Holiday*, hair the shade of pale champagne, whoever she was, she made Cecilia feel small and dumpy, even in her Marilyn Monroe dress. Especially so. Then her father was there, shoving Nicky and Joe off none too gently. Taking the goddess's hand and drawing her farther into the foyer, he called out to the man still standing in the doorway waiting to come in.

He stepped inside.

He handed the doorman his overcoat and hat.

He lifted his head.

All the air in the room got sucked out the door, a wind tunnel pulling at her, making her continue descending the stairs suddenly like stepstones across a raging brook. To him. Older. Broader. A man. Her Aldo. Standing in the grand foyer of her family home wearing a tuxedo, greeting her father like he was an old friend despite the fact his gaze had not yet left hers.

Cecilia's whole body crackled and she shuddered. Enzo's curiosity spared her his concern. She needed a moment to gather herself, though another thousand moments wouldn't suffice, so she continued toward him and knew she'd been doing just that all these years.

"Ah, there she is. My beautiful daughter." Dominic drew her and Enzo over. "This here is Al DiViello and his sister, Theresa."

"Tressa." The goddess spoke, her voice as velvet and sweet as a movie star's. "Two syllables, not three." And southern. More crackling recognition. Cecilia wanted to throw her arms around the woman for not being Aldo's wife, for being the sister he once envied and missed instead. She wanted to throw herself back in time, back to that night Patsy was conceived, and change the course of everything. Ungrateful thing. Disloyal wife. And her little son sleeping innocently upstairs, oblivious to his mother's banishing wishes.

"Good to meet you, Al." Enzo shook his hand. He bowed over Tressa's. "And you, Miss DiViello."

"Such a gentleman," Tressa cooed. "And your name is?"

"Enzo Parisi, the son-in-law."

"What'sa matter, Ceci?" Cami guffawed. "Cat got your tongue?"

Aldo's steady gaze undid her. He took her hand and, as Enzo had done to Tressa, bowed over it. "Hello, Ceci . . . Mrs. Parisi."

His voice, like chocolate and cream and all things rich and delicious, trickled through her brain. Fingers caressed the underside of her palm where no one could see but she could feel. Cruel and wonderful.

"Hi," she managed. "Welcome. Merry Christmas." Her cheeks flamed. Aldo smiled. Cecilia was as his as she'd ever been.

"Come on in out of the cold." Cami shoved the door closed

even though he'd hired a doorman to do so. "The missus is putting out the spread any second. You don't want to miss a bite. I'm telling you, she's the God's-honest best cook in New Jersey."

"My brother's a chef. He cooks for officers and dignitaries on a ship in the Mediterranean. Or, he will soon enough." Tressa left Aldo's arm for Cami's. "Oh, listen to me, boasting. How unlady-like of me. I'm just so proud of him."

"Yeah? Maybe he and Maria could have a cook-off or some-thing."

"I'll beat him, hands down." Maria Giancami blew into the grand foyer, apron askew, hair falling in curly tendrils around her face, and Patsy on her hip. She handed her off to Enzo, who twirled her in his arms. Cecilia gasped. *Oh, please. Oh, please no.*

"And who's this little angel?" Tressa reached out for Patsy. Traitor child, she went to her like she'd known her all her life. "What's your name, honey?"

"Patsy. What's yours?"

"My name's Tressa."

"You talk funny."

"Do I?" Tressa laughed. Even that was like music. "And here I was, thinking the same thing about you."

"Gramma, I'm hungry."

"I'll take her, Maria," Enzo said. "It was nice meeting you, Al. Tressa. Enjoy the party." He kissed Cecilia's cheek, whispering, "And I didn't forget about the sitter. Just have fun. And get that girl away from your mother before she claws her eyes out."

Cecilia barely nodded, barely digested what he said. How could she when her head was ringing, when he held Aldo's child in his arms and didn't see the similarity to the man's sister, who'd have her eyes clawed out if she didn't let go of Daddy's arm and fast?

She took a deep breath. Her undergarments reminded her of their presence, of the fact she needed them to look half as good as Tressa, who probably wore nothing anywhere near as torturous under her red dress. Aldo's sister. Patricia's aunt. How could this be happening?

Cecilia's vision wavered. She put a hand to her head.

"Are you okay?" A masculine voice not Daddy's, not Enzo's. One like chocolate coating her. Warm and sensuous.

Cecilia dared look up, met his eyes. Eyes she'd been gazing into since the moment her daughter was born. Bad idea. Bad, bad idea. Everything about him screamed, *Remember!* Every cell in her body obeyed. The nose once too big, the cleft once too deep, the smile always and still crooked had settled themselves into the face of a man nowhere near as attractive as Enzo—*my darling Enzo. Forgive me. Please! Forgive me*—but infinitely more desired.

"No," she said. "Of course I'm not."

"I shouldn't have come."

"Don't go." Had she screamed it? Inside her head, she had. No one seemed to be looking their way. Yet. "Fifteen minutes. Meet me outside behind the garage."

Cecilia didn't wait for a response but made a show of excusing herself by telling Aldo to enjoy the party, and scurried off in any direction that wasn't his. She was already sweltering in the fur stole but kept it with her anyway. In fifteen minutes, when everyone was busy eating and complimenting Mama on her culinary prowess, Cecilia would be out behind the garage in need of protection against the cold, a shield against the past.

Mama usually made people go outside to smoke. She hated the smell and how it made her lace curtains dingy. She especially hated cigar smoke—like rotten eggs burning in wet newspaper—but the Christmas party was the one exception she made. Guests dressed up in their finest shouldn't have to go outside to smoke like dogs needing to take a piss. At least, that had been Daddy's argument and, for once, he'd won.

That's how it was now. Whatever Maria Antonette Giancami wanted, she got, if it was in his power to give it. And Mama never asked for anything just to get her way. Wherever he'd been, whatever had happened to him, it changed them both so profoundly it made Cecilia weep to think about. It made it all the more important that she never disappoint them, that she live up to their expectations, their love, and the love they showered on her little family.

And yet there she was, in the burlap-covered rose garden behind the garage, shivering in the white fox stole that had cost a
fortune, though nothing even close to the ermine Tressa wore. The
young woman had said something about Aldo cooking for officers
and dignitaries on a ship in the Mediterranean; had he struck it
rich? Did that happen in the navy? No, that couldn't be it. He'd
only been serving for five years, in any case. Maybe he'd married
well. A general's daughter. Did they have generals in the navy?
Cecilia had no idea. Or maybe Aldo was a criminal, like her father
no matter how kind he'd become. Could that be why he went by
the name Al DiViello? Was it a gangster name? Or a name to hide
his criminal activities?

"I knew you'd be even more beautiful than I remembered."

Cecilia spun, nearly turning an ankle in her stiletto pumps. Oh,
how exquisite he was, standing in the scant light of moon, stars,
and Christmas lights trimming the garage. He came closer, his
shoulders dipping, and Cecilia felt his embrace before he took her
into his arms.

He buried his face in her hair. "You smell the same." And he
kissed her lips, her cheeks, her throat, her lips again.

The years careened backward and she was seventeen again,
making love in a rented room in Motel on the Mountain, saying
good-bye, still full of hope that everything would work out. Somehow. Cecilia wept but she met him kiss for kiss. "You taste the
same."

Aldo pulled back, grinned that lopsided grin, and bent his head
to hers. The raw desperation lingered underneath the slow, deliberate teasing of lips and tongues, tempered but not tamed. His
hands slid down her back, pressed hips to his. She felt him,
familiar and foreign, swell against her.

"I've been playing it out in my head all day, and it happened just
like I imagined." He took her face in his hands, and suddenly let
them fall. "This is so fucked up. You have no idea."

"What are you doing here?"

Stepping away from her, he pulled a cigarette case from his
tuxedo jacket, offered her one. He lit his, hers. "Where do I start?"

He exhaled a plume of smoke. "When your father knocked me down today and insisted I come to the party so he could make it up to me? Or back in 1954 when he tried to kill me but I killed him instead?"

Cecilia stood over her son's crib, her hand on his little back. Gentle rise, whispering fall. Up. Down. Sweet and astounding. Tiny as he'd been at birth, he was a chubby baby now. Healthy. He'd turned over early, and even showed signs of walking already.

She remembered Patricia at ten months old, could conjure it as if it were just last week. Unlike Frankie's smattering of duck fuzz, she had so much hair by then. Long. Thick. Wavy, but not curly. Just like Tressa's. Patsy's sweet disposition finally made sense, too. Tressa enchanted. Everyone. Even Cecilia. Even her father, so devoted to her mother. It had been because of her that Daddy'd invited Aldo after knocking him down. It had been because of her Aldo was in Paterson again to begin with. It was because of her Cecilia's life was suddenly coming apart at the seams, even if she was the only one who knew it.

The undigested, indigestible truths Aldo told still whirred above her head, just out of reach. She still had no idea where Daddy had been all those weeks, probably never would. But others did. Would any of them know the part Aldo played? Did Daddy? Was the cordial manner an act to lure him close enough to kill? Cecilia shook that off as quickly as it came at her. The answer was unequivocally no. Dominic Giancami lacked the sophistication. He'd always been brute force, not calculated wise guy. A man, then and now, quite capable of killing Aldo for fucking his daughter.

What would she have done back then? If Aldo came to her and confessed what had happened? What would have become of him? Even through the whirring confusion, Cecilia knew someone would have ended up dead. Or worse. Enzo's wife, Patricia and Frankie's mother, understood that everything had turned out in the best way possible, for everyone concerned. And still she stood over her infant son's crib reliving forbidden kisses, and wishing . . .

"There you are." Enzo closed the door quietly and came to stand beside her. "I saw the sitter downstairs."

"I thought she'd like to get some food before it was all gone. Besides, I needed a breather."

He put his arm around her shoulders. Cecilia leaned into him. Enzo smelled like Aldo, like the cologne she bought every Christmas and put in her husband's stocking. Or was it Aldo who smelled like Enzo now? Tears stung.

"He sure is beautiful, isn't he?" Enzo whispered.

Cecilia nodded.

"Sleeps like a log."

"Thank goodness. We got lucky with both of them."

"We certainly did."

Had he paused too long? Cecilia's heart stuttered. Her fried nerves sizzled and fizzed. She tried to breathe normally, told herself there was no way he could possibly know. It was those fried nerves, the stuttering pulse making her sense a pause that meant something ominous.

A gentle knock sent Enzo to the nursery door. The young lady they'd hired to watch over their son slipped into the room, a big piece of chocolate cake in one hand, a book in the other. "Thank you," she whispered. "I really appreciate it, but I got all I want from the party. Too much noise for me."

"Understood." Enzo chuckled softly. Easy and unaffected. Dear Enzo. He, too, would rather be cloistered in the nursery with a book and a piece of chocolate cake. Of course he didn't suspect a thing. His love for her, for their children, prohibited anything so base. Cecilia sucked down his calm, let it fill her. Or tried.

Enzo waved her away from the crib and together they left the nursery. At the top of the stairs, Cecilia grasped the railing, halting in her tracks. What little composure she'd gathered already seeped out of her ears, her pores. He was still down there. She could hear Tressa's musical laughter even over all the unruly Jersey Italians. Or maybe she was just tuned in to it.

"Something wrong?"

Cecilia caught Enzo's face in her hands and pulled him to her lips. Soft. Familiar. Yes, get the taste of Aldo out of her mouth. Longer, more sensually. Enzo was quick to arouse, and thankfully quick to soothe. She unbuckled his belt, undid the button and zipper, and slipped her hand inside. Enzo pressed her up against the wall. Cecilia let him feel her curves, savor the tender places behind her ear, her throat, between her pushed-up breasts. His breathing hitched. His muscles jerked. He leaned more heavily against her and relaxed. Cecilia bit her lip to keep from crying.

"You're something else." Hot breath on her neck. Enzo stood straighter, handed her his handkerchief, and tucked himself in. "What was that for?"

"Do I need a reason?" She cleaned her hand. "I like to live a little dangerously."

"You used to." Enzo took her tenderly into his arms. She tried not to flinch. If he noticed, he didn't show it. "It's been a while."

"We have sex all the time."

"But not like that." He sniffed at her lips, grinning. "You been drinking?"

Cecilia managed a small, nervous giggle. "Only a little."

"I've missed this, and didn't even know it until just now."

"A hand job in the hallway?"

"No." Enzo kissed her as tenderly as he held her. "Your wild side."

Cecilia lowered her lashes. *Oh, darling, don't miss that girl. She's up to no good.* "Maybe you'll get lucky again later on, if the party doesn't go too late."

"I got lucky when I was a dopey twelve-year-old. Luckiest guy in the world."

She balled the sticky handkerchief in her fist and stepped out of his arms. "Go on down, darling," she said. "I want to change my shoes. These are killing me."

"I can wait."

"Don't be silly. Go. I might be a few minutes. You've shifted things a bit. I have to make some lady adjustments, too."

Enzo waved over his shoulder.

"Put a cannoli aside for me," she called after him.

Slumped against the wall, she kicked off her heels, wiggled feeling back into her toes. What a mess. What a thrilling mess. All
because a young woman wanted to see the brother she hadn't in far
too many years.

Aldo's hands and lips and tongue chased Enzo's over her body;
or did Enzo's chase Aldo's? Cecilia closed her eyes and conjured
the two, one on either side of her, worshiping her in such different
ways. Aldo's intensity. Enzo's tenderness. One made the Cecilia
behind her eyes cry out, the other made her softly moan. Why
could she not have them both? Was it so wrong? Really?

She thought of Trudy, suddenly, wondered what had become
of her after Daddy banished her from their lives. What had changed
him? How had he let go of that love he'd fallen into—if rumor
had it right—before marrying Mama? She couldn't ask him. Ever.
Couldn't ask her mother. She was on her own.

Cecilia went to the room that used to be hers in the house on
Derrom Avenue, into the bathroom still with pink tiles and lace
curtains. She rinsed the handkerchief in the sink, hung it on the
towel bar to dry. Something was awake in her now, something
that had been sleeping since Patricia was born and Enzo made his
choice. It was yawning and stretching and bearing its sharp teeth.
And it would not go back to sleep again. Not even if Aldo left before she returned to the party and she never saw him again. Cecilia
wouldn't let it, because Enzo wasn't the only one who missed her
wild side, and she hadn't known until it walked through the front
door.

Bar Harbor, Maine

JULY 9, 1999

❦

Some secrets stay secrets for a reason.
—CORNELIUS TRAEGAR

At odds. That's what Alfonse was. More and more lately. Especially since Raymond Switcher inserted Enzo into Cecilia and Aldo's tale. Longer stretches between writing, longer stretches to think about Aldo and his great love for a girl who married another man and the turns that might be taken while in someone else's hands. Alfonse found himself with more time than he was comfortable spending with his own thoughts. That had never been a good thing. Not when he was a schoolboy in Italy, always having his knuckles rapped. Not when he was a young man in America trying to find his way in a culture not his own. Goodness knows, not now that he was an old man with far too many things to regret.

Sometimes he'd wander to the gathering room or the library, chat with old acquaintances, old lovers, avoiding Olivia like the plague. Other times he'd seek out the comfort of her and harass her just for fun. There were daily sessions with Dr. Kintz, who really had only polite conversation to make with a man dying a little bit every day. And Switch. There was always Switch. But the man had never been the talkative type, and Alfonse had yet to master that gentle brand of exchange without words.

And then there were times like now, alone in the dining room, early even for the early birds. Time and thoughts rumble-jumbling. Misbehaving. Malcontent. Alfonse made slow circles on the white linen with the tip of his finger. White linen, a grand dining room, crystal chandeliers sparkling in early evening light. How many banquets had he attended? Award dinners? As master of ceremonies, as recipient, as one of the who's-who crowd. He conjured the endless black-tie affairs that led to momentary, luscious liaisons. He could not count his lovers, even if he would do something so banal. There'd been more women than men; that much he recollected. There had been little curiosity. Men held no real mystery. Their baser desires, their secret needs. Alfonse had them, too. Lust, done and thank you very much, as far as his experience went.

But the women—how he worshiped every one of them. For a half hour, a night, a week or two. Ceaselessly mystifying. Each body uniquely perfect. Not a single one able to satisfy him in the same way the nameless, faceless men did. Not a single one of them as loved as his first. Heaven forgive him, not even Olivia. There was only one Cornelius.

And now there was Cecibel, most mystifying of all, because Alfonse Carducci could be no one's lover, could not worship her in that way.

He'd seen her, of course, since the night of July 4. Alfonse saw her every day. In the dining room. In the halls. Each afternoon at precisely four twenty. She was always and in all ways Cecibel. Sweet. Awkward. Guarded even with him. And yet he could not shake the carnality of dreams sparked by her words of love, by her fingers entwined with his.

It had been many years since the last time he'd been anyone's lover, slightly fewer since he'd been his own. Anything even close to orgasmic could well do him in completely. It wasn't sex he wanted—oh, well, yes. He did, actually, but—and he already had her love, her respect, her fangirly worship. What he wanted and didn't have from Cecibel Bringer was more elusive and harder to define. It had something to do with his own mortality, and how she, somehow, kept it at bay.

The sensation manifested in a tightness across his chest that didn't lift so much as fade. He'd had heart attacks before, had been perilously short of breath, but this was different. A half-remembered sensation from an unconjurable long-ago whispered between his ears. Too soft to hear. Something darker than affection. Something compelling, but never kind.

"Evening, Alfie." Switch pulled a chair out from their regular table and sat down. He checked his watch. "Barely six o'clock. What're you doing here already?"

"Cecibel had to leave a little early." He grunted. "She has a date of some kind."

"Finlay?"

Alfonse nodded. He pretended to scratch an itch on his chest. "It's good she gets out of here a bit, away from us old folks."

"Maybe. She seems happy here, though."

Switch had always agreeably accepted what he was given. Alfonse let it go. "How are things going with our Enzo?"

"No asking, remember? Olivia'd hang us both." He rubbed at the back of his neck. "But good, Alfie. Real good. I'll be done soon, then it's your turn. I think."

"Thank goodness. My fingers are itching."

"I know the feeling."

"I will admit, I'm envious." Alfonse laughed, caught his breath. Electricity crackled across his shoulder blades. "I'm invested in writing Aldo, but Enzo is . . . he is . . . a nobler . . ."

"Alfonse?"

He waved Switch back into his chair. It would pass. Any moment. "You've created a noble . . . a noble . . ."

The dining room pulsed bright, dark, bright. Switch became a Picasso of facial features and body parts. Alfonse swallowed, smacked his lips. Sound garbled.

Ambulance.

Dr. Kintz.

Electricity coursed from shoulder blades to chest, down arms to fingertips to hair follicles across his scalp.

Alfonse. Hold on.

Help is coming.

No. This was all wrong. It was too soon. They weren't finished.

He wasn't finished. And Cecibel. He couldn't leave without saying good-bye to her. His muse. His golden monster. His wounded Valkyrie.

A hand like crepe paper in his. Soft words floated like a breeze off the sea—*Darling, darling. Don't leave me again. Not yet*—ear to ear. Out again. Droned like bees in a hive, duly smoked. Subdued. Waiting for the smoke to clear.

～

It wasn't a date, but it wasn't a walk on the beach either. Cutoff shorts and a hoodie didn't seem appropriate. Cecibel had worn her sky-blue sundress with the tiny daisies embroidered along the yoke to her visit with Alfonse and saw no reason to change. He loved that dress. And when she braided her hair only to the shoulder, letting the rest cascade in curls to her waist. It made him so obviously and boyishly happy when she made the effort for him. Like he was still young and wild and had all the time in the world. He didn't have to say the words for her to know they were there, just behind teeth and tongue, dancing in his lion's eyes. That, in turn, made her feel far lovelier than she could possibly be, as she was in his eyes.

Grabbing the white hoodie from her closet, she avoided the woman in the mirror. Finlay didn't care how she looked. It was a relief to step off of Alfonse's pedestal and back to solid ground. Hood up, zippered to the neck despite July's sticky heat, she dashed out the door.

Already after seven. Where had the time gone? She'd even cut her time short with Alfonse and had earned her first pout. He'd get over it, of course, though it tickled her heart to thumping. Alfonse Carducci, somehow affected by her absence. How did such a thing happen? In what world had she fallen into that she would even meet the man let alone become dear to him in any way? In what world did such a thing ever matter to her?

"Hey, sorry I'm late." She trotted the last few yards to Fin's car. "We're still good, right? It's only a few minutes into town."

"We're good." Fin opened the car door for her. "I bought our tickets yesterday anyway."

"You did?" Cecibel got in, pulled her skirt out of the way of the closing door.

Fin got in on his side. "I got nervous about it selling out. I have to see this one on the big screen."

"You're a real *Star Wars* dork, huh?"

"Nerd," he corrected. "Big difference between dorks and nerds. Trust me."

Cecibel put on her seat belt. "I was thirteen when it came out. I still remember seeing it in the theater for the first time. Video just doesn't cut it, far as I'm concerned."

"I saw them all in prison," Finlay told her. "First one came out when I was in juvie, last one when I was in Bolduc. We got some good movies in. They was pretty good about that. Old, of course. They showed all three of them the summer before I got out. Like nothing I ever seen before. Or since, I guess. I used to be in the theater first day of whatever new movie came to town. Not anymore, though."

"Me either." And she let it go at that. She'd seen all three movies in theaters, the moment they came out. With Jennifer. It was their thing. They had to see each movie at least three times. Popcorn. Twizzlers. Huge, sugary colas. And the Indiana Jones movies, too, because they were both obsessed with Harrison Ford. Except for *The Last Crusade;* they only saw that once. Because Jennifer had shown up wrecked. By then, it was a given.

Familiar roads into town turned unfamiliar the moment they crossed into the village center. Cecibel didn't recall it being so busy. Where did all the shops come from? The restaurants? Spotting locals wasn't difficult when the tourists were so obvious, but they were vastly outnumbered. She tried to remember the last time she was in town, and couldn't.

Fin parked behind the theater, opened the car door for Cecibel, and offered her a hand. She took it even if she didn't need his help. It was good to see that prison hadn't robbed him of the small niceties. Cecibel couldn't imagine spending half her teens and twenties locked away from the world. Or could she? The bars of her prison were powdery white, not metal, but they were real enough.

She insisted on buying the popcorn and soda, since he'd bought the movie tickets. Fin argued but she won. They took seats in the back of the theater that smelled of coming rain, imitation butter, and stale sugar. Cecibel kept her hoodie on and up, thanking the air-conditioning gods for their brutal obedience to winter. Chit-chatting while the theater filled, she relaxed, even laughed when Fin pointed out the dorks (not nerds) who came in costume, bran-dishing plastic lightsabers. The lights went down. The horns blared that familiar *blaat*. Yellow words scrolled. Cecibel's hopes rose. Another masterpiece about to become beloved.

"Let's never speak of it again."

They sat in the car, in the lot behind the theater, damp from the raindrops they'd tried to run between.

"Agreed," Fin said. "The fight sequence was kind of cool, though."

"And the score was beautiful. But still . . ."

"Yeah. Wish I could undo the last couple of hours, remember the old ones without . . . whatever that was."

"There's no going back to such innocent times, young Padawan. We've been tainted beyond redemption."

Fin chucked her shoulder. "Funny." He started the car, pulled out of the lot. Bar Harbor sparkled. The wet streets. Every raindrop reflected in headlights. Rain cooled the temperature, freshened the humidity to a balmy thing that beaded on skin like dew. Ceci-bel opened the window once they reached the edge of town. She leaned out just enough to catch the wind and didn't pull back her hoodie, exposing the monster to the quiet, wet darkness.

"I could drop you off closer to the main entrance." Fin slowed at the head of the Pen's long driveway. "Everyone has to be asleep by now. It's after ten."

"Sure. That'd be great. Thanks."

Finlay pulled up the grand drive and around to a lesser-used en-trance. "Tonight was great, wasn't it? I mean, except for the movie sucking."

"It wasn't that bad." She laughed softly. "It was a nice night. Thanks."

"Thanks for coming with me. I don't like to go into town alone. Never know who you're going to run into."

"You still have"—family? friends?—"people here?"

He shrugged.

"Fin?"

"My mom," he said. "Dad died while I was away. My brother left before I got out. Any friends I had?" Another shrug. "Don't got those no more."

"Do you see her? Your mom, I mean. Is that okay to ask?"

"I see her. Holidays. My birthday. It ain't her. It's me. I stay away, for her sake. She stays in Bar Harbor for mine. Let's not spoil the night with all that shit, okay?"

"Okay. Sorry."

"Don't say sorry." Fin smiled. He tucked damp tendrils behind her ear. Her good ear. The one that didn't look like a broken snail shell nevertheless exposed by the breeze she'd allowed to blow back her hair. Cecibel grabbed the end of her braid, to tug it into place, but Fin's hand stopped hers midreach. "Don't," he said. "Just leave it be."

Her belly lurched. Fin didn't let go her hand. He used it to draw her closer. The other hand cupped her cheek, the fair one not the foul. "Wild Tatterhood." His breath on her face. His mouth on hers. He tasted like cola and imitation butter.

Three sharp raps on Fin's hood startled them apart. "Knock it off, you two. Dr. Kintz wants you. Now!"

Sal's massive frame silhouetted Finlay's window. Cecibel's lurching belly threatened to make good. She tugged her hair into place, pulled up her hoodie, and nearly fell out of the car in her haste to be free of it. "What's wrong?"

Sal steadied her. "You don't want to know, sugar. Just come on."

"It's simply unacceptable." Dr. Kintz paced back and forth in his office.

Fin stood protectively beside her, stone-faced. "I've never had to sign out before."

"That has nothing to do with anything, Mr. Pottinger. House rules state no resident comes or goes without signing in and out, that includes resident staff. In light of what happened here tonight, I'm sure you can understand why that is necessary."

Cecibel trembled. *Alfonse, I'm so sorry.*

"I don't see what either of us could've done for Mr. Carducci," Fin said. "Or what his . . . episode has to do with you knowing we was in town."

"Be that as it may, the rules are clear and you are to abide by them. If you want to leave here, you need to sign out."

"You mean we need permission."

Dr. Kintz's lips pulled back over his teeth. "You can view it any way you like as long as you abide by the rule. Are we clear?"

"No, we're—"

Cecibel grabbed Fin's hand. "We're clear, Dr. Kintz."

"Good." He relaxed. Slightly. "Thank you, Miss Bringer. You two may go."

Fin tugged on her hand.

"You go," she whispered. "I want to ask Dr. Kintz something."

"See you tomorrow for our walk?"

She nodded. Fin smiled, narrowed his eyes at Dr. Kintz, and left.

"Can I help you, Cecibel?"

Now it was "Cecibel"; a good sign. "I just wanted to know what happened to Al . . . Mr. Carducci. Is he all right?"

"He will be. Or, as good as can be expected. His blood sugar went too low."

Her skyrocketing blood pressure slowed. "Oh, then it wasn't his heart."

"It's always his heart in some way, shape, or form." Dr. Kintz sat on the edge of his desk. His shirt was rumpled. His eyes were red and rimmed. There was more worry than anger about him and, no matter what Fin thought of his rules, she understood them well enough.

"You're very close to him, I hear."

Cecibel lowered her gaze. "Don't take too much of the nurses' gossip to heart."

"I'm smarter than that." He smiled. He had a good smile, one that crinkled the corners of his eyes. "Mrs. Peppernell mentioned you'd been spending more time with Mr. Carducci than with her lately."

"I don't mind. I love her dearly, but she is a bit possessive." Cecibel shrugged deeper into her hoodie. "She complains but she's happier than I've ever seen her, thanks to Mr. Carducci." *And the words he set free for her.*

"I've noticed. And the car-crash fantasy seems to happen less often," Dr. Kintz added. "It's either Mr. Carducci or the new strain of marijuana Mr. Switcher grew for her."

"You know about that, huh?"

"Of course."

Cecibel met his gaze. "You said 'fantasy.' Did you mean dream?"

"No. It's not a dream. It's something more conscious. A coping mechanism. We all have them. It's intriguing, really. Conjuring control we needed at one time and didn't have."

"By fantasizing a car crash?"

"A car crash she orchestrates, versus a violent event she couldn't control."

"Oh. I see." Cecibel tugged her braid, still damp from the rain. Her own preoccupation with Olivia's dream—fantasy—was no mystery. She didn't even have to close her eyes to conjure the metal-bending impact. It made sense she'd focus on Olivia's figurative rather than her literal. She could ask Dr. Kintz, if she dared go down that road, the one Dr. Marks had failed to lead her onto because of all her kicking and screaming.

"How long will he be in the hospital?" she asked instead. "Mr. Carducci."

"He's still here in his rooms. Far more comfortable for him. But he won't be taking any visitors for a couple of days. Of course"—he winked—"you're an orderly, so I imagine you'll be looking after him in the interim."

"Mustn't shirk my duties." The corner of her lip twitched. She hid it behind her hand. "I'm really sorry about tonight. Except for walks on the beach— Oh, is that okay? Walking the beach?"

"The beach is ours. You're fine." Dr. Kintz put both hands on her shoulders. Cecibel tried hard not to flinch, and failed. He let them fall. "Please understand, it's a simple matter of security, and safety. You, Finlay, and Salvatore are like the bricks and mortar of this place. Without you here, it might well fall apart."

Sal. Who left constantly. Without ever mentioning signing in or out. Or telling her she was supposed to.

"Well, I guess it's getting late," Cecibel said. "Good night, Dr. Kintz."

"Good night, Miss Bringer. Remember, my door is always open should you need anything."

Cecibel nodded and left him rumpled and exhausted, leaning against his desk. She really did like Dr. Kintz, far better than the last two doctors heading up the Pen. They didn't care much about their patients, as long as they stayed medicated and out of trouble. Whatever rules Dr. Kintz referred to had never been enforced before. Maybe he didn't even know Sal left to do his drag shows almost every weekend.

But of course he did. Sal—Miss Wispy Flicker—made a show of parading through the dining room whenever he had a gig. He embodied a fine balance of Shelley Winters, Carmen Miranda, and Liberace, with all the grace of Gene Kelly thrown into the mix. There was no *not* noticing him, and that was the whole point. Whatever his past, he'd come by his present honestly, fabulously, and proudly. And yet he claimed Dr. Kintz, who sought nothing but the truth and well-being of everyone in the Pen, put him on probation because of his alter ego.

It was getting close to eleven o'clock. Might as well be two. Residents typically in bed by nine and up with sunrise slept like the dead. If they didn't, there was medication for that, freely given by staff who worked the night shift for the peace and quiet of it. Only the safety lights illuminated the hallways of the Pen, from the ground up. A muted sunrise. The dining room was pitched in darkness even darker for the rainy night.

Cecibel stood in the doorway, arms crossed against the chill seeping into her skin through clothes still damp. Something wriggled through her, something she didn't much like. Suspicion. Understanding. Curiosity mingling, swirling like cotton candy. Sticky, like a web.

She backtracked to Dr. Kintz's office, already dark, past it to the door she knew led to the basement. Locked. Of course. She pulled her ring of keys from her pocket, careful to keep them quiet even though she was more likely to run into Cornelius Traegar's ghost than any living person.

Flashlights, plugged in and always charged, lined the wall at the top of the stairs. Plucking one from its holder, Cecibel breathed in deeply. Musty. Dusty. As all basements were. This one was a cavern she'd rarely descended into. Wine cellar. Winter larder. Storage cubicles. Ancient, undiscardable furniture no one wanted. More than likely a fortune in antiques and kitsch from bygone days; literary memorabilia and random souvenirs postmodern anthropologists would orgasm over. And the records room where, whether chart or file, Cecibel hoped to find whatever part of her past Dr. Kintz had access to.

It wasn't locked. There was no need when the entrance was. The records were categorized by year first, name second, an inefficient system no one had changed since the beginning, when it made more sense. The chances of anyone digging through such information was far too slim to worry over. As far as she knew, Cecibel wasn't breaking any rules, not even one she didn't know about. She was entitled access to her own medical or employment records anytime she wished. Asking Dr. Kintz wasn't an option; not unless she wanted to get into things with him. Which she didn't.

The records room was a grotto within the vast cavern under the Pen. The oldest records, dating back to 1949, took center stage along the far rear wall, the years reaching out from there like too many fingers on a hand.

1955.

1968.

1973.

Cecibel followed the years to 1990, the year she left the facility farther south, against Dr. Marks's recommendation, and started working at the Bar Harbor Home for the Elderly.

Nothing.

Nineteen eighty-seven. The year of the accident that might not have been an accident at all.

Nothing.

But what she did find, because it was sticking out a little, as if recently returned to its space, was Finlay Pottinger's file. Nineteen eighty-five. The year he came to the Pen as a handyman's assistant. Twenty-six years old (Fin was older than she thought) and fresh from Bolduc prison in Warren, Maine. Medical records and psychiatric history dating back to his teens, to the trial that sent him away for nine years. Nothing she didn't know, including the fact that Dr. Traegar hired him personally. A typewritten letter from the prison warden confirmed it.

> . . . good behavior.
> . . . shining example to the other men.
> . . . paid the price for his actions with grace and humility.

The flashlight dimmed. Cecibel gave it a good shake. It flickered before burning bright again.

> It is with Dr. Plesanti's recommendation I send him to you, satisfied he will be well cared for and gainfully employed in an institution safe for both him and society. I thank you for taking an interest in your hometown boy. He deserved far better than he got . . .

Safe. For both him and society.

Words made a difference. Olivia and Alfonse, Switch and Judi had taught her that in the notes and scribbles within the margins of the brown notebook. Dr. Plesanti wrote *in* an institution, not *by* one. Not simply *employed*, but *cared for*.

Cecibel closed the file, slipped it back into place. Completely, and not haphazardly as it had been. A rule broken, certainly, but she would never tell. Her thoughts scrambled, she tried to remember when Sal had come to work at the Pen and knew only that it was before her, around the same time Fin had.

She found him in 1986. Another broken, unspoken rule. Salvatore Ramos. Hired as an orderly. Became on-site manager in 1992. Performance reports. Probation warnings for minor infractions like Mr. Gardern getting into the toilet paper. The only medical records were from the bronchitis he was susceptible to, and a sprained ankle in 1996. The only personal information was his stage name—Wispy Flicker—written in red pen and circled with a heart.

The flashlight dimmed again. This time it didn't brighten when Cecibel shook it. Slipping Sal's file back into place, she hurried out of the grotto, to the caverns, to the steps like a mountain rising out of the depths. She slammed the flashlight back into the charger, caught her breath, steadied her nerves.

Three resident staffers, two of whom were required to sign in and out, and one who was—she was pretty certain—not.

In not by.

Employed and cared for.

What words hid in her file—chart?

She stepped over the threshold and into the peaceful night, closed the door and locked it. Her missing file, Fin's found one, and Salvatore's. Alfonse's blood-sugar episode. Dr. Kintz. The kiss, the rain, the movie she and Fin would never speak of. She left thoughts like a breadcrumb trail through the hallways of muted sunrise until, reaching her room, she closed the door on all of them.

Cecibel changed into pajamas, brushed her teeth, her hair, and didn't look once in the mirror. She wished for the sleeping aid so freely given to ancient patients; no one worried about addiction as long as it made them sleep through the night. And then she cried into her pillow because such a thought woke the ghost she'd failed to leave outside. One she thought, so foolishly, she'd left behind long ago.

Bar Harbor, Maine

JULY 16, 1999

There are days not even chocolate can make palatable.
                                    —CORNELIUS TRAEGAR

"It's not up to you, Olivia." Alfonse sighed for the hundredth time, a taxing thing for a man with his lung capacity. "Switch says the story leads to Aldo."

"But it could just as easily—"

"Enough now. Darling," he added, and patted her hand for good measure. "I am fine. My blood sugar went low because I was too busy pouting over Cecibel cutting our time together short to eat the afternoon snack I was supposed to. It's been a week. Switch is done with his piece, and now it's my . . . Aldo's turn."

"You are a pigheaded man."

Were those tears in her fiery eyes? Alfonse chanced a darted glance Switch's way, but Switch was again looking at his watch.

"I am, my love." Alfonse picked up her hand and kissed it. "And I'll not be dissuaded. It feeds me, these words of ours. You know that."

"I do." She pursed her lips. "All right. But if you need more time . . ."

"I won't."

"And you better be sure to lead it back to Cecilia."

"As the story dictates. Raymond"—he tapped Switch's arm—"she's not coming. She's forgotten."

"But I just saw her a little while ago. She said she'd be here."

"It might as well have been a month ago. Ten years." Olivia

heaved a deep breath. "It's so sad. To be that young and already losing your mind."

"Don't say that."

"Oh, Raymond, please. Must we stand on nicety, among us?"

"I will bring it up to her later," Alfonse said. "At dinner, perhaps. Ask if she'd like to transpose Switch's chapter now or both mine and his when I'm finished. She's always good about getting it done quickly."

"Have either of you seen the file yet?" Olivia asked. "Not that I'm doubting her abilities, but . . . well, I'm doubting her abilities."

"I have," Switch answered.

"As have I," Alfonse echoed. "She'd show you if you asked, Livy."

"I don't want to see it. Not until it's finished." She took the notebook from Alfonse's lap, caressed the cover. "There's magic here. The hand, the pen—or pencil, in Switch's case—the page. No keyboard, typewriter, or computer will ever be able to capture that magic."

"Only because it's how we started," Switch said. "Ask any new writer and they'll more'n likely tell you otherwise."

"But it's so . . . mechanical."

"I bet that's what the old storytellers said when people learned how to write things down, too." Switch winked. "It's the creative process itself, Livy. The stewing in your brain that brings places, people, and the things they do to life. Not the means of recording it."

"'We are the music makers, and we are the dreamers of dreams . . .'"

A knock at the door turned them all to it. Alfonse checked the time. Four twenty, on the dot. "That'll be Cecibel," he said. "Damn. I wanted you lot out of here by now."

Olivia was already at the door. "Alfonse was just kicking us out," she said. "Oh, Judith. There you are."

"Look who I found." Judith pulled Cecibel into the room. "I thought we could all have tea together."

Cecibel allowed herself to be led, mouthing *I'm sorry.* She was sunshine spreading brilliant fingers to catch him in her hand. Alfonse smiled and shook his head, silently telling her all was well as long as she was there.

Judith gave no sign that she was supposed to have been there an hour earlier. If she noticed Switch, Alfonse, and Olivia already had teacups half-filled with cooling tea, she didn't say. Making cups for both herself and Cecibel, she drew them all into her chattering. The weather. The poorly edited novel her book club had chosen. Switch's lovely garden, and the mint she hoped to beg from him.

Alfonse wished them all away, wanting more than anything to bask in Cecibel's light before taking pen to paper. But he loved them, too, loved their banter, their wit, their memories, and soon he forgot to be vexed.

"Well, if I'm getting dinner, I have to jet." Cecibel pushed off the arm of Alfonse's chair an hour later. She kissed his upturned cheek, then Olivia's. "This was really fun. I've missed it."

"If Alfonse didn't keep you all to himself—"

"Now, now, Olivia. Sheathe your claws. There's enough of me to go around."

"It wasn't you I was lamenting, dear. Such an ego." Olivia patted his hand, then held hers out to Cecibel. "Come, my dear. We can walk to the dining room together. I want to make sure the *poissonier* understands this time that salmon isn't to be cooked through. Barbarian. Honestly, where did he go to school?"

Cecibel took her sunlight with her. Alfonse shivered just a little bit. He'd sit all day alone tomorrow just to be certain he wouldn't have to share her. It was worth a day of boredom. Maybe he'd even get a little writing done. An hour or so in her shared company might just be enough to start.

"Well, goodness, that was a close call, wasn't it?" Judi edged forward in her chair. "I wasn't sure what to do."

Alfonse exchanged a glance with Switch. "Do about what, my dear?"

"Cecibel, of course, and the notebook. Isn't that why we're all here?"

Another exchanged glance, this time a smiling one.

"You're a bit late, Judith," Switch said. "We'd already finished with that by the time you got here."

"Three o'clock, didn't we say?" She looked at her watch. "Oh, dear. I must have read it wrong." Shoulders slumped, but she wagged a finger, grinning elfin all the same. "You thought I forgot."

Switch shrugged. "It happens."

"More often, with me. Well, it was a lovely little time together, wasn't it?"

"It was," Alfonse answered. "Since you are here, would you like the notebook now with only Switch's chapter to transpose? Or after I'm finished? I won't be starting before tomorrow."

"I'll take it now, then, as long as you all still trust me, and have it back to you at breakfast."

"Don't be daft, woman," Switch grumbled. "Of course we trust you."

"Breakfast tomorrow is perfect," Alfonse said, reaching for the notebook on the desk. On the settee? The coffee table? "Where did it go?"

Switch got up, turned over a cushion. Judi checked the sideboard where the electric kettle sat.

"It was here." Alfonse pointed to the side table next to his chair. "Olivia took it from me and set it there."

"Olivia, huh?" Switch arched an eyebrow.

It took a moment, but Alfonse caught on. "Do you think . . . ?"

"Have you ever known her to give up? Ever?"

"Damn, I should have known better."

"I'm a bit lost here," Judith said, "and not because of Alzheimer's."

"Olivia must have swiped it," Switch told her. "There was a little . . . scuffle over who should write next."

"What did the story dictate?" Judith asked. "Aldo or Cecilia?"

"Aldo," Switch answered. "Absolutely."

"Then I'll get it from her at dinner," Judith said. "You'll have it back in your hands tomorrow, Alfonse. Mark my words. No one thwarts an editor on the warpath."

Alfonse let it go at that. Wisely, so did Switch. Easier to let her believe it was a creative difference than have her worry, too, over failing health that was only getting worse.

Switch and Judi left him to get ready for dinner, not that he had anything much to do. He gathered the teacups and set them on the sideboard where housekeeping would take them, clean them, and return them again. It felt good to move around a bit, something he hadn't done much of in the days since he collapsed. Muscles left to atrophy rejoiced rebellion against struggling lungs and heart. Leaning a hand to the window, clutching at the front of his shirt, Alfonse gazed out upon the sunset sky, the reeling gulls, the sea grass buffeted, always buffeted by the ocean wind. And there he saw her, his sunshine, his light, running across the painted landscape of his folly. Braid bouncing. Jacket flapping. Something small and brown clutched to her chest.

Paterson, New Jersey

December 20, 1959

〰️

Enzo

It was impossible not to watch him. The graceful, manly way he moved. A sailor accustomed to rolling his gait to the swell of the sea. His crooked smile, endearing, not gangster. The way he avoided Cecilia while never letting her out of his sight.

Enzo knew him from the moment he walked in the door, his blond and blue-eyed sister only punctuating that sentence with an exclamation point. Cecilia's gasp. The sizzle crackling the air like his good wool suit in winter. If he had any doubts, which he didn't, his wife's ardor on the stairs would have dispelled them. Al DiViello was the one. The man Cecilia imagined when they made love. Patsy's father. The one and only person Enzo Parisi understood completely, because they both had what the other wanted, and could never, ever have.

He'd seen his wife slip out the kitchen door, Al a few moments later, and though his heart crackled around the edges, it didn't split in two. Cecilia loved him, even if she loved their daughter's father, too.

His mother had a plaque hanging in the upstairs hallway—

If you love something, set it free. If it comes back, it's yours. If it doesn't, it never was.

Sunset over the ocean, gulls reeling in the rays. Kind of cheesy, but he'd always appreciated the sentiment when he thought it only applied to kids growing up and leaving home, not his wife leaving him for another man. But the principle held. Enzo was, unlike the beloved-but-nevertheless-Neanderthals who raised him to manhood, evolved enough to grasp that a show of apish jealousy was the only thing that could tip Cecilia's love and loyalty. The past needed to be settled. He'd weather it bravely. His pride had never mattered to him as much as she did.

He watched the kitchen door anyway, sweating in his suit and trying to pretend he was having a good time at his in-laws' party. Enzo hid a choked gasp of relief in his gimlet when she returned too soon and too put together to have engaged in a quickie behind the garage. Still, he didn't dart to her side, but held up his drink and winked when she caught his eye. Strained as her own smile was, it softened her frenzied gaze. She blew him a kiss. Enzo thought he'd cry, but didn't. He wasn't a Neanderthal, but he was still a man.

They rarely stuck together at parties. It had always been their way. Far more fun to mill about, collect gossip, and share it later in bed. Tonight would be no different. If it was, she'd know he knew, and that was the one thing he didn't want to share. Enzo watched Al instead, and Tressa. Mostly Tressa. She was hard to miss, in any case, a snowflake in a swarthy sea. And while many of the women wore red party dresses, no one wore it like Tressa did.

Nicky and Joe left her side only to fetch her another drink, or a tasty morsel from the burdened buffet tables. Enzo's brothers-in-law were handsome boys. Wealthy. Charismatic. And too young. Tressa had to be in her twenties, while neither of them had yet graduated high school. Nicky would, come May. Even if she were his age, she'd be out of his league. Sophisticated, cultured, classy as hell, Tressa could have any man in the place and she knew it.

"That's some tasty dish, eh?" Cami murmured too close over Enzo's shoulder.

He sipped his gimlet. "Nicky and Joe seem to think so."

"I seen you watching her all night. Do I gotta get out the baseball bat?"

"Me?" Enzo faced his father-in-law. "You've got to be kidding me."

Cami tossed back the remainder of his Manhattan, grimaced. "Yeah, I'm kidding you. Mostly. That girl's got nothing on my Cecilia."

"She's a child."

"Twenty-one, her brother says. Nice guy, that Al, eh?"

"I really haven't had the chance to talk to him, but he seems so."

"He used to live around here, before joining the navy."

"You don't say."

"I thought he looked familiar, when I picked him up off the ground today." Cami signaled to the bartender. "Feel like I should remember him or something. I got no fucking memory since I drowned."

"I imagine *nearly* drowning could have that consequence."

The vanishing that rocked the Paterson underworld so hard it tumbled into the quaking rifts. Dominic Giancami's resurrection, only days before his daughter married a minor rival's son, scooped all the rubble into the palm of his massive hand and crushed the family into something new. Something better. Something more solid than it had been since Prohibition. Even as an eighteen-year-old kid, the timing struck Enzo as too perfect to be coincidence. Uncle Cami had never been that smart. If orchestrated, a defter hand than his had done so. But who? And how? In the years since, Enzo found no answers and didn't care enough to search. Everything was as it should be, as far as he was concerned.

Until tonight.

A server brought Cami a fresh Manhattan, neat with a twist of lemon and a cherry. He took a good swig. "I gotta get my boys off that poor girl," he said. "Go over there and say something smart."

"Such as?"

"I don't know. You're the university man."

"And you're the host of the party. You could just tell her you want to introduce her to someone or something."

"You getting smart with me?"

"Uncle Cami, come on."

"Uncle Cami now, eh?" He laughed, elbowing Enzo in the ribs. "Maria made me swear on my balls I wouldn't go near her. Go on. Save the fairy princess. I'll choke the living daylights out of my boys till they get the message to leave her be."

Cami shoved him, gently for Dominic Giancami, in Tressa's direction. Enzo stopped at the bar for another gimlet before doing as he was told. "I've been sent to save you from these two pups," he said. "Nicky, Joe, your dad's about to choke the living daylights out of you for monopolizing Miss DiViello's time."

"Oh, goodness." Tressa touched manicured fingertips to her lovely collarbone. "I wouldn't want you boys chastised on my account."

"Here he comes," Enzo murmured, leaning in. "You better scoot."

"I'm not scared of my dad," Nicky grunted. "I have to see you again, Miss DiViello. I'm not budging until you tell me when and where."

"Nicky, come on!" Joe hauled at his arm.

"Miss DiViello?"

"Tomorrow, at Woolworth's." She giggled. "We'll have a hot cocoa."

"Two o'clock," he called, and allowed himself to be dragged. Cami was right behind his fleeing boys, signaling to the bartender as he passed.

"They really are sweet boys," Tressa said. "So charming and handsome."

"You were very nice to be so tolerant. I'm Enzo, by the way."

"Yes, we were introduced at the door. Cecilia's husband."

"I wasn't sure if you'd remember. It's been a bit crazy in here."

"But fun." She slipped her arm through his. "Thank you for rescuing me. I'm accustomed to masculine attentions, but everyone here is so . . . uninhibited."

"Not like that in the south, huh?"

"It can be," she said. "But not in the social circles I've been kept to. Military, that is. The high-ranking kind. Always so formal and genteel. I like it here."

"But it is overwhelming."

"At first, yes. Would you mind escorting me outdoors? I need a breath of fresh air."

"Certainly. Let me get your stole."

"No need. We'll only be out a moment, and it's rather warm in here."

Enzo led Tressa through the ballroom, to the dining room, and through the French doors leading to the patio decorated with lights, holly, and pine. Music, muted but still quite audible, wove about the tipsy and the amorous swaying to the sound. He hadn't seen Cecilia in a while, but there was Al, leaning on the doorjamb and chatting with a group of young men Enzo remembered from high school but hadn't seen in years.

"It's good to see my brother smile." Tressa let go his arm. "I never knew he was the melancholy kind. He was always smiling in my memory."

"How long has he been in the service?" Though Enzo knew.

"Five years, but this is the first time I've seen him since we were little children."

"Ah, I see."

Tressa laughed, a sound like summer and birdsong. "You're not like the others."

"What makes you say that?"

"Because Dominic and Joseph would have asked why that was so, probably injecting an expletive or two. Would you like to know why?"

"If you care to tell me."

"We're orphans, you see," she said. "Aldo was already a teenager when Mommy and Daddy died, but I was just a bitty thing. My mother's cousin adopted me. They didn't want him and refused to let me see him or even write to him. He went to an orphanage, then lived on his own here in Paterson. When I came of age and into my inheritance, the first thing I did was find him."

"He never tried to find you when he came of age?"

Tressa lowered her lashes, her cheeks pinking.

"I'm sorry. That was buffoonish of me. See? Not so different from Nicky and Joe."

"It's all right." She glanced up, the Christmas lights dancing in her eyes like lightning bugs. "I will confess, I spent most of the year between twelve and thirteen hating him for staying away. I didn't understand why he didn't make the effort when all I did was think about him and wish. Of course, Mama and Daddy wouldn't have allowed it, but I'd have known, at least, that he thought of me. I've come to understand, in the time since then, how painful it all must have been for him. Losing our parents, our brother and sister, and me. Being rejected and left on his own. I don't blame him for putting it all behind him and letting it stay there."

Enzo nodded, sipped his gimlet. "It's good you found him, then. How long before he ships out? The Mediterranean, right?"

"At the end of January, same as me." She giggled. "What I mean is, that's when I go back to school. I'm hoping we can spend the next month together before we both go back to real life."

"How much more schooling do you have?"

"Three semesters." She sighed. "After being up north, I hate the idea of going back to my very southern school in Alabama. I understand you're a Princeton man."

"Nicky and Joe been talking?"

"Oh, anyone I spoke to mentioned it." She waved, all-encompassing. "Everyone is very proud of you and your education."

"I'm the first to attend and graduate any higher-learning establishment," Enzo told her. "It's good to know they're proud."

"Mathematics. I've never been very good with numbers."

"Mathematics is more than numbers. A lot more."

"Forgive me. I should know better. Most people think journalism is just putting a bunch of words together."

"Is that your course of study?"

Tressa nodded. "Do you think it's an unseemly occupation for a woman to pursue?"

"Not at all." But he didn't ask why anyone would think that, being raised by Neanderthals and all. "Princeton has a really wonderful journalism department. Unfortunately, the school doesn't allow female students."

Her red lips tightened. "I came up against that quite a bit. Many schools I applied to wouldn't even let women into their journalism programs. It was frustrating, to say the least."

"But it didn't deter you."

"Absolutely not." She rubbed her arms, gaze going beyond Enzo to her brother. Her eyes narrowed slightly. And then he heard Cecilia's laugh, deep and husky but not quite her own. He turned toward the sound, saw her waylaid by the pack of young men standing with Al, and that the man's eyes devoured her that second before catching Enzo's stare.

"Did you know my brother, back in the day?" she asked.

Enzo blinked until he stopped seeing red. "I'm afraid I didn't. I wasn't one of the popular crowd. Not like Cecilia."

"Then she must have known him." Tressa tilted her head, crossed arms over her chest. "Don't you think?"

"Maybe. I'd have to ask her."

"Maybe you shouldn't."

He blinked again. "Pardon?"

"I'm afraid it's quite colder than I thought," she said. "If you'd like to join your wife, I'll see myself inside."

"A gentleman doesn't leave a lady to pick her way through the hounds." Enzo offered his arm. "May I?"

"Why, thank you, kind sir." Tressa took his arm. She barely nodded at her brother as they passed. But Cecilia watched them, the fox fur Enzo bought her for the party draped around her shoulders. She didn't break away from the group of men, though she did wink. Enzo's crackled heart flaked a trail behind him as he left her on the patio.

"There she is!"

The high-pitched squeal made him wince and thank all the angels in heaven he no longer lived at home.

"Hand her over, Enzo. You, Nicky, and Joe have been hogging her all night."

"My sister, Chrissy," Enzo introduced. "Chrissy, this is Miss DiViello."

"Tressa," she amended. "Pleased to meet you, Chrissy."

"It's short for Christina." Chrissy groaned. "So babyish, don't you think? God, you're so pretty. I love that dress. Did you get it here in town?"

"Meyer Brothers, actually."

"Ooo! My parents would never let me wear anything so daring."

"Neither would mine. Thank goodness they will never know."

Chrissy laughed, a sound as much like music or summer or birdsong as a cat in heat. "She's funny. Don't you think she's funny, Enz?"

"Have you seen Patsy?" he asked her instead, giving Tressa's arm a subtle squeeze. "Tressa wanted to meet her."

"Aunt Maria probably has her somewhere. Poor kid never gets put down to play. I'll find her for you, Tressa. Just wait here. I'll be right back! Don't go anywhere! Promise me!"

Enzo took the same deep breath Tressa did. They laughed together.

"She's quite the little character."

"Where shall we hide you?" Enzo asked. "Coat closet? Bathroom?"

"I have an idea." She took his hand and led him, not to the closet, bathroom, or ballroom, but to the stairs leading to the second floor. Enzo followed behind, slightly stupefied and more than a little alarmed. Closing his eyes, remembering his wife in her fox fur, standing with Al on the patio, he let his awakening, until-now-undiscovered Neanderthal self be led.

"So much quieter up here." She let go his hand. Enzo opened his eyes. Strolling along the hallway, hands clasped behind her back, she studied pictures on the wall. "Your wedding photo?"

Enzo moved in behind her. "Yes, it is."

"So young. You were just babies."

"Cecilia was seventeen. I was nineteen."

"I see."

I'm sure you do. Everyone does. "Our marriage was arranged when we were little kids. It's my good fortune I've loved her almost as long."

"That's sweet." Tressa smiled over her shoulder. God in His

merciful heaven, she was beautiful. "Mama and Daddy tried to arrange a marriage for me, too."

"Tried."

Her soft laughter hit Enzo in the groin.

"Tried and failed. I will marry for love or not at all." She moved farther down the line of photos. "Oh, this must be Patricia when she was an infant."

"Not even a year old, there." He pointed to another. "That's her last Christmas. She wasn't quite four yet."

"So now she's nearly five?"

"In March."

"I see."

Enzo's insides quivered. "Yes, Cecilia was pregnant when we got married." *With your brother's child. But she's mine. Mine.*

"I wasn't going to ask."

"I could see you doing the math."

Tressa spun to face him, steadied herself on his chest, and didn't pull away once she'd caught herself. Marquis-cut sapphire, her gaze, it singed his face from jaw to lips, lips to nose to brow, blazing in his eyes like sunlight on ice. "Numbers fuddle me completely, Mr. Parisi."

"Enzo."

"Enzo." His name. Honey on her lips asking, so politely, to be licked off.

He put his hands in his pockets. "I get the feeling nothing fuddles you, Tressa. Ever."

Fingers like ivory piano keys straightened the lapels of his jacket. A red fingernail traced the line of his jaw, his lips. Nip her finger. Kiss parted lips. Bend to that creamy, dreamy shoulder and leave a claiming mark. She wouldn't scream and slap his face. Tressa would blaze brilliant under his touch, against his kiss. Enzo could almost feel the heat of it, and he'd more than earned the fall from grace.

"Tressa, I—"

"In another time and place," she said, "you're the kind of man I could fall for, Enzo Parisi. Intelligent. Educated. Well-mannered and just a little wild. Handsome, too. You're very handsome, did you know?"

"My . . . my wife thinks so."

Again, soft laughter kicked him in the groin.

"Cecilia, yes. I think I will grow quite fond of her. She's a pistol, as my granny used to say. Yes, quite fond. It's fitting, I think." She backed away. "It must be getting late. It's time my brother and I go. If I'm to meet Nicky at Woolworth's tomorrow, I need my beauty sleep."

She needed no such thing, of course. Relief chased shame set free by the distance Tressa put between them. And he'd thought himself somehow more evolved than the beloved Neanderthals? What did it say about a man who could hold jealousy in check, but barely survive lust?

"Would you fetch my purse and stole?" she asked. "I believe the coatroom was full when we arrived and they put them up here on a bed."

"Okay. Sure. Wait here." Enzo darted down the hall to Aunt Maria and Uncle Cami's room, where coats and bags and stoles were piled high on their bed. His hands shook. His arousal eased. Already his brain sorted through the whys of how Tressa could affect him so primally. Beauty aside, it didn't take a genius to figure out the less obvious aspects. In the end, he'd done nothing to be ashamed of.

But you would have, had she kissed you.

Spotting Tressa's white ermine was easy enough. Her beaded clutch was tucked inside. Underneath it was a man's coat with a navy insignia on the sleeve.

"Let me help you with that." He draped the fur stole over shoulders at least as soft and nearly as white. "I got your brother's coat and hat as well."

"Thank you, Enzo. You're very kind." Tressa snapped open her clutch, pulled her wallet from inside.

"No tipping, thanks," he tried to joke, but she only pursed a smile at him and shuffled through the contents.

"This is for you." She tucked something small and square and paper alongside the handkerchief in the breast pocket of his jacket. "Don't peek until I'm gone. Promise me."

"Um . . . sure?"

"That's not a promise, sir."

"All right. I promise."

"I believe you." She patted the pocket. "And don't let anyone else see it. You'll thank me, I swear to you."

"Okay, okay. You're confusing the hell out of me, Tressa."

"Just what a girl loves to hear from a handsome man." She giggled, once again the girl who'd enchanted Nicky and Joe all evening. "I'll be in touch. Good night, Enzo. Thank you for rescuing me. Twice."

She grabbed him by the back of his head, stood on tiptoe, and kissed his lips. Twiddling her fingers, she left him in the upstairs hallway, outside his son's nursery. The sway of her hips, subtle. The turn of her heel, like magic. And the back of her neck, that luscious neck, taunting him with what he hadn't tasted. He wanted, damn it all to hell, he did. Al and Tressa DiViello walked through the door, into all their lives, and Enzo was no longer a man he recognized. How quickly everything changed. How delicately balanced their lives had been. And he'd never once suspected.

Taking out the bit of paper—a flimsy photo like the kind from a photo booth and not the expensive portraits lining the hall—he broke his promise to her. Enzo stumbled, looked closer at the little girl in the picture. The child that could be Patricia given another year or two. The likeness was not just uncanny, but exact.

And the little boy. Dark hair and eyes. Smiling. Holding his kid sister in sturdy, little-boy arms. On the back, in faded script—

Aldo and Tressa Wronski
Coney Island, June 3, 1944

Bolting for the stairs, he nearly fell over himself and down them. At the door, Tressa and her brother, Aldo—Wronski, not

DiViello—were being waved off by Uncle Cami and Aunt Maria, Nicky and Joe. And Cecilia. His Cecilia.

No one seemed to see him. Only Tressa, who cocked her head to the side and winked before walking out the door with the secret he and she now shared. Close as a kiss, and just as dangerous. Theirs, and theirs alone, because he'd broken the first promise he made to her, but he'd never break the second.

Bar Harbor, Maine

❧

Spring is short. Summer, slightly longer.
We linger long in autumn, but winter?
Winter passes all too quickly into the night that never
ends.

—CORNELIUS TRAEGAR

Skipping dinner was never a good idea, not when one had an appetite like hers. Voracious, her mother used to say, happily doling out a second helping, or a third. Cecibel had always been solid but never chubby. An athlete who didn't necessarily like sports, but was good at them. Like her dad. But Jennifer? She'd been small and curvy, like Mom. Prone to dramatics, like Mom. Cute little button of a girl, like Mom. Jen had always envied Cecibel's statuesque beauty. Funny how that happened. Cecibel had secretly wished to be petite, to have a spattering of freckles across her nose and cheeks, along her arms and chest, to have the springy curls her older sister did. She never envied her drama, though. As a kid, Cecibel believed it was an act. A way to get Mom and Dad's attention. To get what she wanted.

But it wasn't.

Jen didn't cry, she shrieked and shook. It took days to calm her. She felt the world more keenly, so deeply. Sunrise could make her weep. Or a piece of music. Or the perfect kiss. Boys didn't break her heart; they shattered her soul. Disappointment over a failing grade or a favorite television program canceled put her in her room—shades closed, lights out, blanket over her head—keening for days. Puberty, the specialists said.

But it wasn't.

Something had broken inside Jennifer Bringer, before she was ever born, and it never fully healed. It let in all the demons as well as every passing, mischievous fairy. Jen was the confetti at a parade, or she was a squall coming in off the ocean. It made her infuriatingly and alternately amazing, worrisome. It made her best loved. Losing her broke all of them in the same, unhealable way Jen had been. Cecibel most especially, most visibly, and most invisibly, too.

"Hey, you're early." Fin flopped down into the Adirondack chair next to hers. He riffled around in his backpack. "Sal said you didn't come in for dinner. I brought you this."

Cecibel took the thermos from him, unscrewed the cap. New England clam chowder. Her favorite. Dear Sal. Such friends, she had. Fin handed her a spoon.

"Thanks. Mind if I eat this before we head down?"

"Go ahead," he said. "Want me to hold your book again?"

The brown leather notebook on her lap still evidenced the water marks of its last stay in Fin's backpack, but she couldn't leave it on the chair. Switch's chapter, still fresh, wandered about inside her head. Jennifer insinuated herself into the party, a witness to everything Cecibel read. *Your friends understand what you never did. Some of us can't be saved.*

"Sure, thanks." She'd get the book to Olivia instead of putting it back while Alfonse had dinner, as she'd planned, giving her the blame she seemed to delight in taking. Cecibel didn't remember actually taking it to begin with, only that Olivia had left with her, so maybe the sly old thing had swiped it after all.

Spooning chowder was easier and less fraught with personal peril than eating a sandwich. Cecibel ate without feeling overly self-conscious. After so many years hiding the monster away, the recklessness of being free often took her by surprise, but she didn't hide her away again. What was the point when everyone knew she was there?

"So . . ."

"Sew buttons," she said around a mouthful of chowder. Bad idea.

Fin handed her a napkin. "Funny. I was thinking, how about we watch a video back at my place after our walk?"

"Video?"

"You know. A movie. I just got the new *Star Trek* flick. Haven't watched it yet."

Cecibel spooned more chowder into her mouth, chewed the tender bits of clam, potatoes, carrots. The food at the Pen tended to be a little bland, but the New England clam chowder was perfect.

"Bel?"

Sal knew how much she loved it. Fin understood it was less perilous for her to eat. She'd snuck into the records room and pried into pasts that weren't hers. She went on a date and kissed a man. Kissed Fin. Her friend who coaxed the monster out of her cage and didn't shy away from her teeth. Cecibel had swiped the notebook from Alfonse—she remembered now, with clarity and not a shred of shame—who looked dead on and didn't see the monster at all. She read Jennifer further out of her brain opening up and opening up, spilling its contents so long locked away. Something once shriveled like a seed had cracked when Alfonse Carducci arrived in the Pen. It had been silently, discreetly spreading green and growing fingers through Cecibel's body so that now she could almost feel the leaves sprouting from her fingertips, toes, the top of her head. Coax it? Or force it back into its split casing?

Screwing the cap onto the thermos—could she? would he?—Cecibel rose from the chair. "I have a better idea," she said, and held out her hand to Fin.

"Don't close your eyes," he'd whispered. No light but whatever scattered in through the open windows. No sound but for frogs and the occasional bird. And their lovemaking, the groans and moans of it. The sweet words. The caught breath. And through it Cecibel's eyes stayed open. Fin's, too, even when his body hitched and he thrust his last, pushing so deep inside her he pricked her soul and spilled her out. Cecibel the monster who'd never. Cecibel the princess fair who had and had and had. Puddling on the mattress beneath them both. For once and momentarily whole.

"You are so beautiful." He kissed her lips so tenderly, the corner that worked to the corner that didn't.

"Don't say what isn't true."

"But it is."

"No, it's not." She turned her head. "Don't pretend, Fin. Not you. You're the only one who sees me. You and maybe Olivia."

"I do see you, Bel." He kissed her again. "I see this"—he touched her fair half—"and this." He fingered her hair. "And this"—her breasts—"and this"—her abdomen—"and this"—between her legs slick with them. "I see this, too." He traced her scars, her ruined ear. "It's not beautiful, but it doesn't make the rest of you ugly either. You could have it all fixed up tomorrow and I wouldn't love you more. And if you never do, I won't love you any less."

Cecibel's heart stitched. "You . . . love me?"

"Of course I do. Don't you . . . do you? Love me?"

A little boy wanting. A grown man needing. The monster and the murderer. What a pair they made.

"I don't know," she said. "I don't know if I'm capable."

"You are, but I won't push it. I won't push this." He gestured to the bed. "Just don't pull away from me."

"I won't. I'll try not to."

Fin sat up in bed, ruffled fingers through his hair. "It's been a long time. For me, I mean."

Of course it had. Monster had never made love. Not once, until now. Had murderer? Caught up in epiphanic resolve, she hadn't even thought. Thank goodness.

He smiled a goofy, just-laid smile. "So . . . you want to watch *Star Trek* now?"

Whatever her afterglow thoughts, Fin's were of much lighter stuff. How did he do it? She would ask, one day. Not now, but soon. Another door opened. Another small and shriveled something cracked. "Set it up." Cecibel tossed aside the sheets. "I'll make popcorn."

Nights in July were often humid no matter how cool the breeze coming in off the ocean. Cecibel wasn't overly fond of July. August was her favorite month, when it was still hot during the day but rarely humid, when nights chirped autumn sounds. Autumn scented. Autumn chilled. A little more than halfway through July, and she was ready for it to be over. Almost. When every passing day gave her one less with Alfonse, she wished it could stay July forever.

Walking the grounds of the Pen alone—she'd asked Fin not to join her—gave her time between his bed and her own to gather perspective, let the world back in. The real world, and not the one she'd spent the last few hours in. But in those hours between one day and the next, perspective bent in fantastic ways, showed her *is* and *might be* were not entirely different things. Cecibel hummed, matching her tune to the *see-see-saw* of crickets and her step with moonlight patches wending through the leaves. It was no longer today, and not yet tomorrow. It was now and she was, for once, content.

All doors were locked at that time of night. Cecibel had to swipe her electronic key. Again dark hallways of muted sunrise. Again the silence whispering. Tonight, it was a tranquil thing rather than a sinister one.

Cecilia and Aldo and Enzo and Tressa walked alongside her, before her, behind her. She felt them there, escaped from the book in her arms. Guiding. Protecting. Speaking their secrets. In her mind's eye, she was Tressa, though not as clever or strong-minded. Who'd created her? Alfonse, she was almost certain but only almost. He made her into his vision of Cecibel, the woman he saw and not the woman she actually was. It was why she loved him, she realized. Her ugliness, her inadequacies did not exist for him. In his eyes, she was the Cecibel she might have been in another version of her life. A fantasy. His. Hers. Only real so long as he was living.

Standing outside his suite, Cecibel didn't remember getting there, didn't remember taking her electronic key coded to every door in the place out of her pocket again. Emergency use only. She swiped the key.

It was quiet, and dark of course. The plush carpeting swallowed any footfall that might have squeaked her intrusion. She only wanted to put the notebook back where she'd swiped it from. No harm. No foul. At least, she told herself those lies.

Cecibel set it down on the coffee table, Alfonse's nighttime view capturing her. The expanse of lawn a negative cast in shades of blue and darker blue. The sea beyond the dunes. The moonglade cutting a silver path upon it. She closed her eyes and heard the rushing hiss, the roll, the boom. Even during those hospital years, Cecibel had never left the sea. It crashed into every day of her life, from babyhood to this moment in Alfonse's silent room.

As she tiptoed back to the door, the mechanical hiss of an oxygen tank halted her midway. The door to Alfonse's bedroom was ajar, the sound coming from there. Of course. He required oxygen while he slept. Soon, around the clock.

He slept on his back, propped up almost to sitting, his head lolled to one side. The oxygen tubes in his nose hooked over his ears and down his chest. Cecibel crept nearer, so close she could see his eyes slumber-fluttering. What did a man like Alfonse Carducci dream? She wished she could see. Instead, she would read. Every word he wrote, even those painful to her now. Cecibel made that pact, standing over the man sleeping.

Her heart stitched. *I've never been in love.* She loved Alfonse impossibly, ridiculously, truly. Did she love Fin? After a lifetime without even the hint of so deep an emotion, Cecibel was awash in too many kinds to name. Love for Olivia. For Sal and Judi and Stitch. Love for Fin, carnal and honest. Love for Alfonse, a fantasy for them both. And Jennifer. How she loved her sister whom she'd long ago banished from thought.

Alfonse took a deeper breath. Eyes fluttered opened to slits. Cecibel stood perfectly still. *You're dreaming,* she told him, thought to thought. *Dreaming, Alfonse. Dreaming.* He reached for her. Cecibel did not move. His fingers jerked. His hand stilled. He reached again. She edged close enough for him to touch her, or push her away.

Alfonse touched her. Through her shirt, then under it. Cecibel gasped but silently. She wore nothing underneath. Fingers that had undone a million buttons flipped open three of hers, then four. He sat up, swung his legs over the side of his bed. Opening her shirt, he buried his face between her breasts. Cecibel arched to him, to his touch, to his mouth and tongue and teeth. The rest of her buttons came undone. He pushed the shirt from her shoulders. It fluttered to the floor. Alfonse sat back, ran his hands up the curve of her waist, to breasts glistening with his spit. His breathing came in ragged, impassioned gasps. On the monitor, his heart rate stuttered. Any moment, the alarm would sound and break the fantastic hours between today and tomorrow like an egg.

Cecibel blinked. Stepped back, and away. Alfonse lay sleeping peacefully, tubes hissing up his nose, hand twitching at his side. The monitor blinking steadily. She snatched her shirt from the floor, a foreign thing in her hand. Puzzling and alarming. All things were possible in dreams.

She dashed from his room as silently as she'd come, out the window, not the door. Dropping to the ground, she listened for any sign she'd been seen. Silent night. Holy night. She ran topless—sea air and humid July salting her skin—to the beach, where she kicked off her shoes, her shorts, and dove into the rumbling sea. Cecibel washed the fantasy from her skin. The reality of Finlay, too. They were men, and she loved them, but she was not theirs. She was no one's. Only hers. Belonging to someone else had never been a good fit for her.

Trudging naked out of the water, Cecibel slicked the hair back from her face. Hiding had never been a good fit either. Dr. Marks had been right about that, about so many things. Wrong about so many others. Maybe it was time to talk to someone. Dr. Kintz welcomed her. Anytime, he said. But she needed to know something first, and now was as good a time as any. Better, in fact, than cruel morning and all its revealing light.

Air-dried and damp-dressed, Cecibel left her feet bare and her hair slicked back. She walked all the way to Dr. Kintz's carriage house near the entrance of the property. It took only four good knocks to get a response. The click of locks unlocking, a muffled "Just a moment." And then, "Cecibel. Miss Bringer. Is . . . What's wrong? Why are you all wet?"

"Am I an employee or a resident here?"

Dr. Kintz pulled his robe closed tighter. "What was that?"

"Am I an employee or a resident? It's a simple question."

His hair stuck up in all directions. Running a nervous hand through it only made it worse. His chin shadowed, his night-wear disheveled, fumbling for words, he cut a tempting figure for a woman newly flayed to the possibility of men. Something like power rippled through Cecibel. She smiled her gruesome, un-masked smile.

He stood aside. "You'd better come in, Miss Bringer," he said. "I'll make us a drink."

Bar Harbor, Maine

❧

To die, to sleep—
To sleep, perchance to dream—ay, there's the rub,
For in this sleep of death what dreams may come
When we have shuffled off this mortal coil.

—CORNELIUS TRAEGAR
(PEOPLE WILL TELL YOU IT'S SHAKESPEARE.
THEY'RE LYING. IT WAS CORNELIUS.)

Alfonse set down his pen, flexed his fingers. Only three days working, and he was nearly done with his chapter. It poured out of him like lava, charred the book around the edges. Shorter. Necessarily so. Tension building, events spilling, emotions running over. His tightly wound chapter would spark Olivia and Switch to do the same. The pattern was innate. The story might not go exactly where he wished it to, but Alfonse wasn't entirely sure of his desires on that count anyway. He was content with the established pattern, and the rush of adrenaline rising with the story arc.

Tipping his head back against his comfortable chair, Alfonse closed his eyes. Sunshine warmed him through; he was always cold these days, unless sitting in the sun, where recollected dreams flickered behind his lids and reminded him of what it was to be a man. He could still feel the softness of her body, taste the salt of her skin. Cecibel of his dreams, their nightly sexcapades his body would never tolerate. Innocent, he told himself. He was an old man so near to dying he could smell it like tar melting on a summer day. He tasted its metallic tang in everything he ate or drank.

What happened while he slept was his and his alone, not under his control at all.

Such lies, when one thought of little else through waking hours, replayed it on the page. He'd woken, every day of the past four, to his heart monitor emitting that threatening beep, and an erection. A real one, and not the smashing effort that had passed for one the last decade of his life. What a fine way to go, he decided. Cecibel riding him like he was fifty again. Long hair tickling. Breasts bouncing. Head back and lips parted, her hands pressed to his chest. The explosion in his groin would burst his heart, his lungs, but what glory it would be, and worth the days it might cost him. Because Alfonse was down to days, he knew. Two. Twenty. Forty-six. Nothing one could count in months anymore. Maybe he'd see August come and mostly go. He'd probably not see September—oh, glorious month. For that he was sorry.

And the story wasn't even close to finished.

Smoothing his hand over the water-stained cover—he didn't believe Olivia's confession that she'd gotten caught in the rain—Alfonse pleaded with his heart. *Keep going, old man. Give me a little more time.* Olivia would get the notebook next, several days earlier than anticipated. Then Enzo's voice had to echo out of the Christmas party before too much time had passed. Even with the heightened pace, Alfonse could conceivably not get the notebook back for a couple of weeks. He could well be dead by then.

Switch's interference had complicated the simple, desperate tale of lovers—thank all the gods in every heaven. Whatever his, and then Olivia's, first intentions, the magic had taken over. Weave the threads, overlap them here, combine them there, create a tapestry worth marveling over. He could no more forbid himself that than he could command his heart to continue beating.

"Hello, hello!" Judith's singsong preceded her. She didn't wait to be asked inside but fluttered into the room. "Were you writing? I can come back later."

If she remembered. "I was just taking a break," he said. "What do you need, my dear?"

"A look at the manuscript. I was looking over the last chapter I transcribed in such a hurry. I knew I'd mucked something up. Unless Switch wrote about marquis sapphires cutting someone's face. Which I highly doubt. I was afraid I'd forget by the time I got the book back. Even with notes, I do. Sometimes. It's best to address things when they're fresh. Do you mind if I have a look?"

Alfonse handed her the notebook. Sinking into the chair opposite him, Judi thumbed through the pages. "Ah, there it is. Paper? Pen?"

"Right there in that drawer."

Judi jotted down the correct line, and tucked the note into the pocket of her jeans. "Thank you, Alfie. I'll let you get back to work."

"Stay," he said. "I was taking a break, as I said. I could use a little company. I don't get out much more than dinner these days."

Judi sank back into her chair. "I noticed. We've been at a loss as to what we should do. Come visit? Or leave you be?"

"It's usually a fifty-fifty chance." He smiled. "But always opt for visiting. I can tell you to go away."

"You could also buzz any one, or all of us, to come to you."

He looked down at his hands. Cecibel told him they were nice hands. They were, he had to admit.

"Alfonse?"

"I know," he said. "I'll try to remember that."

"You're not the one with the memory problem." She laughed. "Don't tell me you, of all people, are becoming humble."

"Humble? Never." He met her eyes. "I know what it is to avoid a death you cannot fathom. I never came to see Cornelius. I don't blame anyone for not wanting to watch me die."

"Oh, Alfie." She leaned forward, patted his knee. "You were young and full of regret where he was concerned. We're all old and near enough to our own ends to know there is no avoiding it."

"If I was young then, so are you now. I was about your age when he fell ill."

"You cannot compare your sixty-seven to mine," she said. "You never looked or acted your age. I've the mind of a ninety-year-old who's fallen on her head a few too many times."

"You exaggerate."

Judi shrugged. "Only a little. I've no delusions. My descent will not be pretty or romantic. It will be sad and heartbreaking. Having no one in my life used to make me sad, but now I'm glad no one will have the pain of witnessing what I'll become. Then again, I have no one to grieve over me either."

"You're well loved," he said. "Everyone here will mourn you."

"Momentarily. We all come here knowing good-bye is all too near."

"She says to the man nearer to death than anyone else in the Pen."

"As if you've no one to lament you." She crossed her arms. "The whole world knows and loves Alfonse Carducci. You'll not be forgotten."

It was true. Long after he was gone, people would read his novels. Colleges would offer courses on the body of his work. Judith Arsenault's connection to any of it had long been forgotten by all but a scattered few. Everyone knew who wrote *Gone with the Wind,* but did anyone know who Margaret Mitchell's editor was?

"I will be just as dead as any nameless, homeless man brought into a New York City morgue," he said, "and won't know who remembers what of me."

She cocked her head; dark hair only slightly salted swung like a silk curtain at her chin. "Then you don't believe in heaven?"

"I don't believe in hell," he answered, "so contrariwise, no, I do not believe in heaven."

"I never knew you to be a cynic. You've always been so whimsical."

"Me? Whimsical?" He'd laugh if he could spare the effort. "Darling, I'm a writer. I'm the most cynical fool God ever sent rambling."

"I believe the quote is '*sublime fool.*'"

"Was I quoting someone?"

"Bradbury."

"That, she remembers."

"It's how Alzheimer's works," Judi said. "I can remember things from the seventies, sixties, even earlier, like they just happened. I was at the commencement where he made that speech."

"Was it? A commencement?"

"I think so. It doesn't matter. Why don't you believe in heaven?"

"I think you're lying about your short-term memory problem."

"Don't be an ass. As if someone would lie about something so dreadful."

He offered a smile and hoped it still worked its magic. "I was trying to avoid answering your question, dear. Forgive me."

"You're forgiven." Judi grimaced. "What was my question?"

Alfonse hesitated.

"I'm kidding." She shook her head. "Got to have a sense of humor about it, no? So, you going to tell me why?"

Alfonse inhaled very slowly, feeling every molecule of air struggling to find his lungs. "I don't know," he said at last. "I did, a long time ago. All the fire and brimstone good Catholic boys fear. Somewhere along the way, I stopped believing in . . . everything."

"That's not true. If it were, you couldn't write as you do. Cecilia and Aldo would not exist."

"They don't. Not really."

She leaned her palms to his knees. "But they do. You're the god who breathed life into them."

"I like the sound of that."

Judi slumped backward. "You're impossible."

"As I've been told many, many times." He shouldered more comfortably into his chair. "Then you believe in heaven? The angels and all that?"

She flipped a hand. "Not in the traditional sense, no. But I do believe there is more to life than we understand on this human level of ours. So arrogant, we are, thinking we can define whatever it is."

"It's human nature. A need to understand. To put shape to things we can't explain."

"Is that why you write?"

The notion bloomed, presented petals for him to pluck. Astute woman. Always had been, even if she wouldn't always be. "Maybe," he said. "I've never really thought about it."

"I think about such things," Judi murmured. "All the time. But I'm not an artist. I've never been able to create on my own, only mold what others give me. I wish I had words, or paint or music. Something to shape into the divine."

"Judi." He held out his hand for hers. "That molding is divinity in and of itself. Without goddesses like you, gods like me could not exist."

"Such flattery." She squeezed his hand. "You were always so good at that."

"Because it's sincere. My mother always told me truth did not require a good memory. I say nothing I don't mean, and mean everything I say."

"I know you do. It's why everyone loves you, and few are angry when you're through with them."

"You make me sound so callous."

"Cavalier," she said. "Never callous. It's just who you are, Alfonse. Make no excuses for it."

He let go her hands and settled back into his chair. "I suppose I was. Or at least that's how it seemed. I skimmed the surface of my life. I see that now in my failing decrepitude. I loved until I loved too much, and then I moved on rather than risk the downside. Always the high, never the low." A prickling sensation worked up his spine, across his shoulders. What would fail him this time? But nothing happened and Alfonse nearly burst out laughing for the truth chasing fear away. "And that was not a lie until just now, speaking it aloud."

"How so?"

"I felt the lows. Not always, but at least twice. And they stayed with me. Stay with me still."

"Cornelius?"

"And Olivia," he confessed. *What would life have been had I been braver?* "At least Olivia and I came out the other side. I love her fiercely, if not passionately."

"Then who is it you feel this passion for? I wonder," she asked, "that lets you write of Cecilia and Aldo with such raw emotion?"

"Remembered passion," Alfonse lied. "I'm too old and broken for—"

"You spoke of honesty and I believed you. Silly me. But it's not my right to pry, even if I'm fairly certain it's no secret at all. There is something about her that pulls us all, I think. Even Dr. Kintz."

"Her?"

But Judith was having none of it; she laughed her sweet and merry song. "I'll leave your delusion in peace, dear Alfie, and instead ask you this question I just remembered asking myself, when transcribing. Funny how that happens, isn't it? Just pops in for no reason whatsoever, but if I tried to remember it with strings on every finger attached to notes in every pocket, I couldn't do it."

"What's your question, Judi?"

She scooted to the edge of her chair. "Do we know if Princeton even had a journalism department back in 1959? The University of Alabama, for that matter? Did it even allow female students at all? These are facts that must be correct. You know that."

"Only if this were for publication," he told her. "Which it is not. Transcribe, Judi. No fact-checking."

"I know, but—"

"You agreed."

"I did, but—"

Alfonse laughed. Carefully. "You can't help yourself. I had that thought about myself just before you got here. But the chances of this book seeing publication are close to zero. The legalities of three authors with a claim on it would be a nightmare. And thus such details can stand as they are. All of them."

"At least . . ." She paused. He waited. Judi bit her lip. "You must understand, Alfie. This is what I do. It's how I feed my brain, and my brain is starving most of the time these days. When I'm working on this, I feel like me again. I don't forget. I remember. I remember all the rules of grammar and story and character. I notice little details most readers never would, like whether or not there was a journalism discipline at Princeton in 1959. I swore to you I'd make no suggestions, I'd change nothing, but at least let me keep the notes that, should this ever be seen by even a single reader long after we're all gone from this world, I won't have to do that terrible thing of rolling over in my grave because of a half-assed job."

Alfonse steepled his fingers under his chin, as much to think as it was to support his head. How did he get so tired, simply sitting in a chair and chatting with a friend? "All right," he said at last. "Take notes in a separate folder, or in a notebook, however you wish. I couldn't stop you from doing that one way or another. Thank you for doing me the honor of asking."

"It's your project." She flipped her hand again in that way she had. "I've been an editor for a million years, and even I won't trample through an author's flower beds."

"And she says she has no art."

"I stole it from somewhere, I'm certain. There isn't a creative bone in my body."

It wasn't true, but Judith Arsenault had always been more stubborn than she believed. She chatted on about colleges and curriculums. Naval bases and chains of command. The logistics of Paterson, New Jersey. That, at least, Alfonse knew firsthand. He'd lived there, experienced the falls and hot dogs all the way, the row of mansions on Derrom Avenue and the coffee counter at Woolworth's. He'd made love to the posh ladies who shopped in Meyer Brothers, and the poor ladies who worked there, wishing. The curve of a cheek. The clouds of blond waves, brunette silk, red curls. The scent of roses, violets, and sex. The rush of desire. The crash laying him to waste. No tears. Never tears. They'd all known just what he was, just like Judi said.

Bar Harbor, Maine

JULY 23, 1999

*There's no hiding from the truth, no matter how good a
liar you think you are.*

—CORNELIUS TRAEGAR

Almost a week since Fin, since creeping in on Alfonse, since her
witching-hour drink with Dr. Kintz, Cecibel still drifted through
the days. She concentrated on work without concentrating at all.
She couldn't talk to Fin about it. Late-afternoon walks had been
suspended. He said he understood, he'd wait, he'd be there when
she was ready. And that he loved her. This last done with a sweet,
careful smile as endearing as it was frightening.

She couldn't talk to Sal, though she nearly did. He was too
intimately involved, and Cecibel wasn't sure he wanted to know
what she did. Olivia was out of the question. She was liable to say
anything when stoned, to anyone. Certainly not Alfonse, the only
person she didn't abandon in her enforced solitude. Every day at
four twenty, she knocked on his door, made him tea, chatted with
him in the sunshine, of things that didn't matter. Her copy of *Night
Wings* taunted her, tucked as it was into the cushion of Alfonse's
chair. The passage marked. The words echoing out of slumber every day for over a year after the accident, after Jen. His words that
changed meaning with every step she took toward letting them go.

"Is Dr. Marks still practicing? Is she even still alive? She was
pretty old, when I knew her."

Dr. Kintz—Richard, in the deep of night, disheveled and
kind—had handed her a second Scotch and soda and resettled onto

the couch beside her. "Last I heard, yes. But I can find out for sure, if that's what you want."

"I'm not sure. Yeah. Yes. Maybe. I think I'd like to see her."

"I can only tell you what was passed on to me." Richard sipped at his Scotch. Straight up. Neat. "She can tell you exactly what she and Dr. Traegar discussed."

"I'll let you know. Thank you."

And now a week had nearly passed and she'd not let him know a thing. Bits of information, mangled memories, assumptions, and outright lies wouldn't let her say the words that would sweep the detritus out of her mind. Living in the Pen, Cecibel understood better than most that "any day" had more of a chance at being "today" with people Dr. Marks's age. If she didn't speak soon, it could well become too late.

She knocked on Dr. Kintz's—working hours, he could not be "Richard"—office door, and entered when he called his welcome.

"Miss Bringer." He barely looked up from his desk. "Give me one moment."

"Of course."

Moving to the big windows, Cecibel tucked her hands behind her back to keep them from tugging her ponytail in place. Some of the nurses had been appalled and cruel when she stopped hiding the monster behind her hair. They gaped and they gasped. They turned residents around in their chairs so they wouldn't have to see what they saw. But some were kind. Encouraging. And Cecibel reminded herself not to let Olivia's prejudices rub off on her anymore.

"Sorry about that." Dr. Kintz rose from his chair, came to stand with her at the window. "Lovely day, isn't it? Glad the humidity finally broke."

"August is coming," she said. "Have you been in Maine for August yet?"

"I've never been in Maine at all until coming here to live. I understand I'm in for some surprises come winter."

"It's as beautiful as it is harsh. Too harsh for most, but it suits me fine."

Richard smiled. "Of course it does. So, have you decided?"

"I have. Would you arrange it?"

"Sure. When?"

"Whatever works for Dr. Marks. I'm . . . here."

"Excellent. I'll let you know as soon as I get word back."

"Thank you, Dr. Kintz." She turned to go, but didn't. Instead, she gathered her courage and met his gaze—not a hint of revulsion there. "Thanks for your honesty. I know you didn't have to tell me anything."

"It would have been unethical not to, once you'd asked. For the record, I was working up to speaking with you openly. I simply didn't know how much you knew, or if it was in your best interests to say anything at all."

"Good thing it worked out as it did, then, huh?"

He laughed softly. "Yes, it is. I will be speaking with Finlay soon. I was waiting to see what you wished to do about Dr. Marks first. The arrangement made on his behalf is only that, not mandated by the courts."

"It wouldn't surprise me to know he's been aware all along," Cecibel said. "He knew Dr. Traegar, way back when he was a kid. They have a history, and probably had a friendship."

"Good to know. Thank you."

Outside, where it was no longer humid but so much hotter than indoors, Cecibel lifted her face to the light. Sunshine seeped into the crags and valleys of her melted-candle face, a sensation still so alien, but good. Like the ache she'd noticed in bed at night, starting in her neck and fingering up to her scalp. The ache of muscles so long unused, brought back to life with smiling. Speaking. Laughing. Also alien, but good, and only a dozen years in coming. She felt for the note in her pocket, found it there and took it out.

Fin, I'll see you soon. Thanks for being patient.

Yours, Tatterhood

They weren't words of love, but they were close enough. He'd see the things she couldn't say. Finlay Pottinger was a simple man, but he wasn't the kind of simple Cecibel had long believed. Proper grammar and a sophisticated vocabulary didn't make one smart, only well spoken.

Leaving the note on Finlay's door, Cecibel rested her head to it and listened, just in case. She knew he wasn't home. He'd left early that morning to visit his mother for her birthday and wouldn't be back until tomorrow.

"Come with me," he'd said. "Meet my mom."

But she couldn't. It was just one too many things, and Cecibel feared something toppling before she was equipped to catch it back.

Paterson, New Jersey

DECEMBER 21, 1959
(EARLY MORNING HOURS)

━━❧❧━━

Aldo

He shouldn't stare, but he did. He especially shouldn't follow her from room to room. Aldo wasn't even discreet about it. No one would notice anyway. They were all too drunk. He'd nursed a single drink all evening, unwilling to take the chance he'd do or say something that would scare her. He kept the distance she seemed to need. The kiss behind the garage, the fumbled explanations, Cecilia's tears and sudden flight. He couldn't let it end there. The crossroads five years past had presented itself again, in the very same place, with the very same people. Few men got a do-over; Aldo Wronski wasn't going to blow his.

Midnight came and went. Tressa remained the life of the party. Good distraction there, too. No one was looking at Cecilia when his sister was around. Not that she wasn't just as beautiful. In Aldo's opinion, Tressa didn't compare; but his sister was a dove among ravens, soon to vanish like Cinderella from the ball. Even Cecilia's husband was taken with her. She'd been on his arm for a while and he seemed no worse for wear.

On the patio, chatting with guys he once went to school with, Aldo waited for Cecilia to reappear, wearing the white fox fur he overheard her tell friends she needed to fetch in order to fend off the cold. They'd laughed and teased her vanity. One said something about Enzo spoiling her even worse than her daddy did.

A glimpse of white caught his attention. Not a fur, but Tressa still on Enzo's arm. Was something brewing there? He felt a heel even thinking the thought, but how advantageous such an affair would be. Could Tressa survive that fall from grace?

Cecilia stepped through the French doors, wrapped in white fur, and all other thought was water through a sieve. The guys he barely remembered waylaid her from going back to the clutch of women waiting to get a look at the stole. They joked with her, put on a masculine show. Her smile was big and red and forced. Aldo could focus only on her deep laughter hitting him low in the groin. Lust saturated his pores, tweaked the glands in his jaw. *Look at me, Cecilia. Just look at me.* But she didn't. Her gaze darted everywhere but never met his.

"Looks like you got some competition, eh, Cecilia?" The man to his left jutted a chin in Tressa's direction. "I seen her with Enzo inside, too."

"Be careful, Johnny." Cecilia wagged a finger. "You know Al's her brother, right?"

"Oh, right. Sorry there, Al. I was just joking, anyway. Enzo's a stand-up guy. Cecilia's had his balls in her fist since they was kids, anyway."

"Is that so?" Aldo sipped his ice-watered bourbon. "How long have you two been together?"

"Our parents made arrangements when we were children. We've been married about five years."

"Enzo's been toes over tits for her since they was babies." Another drunk jokester guffawed, pounding Aldo's back. "But Cecilia was way too cool for him until—"

"Hey, now, Louie." Johnny grabbed his friend's arm. "How's about another drink? I'm bone-dry here."

Wise Johnny, probably more sober than he pretended, led Louie back inside by the arm. The other two followed, leaving Aldo and Cecilia as alone as one could get in a house so tightly packed with Christmas cheer.

"Until?" Aldo prompted.

Cecilia's eyes remained on the door her alibi had gone through. "Until my father vanished and my arranged marriage got moved up." She met his gaze, her eyes hard. "I didn't have a choice. I think we've had this conversation before."

"Once upon a time, yes. We did."

"I can't do this, Aldo." She stomped her foot, hands fisted at her sides. "I can't be out here alone with you. People will talk."

"Your lady friends are all right there."

"Watching every move I make. You have no idea how gossipy they are."

"Why do you care? You never did before."

"I have to now. There's that choices thing again."

"You hide behind the limitations you obey." Aldo sipped his drink.

"You're a man. Of course you think that."

"I don't have as many choices as you seem to think I do. I never have. Especially where you're concerned."

A tear rolled. Thank heavens. "What do you want, Aldo?"

"You, Cecilia. Always and only you."

"Don't say that."

"I love you."

"You can't."

He laughed, head tilted back and belly churning. The women watching every move Cecilia made clutched together. Aldo lowered his voice. "I never thought I'd see you again, even when Tressa asked me to meet her here in Paterson. It's a big city, and I'm no one. But here I am, at your father's invitation. Morbidly ironic, isn't it. But doesn't it say something? About us? About fate?"

"It can't."

"It can. It does. Don't throw this away."

"You did."

Ouch. Right in the gizzards. Aldo rubbed away the too-real pain. "I didn't mean to. I didn't know. I thought I'd done something unspeakable."

"You didn't trust me to love you enough."

"That's not true." He bowed his head. Was it, though? Things tamped down over years of ignoring they existed threatened to burrow up out of the ground again, right at his feet, swallow him up, and take her with him. The women had moved closer, close enough to hear their words instead of guess at them. Cecilia's plastered-on smile could only last so long.

"We can't do this here, Cecilia."

"We can't do this at all."

"But we have to." He raised his head. "Don't we? Can you just move on from here as if I never showed up again?"

"Aldo, I . . ."

Her hesitation gave him courage. "Please. Give me this. I'm begging you."

"Don't beg."

"I'll get down on my knees."

"Don't."

No, not courage. Desperation. "I will unless you say you'll meet me. Anywhere. Anytime. Just say the word and I'll be there."

Tears trembled her forced smile, but Cecilia met his gaze dead-on. "Your sister is meeting my brother at Woolworth's tomorrow. Two o'clock. Tell her you want to chaperone. I'll tag along with Nicky. He won't want me there any more than your sister will want you. We can take a table in the back. Watch over them like good siblings."

"Thank you."

"I'm going to show off for my friends now," she said. "Don't follow me."

He bowed like a gentleman and Cecilia was gone. Aldo lit a cigarette, blew a plume over his head. It was a start. But definitely not the finish.

Cecilia loved him still, wanted him whether or not she loved her husband, too. He seemed a nice enough guy. Good-looking, tall and broad in the shoulder. Movie-star hair and teeth. Few partygoers had passed up the opportunity to sing his praises to the newcomer who hadn't heard it all before. Yet, for all he knew, Enzo hadn't wanted to marry Cecilia any more than she did him, despite what those assholes said to the contrary. The couple hadn't spent even a few minutes together all night long. But that wink Cecilia tossed her husband when he left with Tressa on his arm—no jealousy there. Because she didn't care if Enzo fucked Tressa? Or because she was that secure in his love?

"Give that here." Tressa came out of nowhere, snatched the cigarette from his fingers. She took a long drag, held it, let it go with a whoosh between smudged red lips. "We need to go."

"Need to?"

"Yes." She took another drag and offered it back.

Aldo put up his hand, took his coat from her. In his periphery, Cecilia modeled her stole. "What's wrong?"

"Nothing. I'm just so tired. All these people, and they all want to chat with little old me. Please take me home." She hooked an arm through his. Her fingers trembled against the wool of his jacket and her eyes were everywhere at once.

"You okay?"

"Of course. Can we go?"

He was ready. Exhausted, in fact. He would see Cecilia tomorrow. It was long past midnight. Today. Sleep, a long hot shower, and the right words. Aldo needed all three before two o'clock.

Paterson, New Jersey

DECEMBER 21, 1959
(AFTERNOON)

Cecilia

"Your sister's going with you, Dominic. That's the end of it."

Cecilia's heart hammered. What the hell was she doing? "If you insist, Mama."

"No fucking way."

"Watch your mouth." Mama slapped Nicky upside the head. "That's why you need a chaperone."

"I'd never talk like that in front of Tressa," Nicky grumbled.

"So she's more a lady than me or your sister now, eh?"

"Ma, come on."

Cecilia let them duke it out. In the end, no one refused Mama. She got her coat and hat from the closet in the hall, stood at the door, and waited. Nicky stormed toward her, grumbling under his breath.

"What'd you go and do that for?"

"Do what?"

"Tell Ma a girl like Tressa would expect a chaperone."

"Because it's true," she lied. "She's a southern girl, not one of the *putan'* you usually go out with."

"She's a woman, not a girl."

"And you're not even out of high school. Don't get your hopes up too high."

"Says you." He grabbed his coat from the closet. "You just make yourself scarce, y'hear?"

"I'll sit all the way in the back and sip my coffee and eat my pie. You'll never know I'm there."

Nicky halted, one arm in and one arm out of his jacket. "Oh, so that's it."

The burn worked up from her neck to her cheeks. "What?"

"Where's Enzo?"

"He took the kids to his mother's. Why?"

Nicky finished putting on his coat, opened the door, and gestured her through. Cecilia took careful steps to keep from stumbling, thankful for the bracing cold of December air.

"Need a little time off, is that it?"

She pulled her gloves on, her relief exhaled in a cloud swirling around her head. "Maybe."

"Why didn't you just say so? I'd have covered for you. You want to go shopping or something?"

"You're trying to get rid of me."

He laughed. "Ain't that been what I been trying to do the last half hour?"

"Isn't," she corrected. "You sound like a hoodlum."

"Yeah, yeah. You want to walk or drive?"

"Let's walk. Parking downtown is a nightmare."

Hands in pockets, jiggling coins as he walked, Nicky looked like every picture Cecilia ever saw of their father at that age. When had her little brother grown so broad? So handsome? No wonder Tressa was taken with him.

It was only a quarter to two when they reached Woolworth's. The place was packed with last-minute Christmas shoppers resting up. Nicky didn't hesitate, but skipped past the head of the line and to a table in the window. The two young ladies sitting there, chatting over cups of hot cocoa overflowing with whipped cream, looked up when he approached. Blushing smiles became furrowed brows. Nicky reached into his pocket and slapped two bills on the table. A moment later, the two women hurried past, already putting on their coats. Nicky waved a waitress over.

". . . can't just do that, sir," the waitress was saying when Cecilia reached him. "There's a whole line of people ahead of you."

"Sure I can. I just did. You got a problem with that you can call my office and lodge a complaint." He flipped a business card between two fingers. The waitress took it, her eyes nearly bulging out of her face before she scurried off. Yes, indeed. Just like their father.

"That was efficient."

"Man's gotta do what a man's gotta do. Now scram, sis."

"Where am I supposed to go?"

"You said you'd make yourself scarce."

"But there isn't a table to be had."

"That neat trick I did worked once. It won't work twice. Besides, I just slugged down two twenties to get this table. I'm almost tapped out. Got any cash?"

"Dominic Marcello Tommaso Giancami, you evil thing." But she took a twenty from her wallet and handed it to him. What was she going to do now? *Go home, Cecilia. Go to your husband and children at his mother's.* "Where shall I meet you? And when?"

"You don't have to, Cici." Oh, it was Cici now. "Ma'll get over it."

"I'd rather not hear it, thank you very much, especially since I instigated the whole thing. Where and when?"

"Back here. Four o'clock."

Cecilia tugged on his lapel, kissed his cheek. "Behave."

Ducking through the crowd lined up at the door, Cecilia told herself she'd agreed to meet Aldo only to talk. To put a period on that part of her life. She wasn't doing anything wrong. No matter the circumstances, they'd both made their choices. Her reaction to Aldo the night before had been raw instinct, muscle memory, shock. She'd had the night to sleep on it, beside her husband, who adored her. They'd made love so loudly Mama banged on the wall to shush them, and giggled into the pillows when the bedsprings in her parents' room started to squeal in turn. Cecilia had fallen asleep in Enzo's arms, content in the knowledge she'd stand Aldo up, that she couldn't betray the life she'd made when he vanished from it five years ago.

But she'd woken crying softly, out of dreams of Aldo holding Patsy tenderly and close. Cecilia knew before slumber fully faded that she'd meet him, that she owed him something for the secret she'd never share. A proper good-bye. They both deserved one. It didn't even feel like a lie.

She saw Tressa coming a block away, not because of her fair hair and white coat, but because heads turned like startled flamingos as she passed. She walked alone, head up, smile in place, her heels clicking staccato on the sidewalk. No Aldo. Not beside her or behind her. Cecilia's stomach lurched. She ducked into a doorway before Tressa could spot her, stayed there until she saw Nicky stand, take his date's coat, and hold out her chair.

"Boo."

Cecilia swallowed a scream. Hand on hat, she spun to face him. "Don't do that!"

"I couldn't help myself." He took her hand from her hat. She thought he'd kiss it, but he shook it like a gentleman meeting a female acquaintance in the street. "Why are you hiding?"

"I'm not."

"Skulking in doorways must be the new fashionable thing to do, then."

Cecilia yanked her hand away. "There isn't a table to be had," she said. "The wait list is at least an hour long."

"How'd your brother get the spot in the window?"

"Never mind. Why didn't you come with your sister?"

Aldo shrugged. "She wouldn't let me. She called me a Neanderthal for assuming she needed a chaperone and forbade me to tag along. So I followed."

"My brother gave me the boot, too." She laughed softly. It wasn't supposed to be so easy, being in his company. "Problem is, being distant chaperones for our siblings gave me a good reason for being alone with a man who is neither my husband nor an old friend. What now?"

Aldo leaned against the doorway, his smile slow and his eyes suggesting things turning Cecilia's insides to mush. Or maybe she was imagining it. No, she didn't think so.

"How about a movie?" he asked. "We could sit in the back and . . . talk."

Dozens of movies flashed through her like silent films, movies they paid to see then didn't watch from the back of the theater where no one else did either.

"Too public." She cleared the huskiness from her voice. *Call it a day, Cecilia.* "Any other ideas?"

"Anywhere we go will be public. Except . . ."

"Except?"

Again that slow grin. Goddammit. He put a hand in his pocket, pulled out a key. Aldo pressed it into her hand. "Les Fontaines," he said. "Fifteen minutes."

She tried to give him back the key. He closed her fingers around it.

"Fifteen minutes," he said again. "If you don't come, I'll tell the desk clerk I lost my key and that will be that."

"I can't, Aldo."

"Yes, you can." Tipping his hat, Aldo left her standing in the doorway near the Woolworth's where her brother and his sister sat chatting over coffee and pie. A few blocks away, her husband visited with his mother, her children playing with all the Christmas toys they'd already collected from family and friends, too many to bring back home again. Home. Princeton. She'd been happy there, her little family, her whole world. She would be again, once Aldo went back to sea.

Heading home—Mama would rage but it was the least of every other evil—Cecilia gripped the key in her gloved hand. On the corner, a mailbox. She halted abruptly in front of it; a woman behind her almost knocked her down. The edges of the key dug ridges into the leather glove encasing her palm. Cecilia pulled down the slot. How many letters had she dropped in boxes all over her city, five years ago when Aldo vanished without a word? How many times did she beg Agnes for letters that never came? The agony of that time welled up, threatened to pull a sob from her. *You hide behind the limitations you obey.* She hid then. She was hiding now. What choice did she have? What choice had she ever had?

The slot slammed shut. Cecilia fled. She didn't think. If she did, she couldn't do it, and she had to. She had to. How many blocks to safety? She hadn't run so far in years. Breathless, she stumbled to the service entrance, unwilling to come across another living soul. Pressed up against the door, Cecilia fumbled with the key. *Just today. Just this once. I swear it.*

The door opened, and she fell into the always-and-forever arms that caught her, pulled her close.

Paterson, New Jersey

DECEMBER 23, 1959

Enzo

If he didn't know what he knew, Enzo would never have agreed to meet her. But he did, and she'd asked. No, she'd threatened. Sweetly. If he wanted this blip in his life to remain a blip, he'd meet with her. Tressa looked like a mild-mannered princess from every fairy tale he'd ever heard, but looks could be deceiving; in her case, they were outright lies.

The tearoom in Les Fontaines. Very European. Very high society. The sort of place Cecilia would never frequent, but one Enzo would have liked to. He'd been to Rome, London, Paris—the three musts for a young man attending Princeton. He'd spent three months of his senior year overseas with an exchange program few were chosen to take part in. He hadn't wanted to go, hadn't wanted to leave Cecilia and Patsy, but it was best, she insisted, for their family. It would open doors for him that might otherwise stay closed. His family, hers, could bully him into just about any job, school, program he wanted, but he'd earned this on his own. It would give him the respectability he longed for, that he wanted for Cecilia, too. Being a Giancami had its perks, but it definitely had its drawbacks, too.

He hated lying to Cecilia. She'd been so on edge since the party. It was never easy going home for the holidays, the enforced proximity to their parents after having over an hour down the parkway between them. Add Aldo to the mix, the fear, the old feelings, the secrets kept too close, and he wasn't sure who was keeping what from who anymore; the tension was like buttercream on a birthday cake.

I know who Aldo is. It'll be okay. It will be. I swear. He'd said the words to her, in his head, countless times over the last few days, while making love in her girlhood bedroom twice and three times a day. Enzo knew every reason for her impossible libido, and hoped the one he feared most was just his waking Neanderthal nudging him in the back.

Enzo checked his watch. Nearly four o'clock. The tearoom was populated by women and little girls dressed in Christmas finery. He knew no one, and suspected no one here would know him. It didn't matter. He was going to tell Cecilia he ran into Tressa in town and she asked him to have tea with her, as soon as he got back to her parents' house. She hadn't been home when he left. They seemed to cross paths quite a lot during the holidays. There were always old friends who desperately wanted to see her. The kids were being spoiled by their parents' lack of attention and the abundance of grandparents. Things would settle down again, once they were home in Princeton. Self-delusion was never his strong suit, but Enzo Parisi was getting better at it every day.

Heads turned to the foyer. Mothers leaned closer to daughters, glossy lips whispering behind manicured hands. Enzo rose from his chair so Tressa would see him. She waved and came his way. His breath caught. He had to concentrate hard to right it. Who knew "breathtaking" was more than a pretty word?

"Good afternoon, Mr. Parisi." She sat in the chair he held out for her. "It was so kind of you to join me."

"How could I refuse?"

Her sweet smile bent a little wickedly. Oh, the power she wielded, so effortlessly. Enzo put a napkin in his lap in hopes of hiding the effect. He gestured to a waiter in a white tux. They ordered a pot Earl Grey and a tier of assorted cookies. After the waiter left them, Tressa leaned a little closer to whisper, "I'm so impressed you didn't insist on coffee. So few men will take tea with a lady, as if tea somehow makes them less masculine."

"I spent a good amount of time in England." He sipped the slightly too-hot tea. "I prefer it to coffee, if I'm being honest."

"And you are never anything but, I can tell." Tressa dropped two sugar lumps into her cup, a third. "I know you suspect me of terrible things, but I promise you, I've only your family's best interests at heart. My brother's. Mine. Everyone's."

Her kiss still lingered on his lips, the scent of her in his nostrils. Powdery, like flowers with an undercurrent of spice. He put his cup to his lips, but even that didn't burn away the sensation just looking at her caused. Taking the fragile photo from the breast pocket of his suit, he forbade his hand to tremble. He slid it across the table to her.

"I knew before you showed me this."

"But your wife doesn't know you know."

He shook his head. "Does your brother know he's her father?"

Tressa waved a dismissive hand. "I love Aldo to the moon and back, but he's an idiot. No, he doesn't know. He doesn't see what's right in front of him. All he sees is Cecilia."

Bald truth. Right in the gut. Enzo wasn't sure he could survive all this honesty. "Forgive my bluntness, but what do you want?"

"I want what you want." She covered his hand with hers. "I want my brother to go back to sea none the wiser. I want you to keep your lovely little family. It's what's best for the children, for you, and for Cecilia. And whether he believes it or not, it's best for Aldo."

"Why?"

"Because love doesn't conquer all," she practically spat. "Not their kind. More lust than love. Pinhole vision. They were children, after all, when Patsy was conceived."

"So was I."

Tressa leaned back a little in her chair. She picked up a cookie, took a tiny bite. "Oh, this is lovely." Another. Red lips. Crumbs. He wanted to lick them clean. She took a sip of her tea, left lipstick on the rim. "When did you first know?" she asked. "It had to be before now."

"When Patsy was born blond and blue-eyed and far bigger than a premature baby could ever hope to be," he answered. "I made a choice right then, Miss DiViello. I love my wife, regardless of who she loved before. And I have loved Patsy like my own. She *is* my own."

"And that," she said, "is the sort of love that conquers all, Mr. Parisi. I don't believe my brother is capable of such a thing. There will be no happily-ever-after for them, but there can be for you. It's better he never knows."

"You don't want your brother to know his child?"

"He doesn't want to know her," Tressa said. "Aldo is very good at casting aside those things too difficult or painful. It's how he survived when our family died and I was taken away."

Ah, more truth. Did she even know what she'd divulged?

"Enzo." She grabbed his hand again. "We can discuss this until the cows come home but we will get nothing but hurt from it. There isn't the time for it to wind down to anything resembling comfortable. What it comes down to is this—I can help you keep your family intact. All I ask is that you let me know Patricia. She is the only real family I have left."

Enzo pulled his hand gently from hers. He leaned back in his chair. "What?"

"Aldo has no use for me." Tears welled but didn't fall. She pointed to the flimsy photo. "I carried that around with me since I was a little girl. I never understood why he didn't come for me when he turned eighteen, but I've come to understand, despite how much it hurts. He didn't want me, just like my guardians didn't want him. I accept that. It's been too long, and he's who he is. But Patricia is my niece. She looks like me. I can't just let her go. So I will help you keep your family, if you let me into it."

"But how can you do that?"

Tressa studied him a moment, eyes narrowed and fingers tapping. "Aldo will get a telegram telling him his dates have been changed and he's required to report for duty on January second. He will go because he must or be arrested. He will also beg Cecilia to come with him. Once he's gone, she will come to her senses. You will make sure she does. And believe me, it won't be with threats and raging. It will be accomplished only with love and understanding. I promise you that."

"You expect too much from me. I'm a man, not a stone."

"A good man, who loves his wife even though she's fucking my brother."

Enzo's heart stilled in his chest. Strange, because he could hear it whooshing in his ears.

Tressa leaned closer. "Do you want her still? If she's fucking my brother right this moment, do you?"

He couldn't breathe. Dammit, his lungs wouldn't inhale, exhale, not even to gasp.

"Because if you don't, say the word," she whispered. "I'll take you to my bed and provide all the vengeance your masculinity requires. Then you can confront them and tell them everything you know. I'll stand beside you as you do. Let all our lives explode and hope the pieces are salvageable in the end."

Enzo squeezed his eyes shut tight. The quiet tearoom susurration of ladies' polite tea-chatter. Bend into it. Tea instead of coffee. London instead of Princeton. He could step out of his fractured life that moment, get almost any position he wanted in another world. Divorce from across the sea. No more rowdy guffawing at parties. No men belching or women chasing children, shouting at them to stop behaving like animals.

No more Cecilia, Patsy, and Frankie.

"What do I have to do?"

"Keep secrets," she told him. "Even from yourself."

"I don't know if I can."

"I do." She poured them both another cup of tea, pretty as you please and coolly. As if the earth were not careening out of its orbit, sending all and everyone flying into space. "I knew from the moment I met you that you are a man of extraordinary character and fortitude." She set the teapot down. Stirred in three lumps. Took another cookie and bit. "I was not wrong."

Enzo made no response but to stir sugar into his tea.

"I didn't come to Paterson with this plan, Mr. Parisi," she said. "I didn't know about you or Cecilia or any of it. All I wanted was to see my brother."

"And now?"

"Now I know a terrible amount more, things I never wanted to. But there you have it. It's up to those of stronger constitution to save the rest from themselves. What matters most is Patricia, and what's best for her is you, her mother, her brother, and a happy life in Princeton."

"And Al . . . Aldo?"

"As I said, what's best for him is to continue on with his career. He's sinfully good at what he does, I'll have you know. It certainly wasn't easy, securing him the position in the Mediterranean, but it was earned nonetheless."

"You got it for him?"

"Little old me?" She chimed that perfect, southern-belle laughter, a dainty hand to her breast. "Didn't I mention Daddy is an old navy man? I'm certain I did. I can't even begin to tell you how many men are beholden to him for their very lives. The war, you know." Tressa sipped her tea. "I don't ask for much, and considering he really did owe Aldo for abandoning him to the orphanage, making the arrangements was just compensation. It took months to work out, but after all I'd dug up on my brother over the last year or so, I wanted him to have his dream come true. I still do. Getting his orders changed was far easier. Daddy had it done in a snap."

"You arranged all that. For a brother you say doesn't want you."

Her lip trembled. She dabbed at her lips with a white linen napkin, leaving red kisses behind. "Things don't always work out as we hope," she said. "I can't undo all his lonely years. I can't go back and have a miserable life instead of my happy one, no matter how guilty it makes me feel, no matter how disappointing it is to be able to win over everyone but him. It was silly of me to think I could. But there's time yet, once he goes back to sea."

Calm had settled over Enzo somewhere along the line of their conversation. He felt little rage against Cecilia or Aldo; more pity than anything else. To be young and impossibly in love, to have your lives dictated rather than chosen. He'd been promised at the age of twelve, to a girl he fell easily in love with. He grew up knowing he'd go to college, have a career that satisfied his soul.

No one expected him to go into the "family business," even if he'd have the power of that family behind him his life long.

But . . .

"Is she?" the Neanderthal asked.

"Is who, what?"

"My wife. Fucking your brother."

Tressa didn't reach across the table this time, but under it to gently take his hand. "I honestly have no idea. Do you want to know? We could go down to his room right now, knock on the door, and see who answers. Just be certain of your choice before you make it."

"Choice." He chuffed. "There isn't one that doesn't hurt like hell."

"Which hurts the least, in the long run?"

Enzo squeezed her hand, didn't let it go. Tressa squeezed back and did.

"More tea?" she asked, the china pot balanced in her hands.

Bar Harbor, Maine

AUGUST 1, 1999

❧❦❧

Nighty-night, Rabbit.

—CORNELIUS TRAEGAR

"What do you think, Alfonse?" Judi leaned close enough for him to smell the peppermint tea on her breath. "It's your story, in the end."

"It's ours." He wheezed. Sweet breath. How many more did he have? Not many. Hopefully enough. "All of ours."

"But the way Raymond left it," Olivia chimed in, "there's no clear character it should go to next."

"That was the point," Switch grumbled. "I'm the interloper here. I can't make that decision. You two have to."

"But we said no planning."

"Then don't plan. Toss a coin. Whoever wins the toss gets to decide."

Olivia and Switch argued back and forth. Once in a while, Judi's voice would chirp a suggestion. All to the tune of the oxygen hiss and click. Eyes batting, breath slowing, slumber falling, Alfonse let them argue. In dreams forming, Aldo and Cecilia were tangled in hotel sheets, glistening and slick and barely sated. A knock at the door sent them both scrambling and in walked Tressa. No Enzo. No Cami or Nicky. Just Tressa in the doorway, glaring.

Tell him I stopped by. I'll check in on him later.

He'll be disappointed to have missed your visit.

It's better that he sleeps.

So far away, those voices lovely and familiar. But Alfonse couldn't place them. They were part of a too-distant future he couldn't guess at yet. Cornelius called him from the kitchen, if a kitchen indeed it was. Gutted but for the hearth and the iron pegs along the stone wall no man could remove without dynamite. Alfonse stuck his head inside, laughing to see his love covered in soot and spiderwebs. He'd never seen a hair on Cornelius's head out of place until Bar Harbor. Until this house.

"I need another bucket of water." He kicked the bucket that sloshed soapy water onto his shoe. "Make that a whole lake."

Alfonse stepped carefully into the kitchen, took Cornelius into his arms. "Why not hire someone to do this?"

"I'd rather spend the money on the renovation than the cleanup." Cornelius spun away from him. "Keep your hands to yourself, young man. I'm working, and I'm dirty."

"I like dirty."

"Oh?" Cornelius raised an eyebrow, his grin turning wicked. "And how do you feel about wet, Alfonse? Do you like it wet and dirty?"

Alfonse jerked Cornelius back into his arms. "You know how I like—"

A wet rag in his face, being squeezed over his head, and Cornelius escaping him to dart across the room. Alfonse picked up the bucket of filthy, soapy water and chased. They slung disgusting things at one another, laughing and dodging and cursing. And when they were out of ammunition, they made love like wild men on the kitchen floor, kissing and clawing and promising things neither one of them could ever hold true. Dreams out of their reach—marriage, children, a home for all—because they were men and not even in the remotest reaches of Maine was such a thing allowed.

On the cold stone floor, wet and streaked with soot, Alfonse held his lover close, felt their hearts beating chest to chest, echoing one another and not in sync. Sticks and bits of cobwebs stuck out of Cornelius's blond curls. A bruise purpled on his freckled shoulder, evidence of their roughhousing that gave rise to more games of chase and catch during those days in the abandoned mansion.

"I love you," he said. "Let's never leave this place."

"Don't be daft." Cornelius shoved him off. "You're young and handsome. A rising literary star. You have places to go, people to meet."

"I sold a single novel."

"The first of many." He pulled his dirty shirt back on, his pants. "This is my business, Alfie. I know a star when I see one."

"Is that why you love me?" Alfonse rose to his feet, naked as the day he was born. "Please say no, even if it's a lie."

"You know it's not. I'll love you even when we are old queens griping at one another about who left his wet shoes in the foyer."

"Do you promise?" Alfonse grabbed his wrist, pulled him close again. Cornelius didn't look at him until Alfonse took his face into his hands. "Forever?"

So blue, those eyes. Like the hydrangea growing wild in the storm-ruined gardens. Alfonse had lost himself in them once and hadn't found his way back out again. His family would never understand. Neither would the friends they had back in New York. Friends who saw them as mentor and protégé. Cornelius had laid claim to many of those in his forty-some-odd years. Alfonse hadn't been the first, but he would be the last.

Dusk had settled over the ocean by the time Alfonse woke. Olivia sat nearby, her chair tipped to the last rays of sunlight, reading through the notebook nearly filled. Beside him, a plate of fruit and cheese and bread. Alfonse shouldered higher in his chair.

"I thought you might be hungry when you woke."

"Did I miss dinner?"

"Not yet. I didn't think you'd want to go down tonight. Shall I get your chariot?"

"No, no." He waved her back into her chair. "This will do fine. Thank you, Olivia."

She pulled her chair closer. "Well, thank you for not doing another sex scene." She patted the book. "I get so bored of them."

"There was no need. We'd seen them at it before. Nothing has changed."

"And isn't that the whole point?"

Alfonse tapped the side of his nose. "I knew you'd get it."

Clutching the notebook to her chest, Olivia rose from the chair. She sat on the edge of his armrest, her arm going around his shoulders and her head resting on top of his. "I've read it several times while you were sleeping," she said. "I think it's Aldo's time to speak."

"I do, too."

"Then why didn't you say?"

"I like to hear you argue." He grinned. "I was dreaming about it. About Aldo and Cecilia."

"Don't tell me. I'll read it in a few days."

"I wasn't going to." He took the notebook from her and set it aside. "Did I hear Cecibel in here earlier?"

"She said to tell you she'd stop by again a little later."

"Good, good." Alfonse would try to stay awake, but he would be sleeping, and she would go away. Probably to be with Fin. He didn't have to see them together to know when they were. "She's changed since I first came here."

"Of course she has." Olivia laughed softly. "What woman fails to be changed by the great Alfonse Carducci?"

"It wasn't me."

"Of course it was. Don't be daft, Alfie."

"You give me far too much credit, but I won't argue. I'm not up for it these days."

"I miss arguing with you."

He patted her hand. "We did have some fun, no?"

"'It was the best of times, it was the worst of times.'"

"'The age of wisdom' . . ."

"'The age of foolishness' . . ."

He laughed softly. The only way he could. "Are we really going to do this, my sweet?"

"Alfonse." His name a breath on her lips, a sob in her throat. "I can't bear it."

"You can. You will. Stay with me while I eat my meager rations, then leave me to write."

"I'll get you something to drink." Olivia darted to the sideboard, came back with a splash of purple, forbidden liquid in the bottom of a stemmed glass.

"Livy, I can't."

"What possible harm can it do now, Alfie?" She handed him the stem, stepped back.

Alfonse brought the rim to his nose. The scent nearly made him weep. The tiniest taste of it on his tongue tipped him into it completely.

"Where did this come from?"

"Judith brought it." Olivia shrugged. "She forgot you weren't . . . well . . . anyway. We three had a glass earlier on. This is all that's left."

"Thank you," he said. "You've no idea . . ."

"I might have some." She sat again. "Is there anything else forbidden that I can sneak in here for you?"

"Viagra?"

Olivia snorted. "As if you need it. I've been here when you wake up, my dear."

"Some things never die."

"Perhaps we should have it bronze-cast and mounted on the wall in the library."

"You'd have to put in supports so the wall doesn't crumble under the sheer enormity of it."

Now she laughed, husky and wicked. "I've personal experience enough to know it's substantial, but not that big."

"You haven't seen it in a while."

"Is that an invitation?"

"Livy, please don't tease me."

"I'm not teasing."

No. She was not. In the fiendish blue of her eyes, he saw her younger, wilder self. Of all the lovers Alfonse Carducci had, she was the least inhibited. He knew her past, her married life; it always astounded him, the madness with which she made love. Olivia reached for him, her gaze never leaving his. The zipper of his pants, undone. The fumbled folds of boxers, aside.

"My heart," he said, already out of breath. "I . . . I can't."

"Then I won't," she said, still gently massaging. "Just relax, Alfonse. I promise not to kill you. Tonight, the forbidden gets tasted. Tomorrow is another day."

Olivia stopped before his heart rate rose enough to send the monitor always attached to his finger to beeping. Alfonse wanted her to continue. He wanted it so badly. But sometimes what one wanted was not for the best, or even for the worst, but definitely not wise.

No awkward segue, no blushing. They were too old, too familiar, too beloved. He tucked himself in, zipped himself up, and ate the fruit and cheese Olivia had fetched him from the dining room. She checked her watch. "If I want dinner myself, I have to go." Rising, she kissed his cheek. "I'll see you tomorrow."

"Yes. Tomorrow. Thank you, Olivia." He took her hand. "What would I do without you?"

"You've done without me many years." She smiled. "You'd do fine. It's just nice for you to have me around again."

Another kiss, this time on the lips, and Olivia left him alone in his suite. Evening light canted through high windows, spilled shadows in crooks and corners. Alfonse inhaled carefully, exhaled long and slow. He tipped the last drop of wine onto his tongue, savored the taste he'd not enjoyed in far too long. How simple life became when one was old and close to death. A splash of wine, an old woman's hand on his cock, a little cheese and fruit made all right with the world. And maybe, if he were very, very lucky, Cecibel would come and bid him good night before slumber took him out of the running.

He dug her copy of *Night Wings on the Moon* out of his seat cushions, fanned through the pages. How long had it been since that day she'd brought it to him? Less than three months, and how she'd changed. How everything had. It seemed like an eternity since he'd been wheeled out of the ambulance and to this room Cornelius left to him, only him. And yet hadn't it only been hours ago they two had chased one another through the house like madmen?

Alfonse flipped to the page Cecibel had, in furious sorrow, marked. The faded pencil, still indecipherable, beckoned. *Find me,* the words said, *and you find her.* Younger eyes, better light, he didn't think either would make a difference.

We fell free from on high, like dragons mating . . . ground came at us . . . didn't care . . . I covered her eyes . . . I didn't want to be saved, and so she couldn't be either.

A sister. One broken before Cecibel could save her. One who'd broken Cecibel completely in the end. Unintentionally. Which of them did this passage speak of? Who covered whose eyes? Who didn't want to be saved?

It didn't matter, Alfonse realized. It spoke of both of them. To both of them. There were mysteries he'd never solve. This was one of them. He hadn't the time to unravel it. He squinted hard, brought the paper pages as close to his eyes as he could before they blurred all over again. It was no use. The words she'd penciled were lost.

Or were they?

As he took a pencil from the drawer in his side table, his heart hammered harder than it had while Olivia fondled him. Boldly, so carefully, he erased what remained of the pencil marks. He just as carefully rubbed the graphite tip over the spot. Letters, long ago written and lost to searching fingers and sorrow were born all over again.

Never again.

Sweat beaded his brow, his upper lip. Never again to love. Never again to care. Never again to fail, to live, to survive, to hope. Everything and nothing and all things in between. Alfonse Carducci's battered heart swelled in an almost pleasant, not painful way. Closing the book, he caught his breath that had gotten away from him just a little. He shoved Cecibel's copy of *Night*

Wings back down the side of his chair, into the cushions. Safe and hidden. For now.

Words and emotions raw and flowing, Alfonse Carducci picked up the brown notebook full of his words, Olivia's, Raymond Switcher's. The story of Cecilia and Aldo, and then Enzo, too. And Tressa, of course. The scene brightened behind his eyes, in the gray matter still working just fine. Lovers in a hotel room. A telegram. A plan. And fates sealed.

Portland, Maine

AUGUST 3, 1999

They say, "There's always tomorrow," but sometimes, tomorrow doesn't come.

—CORNELIUS TRAEGAR

"It was good of you to make the trip." Dr. Marks, a shriveled old woman now, didn't rise from her chair. Could she? How old she'd gotten in the years since their parting. Knobbed knuckles, lined face, white hair. But her eyes—gentle, brown, clear, and kind—hadn't changed. Only Cecibel's perspective had.

"It's good to see you, Richard."

"Lovely to see you, too, Maybelle. It's been too long."

"I wasn't aware you two knew one another," Cecibel snapped. She took a deep breath. "Sorry."

"No need to apologize," Dr. Kintz told her. "This isn't easy. Now that I've gotten you here, I'll make myself scarce. You have my pager number when you're ready to go."

Dr. Kintz, leaving? Of course he was leaving. They'd discussed it at length when she'd asked him, not Fin, to drive her down to Portland to see Dr. Marks. Fin didn't even know she was going. She'd told only Olivia, so she could let Alfonse know why she wouldn't be in to see him that day.

The click of the door closing nicked a tiny hole in Cecibel's stomach. She felt air squeaking in, bile leaking out. Silence filled the space Dr. Kintz left behind, a silence she remembered all too well. Some things never changed. Until they did.

"I knew Cornelius a very long time." Dr. Marks spoke first. "I helped him get certified, he helped me with my book. He was a literary agent before he became a doctor, did you know?"

"Of course," Cecibel answered. "You can't live in the Pen and not know that."

Dr. Marks chuckled softly. "I see the name still sticks. I always liked it."

"It fits." Cecibel shrugged, and fell silent. The same diplomas on the wall, even more yellowed than they'd been, but different furniture. Softer chairs. Wood where there had been Formica and steel. Or maybe it was that perspective thing again.

"I will get down to it," Dr. Marks said. "Yes, Dr. Traegar and I made arrangements on your behalf. I knew about Finlay Pottinger, and what he'd done for him. I asked it of him for you as well."

"How did you know about Fin?"

"The whole country knew about him."

"I mean the arrangement with Dr. Traegar."

"Friends talk." Dr. Marks shrugged, a shoulder to her ear. "What does it matter? All that does is I asked and he agreed."

"What did you ask of him?"

"You already know. Richard informed me. He said he did so with your permission."

"I want to hear it from you." Cecibel's fingers clenched into a fist. "You were the one who did the arranging."

Dr. Marks poured herself a glass of ice water from the sweating carafe on her desk, and one for Cecibel, pushed it to her. "I couldn't do anything more for you here. You weren't ready to leave, but you wouldn't stay, and I felt forcing the issue would do more harm than good. I asked Cornelius if he would hire you, give you purpose in a place where you'd be safe."

"Like Fin."

"Yes and no. People will blame a victim, if given the chance. It's far more comfortable to believe he was complicit in what happened. A bad choice made by a teenager versus a horrible thing done to a child."

"Protect Fin from society while protecting society from him. That's what his chart said."

"You read it?"

"So what if I did?" Cecibel grabbed the glass of water from the desk, spilling most of it. She wanted to hurl it at a wall. She wanted to scream. Mopping it up with a fistful of tissues, she breathed deeply through her nose. "Fin killed the guy who raped him and went to jail for it," she said. "I tried to kill myself and my sister and got half my face ripped off instead. Charity cases. Murderer and monster. Things to be locked away." Like Sal, dressing like a woman and singing show tunes.

Cecibel tossed the soggy tissues into the waste bin. Dr. Marks folded her hands on the desk. Knuckles white. Kind eyes. Waiting for Cecibel to say more, which she never had. She kept it in. Or she told lies and half-truths. Made some things up because they were better, or worse, than reality. Some things never changed. Until they did.

"But I didn't kill her. Jen. I didn't kill her. She was already dead. Jennifer was." Her name, spoken aloud, cast its spell. If she closed her eyes, she'd see her there. "I found her on the playground, at the beach. She was already cold." Eyes closed. Mouth open. "There was no one else around." The surf hissing, gulls crying. Cecibel on her knees in the dark, in the damp sand. Shaking her sister. Shaking. "She died alone under the slide, staring up at graffiti and chewed gum." She snatched a dry tissue from the box. "All I could think was to get her to the hospital. They'd brought her back before." She blew her nose, the images in her head scattering, re-forming. Dragging Jen to the car, shoving her in. "I was driving so fast. I couldn't even be sure where I was. She was in the car next to me, eyes closed and foam on her lips. It smelled so bad." Egg farts. Cecibel choked on the laugh knotting in her gut. "So bad. I can still smell it sometimes. The poles kept whizzing by and whizzing by and the music was blasting. I tried so hard." *Damn you, Jennifer. Fuck you. Fuck you!* "I thought I knew her every trick, every sign. But she was always a step ahead of me."

Arms wrapped around her waist, squeezed the air from her lungs. Cecibel doubled over, trapped the culprit, made her stop. "That curve, the other car." Moonlight had been full. Bright. "I saw it. For one, tiny second I thought how easy it would be to just hit it"—headlights coming the other way, oblivious. Innocent—"to take us both someplace that had to be better than this one." How easy. A relief. No more grief. No more anger. Gone, gone, gone. "Only for a second. That's all it took. I pulled out of it too late."

She sat upright, unwrapped her arms from around her waist, took a deep breath. "Instead of dead, I got this." She covered her ruined face with her palm. "But I'm not a murderer. It isn't murder if she was already dead, no matter what I might have wanted for that second. Is it?"

Cecibel tore at the snotty tissue in her hand. Dr. Marks rose from her chair, after all. Hands clasped behind her back, she came to the other side of the desk and leaned against it. "There has never been any question about the cause of Jennifer's death," she said. "The autopsy report is clear, and you were never charged with any sort of manslaughter. You were told, but you never heard, or elected not to listen. I have the report in the file, if you wish to see it."

Of course there was a report. Like there were charts hidden away in an antiquated record-keeping system in the basement of an old mansion.

"Whatever your intentions toward yourself or your sister are lost, to you and to me. There's no way to know what went on in your mind during the extreme duress of those moments. Your memory can't be trusted, and shouldn't be. Whatever the truth was no longer matters. Only the present matters, now." Dr. Marks tucked white hair behind her ears. She leaned closer to Cecibel. "You survived. You fought your way back when you could well have succumbed to your injuries. And now you're here, face uncovered, where it all began. Why do you think that's so?"

Rumbling vibrated the chair under her, the floor at her feet. Cecibel glanced out the window, but no thunderclouds darkened the sky. She bit her lips closed. Dr. Marks only smiled. Some things never changed, until they did. "I didn't make arrangements with Dr. Traegar because I thought you were a suicidal murderer who needed to be locked away, Cecibel. I did that because you did. You needed a place to heal. A safe place where you could take as long as you needed and never be turned out. You earned a living. You made a life. I took the chance that you would because I believed you were a fighter. And you are."

Why didn't you tell me all those years ago? I did.

Why didn't you make me listen? I tried.

Why couldn't I save her?

"Now, then." Dr. Marks pushed away from the desk. "I'm going to give you a few moments to yourself. Then we will continue this, if you wish."

Drained. Sad. Relieved. Free. From secrets that were no secrets at all, only ones she'd kept from herself. The pain of it all was exquisite. "Thank you."

Her smile, so kind, deepened the lines of her face. "Would you like a cup of coffee? I might be able to scare us up a few cookies, too."

"Sure. That'd be great. I'm really hungry all of a sudden."

Dr. Marks patted her shoulder. Cecibel closed her eyes. A phantom kiss, a tender gesture, ghosted across her brow, but the doctor was already out the door, the soft click nicking closed that tiny hole earlier pricked. No more squeaking air or leaking bile. The specters of memories left unremembered so long fluttering about the room, trying to settle into new, untried places, had no way back inside. Not even Jen. Beautiful, troubled, beloved Jen, whom Cecibel hadn't been able to save no matter how hard she tried.

Cecibel dreamed.

She and Fin were walking on the beach, collecting sea glass. He found a blue one, like her eyes. Holding it up to moonlight, she watched tiny images play across the surface—Jennifer running, Alfonse and Olivia dancing, Cecilia and Aldo kissing.

Cecibel dropped the smooth shard in the surf and watched it roll back into the ocean. On the cresting waves, Jennifer ran, Alfonse and Olivia danced, Cecilia and Aldo kissed. Waving, waving, she waved them out to sea, where from the water a giant clamshell rose. Venus lifted her face to the moon. Golden hair cascading, salt water streaming, her face was whole and lovely and sad. Dr. Marks offered her a hand, assisted her off her precarious perch and onto the shifting, still-warm shore. The wind kicked up, a storm came in, and on it galloped braying hounds. From the moon, an arrow twanged. It cut a path through storm and sea and sand, through Jen and Olivia, Alfonse and the rest, collecting them all on its shaft, and fell, inert, at Venus's feet.

"Miss Bringer." A howling dog. "Cecibel. Wake up. We're back."

Wiping the drool from her cheek, Cecibel shouldered upright. Dr. Kintz took his hand from her shoulder.

"Sorry. Did I sleep the whole three hours home?"

"Most of them." He smiled kindly. "You woke up a few times."

"What terrible company I am."

"Believe me, it was nice to have so much time all to myself without having to talk. Sometimes I feel like that's all I do."

"Well, you *are* a psychiatrist." She laughed because he did, waited for it to fade. "Thanks for today."

"You're welcome. I'm happy to do it, and if you need to go back to see Dr. Marks again—"

"About that." She fidgeted. He waited. She said, "If it's okay with you, I'll skip the ride down to Portland and just talk to you now and then."

"What does Dr. Marks say about that?"

"That she's old and too much of my past." Cecibel shrugged. "It was her suggestion, and I agreed. I mean, if you do."

"That would be fine with me."

"She's going to send you a report or something, just to bring you up to speed in a more clinical way. I'm sure there will be some doctor-to-doctor things in there, too."

"Whatever you're comfortable with. And Cecibel"—he stopped her from getting out of the car—"it doesn't have to be a formal thing. It can just be friends, talking. You're not a patient here. You know that, right?"

"Do you?"

He lowered his head. "I overreacted, and I'm sorry. All I knew was what I read."

"It's okay. I'm glad you did, in a way."

He looked up.

"If you hadn't made a fuss about me and Fin leaving without signing out, I wouldn't have gotten angry, or curious about why. It's all good, Dr. . . . Richard."

"I'm glad."

Cecibel got out of the car, waving to Richard as he pulled away, recalling a snippet of dream and smiling. He'd let her out near the entrance closest to the kitchen. The obvious smells drifted out of the big windows—bread and meat, and the undercurrent of chicken broth that made its way into everything. Dinner was in full swing in the dining room by now. It was too late to make a tray for herself and vanish, but she was hungry just the same and, tonight, didn't feel like vanishing anyway.

Peeking into the dining room through the curtain, she spotted Switch, Judith, and Olivia at their accustomed table. No Alfonse. Her heart stitched. He'd gotten so much worse, so quickly. She'd been briefed on his condition and prognosis long before he ever set foot in the Pen. The reality then nebulous suddenly blared all too clearly. But the others in that most prestigious court, eating and laughing together, told her he was still alive if not well.

She slipped in through the service entrance and went straight to the kitchen. Making herself a plate, she exchanged small pleasant-ries with the staff she'd always hurried past. No one shrank away from her anymore, at least not that she saw. It wasn't easy, coming out of hiding, but it got easier day by day.

Instead of taking her meal to her room, Cecibel sought out Sal. She'd been avoiding him since prying into a story he would will-ingly but never forcibly give. He, Fin, and she were of a kind; she'd always known. Misfits. Damaged. As similar as they were different. While Fin kept his head down and plodded on, while Cecibel hid herself away, Sal flaunted his fabulous self, defiant and proud and, at the end of the day, safe within the Pen.

She found him in the laundry, pulling something full and fluffy from one of the huge dryers. Setting her dinner tray onto a folding table, she cleared her throat.

Sal spun, silver-and-black-tipped fingernails pressed to his chest. "Girl, you nearly gave me a heart attack."

"Sorry. I tried not to scare you."

Embracing the garment, a white and red floral, he inhaled deeply. "Nothing like a pretty dress straight out of the dryer." He shook it out, held it against him. "What do you think? Too Lucille Ball?"

"Vintage." Cecibel picked at the green beans on her plate. "I've never seen you wear anything so . . . so . . ."

"Nonglittery?" Sal laughed. "I'm getting too old for all that sparkle."

"A girl is never too old for sparkle."

"If only the world believed that, too."

The dress swung back and forth on its wooden hanger. Sal was not small, and the dress had volume. Cecibel fingered the fabric, light and smooth. Cotton chintz, she thought, and wondered how in the world she'd know such a thing. A hazy memory—Mom, a yellow room, pins in her mouth, and dancing under a disco-ball sky—flittered like dappled sunlight.

"Where'd you go, sugar?"

"Huh? Oh, sorry." Cecibel let go the dress, picked up a roll off her tray, and pulled it apart. "Very pretty. Special occasion?"

"Do I need one?" Sal laughed. "No, not really. I just liked it. I found it at the thrift store downtown. It's not easy finding anything in my size. I snapped it up, even though it was way too expensive for a thrift-store dress."

"You're going to glitter it, aren't you."

"You know me so well." Sal hugged her around the waist, lifted her in the air. "So how'd it go with your old shrink?"

Cecibel gagged on the bread. "How did you know? I only told . . . Olivia!"

"She's ridiculously easy to get talking once she's had her medicine."

"I should have known better. Put me down."

Sal obliged. "It wouldn't have been hard to figure out. You've been . . . different lately, and I don't just mean that you're showing that face of yours. So? Eat, and tell me what happened."

It didn't take long. There wasn't much really to tell. Keeping secrets, after all, was more about keeping them from oneself than the world that most likely guessed long ago. Or didn't care. Sal had known a little about Jennifer, about the drugs and the chaos, that Cecibel had given up everything to help her, and failed. Not even the momentary suicide fantasy came as any shock, as of course, Cecibel should have known.

"That's why I'm here, you know," Sal said when she'd finished. "I tried to kill myself, but only after a gang of stupid, silly boys tried to kill me first."

"Oh." Cecibel hugged him. "I didn't know that."

He poked her. "You didn't read about it in my chart?"

"That was temporary insanity," she said. "I'm sorry. I really am. I only glanced at it. I didn't dig. I wasn't digging for you, at any rate."

"I know. But you know what, sugar? That hurts, too. You've never asked. After all these years, didn't you ever wonder about me?"

"Yes and no," she answered. "I wondered, but only long enough to remind myself that I couldn't ask when I didn't want to tell, you know? I'm not as brave as you are."

"Brave?" Sal pressed hands to dimpled cheeks. "Yes, I suppose I am. Now, anyway. It gets easier, once you decide to be." Sal pulled more clothes from the dryer. Scrubs. Underwear. Men's clothes but for the floral chintz. "It's not easy being who I am, especially in a small town. I'm from Camden. Did you know that?"

Cecibel shook her head. Sal shrugged and went back to folding his clothes. "They beat me so bad, those boys. So bad. Raped me, too, can you believe that? All the while calling me a fag. I didn't want to live in a world that let things like that happen. My mom and dad, my brothers, they acted like I got what I asked for. That if I'd just stop being queer everything would be fine. I tried. I even dated a girl for a little while. And then I tried to finish what those boys started. Dr. Traegar found me in the hospital in Rockport.

Don't ask me how. He never said and I was too grateful to push it. But he understood about boys like me. He understood that the world wasn't ready for us. So he let me come here, made sure I'd never get kicked out."

"You knew all along?"

"Of course."

"But Finlay doesn't."

"I have no idea. You'll have to ask him."

After I apologize. "We're quite the trio."

"We're a family, sugar lips. Us, the residents, even the nurses and doctors. Better than our own, who abandoned us."

"Not Fin's mom."

"Didn't she?" Sal flicked lint from his shirt. "I've never met her. She never comes here. He has to go to her, and only for special occasions."

"But she stayed here in Bar Harbor when it would have been easier for her to move away."

"I suppose you have a point. What about you, baby girl? If we're talking about deep stuff here, where'd your family go?"

"Away." The word came unbidden. She couldn't take it back. Cecibel's cheeks burned. The haze parting, parting, parting since finding those charts in the basement let in more light. Choices made. Tears cried. How long ago it had been. Back then, Cecibel believed it was all temporary. Back then, she still had hope that Jen would be okay. "Before Jen died. Long before. They couldn't take it. I . . . I have a little brother." Kenny. Holy shit, Kenny. She hadn't thought of him in years. "Jen and I were in our twenties, grown women and already out of the house. He was only ten. When I told my parents I wouldn't go with them, they accused me of doing . . . of being like Jen. They left. Last I heard, they were in South Carolina or something."

"Well, fuck them. Do they even know your sister died? That you nearly did?"

No, they left me to take care of her and never looked back. "I'm sure they must know. And if they don't, it's because they don't want to."

"Come here." Sal opened his arms, pulled her to him when

she got close enough. He smelled of laundry soap and a little like marijuana. Cecibel let him hold her, stiffly at first, and then she was weeping, buried deep into his softness. Mom and chintz and the high school gym bedazzled by the rented disco ball. Her date— what was his name?—Steven. Maybe it was Tom. Whoever he was, he'd been lost to a past Cecibel traded in for Jennifer. Like Kenny. Her own little brother. Mom and Dad, she couldn't feel sorry about. They'd not only given up on Jen, they'd given up on her, too. All the reasons that might be so didn't matter, right that moment, only that they had.

Rubbing her back, Sal crooned sweetly, softly. Familiar tune. Familiar words. "'It's raining men, hallelujah. It's raining men, amen.'"

Cecibel choked on her own laugh. "Are you kidding me?"

"Sorry, sugar. It's my new song. I'm performing this weekend." He pulled back just enough to look at her. "You want to come?"

She wiped her cheeks dry, sniffed back tears. Family. He was her family. Part of it, anyway. Cecibel smiled openly, gruesomely, and Sal didn't even flinch. "Sure. I'd love to."

"Oh, girl! It's going to be a time! Maybe we can get Finlay to come, too. And Dr. Dick."

"Don't call him that." She nudged his plush belly. "He's a good guy."

"I suppose. Oh!" He gripped her shoulders. "Mrs. Peppernell. Can you even imagine? She'd love it. Wispy Flicker's got herself a new audience!"

Almost nine, and still Cecibel had not come to him. Olivia said she would. Then again, Olivia had been mightily stoned when she came to fetch the notebook. She'd have done anything to make him feel better, including pry into his pants when they were alone and her inhibitions were nil. The first time had been nice. The second, too. The rest? Not so much. The sensation he'd spent his life pursuing frightened Alfonse now. If an orgasm was going to kill him, he had a better scenario in mind than Olivia's old, beloved, familiar hands on him.

How he dreamed! Dreams that threatened the beeping monitor and came close—but never too close, after all—to shaming him in waking hours. He'd become the quintessential dirty old man, lusting after a young woman dazzled enough by fame to indulge romantic fantasies of what might have been were he younger, she older, and they'd met in some New York club instead of a home for elderly writers going quietly into that good night.

He got into his pajamas without calling for the nurse. Sitting on the edge of his bed, winded yet feeling quite accomplished, he reached to switch off the bedside lamp; a soft knock at his door halted him. His heart stitched. His groin twitched. Alfonse sat up straighter. "Come in, Cecibel."

And of course it was she, slipping in out of the night from wherever she'd been. Portland, Olivia said, visiting with her old psychiatrist. The implications of that were too much for him, especially when his heart was already pounding so.

"You were about to go to sleep," she said.

"Bed," he told her. "Not sleep. I mostly just lie here . . ." *conjuring exquisite, dastardly dreams.* "I'm glad you came to see me."

"Don't get up." She stopped him from rising. "I'll pull a chair over. I won't stay long."

He did as she asked and got into bed. She propped him up, covered his legs. Old. Feeble. Pathetic. How had this happened? He'd never meant to grow old. Not ever. He was supposed to die in some spectacular way, worthy of newspaper articles full of speculation and gossip, tributes to his never-ending *joie de vivre.* Instead, Cecibel sat beside him like a dutiful granddaughter, concerned and fussing. Exquisite dreams morphed into impotent fury, setting his heart thumping more rapidly than it did when Olivia had her hands on him. He couldn't die this way. Not Alfonse Carducci. If he ever imagined dying in bed, it was with a bullet in him and an angry lover looming, or a lover's spouse. Not this way. Please, God, not this way.

"You've gone very quiet."

"Just feeling sorry for myself," he mumbled. "It will pass." *And so will I.*

"What can I do?"

Take off your clothes and get into bed with me. Let me touch you. Touch me. Selfish, selfish man. Hadn't he always been? He would die, sent into oblivion with a smile on his face. Cecibel would be his lover and his killer, all in one act of love. Scandal. Exactly what he wished for. But not for her. She'd had enough, that much he knew, even if he didn't know exactly what form it took.

"Tell me something, Cecibel. Anything."

"About?"

"Oh, I don't know. Tell me a funny story about Olivia before I came here. There must be thousands."

"At least that many." Cecibel laughed softly. "If I tell you one, will you tell me one?"

"I might be persuaded."

Slipping her arm through his, she rested her head to his shoulder. Alfonse kissed her temple before he could think better of the idea, but Cecibel only snuggled in closer. "I guess it was back in 1996. Switch had just moved in a little while before that and hadn't started growing for her yet. She used to have this guy from town deliver her weed . . ."

Olivia and her provider, the new product he introduced with a free sample and his company while she partook. The hilarity of hearing her explain, in her imperious way, why there was a naked man locked in her bathroom when the nurses came to investigate the banging. Alfonse countered with the night they broke into a restaurant in Greenwich Village back in 1971, made themselves a meal, and drank three bottles of the house wine. She'd been furious when he told her he went back the next day and paid for what they'd taken, let the owners take a picture, and promised to sign it when it was developed. At least he hadn't told them of her involvement, which she'd thanked him for, especially when the photo hit the front page of the *Village Voice,* and yet remained insulted by the omission to this day.

Back and forth they traded stories safely about Olivia. Cecibel's head on his shoulder, her arm through his. Pillow talk of a different kind. Somewhere between one story and the next, Cecibel had shifted onto the bed beside him and Alfonse found it comforting rather than arousing. That alone should have infuriated him all over again, that the one-and-only Alfonse Carducci could have a woman in his bed and feel only contentment. But it didn't. Not this time.

He went with it. Took it a step further. He loved Cecibel, for sure and certain. But not the way he'd loved Cornelius, or Olivia, or any of the dozens of lovers he no longer remembered but loved in their moments. Once he set aside erotic dreaming that left him almost-shamed and breathless, what was left behind?

Love. Pure and simple. It had never been either for him. Always complicated. Always conflicted. Always creased covers and dog-eared pages. This love was the pristine kind, the cherished kind held above the everyday. She was more important. Her wants. Her needs. He'd never wanted children. He'd been too selfish all his life. But, from the very start, not with Cecibel. Never with Cecibel. Her best interests trumped every selfish impulse Alfonse had.

Earlier anger made a play for his attention, tried to trick him back into the safe, the comfortable habit of an ego dying a harder death than his body. Pulling forward the new sensation, he felt it swell in him and swell in him until it was let the tears fall or his heart burst.

"I thought she'd drown, but she managed to get back to the beach before—"

"Cecibel?"

She lifted her head—"What's wrong?"—and looked at the clock. "Oh, crap. It's after ten. Here I am blathering on about Olivia. You're probably exhausted."

"Not at all. I interrupted your story. Forgive me."

"Why are you crying? Should I get a doctor?"

Alfonse gently pressed her head back to his shoulder. All the wicked, impossible dreams of the past weeks were melting like sugar in hot water. He let them go. Sadly. Regretfully. Resignedly. Was this evolution? Did he still have it in him, after all this time?

"I want to tell you a story," he said. "One I've only told one other person in my whole life."

"Cornelius?" His name from her lips brought a smile to his.

"Yes, Cornelius. I told him everything, once. Then nothing at all. But it's not about him. It's about when I was a boy, back in Italy."

"Oh. Okay."

"I was a boy like any other boy. I played soccer with my friends, caused a ruckus wherever I went, and came home dirty for dinner every night. But I also wasn't like the other boys, and I didn't know why until I was eleven."

"What happened when you were eleven?"

"I fell hopelessly in love with a childhood pal. Someone I'd known since the cradle."

"That might do it." Cecibel laughed softly.

"His name was Roberto. I loved him as only a child can love that very first time. It was very confusing for me. I didn't understand how I could be a boy, but wanted to kiss him, to see him naked, to touch him. Another boy. I'd never heard of such a thing. I knew better than to ask my family. I chased the girls, all the while wishing it was Roberto I got caught kissing under the bridge.

"The older I got, the more I wanted him, and the more girls I kissed. It was nice. I liked how it made me feel. Carina Petrocelli was my first lover. I was thirteen, she was sixteen. She rode me like a circus pony whenever she caught me. I let her catch me often. My mother said I would make her a grandmother before her time. My father scolded me in front of her, but patted me on the back in private. I cried myself to sleep most nights. I didn't want Carina. I wanted Roberto, and still I didn't understand.

"When we were young men, Roberto went to fight in France and I came to America. We were twenty, and still best friends. I never told him how I felt, but he kissed me before he left. Kissed me the way I'd always wanted to kiss him. It was the last time I ever saw him."

"Oh, Alfonse. I'm so sorry."

"First love." He laughed softly. "It wouldn't have worked out for us. Not in Italy. Not back then. We writers tell tales of that first love being the only one. It's romantic, but rarely so. I met Cornelius when I was twenty-six. He was almost forty and already a giant in his field. At first, it was all about the writing. Mentor and protégé. It became more, quickly. In this house, our house, when it was still just a shell in need of more repair than I ever thought could be done, he promised me forever."

"What happened?" she asked.

"He gave it to me," Alfonse said in a rush of breath that left him light-headed. "He wanted more for me than I wanted for myself. He feared our relationship would kill my career, so he sent me away to become the great Alfonse Carducci. And I did. We always intended it to be temporary. But the longer we were parted, the less I wanted to be tied to one person, to one man. I love women. I love the feel of them and the look of them and the smell of them. But I've only loved Cornelius in that way I wrote about so many times. Only him. I broke his heart a thousand times over. I left him and didn't return. Not even when he was old and sick and all he wanted was to see me one more time. I should have come to him, Cecibel. I asked him for forever and he gave it to me, but I couldn't give it to him."

Words he'd never spoken. Tears he'd never cried. Freed, at last. Like the words Alfonse thought had abandoned him. Holding Cecibel in both his arms, he buried his face in her hair that smelled like the beach. Always the beach.

"There, now." He sniffed. "You've had two stories for the price of one. The first, told only once before. The second, known too well but spoken of in whispers, behind old hands." He shifted her from his shoulder to look her in the eyes. Dim lighting softened the melted candle of her face, accentuated the beauty of the other half. Tears blurred Alfonse's vision, let him see her whole as she might have been in another set of circumstances. Another Cecibel. Not his Cecibel. The beautiful monster who'd given him back his greatest, truest love. *I've been writing,* he wanted to say. *Because of you.* But he had promises to keep.

He tucked her hair behind her remaining ear, touched her cheek. "Now I need to rest. Confession is good for the soul, but taxing. Do you mind?"

"Of course not." Cecibel pulled out of his arms that let go reluctantly, leaned down and kissed his cheek, then his lips. Alfonse kissed her back, a little of the dirty old man always and forever lingering.

"You're an amazing man, Alfonse. Far more so than any of my fangirl dreaming."

"I've lived an amazing life," he said. "If that makes me amazing, I gladly wear the word."

She laughed softly, took his hand, and squeezed it. "Good night. Sweet dreams."

"Good night. I'll leave the light on for you, until you're out the door."

The door clicked. Alfonse switched off the light. He sat upright in his bed, in the dark and the quiet, too many thoughts whirring through his head. Good thoughts. Regret was a cruel disciplinarian, but effective when heeded. Alfonse regretted much, but not everything. Not the words. Never the words. He'd sacrificed everything for them and would do it all over again.

They whispered. The words. Aldo and Cecilia. Olivia had already taken the book to pen her part. Cecilia's part. He'd not get it back until Enzo had his say. But his fingers itched. His brain bubbled with thoughts he couldn't quite grasp. It was after ten. *Sleep, sleep, Alfie.* Whose voice beckoned? Certainly not his own. He sat up straighter, checked the shadows.

"I can sleep when I'm dead, and that'll be soon enough." Tossing aside the blankets, he swung his feet to the floor and regretted it for the way it dizzied him. Alfonse walked slowly to his easy chair, had to stop and rest. Arms flopped to his sides, his hand landed on the familiar spine of a passion-creased book. He pulled Cecibel's copy of *Night Wings on the Moon* from the seat cushion. His words. Hers. *Never again.*

The garbling rush between his ears cleared. Words formed. The right words, at last. His beleaguered heart thumped more happily than painfully. Plucking a pen from the side table, Alfonse obeyed the call of his greatest love, as he always had.

⌒

Cecibel walked the quiet halls of the Pen. Meandered with no intention of going to her own room, to sleep. Alfonse's story played over and over again. Roberto. Cornelius. A man forced to live against the longings of his heart. Why he'd told his story to her, that night of all nights, was no mystery. He was dying, and soon. She sensed it the same way Olivia did, as Alfonse must. The unburdening revealed him, at last, for who he was. Cecibel couldn't cry. He'd entrusted the only-once-told tale of first love to her. An honor, his heartbreak. This confession, even now, he'd felt the need to make. She would cherish it the rest of her life.

She sat in the library a moment or two, looked into the cleaned dining room waiting for breakfast. Past Dr. Kintz's office, the utility room, Sal's room, her own, she walked through and out of the building entirely.

The sea air rushed up to greet her, a happy puppy left alone all day. It scooted up her skirt and tossed her unbound hair—unbound, but not concealing, cascading, instead, down her back and not over her left shoulder. Free.

Her feet trod a path well known, her nose followed the scent. To the sea. Always the sea. Cure for all things. All things but one. Jennifer had died to the sound of the ocean, its scent more familiar than flowers or grass. All those times Cecibel found her, she'd been at the beach. A last-ditch effort to soothe the demons breaking her from inside. Mighty ocean. Ancient womb. It hadn't been any more successful than she.

Sliding on her heels down the dunes, Cecibel took off her hoodie. She set it on the sand well above the tide and sat. Legs curled up, arms wrapped around them, she listened, listened to the oldest song in the history of the world. The tones unchanging, the continuous symphony never repeated, silenced by familiarity.

She couldn't think coherent thoughts. Not now. Instead she let them fill her along with the sea-crashed symphony. Salt spray dewed her arms, her shoulders, her face half ruined but only half, after all. A monster revealed was a monster vanquished, in old fairy tales.

Upon the moonglade cast upon the black and glistening sea, dancers danced as they had before, in the car, in dreaming safe and dreaming strange. Cecilia, in movie-star finery, her dress throwing foam as she spun into Aldo's arms. Or were they Enzo's? Olivia twirled all alone, hands raised to the stars. Switch and Judi, Sal and Richard, Dr. Marks—they all stomped and splashed like children on the surface of the water, never sinking past the soles of their feet. Alfonse held Cornelius. They swayed slowly out to sea. Alfonse looked back, his hand reached, but Cecibel couldn't get there quickly enough and they were gone.

And there was Jennifer, not tragic, but as she'd been before heroin took away her pain, dispersed it in a circle around herself. She stood apart from the others gathered, looking straight into Cecibel. Eyes smiling, lips parted to show the gap between her front teeth, the one she'd whistled and squirted water through when they were kids. No "I'm sorry." No forgiveness of any kind asked. Just that smile before she turned and walked away.

Cecibel tried to follow her, but arms, strong arms, held her back. A gentle voice told her no. She'd done that once before. It was time for a new story now. Their story, a cliché of rising from the ashes, of building something stronger on the ruined foundation of the past, couldn't start that way.

Your focus determines your reality, Tatterhood.

Didn't we agree to never speak of that movie again?

It had a few good moments.

No, it really didn't.

The arms became a hand, that hand attached to a man she needn't dream of when he waited patiently for her in the waking world that wasn't the past, his or hers, only part of it. She was ready. She was ready. But Cecibel slept contentedly on. In the solitude of crowded dreaming. In the perfect silence of the sea.

Paterson, New Jersey

DECEMBER 31, 1959

⟨⁂⟩

Aldo

In all his travels, across the world, he'd never seen a woman nearly as lovely as Cecilia in a lacy bathrobe, rollers in her hair and a dab of overlooked cold cream on her chin. Sprawled naked on his bed, Aldo watched her at the vanity mirror scrubbing away all evidence of him. Soon she'd replace it with the domesticated mask she daily wore. He didn't care. Not when every day the mask went on lighter, came off easier. She was his and always had been. His Cecilia. His one and only love.

"This is the last time." She said it without turning around, as she did every day for the last eight. Cecilia couldn't look at him and lie, but apparently the mirror fell for it. "I mean it, Aldo."

"Okay." Only it wasn't. Cecilia might believe her own lies but Aldo didn't. Not for a second. She told him she could never leave her husband, her children, but every day she did. She showed up at his door and met him kiss for kiss. Body to body. Skin to skin. Sweat mingling, staining one another with scent and sex. How did her husband not smell it on her? Or did he and not care? Cecilia wouldn't talk about him, not to say she loved him or never had. She wouldn't talk about the future any further than what time she had to leave their bed to brave the world without him. What she did outside the hour or so she gave him, Aldo didn't want to think about. Husband, children, family. Holiday events that never ended in their vast Italian family. Domestic bliss. He'd save her from all that. Yes, he would. Aldo would show her the world.

"Your sister has been spending a lot of time with my brother."

She pulled curlers from her hair, shook it into coiffed waves. "Have you noticed?"

"It's hard not to." Aldo got off the bed, still naked, and wiped the cold cream from her chin. "Makes this easier."

"Does she know? Did you tell her?"

"Of course not." Yet. She'd find out soon enough. They all would. "She's going to your father's party tonight as Nicky's date, you know."

Cecilia glanced up at him in the mirror. "My brother is an idiot. Thinks only with his dick. As if Tressa would let him do anything to her with it."

"How do you know?"

"Because she's a lady," Cecilia told him. "She'd never let him touch her."

Aldo stood behind her, put his hands on her shoulders. In the mirror, his bare torso, his hands, her face looking up at her view of him in the glass. "What does that make you?"

"A whore." She said it without flinching.

"Don't say that. It's not true."

"A woman who fucks a man who isn't her husband is a—"

Aldo descended upon her lips, snatched the words from them like an eagle at a fish. He crushed them in his talons, kissed her breathless. Drawing her from the vanity, back to the bed, he made quick work of the lacy bathrobe, devoured her lips to ankles. He pushed into her and she groaned. Her lips parted. He bit the swell of them. Tenderly. "Tell me you love me."

"I love you," she gasped. "I love you, Aldo."

He moved slowly. Cecilia squirmed underneath him.

"Again."

"I love you."

Faster. "You were mine first, Cecilia." Deeper. "We promised forever." Deliberate. "A promise we kept. There is no shame in that. No wrong."

"Stop talking and fuck me." Legs hitched around his hips. Aldo's brain liquefied. He thought no thoughts, only felt every glorious bit of her moving with him. Cecilia bit his shoulder, his bicep. She arced her body to his, breasts pressed to his chest. Before he lost his mind completely, Cecilia pushed him off her, flipped him like a wrestler, and pinned his shoulders down.

"Tell me you love me."

"I love you."

"Again."

Her hair fell in disheveled curls, framing her tiny, round face. Cheeks crimson. Sweat beading lip and brow. Eyes—those fathomless eyes—pulling every molecule of his soul out of his body and into hers. Aldo lifted her hips, maneuvered himself back inside her. Cecilia's head tilted back, robbed him of her face, those eyes. He took her chin in his fingertips, turned her back to him. "I love you, Cecilia. Forever."

He moved in her, and she in him. Gazes locked. Tension building. Sex crashing in a silence they'd never shared before. This was it. The moment beyond all other moments. Aldo and Cecilia. Cecilia and Aldo. The two of them, together. Inseparable by time, distance, and circumstance. It was written in the stars.

She left without speaking another word to him. No kiss good-bye or warning of a last time. He'd see her at the party in her parents' house, later on. She never asked him not to come, and he'd never once considered skipping it. Tressa had insisted, in any event. She couldn't go without him, even as Nicky's date. Because she was his sister, because he loved her, and for more reasons than he cared to think about, Aldo let her think he was doing it for her.

Beautiful, sweet, smart, cunning Tressa. Without knowing her more than these last few days, he knew Dominic Giancami Jr. was not her kind of man. Enzo Parisi fit the bill, in fact—yes, please—if he would. Educated and sophisticated. Good-looking. Nicky was that. Good-looking. If a girl was into that Latin-lover thing. But he was rough around the edges and as far from sophisticated as Aldo himself.

He wiped the steam from the bathroom mirror, inspected his

chin. Lathering up, Aldo squashed the thought that maybe Tressa liked Nicky for all the wrong reasons. That maybe, if he'd been nicer, more available, a better brother, she'd go for a man worthy of her rather than one just like him.

Clean, shaved, Aldo slicked back his hair. He'd have to cut it before reporting back for duty. No commander would suffer a sea-man with long hair, let alone an admiral's personal chef. Salfrank had made it very clear that he'd accept no less than neat, orderly, regulated crewmen from head chef to dishwasher, no matter their rank.

Aldo would accept nothing less from his crew either.

The galley on board the USS *Opal* awaited him. Gleaming white and steel. Everything new and top-of-the-line. Aldo had a *brigade de cuisine* at his disposal, just like any chef in a Parisian restaurant. On a smaller scale, of course. The ship wasn't a big cruiser, or a destroyer. More like a yacht. A very big one. The meals served upon it would be elegant, significant, and frequent, prepared for officers and dig-nitaries, royalty from time to time. They would taste his food and marvel at his skill, his impeccable palate, his artistry. And he, a man not even thirty.

Prepping for the mess, feeding a hundred men at a time, was one thing. It took a lot of sweat, perseverance, but little skill. Yet the abundance of food always surrounding him, day in and day out of his existence in the galley, had allowed him to experiment with the many ways one could prepare a potato, a carrot, a tough piece of beef. No longer forced to take what he could afford and like it, Aldo didn't. His palate elevated. The nuances of that lowly potato when roasted rather than fried, when treated with butter and herbs and salt, opened up a world of flavor wherein food was consumed with the eyes first; it changed his whole perspective. It was the difference between dining and eating, between drinking Chianti from a crystal glass and straight from the bottle, between food to sustain and food to experience.

It was the difference between frying dogs at Falls View, and creating masterpieces on a yacht in the Mediterranean Sea.

He looked again into the mirror, and saw not Aldo Wronski who'd left Paterson behind, but a chef. A sailor. The man he'd become away from this place. Did Cecilia see it? See him? Did she even know he was a chef? He couldn't remember if he'd told her, or about the plum assignment he'd gotten in European waters. They didn't talk, Cecilia and he. They sweated and fucked and growled words of love, undying and real, but they didn't talk. They didn't need to. Had they ever? Aldo couldn't remember for the life of him.

Only a little after three o'clock. Too many hours to kill before the party, and Tressa was out shopping for a new dress to wear. The woman could shop, and did so anytime she wasn't with either Nicky or Aldo himself. Aldo had attempted to go with her once and ended up wanting to claw his own eyes out of his head before viewing yet another dress that looked just like the last seventeen she'd tried on. They had breakfast together every morning and dinner every night, even those evenings Nicky joined them, or rather, Aldo joined Nicky and Tressa. She guilted him, both times, into tagging along.

"I won't go out with him at all if it means leaving you to have supper on your own."

And that had been that, no matter what either of the men had to say about it. Thankfully, Tressa occupied her days between breakfast and dinner with shopping and new friends, with lunches and teas he sometimes attended. The girls flirted with him, a man in uniform, and he flirted back, biding his time until he ditched them all for Cecilia and an hour or two of bliss.

Now time was winding down. Soon it would all change. This limbo between Christmas and New Year's would trip them all into a future none of them had seen coming before the Giancami Christmas party. Tressa would be disappointed, but would get over it soon enough, he was certain. Cecilia, on the other hand, had a choice to make, and Aldo had no doubt what the outcome would be.

He opened the drawer where he kept his socks, moved the last clean pairs aside, and pulled from the bottom the telegram that had been awaiting him. On the floor. Overlooked. Stepped over by both him and Cecilia in their fervor to get at one another.

WASHINGTON DC DECEMBER 27 1959
LEAVE CUT SHORT YOU ARE NEEDED URGENTLY REPORT
FOR DUTY JANUARY 2 SHIP DEPARTS NYC JANUARY 3 SEE
YOU ON THE OPAL

From the admiral himself. Pride had swelled before Aldo realized the implications. He didn't have until the end of January to woo and win Cecilia the way he should have years ago. There would be no apartment in New York to whisk her to once she'd left her old, forced life behind, no time to deal with the formalities, the frustrations. There was only a new life for them both, the one that should have been had circumstances not tricked them into believing otherwise.

He set the telegram on the dressertop, pulled from the drawer a white envelope. Inside, an itinerary—a ship bound for Lisbon, then a train to Barcelona, where, somehow or another, he'd be waiting for her. The travel agent in Fair Lawn, an abutting town grown big enough for Aldo to hope Cecilia's name rang no bells, had been so eager to make the arrangements for him, especially since he handed over every last dime he had, in advance. She practically swooned over the story about the love of his life, the leave cut short, and the wedding they would have somewhere in Spain the moment she arrived. A man in uniform was rarely suspect, especially when he had clear blue eyes, foppish dark hair, and a slightly crooked smile plastered on his love-stricken face. She'd taken the information, made the arrangements, and handed him the itinerary.

"I'll have the tickets for you in a couple of days," the woman had said. "Make sure she has a passport."

Aldo said she did, and hoped he wasn't lying.

He finished dressing and left his lonely, still-sweaty room. He couldn't pick up the tickets until after five o'clock. The travel agent was working overtime, just for him. Maybe Tressa and her friends would have forgone the Meyer Brothers tearoom in favor of the one in Les Fontaines. Fresh out of Cecilia's arms, he had no interest in flirting, but the prospect of some company to kill the hours until he put his plan into effect appealed.

Standing at the entrance, scanning the cluster of women and girls far smaller in number than they had been before Christmas, Aldo didn't see his sister. As an American man of his age, and military to boot, popping into the tearoom of the hotel on his own wasn't without scandal, but Aldo actually liked tea. He especially enjoyed the Russian tea cakes at Les Fontaines. Confections made of flour, sugar, nuts, and lots of butter if his palate guessed correctly, so simple they crossed back into elegant. Despite and because of the cold feelings between the United States and the Soviets, there would be a fair amount of friendship-making attempts in the anonymous Mediterranean Sea. Perfecting the sweet staple of every Russian soldier's childhood would surely win some points.

"Al, over here." A masculine voice, and vaguely familiar. Aldo searched for the man to go with it and found Enzo Parisi, hand raised and beckoning. An uncomfortable sting shivered up his spine, settled in his gut, and turned it. How long had Enzo been there? Long enough to see Cecilia leave? Aldo tugged on his jacket lapels. He was an officer in the United States Navy. Tea in a posh hotel with his lover's husband could not faze him. He joined the man at his table.

"Hello, Mr. Parisi."

"Enzo, please. Sit."

Aldo complied. "What brings you to *Les Fontaines*?"

Enzo's smile never wavered, but his glance was long. "I met your sister here for tea just before Christmas," he said at last, "and wanted to come back. I was hoping to run into her, in fact. A man having tea by himself in a fancy hotel is suspect, but I really like tea, and their cookies."

"You and me both." Aldo laughed without meaning to. "I'm thinking of stealing their recipe for Russian tea cakes."

"Are those the crumbly ones with the powdered sugar and nuts?"

"Yup. I'm not a pastry chef, but I think I could duplicate them."

Enzo signaled the white-tuxedoed waiter. "A plate of your

Russian tea cakes and a pot of"—he looked to Aldo—"Darjeeling black?"

"I'm game."

Nodding to the waiter, Enzo turned that movie-star smile back on Aldo. "Looking forward to this evening?"

"Sure." Aldo shrugged. "Last party was a hoot."

"My in-laws know how to entertain. Tell me, as a chef, what do you think of Maria's culinary efforts?"

Culinary efforts? Aldo bit the inside of his cheek. Was Enzo talking worldly man to worldly man? Or being condescending? "She's a fine cook," Aldo answered. "I enjoyed everything I ate."

"I understand you're quite the accomplished man with food." Enzo altered the topic without batting an eyelash. "Tressa never tires of telling us all how talented you are."

"She's my kid sister." Aldo tried to smile. "She has to say nice things. I've never cooked for her."

"That's a shame."

The waiter returned with a pot of fragrant tea and the cookies Aldo's mouth would have watered for if he weren't sitting across the table from the man whose wife he'd recently fucked. Play it cool. He didn't know. He couldn't. Aldo snatched a cookie from the plate while the waiter poured. Yes, flour, sugar, butter, nuts, and vanilla. Maybe a hint of nutmeg and cinnamon.

"What made you join the navy?" Enzo blew across the surface of his tea. "At loose ends?"

"I had no real prospects other than short-order cook at a local joint. The navy seemed like a good option."

"Any regrets?"

"Plenty of them." Aldo sipped the tea, too hot, and pretended it didn't burn. "But I'm glad I did. Why?"

Enzo shrugged. "Just curious," he said. "I think we all wanted to be in the military when we were kids."

"Did you?"

"Of course. I was seven when my uncles and cousins went to fight overseas. Old enough to know it was important, too young to understand the horror. I saw them as heroes, every one of them.

Especially the ones who never made it back home. I know differently now, but back then, all I wanted was to join the army."

"Not the navy or air force?"

"They were army. I wanted the same. Besides, I'm not all too keen on flying. You?"

"I've flown a few times. Never jumped out of a plane, though."

"Lucky you."

The men chatted amiably, and yet Aldo couldn't shake the feeling that Enzo was coiled tight and ready to spring. *So how long do you plan on fucking my wife?* The question was there, in between every word they spoke. It was in the other man's bright eyes, in the tilt of his charming smile. Aldo loosened his tie. Heat trickled out of his clothes to steam his face. Or maybe it was the tea grown tepid in his cup. Or maybe it was his imagination running away with him.

"I guess I should get going," Enzo said, looking at his watch. "My wife will castrate me if I'm late to the party."

"My sister says arriving late is fashionable."

"Not when it's Dominic Giancami's party and you're married to his daughter." Enzo rose to his feet, extended a hand. "I'll see you later, then."

"See you later."

The man's handshake was firm (too firm?). His smile (sneer?) crinkled the corners of his eyes. Aldo dropped back into his chair, slumped and suddenly exhausted. Enzo tipped the hatcheck girl, donned his overcoat, and, hat in hand, left the tearoom.

The last, surreal hour of his life played in Aldo's head. He'd gone from Cecilia's arms to Enzo's charming clutches with only a shower in between. He felt dirty and raw and, for the first time, guilty as hell. He went back to his room, tossed his uniform jacket on the bed still Cecilia-rumpled, Cecilia-scented. Would Enzo know his wife's scent in the room? Had he smelled her on him? Aldo stripped out of his clothes, left them where they lay, and got back into the shower. Hot water scalded. He leaned his head to the tiled wall and let it burn. Cecilia was his. She had been from the moment they met. Enzo's part in their triangle was unfortunate, but had nothing to do with them. It had been determined by his parents and hers, long before Aldo Wronski ever knew Cecilia Giancami existed.

That makes Cecilia his.

No! It didn't. An agreement between rival families bound hands in marriage; it didn't inspire love. That, Cecilia had given Aldo, mind, body, and soul. Whatever she felt for the man she married and the children he gave her had nothing over the forever she promised him. Nothing.

Turning off the water, Aldo stood as he was, water dripping from his hair, his body. Cecilia was his. She loved him. He loved her. That was all that mattered. No husband, no children, no life that didn't include him could change what had been written in the stars. To fear otherwise was a sacrilege to the only religion Aldo had ever ascribed to.

Toweling off hurt, so he patted himself dry. The silk shirt Tressa had bought him clung to the damp pain left on his skin. The jacket pulled Aldo's shoulders down. He squared them, a valiant effort, and triumphant. Enzo Parisi was a good-looking man. Charming, rich, intelligent. But Aldo wasn't so bad, himself. A navy man of many travels, a man of culinary art and adventure, dressed in evening attire not quite the tuxedo he'd worn to the Christmas party, but elegant and formal enough for New Year's Eve. He looked dashing, if he did say so himself. Tressa had impeccable taste. It was going to be a job to keep all her new friends off of him the night long, but he would even if he had to hide in a closet.

Aldo plucked the itinerary and the telegram from the drawer, tucked them into the inside breast pocket of his suit. He'd pick up the tickets and give everything to her tonight, at the magical stroke of midnight. Not only a new year suspended between yesterday and tomorrow, but a new decade hovering between then and now. Powerful magic, indeed.

Tomorrow, he would leave Paterson. Not even Tressa knew. But Cecilia would. She'd read the telegram, the tickets, and in a month, they'd be together in Barcelona. The romance of it all took his own breath away. Cecilia could be no less affected.

Paterson, New Jersey

DECEMBER 31, 1959

❦

Cecilia

Tears froze on Cecilia's cheeks before she could wipe them away. It hadn't been so cold when she left the house, left her husband and children playing on the floor in her parents' parlor. Christmas toys—blocks and dolls and another new baby carriage for Patsy— everywhere. When she and her brothers were little, toys weren't allowed anywhere but the playroom. Such rules didn't apply to grandchildren meant for spoiling. No rules at all, for them.

Enzo hadn't said a word as she hurried for the door, her coat already half on, her hat askew. He'd only smiled and waved, made baby Frankie wave his tiny hand. She'd almost taken her coat off again. Almost. But Patsy chose that moment to grab her daddy's attention, giving Cecilia permission to duck and run.

Patsy. And Frankie. Tears froze anew. The rapid click of her heels on the pavement echoed the beat of her broken heart. Head down and hands shoved into her pockets, Cecilia picked up her pace. It wasn't fair. It had never been fair. Not to her or to Aldo, not to Enzo, who could have married someone worthy of his love instead. She'd never been worthy of that abundance, that purity, not from day one. It wasn't even her fault. She'd fallen in love. Girls had been doing that forever. Boys, too. Aldo had fallen in love with her. And so had Enzo.

A scream formed in her throat. Cecilia swallowed it down. The fantasy of having both men played incessantly through her mind. It was so easy a solution, so right. She could love them both, have them both, and not have to choose which of her children got to be with their father. Damn society for forbidding such a thing. Damn possessive, masculine egos. If Enzo said he wanted Tressa—which he did, Cecilia knew full well—she'd share him. Wouldn't she?

Hurrying up the steps of her parents' home on Derrom Avenue, Cecilia stumbled. She caught herself, her breath, and pushed open the door. "Enzo? Mama?"

"In here," her mother called softly. Cecilia followed the tinny sound of kiddie music to the parlor. Mama sat in the wingback chair with Frankie in her arms. Patsy, chin on fists and little legs swinging, watched *Howdy Doody* on the new twenty-one-inch television set Daddy got Mama for Christmas.

"Where's Enzo?" Cecilia asked quietly, taking her baby into her arms. He stirred only to suckle in his sleep. So perfect, her son. Cecilia's heart swelled.

"He went out," Maria answered. "He didn't say where to. Where have you been?"

"Just met some friends."

"What friends?"

"Some of the girls." Cecilia kissed Frankie's soft cheek. She closed her eyes and swallowed the lump rising. "Why?"

"You're spending an awful lot of time with young ladies you couldn't give the time of day to most of the year."

"It's the holiday season, time to live it up a little."

"You're living it up an awful lot more than a little, eh?"

Cecilia lifted her head. Mama's mouth was a thin, grim line, a countenance that had been stiffening Cecilia's spine since her earliest memories. Placing Frankie in the folding crib set up near the radiator, she gathered her composure. Patsy, engrossed with puppets and cowboy songs, hadn't yet acknowledged her mother's presence and likely wouldn't until the show was over.

"I'd like a word with you, Cecilia Marie."

The second name. Thank God she hadn't added the confirmation name, too. Still, her spine stiffened and her fingers trembled. Following her mother into the hallway between parlor and kitchen, Cecilia took shallow, even breaths.

"What is it, Mama? Was Pasty a good girl?"

"Of course she was." Maria waved her off. "Come. The children are fine. I'll make us coffee."

Coffee, not tea. Maria had no interest in tea. She brewed her coffee strong, from dark-roast beans, the way her own mama did, and made no apologies for it.

Cecilia grabbed the tin of Christmas cookies from the pantry shelf and pried off the lid. Slightly stale, but still sugary and chocolaty and gooey in turns. She took a sugared Christmas tree out and bit. It crumbled in her mouth.

"You keep that up and we won't be able to get you into another slinky dress next year."

"You saying I'm getting fat?"

"I'm saying you're not as slim as you used to be."

"I've never been slim, Mama. Men like my curves."

"Men, eh? Not Enzo?"

Cecilia's cheeks burned. She took another cookie from the tin. "What did you want to talk about? Not my figure or choice of words, I'm sure."

"Can't a mother enjoy a chat with a daughter she doesn't see nearly enough of since she moved all the way down to Princeton?"

"I've lived there five years. You were all for it. And we see you all the time. I make sure of it."

Maria plugged in the percolator, brushed coffee grounds from the counter into her hand, and dumped them back into the can. Taking a cookie for herself, she eyed it carefully before biting. "Andrea makes better sugar cookies than Dolores. Dee doesn't sift her flour. Makes a big difference."

The aroma of coffee wafted; the percolator bubbled. Cecilia checked the clock, still another fifteen minutes of *Howdy Doody* to keep Patsy occupied. After that, she'd be able to escape whatever had her mother's face grim despite the superior cookie and chat with her supposedly missed daughter.

"Is all the cooking for tonight done, then?" she asked.

Maria met her gaze. "I'm having it catered."

Cecilia barked laughter. "You're kidding me, right?"

"No, I'm not kidding. I did all the showing off I needed to at Christmas. I'm getting older. I can't keep that up forever."

Older? Yes. Though her hair was still the jet black it had been all her life, it was done at the hairdresser's now. Smile lines around Maria's eyes remained even at rest. How old could she be? Cecilia used to know, but didn't now.

"You know, Ceci, I was young once, like you."

"I know that. I remember."

"You can't remember me at that age. You were a baby. My first. My only daughter. I had all of you kids before I was twenty-five."

"Is that why you stopped?" Cecilia asked. "Too many, too fast."

Maria's eyes narrowed. Her lips pursed. "You remember Trudy."

Cecilia looked away.

"Of course you do. Everyone does, even though she's been gone for years. I'll never live her down. Ever." Maria lunged for Cecilia's hand across the table. She held it way too hard. "When a man cheats, it's his wife's reputation that's ruined. When a woman does, she ruins her own, but it's far worse for her husband. No one respects a man who can't keep his wife in line."

"In line?" Cecilia pulled her hand away. "Are women dogs now?"

Maria shook her head, her mouth working words that wouldn't cooperate. "I learned the hard way"—she managed to get out—"just what women are in this world. You think you're modern and different, but you're not. You're the same as the rest of us. The only power over your own life you'll ever have is through your husband. Trust me on this one."

Bile rose from her churning stomach. Cecilia took another cookie, ate it so fast she choked. Maria leaped to her feet, pounding her daughter's back.

"I'm fine, Mama." Cecilia held up her hand. "Stop."

But Maria put her arms around her, held her close. "I did the best I could for you and you've been happy no matter what else you've been. I know love. I know how it can tear up a woman's soul. It's big. So big. Consuming. But it flares and then it fades, and what you're left with is all the hurt it leaves behind."

"Mama." Cecilia pried her off. "What are you talking about?"

Maria hugged her tighter, and let her go. She sat opposite again, her hands bunched in her lap. "I married for that kind of love. Your father, my God. He tore up my soul. I knew about Trudy. Everyone did. She and I were friends when we were kids. But we all knew he'd marry me, just like his parents and mine wanted.

"I tried to make him happy, to make him forget her, but he wouldn't. Or he couldn't. So I understand all sides of it, in my way. I'm not a stupid woman. I didn't blame her or him or even myself. And I don't blame you."

Tears pooled. Cecilia blinked them away. Maria thumbed them from her cheeks. "When your father vanished, I did my best for you. For all of you. I'm proud of that, even if . . ." Mama's head bowed, but she looked Cecilia square in the eye when she spoke again. "I want to tell you something. Something very few people know about, and will never speak a word of."

"You don't have to."

"I think I do. You are my daughter, a woman now. It involves you, so you should know."

"Mama, please—"

"Just listen, Cecilia! For God's sake, listen."

"I'm sorry."

Maria took a deep breath. "When your father vanished, I was afraid. For you, for the boys, and for myself. If I could have remarried quickly enough, I would have given you a few more years, but as it turned out, moving up the nuptials worked in your favor, eh?"

"Mama, I—"

"Hush, child. You willful thing. Let me speak."

Cecilia bit her lip. She nodded.

"Your father turned up sooner than anyone knew," Maria told her. "By who and where doesn't matter. Women who stick together have power. Remember that, Ceci. Anyway, I managed to keep him there, out of sight, until it was safe. For you."

"I don't know what—"

"Oh, please, Cecilia." Maria grimaced. "Don't play stupid.

I suspected you were pregnant before you went out with Enzo the first time. We're the only two women in the house. It wasn't hard to notice you skipped a period. Then Patsy was born with blond hair and blue eyes, and still I hoped I'd been wrong. But this Christmas . . . that Tressa woman. I wasn't wrong, was I?"

Cecilia's chest ached. If she'd thought her heart broken before, she was horrifically mistaken. It had only been splintered, not shattered. The jagged pieces of it shredded her insides now. She dabbed her mouth, expecting to come away with bloody fingers, but found only cookie crumbs. "Enzo has known from the day she was born," she whispered. "I asked him to make his choice, and he did."

"And so did you."

"I know."

"Does he know? This Al fellow?"

"No."

"Then what are you doing?" Maria growled. "Why would you jeopardize everything for a fling gone cold five years ago?"

"It never went cold, Mama." Cecilia clutched her mother's hands. "I love him."

"Love." Maria chuffed. "It comes in all shapes and sizes, my girl. You love Enzo, don't you?"

Cecilia nodded.

"That kind of love trumps the soul-ripping kind. Trust me on that. I'd take it a million times over."

"But . . . you love Daddy. You said you always did."

"Did," Maria corrected. "He crushed it. He crushed me. When he vanished, I was scared but not heartbroken. I was actually . . ." She shrugged. "Hopeful. Maybe it was his brush with death. Maybe being in the water so long did something to his brain. He lost all memory of the time shortly before and after his dip in the river. I don't know what it was, but he came back a different man and I thought, at last, I'd have what I always wanted. He sent Trudy away. He treated me with love and affection. But it was too late. That's what happens to the soul-crushing kind of love when there's too much hurt involved."

Cecilia tore free of her mother's gaze. Everything she said made sense. And nothing. Sense married her to Enzo when it was Aldo she loved, when it was Aldo's baby she carried. Sense made her a dutiful wife and mother when she'd never aspired to anything of the kind. She had dreams squelched as soon as she could dream them, because sense told her she'd never attain a single one of them. But that life made out of sense and duty gave her Frankie, too. And Enzo, whom she loved and had been happy with if not fulfilled until Aldo walked through the front door.

Maria pushed to her feet and got the coffee. She poured two cups. Sugar and cream, they liked it the same way. Dark and rich, sweet and creamy. Setting a cup in front of Cecilia, Maria sat back down again. "It isn't fair," she said. "It never has been. Men rule this world, or think they do. The old saying about behind every great man is a great woman is true. A greater one, in fact, because she has to be smarter. Sometimes it all works out. We get to marry the men we love, or learn to love the men we marry. Life for women is all compromise, choosing the lesser of evils. As long as we're quiet about it, we women can manipulate our lives to the best advantage. Know what your best advantage is, Cecilia. For yourself and for your children. My grandchildren, because they come from you no matter who their fathers are."

Sipping her coffee, Cecilia closed her eyes. Words scalded her mouth hotter than the liquid in her cup. Scream them? Or swallow them down? Her throat burned, her stomach. The pain mingled with the shards of her broken heart that cut deeper with every breath she took.

Little feet thundered their way. Patsy threw herself into Cecilia's lap, nearly spilling the coffee all over the place.

"Can I have a cookie, too?"

"Of course you can, baby," Maria answered, and pushed the tin closer. Patsy took three, jamming one into her mouth before anyone could object. As if anyone would. No rules. Not for her. Not yet.

Her baby. Her little girl. Already so bright and beautiful, believing the world was hers, and it was. Cecilia was like her, once upon a time. There'd never been any doubt in her mind that she was the center of the universe. But things changed, the way they'd been changing in little-girl lives for as long as history recorded such things. It wasn't fair. It never would be. But it could be more fair, in the increments those powerful women sticking together made happen, or in the giant steps taken by a fearless woman walking alone.

❦

Enzo

He shook the whole walk home. How he had sat opposite Aldo Wronski a full hour, chitchatting amiably about things he would never remember crossing his lips, eluded him. Enzo had been waiting outside the hotel, just as he had been all the days since tea there with Tressa, to see Cecilia emerge hours after leaving her parents' house. He never followed her. Not once. Yet he found himself there daily. Waiting. Cecilia had yet to disappoint.

Fury wouldn't come. Only fear. Maybe the fury would come later, if she didn't leave him. Enzo hoped he'd be far too relieved, too happy and grateful, for that. Confusion refused to let him think straight, and if he couldn't think straight, he wouldn't act. Crimes of passion got dismissed as understandable, for being beyond one's control, but the damage couldn't be undone. Enzo Parisi was an intelligent man. A man who lived by reason and logic. A man who loved his wife. And yet he was a man, he'd discovered, as primal as any other he'd known, because what he wanted to do was wring Aldo Wronski's neck and throw him at Cecilia's feet. Instead he'd taken tea with him, like the gentleman he fancied himself to be.

Trotting up the steps of his in-laws' house, he held his breath. She'd be home by now, his wife. Probably getting Patsy to nap so she could stay up later that night. Aside from hired staff readying this and setting up that, the house was strangely quiet. No television or radio. No voices casually chatting. A vacuum, the soft whispers of staff trying to go unnoticed, and the ticking of the big clock in the foyer.

Enzo took off his coat and hat and hung them in the closet. He took the steps two at a time and was outside the nursery door, hand on the knob, before thinking a coherent thought. Cecilia's deep voice, singing on the other side of the door, made him drop his hand to his side. He listened. He closed his eyes. He refused to weep. Men didn't do such things, especially not Neanderthal cuckolds.

He opened the door carefully, but it squeaked. Cecilia glanced over her shoulder, her hand on Patsy's back never faltering in its rubbing. Their daughter lay on her tummy, golden curls splayed across her pillow. Enzo stayed where he was, and in a moment, Cecilia's singing ceased. She kissed Patsy's little cheek, brushed back her silky hair. Waving him ahead of her, she followed him out the door and closed it softly behind her.

"How's your mother today?" she asked in the hallway, arms crossed over her chest. Protecting. Protective.

"She's fine. Looking forward to tonight. How was your afternoon with the ladies?"

"Fine." She shrugged. "But it'll be good to get home."

Home. Enzo's heart nearly burst from his chest. He took her into his arms. What was it he smelled in her hair? A familiar scent, but not hers. He closed his eyes, closed off his thoughts, and simply held her.

"I love you," she said.

"I love you, too."

"No." She pulled away. "I really, really love you."

He smiled. "So you said. You okay?"

Another shrug. Enzo took her hand and led her away from the nursery door, into the room they shared while in this house. "Talk to me."

"There's nothing to talk about. I love you. That's all. You . . . you deserve better than me, is all."

"There is no better than you. Stop."

"You deserved someone who didn't trick you into marrying her."

"Cecilia."

"No, listen to me. We never talked about it. Ever. We need to."

"No, we don't."

"Maybe you don't," she insisted. "But I want you to know if ever you wanted to—"

"Don't say it, Cecilia."

"—be with someone else. If you fell in love for real—"

"Stop it! Stop talking!"

Cecilia's mouth hung open. In all the years they'd been married, he'd never once raised his voice to her. Enzo pushed fingers through his hair, took her shoulders in his hands, grasped them a little too tightly. "I love you, Cecilia. I love our children and our life. What happened back then doesn't matter."

"But it does." A whisper. Her lips trembled. "I don't know what's wrong with me. I feel like two people and I don't know how to become one. I'm not sure if I can."

He held her gaze a long time. Speaking words that could not be then unspoken held no appeal. Not to him, college-educated man of the world, but to the Neanderthal . . . "What's happened this Christmas to make that so?"

A tear rolled, then another. Cecilia blinked and broke eye contact. "It's not just this Christmas," she said. "It's been always. From the time I was a little girl. There's the mouthy, spoiled Cecilia who pushed but never went out of bounds, and then there's the totally insane woman who wants to be traipsing across Australia making friends with the bushmen. One of me is so happy being your wife and the kids' mother. But the other . . . she's not happy and never has been. She's trapped and about ready to start chewing off her own foot to get free."

Aldo. The hotel. Her trap sprung. Neanderthal shook her until her head snapped off her neck. Gentleman pulled her into his arms and kissed the top of her head. "I don't want to be your trap."

"You're not. I am. It's me. All me. You're perfect and always have been."

"I'm not."

Cecilia pulled away enough to look up into his face. She touched his cheek. "You are to me."

If he kissed her, he'd taste Wronski on her lips. Making love to her, he couldn't even consider. His mind raced and raced, threatened to burst his heart for the pounding of it all. Letting her go, he stepped away. Enzo needed to think, but didn't want to. Ever.

"It's going to get busy around here soon," he said. "You need time to change and everything. I'm going to have a shower."

Yes, a shower. Wash all this off of him. He turned away without looking at her. In that pink-tiled bathroom, he stripped and got in the tub. Cold water braced, became warm, then hot. Enzo let the water pour over him until he could no longer stand it. Adjusting the temperature released those banging thoughts cold and heat had held at bay.

If Cecilia didn't leave him, how would he ever be with her again? Before suspicion was proved truth, he'd made love to her two and three times a day, he thought, to help her resist the pull into Aldo's bed. Since then, he hadn't been able to touch her in any intimate way. Knowing *his* hands had been on her, *his* cock in her, was too much for him. And if she became pregnant again . . .

A great sob erupted from deep in his chest. Enzo sputtered, choking on it rather than letting it go. And failed. He wept as he hadn't in all his life. Raising Patsy as his own had never been an issue. Raising another of Wronski's offspring? Neanderthal wouldn't do it. And yet, there was no way to know whose child she carried unless it was once again born too blond and blue-eyed to refute.

If she carried any child at all, educated man said. After Frankie's birth, the doctor had asked him for permission to prescribe a new form of birth control. A pill, of all things. Skepticism aside, Enzo had seen no reason not to try it. In all the months of their very active sex life, Cecilia hadn't conceived. Maybe the damned thing worked after all.

Please. Please work.

The water cooled. Enzo turned it off. He rested his head to the tile and breathed. His whole body hurt, inside and out. He wished they'd never come to Paterson for the holidays, that Tressa hadn't asked Aldo to meet him here, now, of all places on the planet.

Wishing is as good as regret. His grandmother, finger wagging, used to tell him that. Only what *was,* what *would be,* mattered. He was in Paterson, with his wife and children, her lover, and her lover's sister. Where would they be next week? In two weeks? That, he could affect.

Cecilia said she was two women. Enzo knew, at the wise age of twenty-four, he was two men. He understood the dichotomy of being. Neanderthal wanted to beat the living shit out of Aldo, take Cecilia and his kids, and disappear from the face of the earth until it was all forgotten, but Neanderthal was stupid. All brute rage and no reason. Enzo hadn't even known of his existence until this Christmas, but he knew the wild woman trying to chew off her own foot to free herself would fight back. Tressa was right. Understanding. Patience. If his wife left him, it wasn't going to be because he chased her away.

And if she stayed . . .

There were, if possible, even more people in the house for New Year's Eve than there had been for the Christmas party. Every room was hot and stank of sweat, alcohol, and the food being offered by waiters dressed in white tuxedos just like in the tearoom at Les Fontaines. Enzo didn't need that reminder, but there it was. Unavoidable.

Nine o'clock. Tressa and Aldo hadn't arrived yet. Nicky paced the foyer, bumping into people and making a general nuisance of himself. And then there she was, Tressa DiViello, taking off her white ermine stole and handing it to the doorman. She sparkled. The blue beads of her gown caught every light in the house. Not slinky, but formfitting, it embraced every curve of her, a jealous lover unwilling to share.

Nicky stopped dead in his tracks, mouth agape. "I just died and went to heaven."

"Don't be silly." Tressa took his offered arm. "I'm sorry to be so late. My brother had a small problem he had to take care of. He'll be right in." She turned her disastrously beautiful gaze to Enzo. "Hello, Mr. Parisi. Happy New Year."

"Miss DiViello." He bowed his head. "You look lovely this evening."

She ran a hand across her abdomen, flat but luscious. "Why, thank you. A girl likes to hear such things."

"He just beat me to it," Nicky stammered. "You look gorgeous. Like a living doll. An angel."

"Thank you, Dominic." But her eyes were still on Enzo and he couldn't look away.

If ever you wanted to be with someone else . . .

And he did. Neanderthal wanted Tressa, knew he could have her. All he had to do was take her hand from Nicky's arm.

"Oh, here he is," Tressa said.

Aldo Wronski walked through the door, handed his hat and coat to the doorman. He patted his jacket pocket; relief eased the worry in his face. He offered his hand to Nicky, then Enzo without flinching. "Hey again," he said to Enzo. "Long time no see, eh?"

"Yes."

"Sorry I made us so late. My orders were changed and I had some scrambling to do."

Orders changed? So Tressa had actually done it. Enzo's heart stuttered.

"Thank goodness my brother has no real attachments here." Tressa laughed sweetly. "Other than me, of course."

"I really wanted to spend a few weeks with you," Aldo told her.

"Some things can't be helped. But you will write to me, and I'll write to you. When school lets out for the summer, maybe I'll join you in the Mediterranean if you can manage some leave."

"What do you mean?" Nicky butted in. "School? Summer? Ain't you staying here in Paterson anymore?"

"It was never Paterson, Dominic. I told you that. Remember?"

He blew a breath through his lips. "New York, Paterson, what does it matter? Same difference. I thought you was staying up north."

"I never said I wasn't," she said. "We can discuss this at a later date. I'm not too much of a lady to admit I'm starving. Lead me to food, Dominic."

"You got it."

Enzo stood his ground, his insides battling. Aldo didn't try to get around him. Maybe if they stood there long enough, something would happen. Anything. But nothing did, and Enzo couldn't take it any longer. "So you have to ship out?"

"Yes. Tomorrow."

"And you just found out?"

"A few days ago. I've been busy. Tressa, you know . . . she likes to be entertained."

"Doesn't the navy make your arrangements for you?"

"Sure, but there were a few strings left hanging that I thought I had more time to deal with before shipping out."

"You didn't mention any of that earlier," Enzo said. "I kept you from getting it done."

"Nah, you didn't." Aldo rubbed at the back of his neck. "It all worked out just fine. Don't worry."

"Oh, I'm not worried. Just being courteous."

Aldo's gaze narrowed. Enzo smiled, feral and dangerous, and it felt so good. "Go get yourself something to eat," he said. "You must be hungry."

"I am, thanks." Aldo maneuvered around him and was gone. Making a beeline for Cecilia, no doubt. Enzo had been doing his best to behave as he always did, mingling and chatting without his wife glued to his side. He'd kept an eye on her, though, always knew where she was. Tressa and Aldo's arrival had made him lose sight of her. His gut lurched. Heading to the ballroom, he looked everywhere at once. Dining room. Parlor. Even the kitchen. No sign of Cecilia.

No sign of Aldo either. But there was Tressa, still with Nicky, nibbling on finger food from a china plate as white as her perfect teeth. Not even that sight was enough to dislodge his panic. Enzo ducked outside, but Cecilia wasn't there, draped in her fur, smoking and gossiping with friends as he'd hoped. Aldo wasn't out there either. Where were they? Where the fuck were they?

"Breathe, Enzo." Tressa's voice in his ear, her hand on his shoulder. "After tonight, it's over. Trust me."

"I can't do it."

"You can. You must. I kept my side of the bargain. You will keep yours."

"She's my wife!"

Eyes turned their way. Eyes too interested in knowing why the golden son of the family would be in so heated a discussion with the beauty from the south. Enzo took a deep breath, forced himself to smile. It did not feel good, this time. Offering his arm, he nearly jumped away from the spark as she took it. Her lips parted. Enzo wanted them. On his mouth. On anything she would consent to putting them on. Tressa's fingers tightened on his arm, her nails digging into his flesh through his clothes. He tried not to look anywhere but ahead and led Tressa back into the house, and, once inside, pulled her into the unused service pantry that opened into the old servants' quarters, now Nicky and Joseph's rooms.

Tressa's arms were around his neck before his lips found hers. She tasted like champagne. Hands pressed to her hips, Enzo pulled her roughly to him. Tressa ground against him, the beads of her dress making little tearing sounds against his suit pants.

"I want this if you want this," she whispered, "but be sure you truly do."

Enzo pushed the skirt of her gown up her thighs. She wore no stockings, no girdle or garter. Nothing at all underneath. Warm, soft, smooth skin. The heat of her radiated, drew him in. Somewhere, in this house, Aldo was doing the same to Cecilia. Enzo said it over and over in his head. Pants around his ankles, buried deep in Tressa, he fucked her like he'd never fucked his wife. Carnal. Animal. Feral. Like his smile had been. And it, too, felt so good.

He finished in moments, spilling everything he had into her and hoping, hoping it resulted in something that made the situation somehow fair. Enzo hadn't realized he'd lifted her, pressed her to the wall, but he had. Lowering her to her feet, he slid her gown back down. It swooshed to the floor in a thousand tiny clicks. Enzo tucked in, zipped up, but couldn't look at her.

"Don't fret," she said. "You weren't my first, and I don't expect you will be my last. This doesn't put any claim on you. Unless, of course, you want it to."

"But . . . ?"

"Stop." She laughed softly. "We both know what this was. I've needed it since I met you. You needed it since you met my brother. We both got what we wanted. It was inevitable. Written in the stars. Now we should get back to the party before someone notices we're missing."

Enzo followed her back the way they'd come. At the door returning them to the world of partying and betrayal, Tressa turned on him. She straightened his tie, smoothed his hair. She kissed his lips sensuously. "She was Aldo's first," she said. "But she will be yours the rest of your life."

"Promise me."

"I can't promise, but I can come close. Just a little while longer, Enzo. Tomorrow, he'll be gone."

"And you?"

"Oh, I'll be around," she said, "in the event you want a proper fucking in a proper bed. I know I'd rather enjoy that."

"What about Nicky?"

"What about him?" She tucked the pucker of his shirt more securely into the waistband of his trousers. "He's a boy, right now. A very handsome, wild, uncouth boy. In a few years, he will be a handsome man, and, with a little work, capable of fulfilling my needs. In the meantime, I'm not going anywhere. I have done all I've done for Patricia, present company excluded. That I did for me."

And there she left him in a cloud of her perfume, their sex, and his bafflement. He didn't have shame in him, not yet. He would, soon enough. Neanderthal, at least, was content. Peaceful. Agreeable enough not to go searching for trouble.

Milling among the partiers, Enzo caught sight of Tressa once again on Nicky's arm. His brother-in-law levitated a foot or two off the ground, just having her there. What would he do if he knew? Enzo sneered. He knew exactly what Dominic Giancami Jr. would do.

There was Cecilia, handing Patsy off to Maria. Is that where she'd been? Trying to get the child to sleep while Enzo fucked her lover's sister in a deserted hallway? Shame tapped his shoulder. He slammed it back. Days and days standing outside Les Fontaines rejected it. If she hadn't been with Aldo tonight, she had been this afternoon, and every afternoon since that first. What he'd done with Tressa, to Tressa, what she'd done to him, Enzo Parisi had earned.

Payback was not sweet. It was bitter and it was heavy and it left him feeling betrayed in ways he'd never even considered before.

Cecilia caught his gaze and smiled. He smiled back and waved, but when it looked like she'd come his way, he pretended to have caught the attention of someone just beyond her. In this way he avoided her most of the night. And Tressa. And Aldo Wronski, that stupid bastard who had no idea his own sister conspired against him. For him, if her truth were told.

Eleven thirty. Quarter to twelve. The countdown on the radio began. There stood Tressa, pressed up against the radio, clutched close to Nicky's side. He wasn't letting her go and chancing some other man getting New Year's first kiss. Enzo's gut clenched. Guy Lombardo's voice rose above the partygoers in Times Square. Ten. Nine. Eight.

He pushed through the friends and family gathered around the radio, glasses already raised. Where was Cecilia? As if he didn't know. He should never have avoided her, never once lost sight. Wronski could not get her first kiss of the new year. The new decade.

Seven. Six.

Outside. To the deserted patio. Cecilia and Aldo. Aldo and Cecilia. It had always been, always would be.

Five. Four. Three.

His wife, and the man she'd loved since she was a scared and pregnant teenager tricking another boy into believing he'd done the deed himself.

Two. One.

Aldo pressed a white envelope into her hands, gathered Cecilia into his arms, and kissed her hard, kissed her long. She froze a moment before thawing against him to puddle at his feet.

Happy New Year.

Enzo backed away, his eyes never leaving the pair locked in oblivious passion. Not even when he could no longer see them. Not until the crowd gathered around the radio pulled him into their collective embrace and covered him in kisses, well-wishes, and glad tidings for the new year.

Maria bundled Patsy into his arms. Cami grasped him about the shoulders, jostling him and slobbering a kiss on both his cheeks. Enzo held his daughter close. *His* daughter, not Aldo Wronski's no matter what her blood. It was 1960 now. A new decade. He'd leave the strange and wonderful 1950s behind, for what they were worth. Enzo Parisi would look forward, not back, no matter how much good there had been.

Bar Harbor, Maine

AUGUST 12, 1999

A merry band of hooligans, we. Writers, wordsmiths,
scribblers of the inane. Here's to all the slashers of prose,
the refiners of plot. To all those who make the illusion real.
And here's to all my beautiful lunatics who bleed, vomit,
and piss words every day of their lives.

—CORNELIUS TRAEGAR
NEW YEAR'S EVE, 1949

"He said he wouldn't make the decision and he meant it." Olivia bit the end of her pen, her eyes on the notebook. Alfonse took a slow, careful breath. They were harder and harder to come by. The oxygen tubes up his nose hissed a second sort of heartbeat morning, noon, and night. He was so tired. Always so tired. He didn't want to die, but he was well and truly done living now.

"It's Cecilia's decision," he said. "You should make it."

Olivia looked up from the notebook, eyes wide. "I couldn't make it for myself, what makes you think I can make it for her?"

"You're a writer, Livy. It's what you do. Live the lives of others."

"Orchestrate, not live."

"Is it not the same?" His body. Hurt. Bone-wearied and chilled. "It must be you."

"It's your story, Alfie," she said gently. "You should decide on the most pivotal moments like this one. It's probably the most important of all, this transition. How did you envision it, before I shanghaied the thing?"

"We said no planning."

"I know, but this is different. Tell me."

Inside his heart, a tiny, electrical ping. It didn't hurt. In fact, it felt rather nice. "I never did," he said. "In truth, my darling, had you not taken it upon yourself to forward my story, I don't know that it would ever have gone as far as it has. I'm tired, and I'm losing focus. I might have given up."

"You?" Olivia chuffed. "Not likely. All right, then tell me now. If you were to write the next part, would Cecilia meet Aldo in Barcelona, or would she go back to Princeton with Enzo?"

Passion or contentment. First love or true love. Creased covers or pristine pages. There was no right answer and there had never been. One path taken left a multitude of paths untrodden. Alfonse had ever been one to let the path dictate itself to him. Choosing had always been too hard, too heartbreaking.

The electrical ping deep in the atriums and ventricles of his heart became a zing buzzing his fingertips. His head lightened. Alfonse blinked. He forgot how to breathe. His lungs wouldn't fill. Olivia was already on her feet. Talking, talking, as ever talking. *Are you all right? Alfonse, speak to me. I'm fetching the doctor.* Over her shoulder, a shadow leaned low, became a once-beloved face.

The zing resumed its ping. He remembered how to form those bone-wearying breaths. Grasping Olivia's hand before she could hurry away, Alfonse managed to whisper, "Fetch Cecibel."

～

It was quiet for a Thursday, though most days in the Pen were just so. Mr. Gardern hadn't gotten into the supply closet all week, at any rate. Cecibel undertook her daily duties as she'd always done—diligently and competently. And yet, these last couple of weeks, day after lovely day, flew by when before they'd seemed eternal. Afternoons with Alfonse. Evening walks with Finlay. Hours pleasantly passed with Olivia. She couldn't remember it raining; of course, it had.

And the notebook. The story. Cecilia and Aldo and Enzo. And Tressa, whom she always envisioned with half a face. It had somehow bled into her days in ways she didn't notice until she turned to better hear what one of them was saying and found herself alone. She'd hated giving it back to Olivia, who was to give it to Judith for transcribing. But there had been nothing left to read, not until one of them decided Cecilia's fate. Cecibel honestly didn't know which way she wanted it to go. Anticipation was almost sweet.

Sitting outside the deli, on a picnic table carved up with initials of patrons long gone, Cecibel leaned back on the heels of her palms, face to the glorious August sunshine. There was no month more agreeable than August in Bar Harbor. Cool yet warm. Blue and sunny skies adorned with just enough cloud cover to soften the burning rays, it was her favorite month.

"I got you chicken Parm." Finlay tapped her shoulder, handed her a still-warm sandwich wrapped in white paper. Cecibel lifted her face (the fair side; there was only so far she could go) to his kiss. Finlay sat on the table beside her and unwrapped his sausage and peppers.

"You have oil on your chin." She laughed, wiping it away with a paper napkin. "That good, huh?"

"Want a bite?"

"No, thanks. I don't do sausage. All that mystery meat."

"Not when it's good stuff. They make this in-house. Come on." He held the sandwich out to her.

Cecibel took a bite. "Oh, wow. That *is* good."

"Told you."

They ate their sandwiches in the summer sunshine. Cecibel only talked from behind her hand, the habit too ingrained to simply abandon. Food didn't fall out of her mouth as much anymore. Or else, she'd stopped noticing. And when Fin wiped away a spill for her as she'd just done for him, Cecibel didn't cringe and want to vomit. Not so much, anyway.

Walking to the deli and back to the Pen took longer than riding in Fin's car—they both had only an hour for lunch—but the deli wasn't far and the day was so lovely, biking seemed the best of all worlds. Pedaling the quiet roads, they raced and laughed like kids rather than a man and woman with seventy-five years between them. Cecibel felt like a kid, with Finlay. They'd both been robbed of younger years. Reclaiming them together seemed natural. They did so and more, reclaiming, too, the bits of themselves left too long abandoned to fates forced on them rather than chosen. The freedom of it all couldn't have happened in a better month, as far as Cecibel was concerned.

They coasted their bicycles into the maintenance shed, leaned them against the wall. Old bikes, years unearthed from the innards of Fin's greasy, rust-encrusted domain, had been brought back to life without too much effort. A little elbow grease, oil, and a dab of paint worked miracles when done by Finlay's hand.

"I guess it's time to get back to work."

He grabbed her around the waist before she could leave him, pulled her in, and kissed her.

"What was that for?"

"I just wanted to. Can't a man kiss his woman?"

She laughed. "So I'm your woman now?"

"Aren't you?"

Was she? She tried to detach herself, gently.

"Move in with me," he blurted.

"Fin, please. It's kind of soon for that. We're getting to know one another."

"We know one another." So serious, his eyes, his expression. "We know one another better than most anyone else ever will. I want to wake up with you next to me. Every day, and not just sometimes. I want to be able to touch you at night, just to know you're there. Aw, fuck it. Forget moving in. Just marry me."

Cecibel's skin caught fire then froze, goose bumps spreading up and down her arms. "Huh?"

Finlay let her go to take her hand. "I don't have a ring," he said, "and I blew out my knees in prison, so I can't go down on one of them. I don't have much but all I have is yours. My heart, my soul, every day of the rest of my life whether you say yes or no. I love you, Cecibel." He cupped her cheek. "My Tatterhood. What do you say?"

"I . . . I . . . Finlay." Cecibel pressed palms to cheeks. One smooth and soft. One hard and lined. He loved both. He really did. But she wasn't a princess in a fairy tale. Not even the tattered kind. Happily-ever-after was not in her stars. Not this kind. Not this way.

"Cecibel! There you are!" Sal was running, actually running, down the dirt path leading to the maintenance barn. Cecibel and Fin bolted, met him on the path. Hand on his heart, panting, sweating, Sal doubled over. "Cec, go quick. It's Mr. Carducci. He's asking for you."

〜

Calm. Contented. Almost, at any rate. He'd be content once Cecibel arrived. She would. He had no doubt. Alfonse couldn't go until she did.

Doctors hung back. Nurses. They wouldn't disturb his last minutes with attempts to undo what a lifetime of abuse had foretold. Olivia sat in a chair beside his bed. Judith was there, and Raymond, too. Dear Switch. Tears in his eyes but otherwise silent. Alfonse had always liked that about him, wished he'd told him. Maybe he had. Words, he'd used them all up. So few left, he saved them for Cecibel. If only she would get there so he could go.

"You can't go," Olivia whispered in his ear. "We're not finished. Not me and you. Not Aldo and Cecilia. What will I do without you? What will they do? Don't go, my love. Please don't go."

I have to, darling Livy. There's no choice in the matter. Cecilia and Aldo, Enzo and Tressa, you—you'll all have to do without me. It's time. Past time.

Cornelius sat in the easy chair where Alfonse had spent much of his time in the Pen, just watching the goings-on. Grinning. Knowing. Waiting. *You thought you could escape me forever, but you can't. I promised it. And here it is. Our forever. At last.* Always joking, never serious, his Cornelius. Even in death, both of their deaths, he teased. Alfonse couldn't wait to be with him again, tell him all the things he never had the courage to go back and say. But not until Cecibel came to him. They'd both wait a little longer.

And then there she was. His angel. His monster. How he loved them both. Equally. Passionately. Perfectly. What he had done to deserve this last, previously unexperienced love at the end of his sinful life, Alfonse didn't know. But he was grateful.

He followed her approach with his eyes, glad she took his hand rather than waiting for him to do the impossible and reach for hers. The tiniest tug, all he could manage, was enough to bring her close.

"Alfonse. I'm so sorry. I came the moment—"

"Shh." One less breath to breathe. "Cushion." One less. "Chair." How few now. So few he could count them on two hands. Maybe a foot, too. "For you."

Alfonse let go her hand. Cecibel's tears were bliss on his skin. She turned from him, went to the chair where Cornelius sat waiting. Still grinning. He didn't move when she reached into the cushions, but made a face as if he'd been goosed. To laugh? Or breathe a few more breaths? He breathed.

Cecibel came back with the book—*Night Wings on the Moon*. Not his masterpiece, but the thing that linked them long before they'd ever met. He blinked. She understood. Cecibel flipped to the title page.

"I don't understand."

He blinked again. Attempted to smile. Cecibel flipped through the dog-eared pages, found the place he'd left his last words.

"Read," he said. Only a few breaths more. He'd hold them just long enough.

Olivia stood at Cecibel's shoulder, a hand tenderly comforting there, but her eyes were on him and his on hers. She would understand. Of course she would. And she would see it done, even the parts he'd not written had he enough foresight to have known he should.

"'Never and forever are not opposites,'" Cecibel read. "'They are two parts to a whole. Like love and pain. Joy and sorrow. Life and death. Like monster and princess. But between love and pain there is comfort. Between joy and sorrow there is contentment. Between life and death'"—her voice hitched—"'there is experience. Between monster and princess, there is courage. And between never and forever, there is everything.'"

Cecibel took his hand again, kissed his fingertips, so cold. Alfonse felt the tears and did not stop them this time. So many words he had left to give her. So many. And none.

She continued, "'You gave me words, those my truest and most abiding love. I can never sufficiently thank you for that, except to bequeath to you my suite in the Pen . . .' Alfonse, no."

"Hush, child," Olivia said. "Don't argue with a dying man."

Cecibel bowed her head and wept.

Please, darling love. Please. I can't go until you let me. I can't go until you're done.

"'Except to bequeath to you my suite in the Pen, Cecibel Bringer, my dear child, my last love, as well as my share in the Bar Harbor Home for the Elderly, its proper name. It was ours, Cornelius's and mine. Now what of it still mine becomes yours. I have no doubt he would have approved'"—her voice, so thick—"'but it is, as always, what I want that matters. All my love ~Alfonse Carducci 8/1/99.'" She held up her finger, a smile making its way through her tears. "There is a P.S.," she said, a hitch more like laughter in her throat. "'Any lawyers or accountants or long-lost family members who dare contest this gift be duly warned—I will haunt you to your end of days.'" Cecibel lowered her head to his chest and wept. "Oh, Alfonse."

Over and over. Over and over. His name whispered from her lips. The sound became a song Alfonse remembered from long ago, when he was a boy and his mama was his world; became Roberto shouting at play; became Cornelius's laugh, Olivia's scolding, hundreds and hundreds of voices calling out, calling him.

Alfonse.

The cheering of multitudes. People who'd read his work and been somehow changed, if only for a little while.

"Alfonse." Cecibel's voice again. Hers and hers alone.

One breath left. "Cecibel."

And none.

New York City

APRIL 1977

Tressa

New York. City of her heart. The place she'd dreamed of all her young, underestimated life. Her home. Her job telling its stories day after brutal, beautiful day. Tressa had made it happen. She made everything in her life happen. The good. The bad. No excuses, done by her own machinations. She regretted nothing. Even now.

"It's still so cold. This better be worth it, Aunt T."

Antee. So insectlike, so diminutive. Tressa put her arm around her niece's shoulders. You could take the girl out of Jersey, but you couldn't take the Jersey out of the girl. Patricia's accent had only intensified over her years in New York City, while Tressa's southern drawl softened into something more elegant. Nicky always liked her drawl. She tried to keep it, for his sake, but the r-lessness was more Katharine Hepburn than Scarlett O'Hara. He didn't seem to notice, in any case. Or he'd ceased to care, after all.

"It will be. I promise. You have to trust me."

"Haven't I always?"

Her smile, like Tressa's own. Always easy and sweet. Looking at her was like looking into the past Tressa loved to imagine, all she might have been had she not been orphaned and sent to live with relatives who adored and spoiled her, who kept her apart from any and all family not theirs. Guardians she called Mama and Daddy but weren't, she was never allowed to forget. They formed her into the perfect southern lady, the epitome of grace and beauty.

But you couldn't take Jersey out of the girl.

Two long blasts turned her attention to the harbor. The Circle

Line. She smiled. Not a real boat, Aldo always said. He'd been on so many ships, all over the world. She, for a time, visited him in ports from sea to sea. Then came misfortune. Hers. Cecilia's. Enzo's. Her chosen family. Chosen for Patricia's sake, if nothing else. She'd come to love them all, even Nicky, despite the ain'ts and gonnas. Despite never getting Enzo out from under her skin. Lust at first sight. Love, over time. Cecilia hadn't noticed, or she pretended not to, until she couldn't anymore. And Nicky. Poor Nicky. Damn him to hell.

Prima la famiglia.

None of it ever touched Patricia, because of who she was to them all. Daughter. Granddaughter. Niece. Beloved and innocent and beautiful to her soul. That was the important thing. The only thing that mattered.

Prima la famiglia.

"You okay, Aunt T?"

Tressa forced the melancholy away to smile down upon her niece. Patricia had gotten Tressa's beauty, but not her stature. That, she got from Cecilia. Tiny, like a china doll. A bird. But not fragile. Neither Giancami women nor Wronski had ever been made of such stuff.

"I'm fine, darling. Tell me. How's school?"

"Not again." Patricia groaned. "We've talked about it and talked about it. I've got another year until graduation and it can't be over soon enough. I'm sticking it out because I promised Daddy I'd be an educated woman, and that's the only reason."

"Enzo would have been very proud of you." Even after death, he still made her heart thump. "When did you see your mother last?"

Patricia chuffed, an unladylike sound so like Cecilia it nearly brought Tressa to tears. "Christmas, I guess. You know, the big party."

Her throat constricted. "I remember it well."

"You could still come, you know. You and Uncle Nicky are still married. Maybe it could mend some fences. It just doesn't make sense. You're the one who found Daddy dead, rest his soul. I never understood why Mama and Uncle Nicky got mad at you."

"Angry, darling. Dogs go mad. People become angry." Tressa shuddered, crossed herself. The betrayal. The blood. The best of them gone. The worst of them still hanging on to the tatters. "Grief does terrible things to us all. At least I still have you?"

At least. The very least. The price of keeping her secrets. "When will you see your mother next?"

"Easter, maybe." Patricia shrugged. "She's so wrapped up in Frankie she hardly notices we don't talk. It's okay." She smiled, though her lips trembled. "I'm used to it, since Daddy died, anyway."

Tressa kissed her forehead, both her cheeks. This child, more like her own than any she might have borne, a woman now. How many promises she'd made on her behalf. To Aldo. To Enzo. Cecilia and Patricia and herself. Tressa had kept them all, even when they hurt so much she thought she'd break. *I'd do it all again, a thousand times over.* "You know, the master's-of-fine-arts program at NYU is—"

"—not happening." Patricia laughed. "Aunt T, you've done enough. And besides, I hate school. I want to travel. See some of the world. Like you have."

"That was a long time ago."

"When you were my age." Patricia nudged her. "Was it a man you followed around the world? Is that why Uncle Nicky made you settle down and marry him?"

"Is that what he told you?"

"A million times." Patricia laughed. "That's why I don't get why—"

"A man, yes." Tressa inhaled deeply. "But not a lover." Slowly. "My brother."

Patricia cocked her head. "You have a brother?"

"I do."

"Why don't I know about him?"

Because I promised. "I'm sure I mentioned him."

"I'd know if you did. He'd be my uncle."

Laughter threatened. Tressa swallowed it. "Not really. I'm your aunt through marriage."

Patricia squeezed her arm, rested her beautiful blond head against Tressa. "Everyone in Paterson is related to everyone else in some way," she said. "I'm sure there's blood between us somewhere. How else would we look so alike?"

"I suppose." So close to the truth, and yet oblivious to it. Had she ever been as naive as Patricia? No. Not ever. Cecilia had been. The proof clutched her arm, stood shivering upon the docks. And for the first time, the only time, Tressa doubted. Promises would be broken. At last. At long last. And everything was about to change. Her world. Patricia's world. Everyone's to some degree. But her niece was a woman now, just as Tressa had been when she stepped onto this path, finally coming full circle.

A polka-dot blob of bobbing uniforms came en masse along the pier. White-clad seamen, dark-clad officers, sailors all. Tressa's heart stuttered. She took both Patricia's hands in hers. "Remember I said your birthday present would be late?"

"Sure, but the pearls were more than enough."

"Pearls are tradition. Every girl must have them." Tressa's gaze darted to the sailors ever closer. She was not hard to spot. Still tall. Still beautiful. She wore her signature white coat, just to be certain. The first men passing eyed both her and her niece as men always did. "Your gift just came in."

Patricia stood on tiptoe, searched beyond her aunt to the pier beyond. "Is it a car? An Italian convertible! Did it come in a big crate? Oh! Will they have to get it off the boat with a crane?"

Tressa laughed. "No, darling. Not even I can afford such a luxury." Though she could, of course. Her trust fund was—thanks to good lawyers and investment brokers who had no problem keeping secrets—inexhaustible. "It's a bit simpler than that, but I hope, even better."

"Better than an Italian convertible?" Patricia sighed, hand dramatically at her brow. "Impossible!"

This darling girl. The best of them all. Even Enzo, with whom she shared no blood, but a bond that had been unshakable. Tressa

314 ~ TERRI-LYNNE DEFINO

clenched her teeth. Thoughts for another time. Not now. Maybe not ever again.

A man waved. Big, over his head. Tressa gasped. Still so handsome. A career made. Success had. He'd been heartbroken, of course, when Cecilia never appeared in Barcelona. It had taken every trick in Tressa's arsenal to convince Cecilia not to, to make her brother accept his fate. But he'd known happiness and fulfillment of a different kind. The kind without a family that could be taken from him in an instant. She hadn't been wrong. She hadn't been. The proof was coming toward her, tanned from the sun in Saint-Tropez, his last destination before this extended leave he was considering making permanent. Tressa had nothing to do with that decision, though it had everything to do with hers.

She waved back to him. He was near enough now for her to see his gaze move from one woman to the other, to note the question forming a line between furrowed brows. Tressa's heart beat so hard her head lightened and her vision swam. Squeezing her niece's fingers, she kissed the tips. "You must trust me. Okay?"

"You said that already. Aunt T? What's going on? Who is—?"

"Tressa?" His voice, beautiful and deep. His expression already softening, changing and changing again.

"—he?"

Tressa stood between them, one last moment before letting it all go. Stepping aside, she gently pushed Patricia forward. "Happy birthday, darling."

Bar Harbor, Maine

JUNE 2014

❈

About Alfonse Carducci, say, "There was never a wine
he would not drink, a woman he would not love,
a man he could not best, or a song outside his key,"
and you will have spoken only half the truth.

—OLIVIA PEPPERNELL

Cecibel clicked save. She closed her eyes, slumped back in the chair. The sunset coloring the sky all shades of purple, pink, and blue seeped through her eyelids—two of them, since the last surgery, and an ear. Scarring tamed but never erased—the last rays dipping into the always-gray sea. She'd seen it too often to need her eyes.

You were his muse. Do with it what you wish.

Sitting forward again, Cecibel brushed aside a tear and saved the file to the thumb drive, logged out of her computer. She hadn't intended to. It just happened. It was this room, hers, and seldom used. It was the cherished memories of a time more magical than real. More real than the prior, unmemorable existence. It was Alfonse and Cornelius, Switch and Judi come to collect Olivia, the last of them to leave. It was Aldo and Cecilia, Enzo and Tressa waiting a decade and a half for their endings. All Cecibel had meant to do was save the ancient floppy onto a thumb drive before all Judi's work got lost to technology.

A knock, and the door opened. "Hey, you ready?"

She sniffed, and she nodded. Fin took her into his arms.

"I can't believe she's gone."

"She was ninety-nine, Bel. Kind of time, don't you think?"

"I wanted her to live forever." She stepped back but not out of his arms. "Where's Joy?"

"With Sal." Fin kissed the tip of her nose. "And Richard. He says this needs to be done today. No knowing who's going to show up tomorrow and raise a fuss."

"They can all go to hell."

"There's no one left to go," Fin said. "She outlived them all."

Cecibel breathed in slowly, out carefully. Ungrateful children. Misinformed. Willfully oblivious to the end. Dead and gone, like their father. Olivia had cried for them anyway.

"We were her family. All of us. She belongs here, not in that family's crypt. This is what she wanted. What's right."

"Then let's get out there and get it done."

Fin held out his hand. Cecibel took it, and he kissed their joined knuckles. Simple. Sensitive. Sensible. She'd made him wait and wait and wait. Through all the surgeries. Through the birth of their daughter, and the change of her career. The first book published. The second, the third. He waited still, as if the question of their forever needed to be asked, or validated with ceremony and paperwork. Cecibel would marry him. Someday. Maybe. They were happy in the space above the maintenance barn, she and Fin and Joy. Their Joy. She had curly blond hair, and freckles. She laughed all the time, except when she was screaming. And she was their everything.

At the edge of the cemetery, a small gathering waited. The day's last rays streamed down over the sea. Dusk lasted forever in June. The fey half-light. The magic therein. Olivia had been specific in her wishes. The time. The variety of tree. The exact spot. She'd spent the last five years of her life planning her ultimate send-off from a wheelchair, and though Cecibel was an orderly no more, she had usually been the one pushing it.

Don't argue, my dear. It was decided long ago, just after Alfonse died.

Olivia had pressed the notebook—brown leather and gilt edges— and Judi's floppy disk into Cecibel's hands. She'd returned the book to the drawer where Alfonse once kept it. Where it belonged. For now. It took some doing, finding a computer that could still read a floppy. And now their story was finished. Aldo and Cecilia and Enzo and Tressa. Cecibel's insides trembled, even while her heart danced.

"Good, good. You're here." Dr. Kintz kissed her cheek. "Sun's going down fast."

"Where you been, sugar bean?" Sal let go of Joy's hand and nudged her gently to her mother. "You okay? You look like you seen a ghost or something."

If only. Cecibel smiled, smoothed Joy's wild hair. "I'm here now. We ready?"

"Ready, Freddy." Sal handed her the plastic cylinder. Fin stood by with the shovel. The tree had already been set in place, at the edge of the cemetery, where it would grow, reach limbs over, roots under. Protecting and protected.

Cecibel unscrewed the lid. How a whole person fit inside seemed ridiculous, and yet there Olivia was—ashes and bits of bone and teeth. Moving away from her daughter—old enough to understand death, not old enough to comprehend the enormity of Olivia's life—Cecibel held the container to her chest.

"Could you give us a moment?" she said over her shoulder. They moved off. Fin suggested Joy pick some wildflowers to leave when they were done. Cecibel hugged the container closer.

"I don't know how the story would have ended had you, Alfonse, and Switch finished it. I don't think any of you did either. But Tressa . . . he made her me for a reason. I hope this was the reason. I hope it's all right." Cecibel laughed softly, tearfully. "You planned it, the moment he died, didn't you? You'd never have given it up before that, but after? I can see it now, the three of you hatching your plot. How did you keep it from me, all this time? I looked and looked for that notebook." She sniffed. "How I'm going to miss you, Olivia. How I miss all of you. Rest well, my dear friend. Rest well."

Wiping the tears from her cheek, she looked over her shoulder, called the rest back with a glance. Cecibel squatted beside the hole and shook Olivia's ashes into the roots of the tree. Wispy clouds of errant ash drifted up, curled along the ground like smoke. *Come back. Come back.* Joy tossed the flowers she'd collected into the hole. Sal sprinkled glitter and Fin a handful of earth.

Richard stepped forward, pulling a baggie from his trouser pocket. The skunky scent wafted out as he opened it. "Just a little send-off, for old times' sake," he said, and shook the marijuana into the hole.

"Damn, that's a waste of good weed." Sal tsked. "A sister could have used a pinch of that."

"Sal, come on." Fin gestured to Joy, but the child was staring into the hole, oblivious.

Cecibel put her arm around her daughter's shoulders. "You okay?"

Joy shrugged. "It's just weird."

"How so?"

"Her not being here. She's *always* been here."

And now she's not. That's just how it goes. "I know. It's going to take getting used to."

"Yeah." Joy looped her arms around Cecibel's waist, twisted fingers into the end of her long braid like she used to do when she was a baby seeking comfort.

"Ready?" Fin held the shovel up. Cecibel nodded. Sal. Richard. Joy's arms tightened.

One shovelful. Two. More. The pile beside the tree shrank as the hole was filled. Cecibel's heart constricted. Alfonse, then Switch, and Judi. Now Olivia. Old people who'd lived their lives. The natural progression of things tempered sorrow. There was no tragedy in an old person's death. Cecibel held her daughter just a little closer.

"That's that, then." Richard clapped, rubbed his hands together. "Olivia provided for a special supper. She made me promise the chef would use salt in her honor."

"Thank the little baby Jesus!" Sal waved his hands in the air. "I didn't know we even had any around here."

"Low-sodium salt."

"You're no fun at all, Dr. Dick."

"I can still fire you, Salvatore."

"But you won't." Sal blew him a kiss. "Who else could organize your chaos?"

Heading back to the mansion, the men bickered like an old married couple. An unexpected pairing. Professional. Personal. Cecibel wasn't sure which had come first, but they worked in a way that made both these men she loved happy.

"I have to put this away." Fin held up the shovel. "I'll clean up and meet you in the dining room."

"Wait for me, Daddy," Joy said. Cecibel let go of her child, ignored the little pang of envy. Her preference had been clear from those earliest days when surgery or writing kept Cecibel sequestered from them both. Joy loved her, certainly. She simply loved Fin a little bit more.

Hand in hand, father and daughter left her alone with the newly planted tree, the scent of turned earth, the silence, and the sunset. Cecibel sat on the low stone wall, let the whole of it all settle around her. That time in her life, that greatest of times, was over now. Truly and completely. They were gone, but not forgotten. Never forgotten. How could they be when there were college courses dedicated to their writings? When their books never went out of print? When she had the last work of those former kings and queens even greater in death than they'd been in life to either keep for herself, or give to the world?

Plucking a fistful of wildflowers from the wall, Cecibel tried and failed to still her pounding heart. She placed the small and simple bouquet on the headstone closest to the newly planted tree, rested her hand to the summer-warmed stone.

"What do you think, Alfonse?" She closed her eyes, wished and wished and wished. But no answer came. No ghostly voice. No inkling. No shiver. Such things happened in the novels she wrote, not in real life. "It's up to me, then, huh? Okay."

Cecibel pulled her cell phone from her pocket. Her finger poised over the screen. She curled it back into a fist, fingernails digging into her palms. She was not a literary great; she was not certain those existed anymore. Not like Hemingway and Woolf. Not like Carducci and Peppernell. But she'd been their muse. And, in the end, they were hers.

She tapped the screen. The ringing on the other end—with all the ring tones available now, why was it still that old-fashioned sound?—reverberated in her belly. A click. A voice. "Hello, Diana Stewart speaking."

"Diana, it's me, Cecibel. Cecibel Bringer."

"Why didn't you call my cell? How are you? Do you finally have something new for me? I've been waiting for—"

"Diana, listen, before I lose my nerve."

"Okay. I'm listening."

Cecibel licked her lips. She walked in the direction of the mansion, phone to her ear and heart in her throat. "I have this manuscript," she said, "and I guarantee it's like nothing you've ever seen before."

ACKNOWLEDGMENTS

I want to start by thanking the city of Paterson, New Jersey. City of my birth. Always in my heart. Cecilia and Aldo's Meyer Brothers, Falls View, Derrom Avenue, and the falls are all real places. It's the Paterson of my parents. If anything doesn't ring true, blame them for remembering too nostalgically.

If Paterson is the city of my heart, Bar Harbor, Maine, is the town of my dreams. There is no Bar Harbor Home for the Elderly, but how grand if there were. You never know; it could happen. If it does, that's where you'll find me someday.

My agent, Janna Bonikowski, makes everything I write better. Whether we're on the phone, shooting emails back and forth, or sending one another strange texts at odd times, she's part of my every day, and I thank every lucky star in the sky she's mine.

Thanks go out to The Knight Agency, for always going above and beyond, and for answering all my curious oyster questions, no matter how bizarre.

Rachel Kahan, fierce lady, without her belief in me and this story, there would be no acknowledgments page on which to thank her. I am forever grateful.

A huge thanks to my daughter, Jamie. She knows why.

And, though she has no idea who I am, and likely never will, I feel the need to thank Dame Helen Mirren, whose brilliant catalog of work gave Olivia life, breath, and heart.

Last thanks goes to my always, my best friend, my love, my Frankie D.

TERRI-LYNNE DeFINO was born and raised in New Jersey, but escaped to the wilds of Connecticut, where she still lives with her husband and her cats. She spends most days in her loft, in her woodland cabin along the river, writing about people she's never met. Other days, she can be found slaying monsters with her grandchildren. If you knock on her door, she'll most likely be wearing a tiara. She'll also invite you in and feed you, because you can take the Italian girl out of Jersey, but you can't take the Jersey Italian out of the girl.

*The Bar Harbor Retirement Home for
Famous Writers (And Their Muses)*

READING GROUP GUIDE

〰〰〰

1. What do you think life in the Pen was like before Alfonse's arrival? What changed when Alfonse arrived?
2. Alfonse tells Cecibel that "love is not passion. . . . Love is sweet
   and good and righteous. Passion is wild and messy and dangerous." What is the driving force behind Alfonse's relationships
   with Olivia, Judith, Cornelius, and Cecibel? Is it love or passion?
3. "If you go by what the critics and sales figures say, my greatest
   work was *And the Ladies Sang*. A good book. One I'm proud
   of, naturally. Nineteen eighty-four was a powerful time for
   women, and the book spoke to several generations fighting the
   good fight. But if you're asking which book rests most kindly in
   my heart, it's *Green Apples for Stewart*." On the strength of this,
   what do you think Olivia's greatest works were about?
4. Throughout the novel Cecibel uses her hair to conceal her scarring and to maintain a sense of "vanity she no longer had a right
   to." Does Cecibel hide her scars purely for her own vanity, or
   does she have other reasons for hiding her scars?
5. Cecibel serves as the muse behind Aldo and Cecilia's story. In
   what ways does Cecibel inspire the characters in Alfonse, Olivia,
   and Switch's story? What are the parallels between Cecibel and
   Cecilia?
6. Cecibel thinks of herself as a monster. Is Cecibel a monster?
   What makes her view herself this way?

7. Finlay was sent to prison for murdering his local teacher after enduring years of abuse. Do you think Finlay deserved to go to prison for his actions? How do the other characters in the novel view Finlay in light of his crime?

8. Discuss whether Cecibel is an employee or a resident of the Pen. Are the other staff members simply employees, or are they residents?

9. "[Cornelius] and I dreamed up this place when we were young men conquering the literary world. We took it from the greats. Faulkner, Joyce, Cather, Parker. We robbed them blind and flew their tattered flags in their faces." Do you think the Bar Harbor Home for the Elderly lived up to Cornelius and Alfonse's expectations?

10. What do you think happens to the characters in the years following the novel's end?